Icing It

A CHICAGO RACKETEERS NOVEL

EMMA FOXX

About the Book

Sex is a fantastic stress reliever.

Or so I'm told by the two hot guys who offer to help me get over some of my work-induced anxiety by getting under *both* of them.

I say yes. For one night.

And proceed to have my world rocked. For three days.

I can *not* afford that kind of distraction. As fun as it was, I have a business to run, a loan to pay off, and a life to live that does not include any extra commitments or responsibilities. Especially not a golden retriever hockey player and a bossy billionaire who are in love with each other and want to make *me* the third in their long-term plans.

And let's not even talk about the *third* guy who wants to date me. He's my brother's coach. And twelve years older than me. But he's also a single dad to a pretty great teenage son, and his competence and gentlemanly behavior are really hard to resist.

Of course, there's also the not-so-gentlemanly things he says and does behind bedroom doors…

Then they all go and fall in love with me. Even though one of them is definitely not interested in making this a full-time foursome.

And the icing on top?

I've fallen for them, too. All of them.

How can I possibly choose?

Worse, how can I possibly walk away?

Icing It is a steamy, fun why-choose rom com! No cheating, a guaranteed HEA, and the guys are all about her. If you like Lily Gold, Emily Rath, and Lauren Blakely, welcome to the world of Emma Foxx!

CHAPTER 1

Cameron

THIS HOCKEY GAME just got way more interesting.

Because Luna McNeill is sitting one row in front of me, I can hear every word she says.

And see her phone screen.

"I'm trying to find three hot guys to have a hookup with," she tells her friend, scrolling through her phone with her thumb.

Unless this girl wants to fuck a scone, she is *not* on a dating app. Right now, she's cropping the image of a sticky bun with a drizzle that makes my mouth water for more than one reason. She's always working at the Chicago Racketeers' games. She looks at images of baked goods, searches for new recipes, checks her email, and makes notes to herself.

As a workaholic myself, I love a good multi-task. This is why while Luna watches her brother, Crew, out on the ice and does pastry research on her phone, I watch my best friend and Racketeers defenseman, Alexsei Ryan, as I look at dating apps.

Alexsei mentioned he was up for us having a hookup with a girl sooner than later, and I'm never going to say no to that. The woman definitely matters to Alexsei. He has a specific type.

Blonde hairstylist wearing elaborate makeup. No. Not what Alexsei is into. Too high maintenance.

Swipe.

A brunette on a motorcycle.

Immediate swipe.

A cute girl named Lex, with a big smile who likes CrossFit. You would think that would be a maybe, but it's actually a hard no. Alexsei doesn't date athletes. He likes to be the strong one. He has a thing about fireman-carrying girls to bed and comparing his big, bulky hands to their petite ones.

Swipe.

I zero in on Luna's hands. She has delicate, long fingers, and always has very pointy fingernails in dark polish colors that probably have names like Suck His Blood and Midnight Goddess.

The kind of nails that would look sexy as hell wrapped around a man's cock.

"I want to be Dani, too," Luna adds, glancing over at her friend, who blushes.

I stop searching for potential hookups and listen more closely to Luna's conversation with Crew's girlfriend, Dani, curious about where their discussion is headed.

Dani is in a very public poly relationship with Crew, the Racketeers physician, and the team owner, who is sitting on her other side, a hand possessively resting on her knee. Hockey fans gobbled up the KissCam beginnings to their relationship, but none of that interests me.

Luna, on the other hand, does. She's witty, sharp, and smart.

While not exactly Alexsei's type, which leans toward sweet as sugar and submissive, she is interesting. I can almost guarantee she's uninhibited and a whole lot of sexy fun.

"If that's what you want, I'm sure you can have it," Dani says in response to her. "Do you know how many guys in Chicago would jump at the chance to be with a girl like you?"

I agree with her best friend's assessment. This is a woman who can get whatever she wants.

"I've been practicing abundance meditations every night and

releasing my intentions to the universe, so I'm reasonably confident."

I can't decide if she's being ironic or serious.

"Plus, I'm cute, and I make baked goods. Men should appreciate me."

Cute is a modest understatement. Luna McNeill is a hot girl.

She has purple tips in her blonde hair, a sassy smile, and long eyelashes. I wonder if she has a tattoo. Like a cupcake somewhere only a lucky few have seen. That needs to be licked.

I lean a little closer to Luna as the crowd gives a collective cheer at something that happens on the ice, my phone going slack in my palm. I can't hear what she's saying now, if anything, which irritates me.

Alexsei skates right up to the boards just then and taps the plexiglass, causing the two girls to jump, and Luna to finally look up from her phone. I haven't been paying attention to the game at all. I don't even know the score.

He points his stick at me, giving me a familiar grin. "You're my ride home tonight."

I give him a nod of acknowledgement. Whenever I'm at a game, he likes me to chauffeur his ass around afterward so he can rehash the whole game without crashing his SUV. Alexsei sucks at multitasking. He doesn't need me to participate in those play-by-play dissections, just interject an "uh-huh" here and there. I don't mind, because I'm not what anyone would call a chatty guy. I don't need to talk. I like to *do*.

"The universe has delivered," Dani says with a giggle.

"What?" Luna asks Alexsei, sounding a little bewildered but mostly intrigued. "I'm giving you a ride home? Um...sure, okay." She shrugs. "Do you like chocolate chip pancakes?"

Her words are like a punch in the gut. Lust rears up, hot and eager, as I envision a night when Luna comes to our place for some naked fun, culminating in breakfast. I'm not a man who is led by his stomach—my dick definitely trumps my stomach—but I also won't turn down pancakes.

Alexsei laughs, shakes his head, and points at me again.

"He means me," I say.

Both Luna and Dani swivel around and gape at me.

"I'm his best friend and roommate, Cameron." I lift a brow. "But yes, we both like chocolate chip pancakes."

"Oh, shit, sorry," Luna gives me a weak smile. "Hi." She turns back around. "Well, that's embarrassing," she mutters to Dani.

I doubt this woman spends much time being embarrassed. I bet she lives her life on her own terms. I fucking love that. But I also love that I just rattled her a little.

I'd like to rattle her a lot.

No. Her words were definitely not embarrassing. More like the answer to my problem.

No need to fish for a woman online when I have a perfect candidate right in front of me. Alexsei already has a thing for Luna. He hasn't told me that, but I see how he looks at her. I just never got the impression she returned that interest. But now…

They would be damned good together. She's feisty, and he's a people pleaser. He'd be all about her. And she would probably think she could boss him around. She'd be wrong, though. Because I'll be there.

And I'm the boss.

"Not as embarrassing as having your butt on the jumbotron." Dani laughs. "And hey, there's two right there. You only have to collect a third to be like me."

A third is not on my agenda.

The buzzer ends the period.

I glance up to check the score and shoot off a text to Alexsei. He'll see it when the game is over, but I want to give him a heads-up.

> Working on something. You already like her.

Crew McNeill skates to the bench and then, as the players all take the tunnel to the locker room, he leaves the line and leans in to kiss Dani.

The crowd goes wild.

"You're on the KissCam again," Luna says to her. "Make it count."

Personally, I would rather shove red-hot needles in my eyes than kiss someone for the KissCam.

I have a feeling Luna McNeill would be in full agreement with me.

CHAPTER 2
Luna

"DON'T LOOK," I say, shifting on the balls of my feet as I pretend to glance down at my phone, "but Alexsei's grumpy friend is staring at me right now."

I regret it the minute I say it.

"He is?" Dani asks in pure delight, turning around quickly and peering across the back hallway of the arena.

I wince.

Telling Dani not to look is basically guaranteeing she'll look. She is the nicest person I know, hands down, but she's also the one who would die first in a horror movie. She has zero guile. Less than zero. Negative guile. She would stop to help the killer restart his sputtered-out chainsaw. That's how generous and sweet she is.

She's also in full matchmaker mode now that she is dating my brother, Crew, Dr. Michael Hughes, and Nathan Armstrong. She wants me to be in love, too, and that's just not happening. I am way too focused on my bakery business to get wrapped up in all the complications of a relationship.

I wouldn't mind having sex. But more than that? Hard pass.

"Dani!" I hiss as she cranes her neck and makes it beyond obvious what she's doing. "Turn back around."

She obeys, but she's grinning. "He is definitely staring at you. You should go talk to him."

"No. He's… very intense." He's *hot*. That's what he is. Like, he's full-blown nerd sex appeal, with his expensive-looking glasses, a tight black sweater that shows off a lean but muscular build, and thick, dark hair with a hint of curl. Not to mention cheekbones that could cut glass and full lips that look like they were made to be wrapped around my nipples.

I almost smack myself at the thought. Which confirms my point.

No nipples, damn it. Nipples don't exist in business plans.

Hot is too distracting right now. Hot is bad. Hot is dangerous. If I talk to any guy or have a hookup, it should be only with a semi-attractive one sporting a lukewarm personality, not one whose stare holds the heat and intensity of a laser beam. Like Kyle, my Tinder date from a month or so ago. If I'm desperate enough for mediocre sex, I can reach out to him.

But intense, smoldering sex with Laser Beam Boy? Nope. Not doing it.

The business I share with Dani, Books and Buns, is exploding from the publicity surrounding her Racketeers romance times three and I'm determined to capitalize on the hype. This bakery is my dream, a spark lit in childhood with weekends spent in my grandparent's cozy kitchen, baking up a storm with my grandma Betty. I want Books and Buns to be a household name, and to that goal, I have a full Thanksgiving dessert menu with preorders running in the hundreds. I need to implement a baking and pickup day plan and sort out what I want to present to customers for the Christmas season. Then there's New Year's Eve trays and New Year's Day brunch pastries, and then we practically roll right into Valentine's Day with chocolate-dipped strawberries and heart-shaped cookies. This is prime baking season and I'm not going to blow it because I have a lady hard-on for a man who's only said half a dozen words to me even though he's been sitting behind me at every home hockey game for a month.

Not that I've noticed.

"You think he's cute," Dani says with a smile.

"He's actually fucking beautiful," I say begrudgingly, super annoyed by that fact. "But grumpy." I can't resist the urge to know if he's still watching me, though. "Is he still staring? Look, but don't be obvious."

Dani pulls her phone out and announces loudly, "Let's take a selfie!"

I roll my eyes. "Not obvious at all," I mutter as she gestures for me to stand beside her.

She holds her phone insanely high so that when she flips her camera, we can see Cameron behind us over our heads. He is one hundred percent staring. He's leaning against the wall, his arms crossed over his chest. He doesn't look away. The opposite, in fact. He clearly knows we can see him and he drills his gaze into the camera.

My nipples approve.

My brain is outraged. Yet curious. What is his deal, seriously?

"Smile," Dani says.

I obey, flipping my hair and tilting my head to give a good angle. Then I do something I haven't done in years. I blow a kiss at the camera. I can't help myself. I want a reaction from Cameron. I want to break that stare.

I'm rewarded with the slightest smile and him looking away. Finally.

"Aw, I love that!" Dani says, pulling her phone back down and scrolling through the multiple shots.

"Send that to me." Not because *he's* in the background or anything. But because Dani and I look cute. "What is taking Crew so long?" I say, checking the time on my phone. "I have to go."

I need to do the employee work schedule for our pre-Thanksgiving baking days. It's going to be all hands on deck, and we don't have that many hands yet. We only have two employees, so I've been interviewing temporary workers for the holiday season.

"You seem really stressed," Dani says.

"I am really stressed. I have like nine million things to do." She may be living on love and sex endorphins these days, but I'm being fueled primarily by caffeine and determination.

"Hey, Luna?"

It's him. Grumpy Adonis. I turn automatically. "Yes?"

Damn it. My voice sounds breathy, flirty.

He peels himself off the wall. "I know a fantastic stress reliever."

I do, too, and it's not green tea or yoga. "Are you eavesdropping on my private conversation?" I demand, because being rude is my only defense against his chocolate brown eyes and whiskey-smooth voice.

"I'm not trying to listen. You're three feet away from me and the acoustics here are amplifying your voice." The corner of his mouth turns up. "You think I'm grumpy, but beautiful."

Oh, Jesus. He heard all of that. "How do you know I was talking about you?"

He looks left and right before pushing his glasses up on the bridge of his nose. "Who else here is Alexsei's grumpy but beautiful friend?"

No one can possibly fit that description. The hallway is full of women—girlfriends, and wives, plus a few press personnel.

But I'm desperate. Sammy the Malamute is walking toward us. "Him," I say, pointing to the unknown person inside the mascot suit. It could even be a woman in there for all I know, but it doesn't matter.

Cameron's eyebrows lift. "You think the guy in the mascot costume is grumpy?" But then he shrugs. "I guess I would be grumpy, too, if I was dressed like a dog."

I nod, relieved he is going to let me off the hook. "Well, have a good night."

I turn back to Dani, only she's now snuggled into my brother, kissing him tenderly. He wraps his arms around her tightly and pulls her closer, looking besotted.

I'm thrilled for them. They're a good fit and for years I've wanted Dani to find a man who worships the ground she walks on. But their timing sucks. I'm left standing here awkwardly, searching for any reason not to look at Cameron. I might be forced to talk to Sammy, who is also staring at me. I think. It's hard to tell with his tiny eye holes beneath his glass dog eyes.

The air behind me shifts as Cameron moves in closer to me. I know it's him without looking because my nipples get hard.

"Sex," he murmurs in my ear.

I nearly jump out of my skin. "Why the fuck are you so close to me?" I demand, even as a shiver rolls over me from the whisper of his warm breath on my skin and the rumble of his voice. "And what about sex?"

My voice drops on the last word, like my mother's does when she talks about cancer. I've lost my cool. I'm never this not-cool. This is officially a red flag situation. Guys don't rattle me like this.

"Sex is a great stress reliever."

We're inches apart. I swallow hard. God, he smells good. Like expensive cologne. Like warm flesh. Like... *sex*. I'm not even sure how that's possible. Maybe it's the power of suggestion. Maybe he's hypnotizing me or I manifested too hard. I did request the universe send me a hookup that I didn't have to work for, but maybe I needed to specify the mediocre part. No hot distractions need apply.

Cameron is waiting for a response. Just... waiting. He's unbelievably in control of himself. His body is still, his gaze steady.

"Sex is a very quality stress reliever," I say, because there's no denying it. I could use an orgasm or seven to relax me. "I agree."

"Alexsei will be out in a minute. Why don't you come home with us?"

I blink. He has just thrown it out there. Just like that. "Um..."

I should say no, but I can't seem to remember why.

"You did offer him chocolate chip pancakes. I assume that means you like Alexsei."

"I mean... sure." I'm not sure what the hell is happening here. "I barely know him, but he seems... fun."

"Do you think he's grumpy and beautiful?"

"No." Alexsei seems normal. A cheerful, grinning hockey player with a great body and good hair.

"He likes you."

"Okay." When I thought he was asking me for a ride home, I wasn't sure why, but I was willing to see how it might play out. "Why hasn't he told *me* that?"

"He's afraid your brother might get annoyed if he asks you out."

That makes me instantly bluster. "My brother doesn't factor into my dating." I've always said I wouldn't date a hockey player, but that's not because it might bother my brother in some sort of way. It's because they all have big egos.

I glance back. Crew is whispering something in Dani's ear and she's giggling. My brother isn't even aware I exist right now, so I have no idea why he would have any opinion about who I do what with.

"Then you should come home with us."

"I…"

I should say no. I have so much work to do.

"You can work tomorrow," Cameron says, like he just pulled a Vulcan mind meld on me. "Let's have some fun for a few hours."

Fun sounds… *fun*.

"The three of us?" I ask, because I need clarification for my nipples and my suddenly damp inner thighs. I have no idea when my pussy got wet, but it absolutely is.

Cameron nods.

Then suddenly Alexsei strolls up to us, clapping his large hand on Cameron's shoulder. "Thanks for waiting."

He smells like soap, and his suit jacket is straining at the shoulders. He's a big man. He gives me an easy smile. "Hi, Luna. How's it going?"

He doesn't look like he wants to ask me out or ravage my naked body. He just looks like Alexsei. Upbeat. Confident. Extremely good-looking.

"It's going," I say, then give myself a mental eye roll.

What the hell was that?

Pulling it together, I say, "Cameron invited me to go home with you guys. For sex. And pancakes."

Alexsei's eyebrows shoot up. Then he grins. "Oh, yeah? Did you say yes?"

Feeling on more sure footing with Alexsei, who is easy to read, I give a nonchalant shrug. "I didn't answer him yet."

Alexsei reaches out and flips the ends of my hair and winks. "You should say yes."

I think about going home alone to my apartment above the bakery, where I haven't done laundry or dishes all week. I picture scrolling on my phone, unable to sleep because my brain is spinning with to-do lists before heading downstairs to obsessively check inventory or clean the oven again. I may be a lousy personal housekeeper, but my kitchen in the bakery is sparkling clean.

Dani will be at Nathan's apartment getting railed by three guys.

I could be getting railed by two guys.

"Sex is a great stress reliever," I tell Alexsei.

He nods, suddenly solemn. "It really is. Do you need that, baby?"

I glance over at my best friend. Dani is now kissing Michael Hughes, his hand possessively on the small of her back. She's glowing. Her skin looks like an Instagram ad for beauty products. When I looked in the mirror this morning, my skin was dull and lifeless and I swear I'm losing my hair. I even walked past my vibrator and ignored it because I wanted to get my dough proofing by six.

If that isn't stressed, I don't know what is.

I nod. "I need that. I really need that."

"Then let us take care of you," Cameron says.

God, something in his voice just makes everything in me say *yes, please.*

Everything except that one tiny corner of my brain that's chanting, *To-do list! To-do list!*

But now, if I go home, I won't be able to sleep because I'll be thinking about how I could have been having sex with these two tonight. That will not make my to-do list any better.

I look at them both for a long moment. I really like how we're just laying this all out there. We all want to have sex tonight. With each other. And now we all know it.

This is actually really great.

I nod. "Yes. Sure. I'm in."

Alexsei gives a grin that makes my pussy flutter riotously. "That's an excellent decision."

It does feel like an excellent decision. Or at least an exciting one. "I'm on the fence about making you pancakes, though. I may not stay that long. I'm very busy."

"You can't offer, then take it back," he says, giving me an adorable pout. "I mean, chocolate chips? Come on."

I'm not normally a fan of pouting men, but he looks pretty damn cute doing it.

"I never offered to make them. I just asked if you like them," I tell him, regaining my equilibrium.

Alexsei laughs. "Sassy girl."

"Semantics," Cameron adds dryly.

"No. Facts." I shove my phone in my back pocket and spin on my heel. I tap Dani on the shoulder. "Bye."

She gives me a finger wave, now lip-locked with Nathan Armstrong.

I turn to my brother. "Good game. See ya."

"Thanks." Crew is only half paying attention to me. He's eyeing his girlfriend with loving amusement. "See you at Thanksgiving." Then he fully turns to me. "You're making cornbread, right?"

Food always takes priority for Crew. I cross my arms. "Maybe. We'll see. I'm really busy." How many times do I have to tell people that?

"Don't show up without cornbread. I'm serious, Luna."

"What are you bringing?" I demand.

"My charm and good looks."

Now, I fully roll my eyes. "I might choke on that." I wave to him and turn back to Cameron and Alexsei, who are talking in low tones.

Alexsei puts his hand out, gesturing for me to go first.

"Wait, what are you doing with those two?" Crew demands.

"They're walking me to my car," I call to him over my shoulder. "Safety first."

Crew is so wrapped up in his own love life, he buys my excuse. He actually reaches out and shakes Alexsei's hand. "Thanks, man. I appreciate you looking out for my sister."

"No problem." Alexsei gives nothing away.

But as soon as we're out of ear shot he does wince. "I feel a little bad about that," he admits.

I'm between the two men, nerve endings strumming in anticipation. "Don't worry about it. He'll never know."

"What if you fall in love with me?" Alexsei teases.

I snort. "Marking myself Safe From Falling in Love With a Hockey Player Today."

He just laughs.

CHAPTER 3
Alexsei

LUNA FUCKING MCNEILL is in the elevator in my building on the way to my apartment.

Finally.

I really did believe we'd get here, eventually, but *damn*, this was faster than expected. And easier. Not that I think she's easy. She actually has *not-easy-don't-even-try-it* written all over her.

But that's the thing. I have not forgotten for a second that the person who actually got her here is Cameron. Cameron never shies away from a challenge. Cameron sees, *don't-even-try-it* and gets that *fucking-bring-it* look in his eye and the thing—or person—doesn't stand a chance.

He looks like a nerd. Sure, a rich, well-dressed, I-don't-give-a-fuck nerd, but still a nerd. But this nerd is worth several million dollars and, well, he really doesn't give a fuck.

And he's my best fucking friend. I'm staring at the perfect, petite, blond proof of it right now. He acts like he doesn't listen to me when I go on and on about the things I get excited about. A new sub shop. A new TV show. A new Reddit forum. An amazing, gorgeous girl.

But he does. He listens. And he got Luna into our apartment tonight.

I sneak a look at her out of the corner of my eye. She's leaning against the back wall of the elevator, scrolling on her phone as if we're in an office building on our way up to start our day in our cubicles.

But we're not.

We're on our way up to our apartment. For sex.

I feel like it's my birthday. Or Christmas morning. Or the day I found out I'd been drafted to the pros. Or all three rolled into one.

Except none of those involved a naked woman. Okay, maybe the night I was drafted did.

But none of them involved Luna McNeill.

I barely know this woman, but I know she's gorgeous, sassy, smart, and funny.

I don't typically go for sassy, but I've had women that are all of those other things, and there's just something about Luna that feels different.

I think, maybe, weirdly, it's that she's not all that impressed with me. Or professional athletes. Or hockey players. Or maybe most guys in general.

Which is why her leaning against the elevator, scrolling on her phone, as Cam and I are taking her home to fuck her all night, seems very in character.

I'm used to puck bunnies. I can admit it. As far back as high school, I had girls interested because I'm cute and because I'm downright magical on the ice. Not my words, but more than one person has used them to describe my play.

Luna doesn't care.

And that makes me want to be magical to her in some other way.

And I will *never* say that out loud to anyone. Ever.

Luna's brother Crew, is our new all-star, everyone's-talking-about-him, high-scoring player. Luna's grown up around hockey. Good hockey. Which means she's grown up around good hockey *players*. She knows how we tick. If she wanted to date a hockey player, she'd be dating a hockey player.

So the fact that she's with me right now, feels like something special.

And as the elevator stops on the top floor and the doors swish open and Cam rests his hand on her lower back, escorting her into our apartment, I try not to think too hard about the fact that she might be here because of my roommate.

Maybe I'm the tagalong. The side dish. Maybe she's here for Cameron and I just happened to come in this package deal.

I shut those thoughts down. It doesn't matter. She's here and there's something else I really love about my best friend and roommate—when it comes to me, he's very generous.

"Do you want a drink or something?" I ask her.

She shrugs out of her coat and hands it to Cam.

My gaze scans her body. I checked her out earlier tonight when I saw her coming down the steps at the arena to her seat behind the glass.

She's in a Racketeers T-shirt, tight jeans, and black boots that go up to nearly her knees. She looks like thousands of other women at the game tonight.

I didn't notice any of them. But I saw her the moment she walked in and looked at her too often throughout the game.

She flicks her hair back as she turns from checking out the kick-ass view through our living room windows and smiles at me. "No, I'm okay."

Cam looks down at her coat as if wondering how he suddenly ended up holding it, but he turns and hooks it on our coat tree.

Okay, she doesn't want to drink. I want to just sweep her up into my arms and carry her into the bedroom, but I'm aware I need to be at least a little cool here. "Are you hungry?"

Her smile grows. She shakes her head. "No, I don't need any food."

"Not even pancakes?" I ask, taking a step closer.

I'm Alexsei Fucking Ryan. I am a professional hockey player. I'm a *good* professional hockey player. I'm good-looking, I'm rich, a ton of women want to sleep with me. Why the fuck am I acting nervous and like I don't know what to do with a woman in my place?

She tips her head. "Pancakes are morning food." Now *she* takes a step toward *me*. I also really like that.

"Morning is several hours away," I point out. My gaze drops to her mouth. She has a great mouth. A mouth I very much want to taste. A mouth, I very much want to see wrapped around my cock.

She wets that luscious mouth. "Yep."

I lift my hand and drag my fingers through her long, silky hair. Some strands are so blond they're almost white. I'm mesmerized for a moment, watching the purple tips slip between my fingers.

"For fuck's sake, just kiss her."

The gruff, seemingly exasperated order comes from Cam.

He'd standing behind me. Luna's gaze flickers to him and I see heat flare. Good. She needs to want us both.

Her gaze returns to mine. "Yeah, just kiss her."

I am very good at following directions. It makes me extremely coachable, a great teammate, and the only man Cameron shares women with.

All three things that serve me very well.

I slide my hand to the back of her head, bring her in, and seal my mouth over hers.

Her hands fist the front of my shirt, and she gives a little moan. That sound shoots straight to my cock. I'm already hard for her. Hell, I've been half hard since I saw her standing in the back hallway outside of the locker room. I've wanted to kiss her since almost the first moment I met her.

And I can feel Cam watching us. That makes it even hotter. My buddy is definitely a voyeur and there's something about him watching me kiss, touch, and fuck the women we share that makes it so damned good.

I lick my tongue over Luna's lower lip, tug that lip between my teeth, then, when she gasps, slide my tongue in along hers. She comes up onto tiptoe, arching closer. My other hand snakes from her waist to her ass, cupping her and bringing her up against me. I know she can feel how hard I am for her.

I feel Cam's hand on my shoulder and then can tell he's sliding his other palm down her back. He stops at the curve of her low back and presses her into me even tighter.

Her moan is louder and longer this time.

I drag my mouth from hers, along her jaw to her ear. "I'm really fucking glad you said yes to this."

She sighs. "Me, too."

I run my scruffy jaw up and down the side of her neck. I feel the shiver that goes through her. I grin against the curve where her neck meets her shoulder. "So I've been thinking about fucking you since I first saw you, but I'm also open to requests. What do you want tonight?"

All she says is, "*Anything*."

I lift my head to meet her gaze. "You sure?"

"I'm sure."

"She got in the car with us," Cam reminds me. "It wasn't actually for pancakes. We all made it pretty damn clear what this was about."

Her gaze goes to him. "Oh, I'd better be getting pancakes out of this."

See? Sassy. I love it and I can't wait to see how Cam handles it. He's not any more used to that than I am because he always picks women he knows I'll like. Sweet, passive girls. Luna is a departure for us both and I can see how much he likes that about her, despite his seeming impatience. I know him well enough to see that simmering beneath the surface of his grumpy exterior, he's turned on by Luna.

Probably more so than with any woman we've ever been with.

"No worries. You will *definitely* want to make us pancakes in the morning," he tells her.

I watch her brows arch. She's still looking at Cam.

"Is that right?" she asks. "I'm making the pancakes?"

I decide to let him take it from here.

"You'll be wrung out on pleasure and so fucking *grateful* to us that you'll be willing to do anything. I'll say 'pancakes' and point to the kitchen and you'll hustle your sweet ass—naked, of course —out and start cooking for us," Cam tells her.

I can hear the tightness in his voice even as he teases her. He wants her. He wants this. But I watch her face.

Her eyes are hot, even as her mouth twitches at the corner. "Wow. I can't believe I come across as a woman who responds to orders. I really need to work on seeming more standoffish than that."

Cam moves his hand from her lower back to cup her face, dragging his thumb over her lower lip. "Sweetheart, I've been sitting behind you at hockey games all season. I know you better than you think."

Surprise crosses her face, and I wonder what he's talking about. Of course, I knew he sat behind her, but he's never said he's spoken to her. Not in any of the times I've gone on and on about how gorgeous she is, how funny she is, how I'd love to ask her out.

But looking at her now, having finally kissed her, and anticipating all of the things we're going to do tonight, it's obvious he's been watching her more closely than I realized. Which I understand. Luna is drawing me in as if she has a gravitational force of her own.

And I never want to get out of it.

She swallows, then says, "I see. You're one of those super insightful guys. And you're going to be the big studs to change my mind about everything? About men and relationships and my place in the world?"

Cam drops his hand, steps back. "No. Just about how you like to be fucked."

His short answer and the word *fucked*, seems to shoot a bolt of lightning into the room and through both Luna and me. I feel Luna tense, and I feel heat flooding through me. She sucks in a little breath and her gaze comes back to mine.

"Why don't you fuck me and we'll find out?"

"That's enough talking," Cam says. "In the bedroom."

"Bedroom. So traditional," she says, but her voice is breathy.

"Yeah, well, I have high standards. And girls only get fucked on my dining room table or over the back of my very expensive sofa after they've earned it."

She narrows her eyes at him, but I think she's fighting a smile again.

"Earned it, huh? Being here is such a privilege?"

I have to adjust myself. I'm getting hard as a fucking rock. I like this dynamic between them, and it's clear Luna likes it as well.

"Yes. The jury's still out on these pancakes, and you've now made them into a big fucking deal. Deliver on those and I'll think about letting you come on my other furniture."

I don't look back, but I can hear when he turns and starts toward the bedroom. His bedroom. When we share, it's always his bedroom. He calls the shots.

I look down at her. "You still in?"

She's staring after him, but when she looks at me again, she nods. "So in."

Her quick, enthusiastic answer makes me grin. "Yeah?"

She runs her hand up and down my chest. "Yeah," she says, her voice husky. "Take me to the bedroom."

So I do the only thing I can. I lean over, hook her behind the knees, and sweep her up into my arms. She gives a little shriek of surprise, but she looks delighted as I grin down at her, turning and starting down the hallway.

When we get there, Cam already has his shirt off, the bedside lamp on, casting a soft golden glow to the room and the duvet pulled back.

I let Luna's feet swing to the floor. But I don't let her get far. I cup her face and bring her in for a deep, slow kiss. She responds immediately, looping her arms around my waist and pressing close.

She's so fucking sweet. I could kiss her for hours. Just run my hands over her body.

But Cam's in a hurry. Or at least he's eager. That's probably a better word.

He moves in behind her and runs his hands from her shoulders to her hips. His hands slide around to the front of her jeans, and he unbuttons the button and starts untucking the shirt.

"Take your shirt off, Alexsei," he orders softly.

I let Luna go, reluctantly, and lean back, only far enough so that I can start unbuttoning my shirt. She's watching my fingers move down the front of my shirt, but she also leans back, letting Cam drag the T-shirt over her head, tossing it to the side.

Then Luna McNeill is standing in front of me in nothing but a bra and blue jeans.

My mouth goes dry. "Fucking hell, you're gorgeous," I tell her.

She smiles. "You, too." Her gaze tracks over my chest and down my abs as the shirt parts and I shrug out of it.

She lifts a hand, tracing the pads of her fingers over my pecs and up over the slope of my shoulders, then down my upper arms and over my biceps.

"This is hot," she comments as she swirls her fingers over the tattoo that runs from my elbow, up my upper arm and cups my shoulder.

It's a Ukrainian flag with writing below it, but I don't want to talk about me right now. I want to bask in *her*.

"Do you have any tattoos?" I ask.

She quirks a brow. "Let's find out."

I groan and lower my head for a kiss.

Cam unhooks her bra and draws it down her arms. She drops her hold on me to let it slip to the floor.

Then, of course, I have to lean back again.

She's fucking perfect. Perky breasts, with hard, dark pink nipples that are begging to be touched.

I lift my hands, cupping them both and running my thumbs over the tips.

She groans. "Yes. Harder."

There's a rumble from Cam and I look over her shoulder at him.

He's watching me touch her. I grin at him as I tug on her nipples and she gasps.

"Yes," she encourages.

I lift a brow as if asking if he would like a turn, because he looks like he might. But he says nothing, just grips her waist as if holding her still for me. She lifts an arm looping around his neck, arching her back and pressing her breasts toward me.

Damn, they look good together. I squeeze her nipple again, and she gasps my name.

"Suck on her," Cam commands.

I don't have to be asked twice. I lean over and take a nipple in my mouth, sucking hard.

She gasps, and her other hand goes to the back of my head, holding me close, her fingers curling into my skull.

I love that breast for several long, delicious moments before moving to the other. When she's writhing, both breasts wet, the nipples obviously aching, I lift my head.

Then I watch as Cam lowers the zipper on her jeans and starts to push the denim and the pink silk of her panties over her hips.

"Take her boots off," he tells me.

I drop to my knees in front of her, not at all surprised to find myself kneeling in front of Luna McNeill. I look up at her with a grin. "Give me a foot, Princess."

She obeys, leaning back into Cam more fully, her arm still around his neck. I slide one boot off. Then she offers me her other foot without me asking. I toss them both toward the door without looking. I'm too focused on hooking my fingers in the waistband of her jeans and shimmying them down. Her trim hips, toned thighs, and her bare, gorgeous pussy come into view.

"Holy shit, I feel like I'm dreaming," I tell her.

"Not dreaming, champ," she says. "I'm definitely wide awake."

I sweep her jeans and panties off, not even sure where they land when I toss them. I run my hands up the outside of her legs until I'm gripping her hips and my face is level with her pussy. Then I notice her tattoo.

"Oh, *yes.*" I lean in and lick over the little cupcake inked on her left hip bone. I look up. "Perfect."

She smiles down at me. "You like that?"

"So fucking much." I lick it again. "Sweet as the ones you bake."

"What the hell are you two talking about?" Cam leans over, looking down her body.

I draw my thumb over the tattoo. "Our girl's ink."

When he spots the cupcake, his eyes narrow. He looks smug. "I fucking knew it."

I see his hands squeeze her tighter and I smile up at him before leaning in to press my mouth against her mound. "I'm going to spend a lot of time right here tonight."

"Promise?" she asks, her voice husky.

"Alexsei loves eating pussy," Cam says gruffly.

I look up at him. His jaw is tight, his voice rougher than usual.

I meet Luna's gaze. "I'm not just a champ on the ice, pretty girl." I squeeze her hips.

"That's the way to get extra chocolate chips in your pancakes, you know," she tells me.

I lean in and kiss the crease where her thigh and pelvis meet, just below the tattoo. "Sweetheart, I don't think we have enough chocolate chips in this house for you to properly reward me for how fucking good this is going to be."

She gives a breathy laugh. "I don't know how we're all fitting in here with your egos."

Suddenly I'm almost tipping forward as Cam moves her back, taking her to the foot of the bed. He nudges her down to sitting. "You two talk a lot." He stands right in front of her, towering over her. He lifts a hand, pressing his thumb against her lips. "It's no wonder you're stressed. Your brain never stops."

"I—" She starts, but it's muffled and Cam doesn't let her lips part.

"No," he says firmly. "You're going to shut up now."

Her eyes widen, and her hand comes up to circle his wrist. He doesn't move his hand, though. He leans in, pinning her with a gaze. "You're going to be a good girl and take everything we give you. You're not going to overthink it. You're not going to ask a bunch of questions. You're not going to say anything except, 'yes', 'harder', 'more', 'please', and—" He pauses. "Macaron."

She frowns. He lets her pull his hand back now. "Macaron?"

"That's your safe word, sweetheart."

Her brows rise. "I need a safe word?"

Cam says simply, "Yes."

I feel a jolt of lust hit me low and hard.

Luna's cheeks flush and I watch her lips drop open. She stares up at Cam. I wait for her to push him back. To stand up and stomp over and gather her clothes. To tell us we're both way too much, way too fast, and this was not what she signed up for.

Seconds tick by. Cameron stands just watching her.

And finally, she nods.

I swear to God, my knees actually wobble. I don't think that I have ever been this turned on in my life.

Yes, she's my crush. My dream girl, though I barely know her. But this whole night seems so surreal. And this energy between her and Cam is something I've never experienced before.

Cam and I have shared before. Actually, multiple times. We even had a short-term steady girlfriend that lasted about six months. And still, I have never felt an electricity like this.

I can't fucking wait.

Cam steps to the side.

"Come here," he says.

Somehow we all know he's talking to me. I step up in front of Luna, next to him.

"How about we use that pretty mouth for something other than talking?" he asks.

She swallows and her gaze drops to both of our flies, where we are both obviously very hard. But again, she nods.

Fuck. Yes.

Luna's eyes stay on his hands as he starts to unbuckle his belt.

I start unbuckling as well. I pull my belt through the loops and she watches, the pink in her cheeks getting darker and spreading down her pretty throat.

I can't help but reach up and cup her cheek, running my thumb over the heated skin. "You okay?" I ask.

She nods. "Yes."

"She didn't say her safe word," Cam says.

Luna looks at him, then back to me. "More."

One of the words Cam gave her to use.

Okay then. This girl is with us. And I'm going to stop asking questions and just enjoy her.

We both shuck out of our pants and our boxers.

Luna drinks us in. She doesn't act shy, her eyes widen slightly, but she doesn't lean back or look away. In fact I watch as her sweet pink tongue darts out again, wetting those lips that I don't think I'll ever get enough of.

Her hands are curled around the edge of the mattress. She's sitting in front of us, bare naked, but she's not moving to cover herself at all.

Her confidence is such a fucking turn on.

Cam steps closer, moving until his knees sandwich hers. I do the same on the other side. He cups the back of her head, then moves her toward me. "Suck his cock."

She leans over and takes the base of my cock in her hand. She strokes up and down my length and it's possible I might embarrass myself. Her touch is perfect.

She strokes me, swirling her thumb over the top, gathering up the precum already wetting my tip. She brings her thumb to her mouth and licks.

I swear I'm panting. That's the sexiest thing I've ever seen.

She smiles, then leans in and guides my cock to her lips. She sucks just slightly, swirling her tongue over the tip, then taking me in just a few inches.

I have to lock my knees and take a deep breath. My hand goes to the back of her head, Cam and I holding her together. I look over and find that she's gripping his cock in her other fist. She's pumping him slowly up and down. He's also bracing his knees and breathing in through his nose and out through his mouth. His gaze, however, is locked on where she's taking me into her mouth.

She takes me deeper, sucks, then draws me out slowly, letting her mouth drag along my length, licking and sucking as she goes.

"Faster and deeper," he tells her shortly. "Right, Alexsei? That's what you want."

"That's what I want."

Then he makes a hissing noise, and I noticed that she's gripping his cock tighter and stroking him faster.

But she also does what he tells her to me. She starts picking up her pace, and I swear to God, it's heaven.

I curl my hand in her hair, gripping tighter, trying to hold on. I don't want to move away from the blissful wet heat but I can't take this much longer.

"Luna, baby, I gotta stop." My words are ragged.

She picks up her pace, sucking harder.

"No, baby. Not coming like this." I tug on her hair.

She doesn't let up.

Cam grips her jaw with his hand and pulls her off of me. He tips her head until she's looking at him. "You need to be a better listener, pretty girl."

She strokes her hand up and down his cock. "He needs to have a less perfect cock for *that* to happen."

"He does have a great cock," Cam says.

Which makes me suck in a deep breath. I love it when he gets like this—making it clear to whatever woman we're with, he wants *me*, too.

Then he pushes, and she tumbles onto her back on the mattress.

"Make her scream," he tells me.

I know what he's saying. He wants me to eat her pussy. He loves to watch me do that because it's not his thing. He never goes down on girls. But he likes seeing their eyes roll back in their heads when I worship them with my tongue.

I immediately go to my knees and move between her legs.

She props herself up on her elbows and looks down at me with a mischievous glint in her eyes. "You're a champ, right?"

"Nothing but five-star reviews."

She laughs. "Well, don't let what's about to happen go to your head. I haven't even been that friendly with my vibrator in a while. So this probably won't be that much of a challenge for you."

I move in and swipe my tongue in a long slow lick up her inner thigh. "How hard do you come with your vibrator?" I ask. Then I give her inner thigh a little nip. "One to ten?"

"You mean what setting do I use?" she asks. "Or how hard is my orgasm on a scale of one to ten?"

I lean in and suck on the spot that I just lapped. "Both. But I want to know about your orgasms on a scale from one to ten. Ten being your seeing stars and nearly pass out."

"I'd give him a solid six when his batteries are fresh."

"Oh honey, I can do a six half-drunk and at the end of a long series," I tell her, licking along that hip crease. "And your vibrator is a 'he' and not an 'it?' Who do you think about when you're using him to get yourself off?"

"You won't be anywhere near a fucking six if you keep talking," Cam says, clearly exasperated. "Eat her pussy, because if I don't hear *someone* coming in the next ten minutes, I'm going to be really fucking annoyed."

She looks up at him and beckons him forward. "I can help you out, big guy."

He shakes his head. "I'm okay."

Her eyebrows rise. "What do you mean, you're okay?" Her gaze drops pointedly to his steel hard erection.

"I said, I'm okay. That's what I meant."

She looks at me. "What's with him?"

"He likes to watch me do this." I lean in and give her pussy a nice long lick, from opening to clit. "Didn't you know this was a spectator sport?"

She gives a groan. "Oh my God. That is a pretty sight."

"Hold on tight." Then I set to work showing her why a six on a one-to-ten orgasm scale is nothing.

I lick, suck, and tongue fuck her for a few minutes. She's gasping and moaning, exactly the way I like it. She also tastes absolutely fucking delicious. I could do this all night.

But I definitely want to see and hear her come. I need to know what all of Luna's orgasms are like.

I also need her nice and soft and wet and hot for when I fuck her. Because that is not going to be slow and sweet.

I fasten my mouth on her clit and suck hard, easing two fingers into her. She's fallen back onto the mattress already and has her arm flung over her eyes. Her other hand grips the duvet as she bucks against my mouth.

I give Cam a quick glance. He's watching us, his cock in hand, stroking slowly.

This is how it usually goes. He really does love watching this particular activity. His eyes are fastened on my mouth, rather than on Luna's face or the rest of her body. I give a long lick so he can see everything, then curl my fingers against her G spot and press. His gaze shifts upward. I know he wants to see her expression as I take her to the edge.

I can't see her face, but I imagine it's a beautiful fucking sight when she cries out, "Yes! Fuck, Alexsei!"

I like that very much. I do it again. Same reaction.

I stroke along her inner wall, sucking her clit at the same time.

"Yes, more! Oh, my God!"

I look at Cam. Those weren't on the list of words he'd given her to use, but I don't think he'll mind.

I look up her body at her. She throws her arm off of her face and takes in a big, deep breath. Then she looks over at Cam. "Come here."

His gaze flies to her face. He frowns. "You don't call the shots."

"Come kiss me. Play with my nipples."

"Luna, you're Alexsei's." He says it firmly, but he does palm her breast, roughly.

She arches into his touch as I suck harder on her clit and thrust my fingers faster.

"Yes! Alexsei!" Luna gasps.

I'm going to get her there. I do have her. Just like Cam said.

"Kiss me, Cam!" she shouts a second later.

Cam suddenly takes a step forward and leans onto the mattress, bracing his hand next to her hip, glowering down at her. "No. You're going to be a good fucking girl, and you're going to come all over Alexsei's tongue. Do you hear me? Your pretty pussy is going to flood his mouth. You are going to come apart all over his hand and face. You're going to do exactly what we tell you to do, Luna, right *now*."

I don't know if I finally sucked hard enough or if it was his commanding words, but Luna's pussy suddenly grips my fingers tight and she cries out, "Fuck yes!" as she tips over the edge, coming hard, exactly as Cam ordered.

I slow my thrusts and kiss my way down her inner thigh as she comes down from the height. When her pussy stops fluttering, I ease my fingers from her, lifting them to my mouth and sucking them clean.

Fucking delicious.

I watch as she throws her arm over her face again, breathing raggedly, squeezing her thighs together.

I also watch Cam watching her.

He's still leaning over the bed, just watching her float down from her climax.

When she finally moves her hand away from her eyes and looks up at him, she says, "What is your problem?"

Cam growls, and the next thing I know he's moving me out of

the way, scooping her up, and sitting down on the end of the bed with her in his lap.

But not cradling her.

No. This is not some kind of after-care thing.

He has her turned over in his lap, face down, ass up and I realize only a second before it happens what he intends to do.

His big hand lands on her bare ass with a sharp smack.

It only takes another second to see that she likes it. A fucking lot.

CHAPTER 4
Cameron

THIS WOMAN.

I don't understand why she's driving me so crazy.

Women never drive me crazy.

I don't usually *care* about women or what they think of me. Except for my mother. My mother is the only woman whose opinion matters to me.

When Alexsei and I bring women home to fuck, it is literally only to fuck. And it's only because Alexsei wants them here. It's not something I need. I do it for Alexsei.

Tonight was supposed to be the same. He's had this thing for this girl for a while, and I'll admit that she's been intriguing me for months sitting behind her at hockey games.

So tonight, when I heard her talking about being stressed, I decided to do something about it finally. All of it. Her stress. My intrigue. Alexsei's interest.

But bringing her home for Alexsei was… for Alexsei.

Yet now, here I am with her naked, post-orgasmic, in my lap, her bare ass under my hand.

And I'm spanking her.

She is momentarily shocked, but then she gives a soft moan of approval. She even lifts her ass, ever-so-slightly, in blatant invitation.

So I lift my hand and smack her again.

Now she blusters. "What the hell are you doing?"

"I have the feeling that you have not been spanked enough in your life," I tell her, my hand just resting on her ass right now.

She flips that pale blond purple-tipped hair over her shoulder and smirks up at me. "I was *never* spanked."

"Shocking." Her fake outrage is amusing me.

"People adore me. People think I walk on water. No one ever wants to spank me."

"Yeah, well, I fucking do."

I lift my hand and smack her again. It's not hard. I'm leaving gorgeous pink prints on her ass, but it's not hurting her. It probably stings. But more than anything, it surprised her, and now it's turning her on.

It surprised me, too.

And it's turning me on.

Which is a little confusing, but not enough to make me stop.

"You need someone to make you behave. You also never stop working and planning and thinking. You never get out of your damn head. I told you how this was all going to go. You just needed to lie there and take it. But you started trying to take charge."

"I just wanted you to kiss me! Excuse the hell out of me."

"And then I said no."

"I was going to come. It would've helped me get there faster."

"You had Alexsei's face buried between your legs. You need to stop thinking. You need to just feel. You need to just let go."

"And you kissing me would've helped with that."

I lift my hand and lower it, smacking her again, this time a little harder than before I'll admit.

She gasps. "Stop that."

Her tone indicates she wants the exact opposite.

I spank her again. "No. You're not in charge."

"You should ask."

"You'll learn that's not me. You also have a safe word. That you are not using."

"I—" she pauses. "I forgot."

I swat her again. "Liar."

She glares up at me. But she also bites her lip, the little flirt. "I did."

"Bullshit. You don't forget things."

She doesn't respond. She wiggles on my lap.

I look down at my hand resting on her pale, smooth ass. My handprint looks good there. And I'm agitated by that.

I don't really do women. So the fact that this one is under my skin is really bugging me.

So I spank her once more, just for good measure.

"Stop." Her voice completely lacks force. She sounds breathy. She's rocking down onto my cock a little.

I run my hand over her ass. The warmth satisfies me. Then I run my hand down the back of her thigh. "That's not your safe word." I'm surprised by how husky my voice is.

Then I think of the other person in the room with us. I look up at Alexsei.

She's here for him. He's the one who likes her. Is he pissed about this?

He does *not* look pissed. He looks intensely turned on.

Fuck. I love that look on him. That tight jaw, that ragged breathing, that heat in his eyes. And of course his huge, hard cock.

This man is magnificent.

And I only ever see him like this—well, naked at all—when we have a woman here with us.

I run my hand over Luna's ass and down her thigh again. I should be nicer to her. Thanks to her, I get to see that look on Alexsei's face.

"You do remember your safe word right, sweetheart?" I ask her, watching Alexsei.

She wiggles some more. "You're kind of a dick."

Her squirming is rubbing her *against* my dick even more. I squeeze her ass. "That's not it."

I run my hand up her inner thigh. "Do you remember?" I repeat.

She's breathing fast and I can tell that this is turning her on. She doesn't just have a safe word, she could easily push up off my lap. She knows it. She knows that I know it.

My eyes are on Alexsei. His eyes are on my hand. As I get closer to her pussy, he steps forward.

He wants to see this. He wants to watch me touching her. His gaze is locked on her body, so I can study his. The small gash on his chin, the scruff along his jaw, the thick column of his throat, the contours of his shoulders and chest, the ink on his upper arm, the ridges of his abs, the deep V of his hips. And that magnificent cock.

Luna's thighs part, almost instinctively, as I run my hand up higher on her thigh. Her heart is pounding where her chest is resting on my thigh.

"Do. You. Remember?" I ask.

Finally, she puts her head against the duvet and says, "*Yes.*"

My fingertips are at her pussy, and the heat is intense. Her inner thighs are sticky, partly from her orgasm just a few minutes ago, but possibly from what I've just done to her as well.

Does she like getting spanked? Bossed around? Dominated?

It's pretty damn clear that it's yes to all of the above. Whether she knows it or not.

This woman desperately needs to be tied up, edged, and then taken into oblivion by orgasm.

I watch Alexsei as I move my fingers up between her thighs and press my middle finger into her pussy.

Fuck. She's tight. And so damned hot and wet.

And I can't deny that the moan she gives as I finger her makes my dick twitch.

So does the look on my best friend's face.

I slide my finger deeper. She moans. Alexsei clenches his fists at his sides.

He's not used to being the one who watches.

I give her two fingers. Alexsei steps closer again.

He just needs to do one thing, and I'll let him have her.

"She's fucking tight, isn't she?" I ask him, taunting him.

He swallows hard.

He gives one jerky nod.

I slide my fingers deeper. She moans again and widens her legs. Alexsei's gaze is glued on my hand, moving in and out of Luna's pussy.

"She's gonna feel like a vice around your cock." I watch his eyes darken.

Then finally, *finally*, he does what I've been waiting for–his hand goes to his cock and he squeezes, then pumps up and down the length.

My cock hardens beneath Luna. If she thinks that's for her, fine. Hell, it is. But it's for Alexsei, too.

Alexsei is watching me finger fuck the girl he's been low-key obsessed with for weeks while I watch him jerk off.

This is going very well.

I don't know exactly what's going through either of their minds, but I do know that neither of them is getting off like this.

I tease her clit and her, *"Fuck,"* makes Alexsei's gaze fly to her face.

She turns her head so she's facing him, her cheek against the duvet.

I reach with my other hand to brush her hair away from her face so he can see her fully. Her eyes are shut, her cheeks pink, her lips open as she pants.

He steps close and puts his hand against her face. "You're so fucking gorgeous," he tells her.

Her eyes fly open, and they lock gazes. He strokes his cock right in front of her and she licks her lips.

But she doesn't say anything. I've finally shut her up.

I feel her pussy tighten around my fingers and her reaction is not about me now. It's about Alexsei.

Perfect.

I slide my fingers free and give her a sharp smack on the ass.

She opens her mouth to speak—of course, she does—but I flip her onto her back on the mattress and stand, pushing my friend between her knees. "Fuck her."

The command is simple. Alexsei sucks in a quick breath, but he leans over and braces his hands on either side of her. He goes in for a deep, long kiss.

Luna wraps her legs around his waist, her hands moving to the back of his head, holding him close. She returns every stroke of his tongue.

I go to the bedside table and withdraw two condoms and a bottle of lube. I toss a condom onto the duvet next to his hand and keep the other.

He's still caught up in the kiss, though, one of his hands cupping her breast, playing with her nipple.

She's moaning and writhing beneath him, so I decide to be helpful. I'm a great guy like that.

I rip open a condom, then move behind Alexsei. I slide my hands down his sides. His muscles jump beneath my touch and I relish it. His skin is hot, his muscles hard, his body big, strong, powerful. This is the only time I touch him like this. But it's always so fucking good.

The first time was back in college. It was a complete surprise to him. Not only that I touched him, but that I wanted to. And that he liked it.

He brought a girl home for the sixth time since we'd moved in together two months before. I usually got lost when he was 'entertaining' but that night, for some reason, I was being an exceptional prick and told him I wasn't going anywhere.

He looked at the girl, gave her a wink, and asked if she minded if they had an audience. She'd said no. So I'd stayed.

But the 'audience' part had only lasted for a few minutes

before I was joining in. When the girl stretched out her hand and invited me in, I decided why the hell not. I told him it was my apartment, too, and if they were going to interrupt my evening by fucking on the couch, I was going to get something out of it.

And while Alexsei was the only one who fucked her, and I hadn't actually fucked anyone but my hand, I'd done plenty of looking and touching both of them.

Alexsei had gotten used to seeing me naked, me seeing him naked, and having hands other than feminine ones on him.

And he hadn't minded.

The next time, it was his idea.

Since then, he's gotten accustomed to having my hand, my mouth, and other parts of me involved with his girl. And him.

And he enjoys it.

I run my hand over his abs and they clench. But he doesn't let up kissing and touching Luna. He knows how this goes.

I reach around and stroke his cock. Firm and slow. Exactly the way I know he likes. I go rougher with him than any of the women do, and I know it works for him.

We haven't talked a whole lot about what he likes from me. Not during, and not after. But I can read him. I've known him well for a very long time and I care. I care what makes him happy, what makes him feel good, what makes him want to keep doing this. So yeah, I pay attention.

I jerk up and down his cock a few times and absorb his groans.

It doesn't matter what's making him feel good, if it's me or Luna or a combination, as long as Alexsei is the center of attention.

Oh, I know Luna thinks she is. I know this feisty little thing showed up tonight to be in the middle of a double-team. I know she thinks this is all about her.

She's wrong.

Finally, I roll the condom down his cock and give it a squeeze. With my mouth next to his ear, I say, "Take that pussy you've been dreaming of."

He shudders and pulls back, looking down at her, breathing fast. "Need to fuck you, beautiful."

She nods. "Please."

I position his cock at her entrance and then he thrusts. There's no easing in. He just takes her.

And Luna seems fine with it. She gasps, moans, and gives him a heartfelt, "*Yes*."

"Goddamn, you feel good," he tells her through gritted teeth.

I keep my hand resting on his lower back as he thrusts in and out of her slowly.

"Is she gripping your cock the way you like?" I ask. "Is she being good for you?" I look at his face, not hers.

"Fuck yes," Alexsei says, his jaw tight. "I could fuck her forever."

Luna arches her neck, and her fingertips dig into his shoulder blades. "More," she pants.

He picks up his pace, thrusting deeper.

"Yes, like that," she urges him on. "You feel so good. You're so big. So deep."

This woman and her mouth. She's constantly reminding me that she's here. I normally like the quiet ones. I like it when I can just get lost in the groans, moans, and grunts.

But her voice is landing on my ears differently. Like a soft, raw flicker of her tongue up my cock might feel. Like velvet. The image of her fingernails pops into my head and suddenly, I'm envisioning them wrapped around *my* cock.

"Kiss her," I tell Alexsei, pressing on the back of his head.

He doesn't need the urging to take her mouth in a deep, hot kiss. I move in behind him. I can get him deeper inside her. And I can get lost myself. I squeeze lube onto my fingers and then along Alexsei's backside.

He shivers, but it's not surprise, its anticipation. He knows exactly what's going to happen. This is always what happens. I work my palm over him, massaging his ass, slowly working my finger inside him.

"Fuck, yes," he groans against Luna's neck.

Her eyes are closed and she's moaning as he thrusts harder. "Yes, God, you fill me up so good."

I grit my teeth, unable to look away from her face now. She's overcome with ecstasy, and she really is gorgeous like that. I work another finger into Alexsei's ass, stretching him, getting him ready.

"Damn, more, Cam," he mutters.

My cock aches. I love when he uses my name in bed. He might be buried deep in Luna's pussy, but he's thinking of me, too.

I stretch him, pumping my fingers deep, loving the way he clenches around them. I lean over and say against his ear. "You ready?"

"Fuck yes."

I press the head of my cock to his ass, squeezing his shoulder for leverage, and start to slide in.

He stops thrusting into Luna, and she looks up at him. "Wha —"

His lips find hers, and he kisses her deeply as I ease the rest of the way in.

Fuck, he feels good. So fucking good. I grip his shoulder with one hand and his waist with the other. I let him get used to having me there, then when he takes a deep breath, I ease out and thrust back in.

He tears his mouth away from hers. "*Fucking hell,*" he grits out.

Then he starts fucking her again, in rhythm with me fucking him.

My thrusts drive him deeper into her and I pick up my pace, feeling my balls draw up as his muscles milk me. It's been a while for us, and even if I've been seeing other people, no one ever does to me what Alexsei does.

I'm quickly climbing toward my orgasm. Almost too quickly. But I don't need to take them with me. They've got each other and I have no doubt that Alexsei will make sure Luna has another before he finishes. He's a good guy that way. And he'll definitely want to feel her milking his cock.

But the way she's gasping and arching her hips closer, I don't think she's too far behind.

He raises his head and looks down at her, his hips still moving. "This is fucking amazing."

She nods. "It is. I'm so glad I said yes to this."

I start thrusting harder and faster, which pistons him inside of her harder and faster.

They both groan, and I can't help the satisfied grin that tugs at my lips.

I squeeze his waist and say simply, "Alexsei."

He knows by the tone of my voice and the rhythm of my body that I'm getting close.

He reaches between them and finds her clit. "Come for me, pretty girl. Want to feel this perfect pussy gushing all over my cock."

"Oh God," she half gasps, half laughs. "You're so sweet. I never pegged you for a dirty talker."

"It can get better," he tells her. "This cunt is the tightest, hottest, sweetest I've ever had. And I want it again and again. Squeeze me, Luna. Fucking take it."

She gasps, then arches her neck again — that long, pale, smooth neck that would look great with a bite mark on it—where the hell is that thought coming from?

Then she cries out, gripping his shoulders tightly. "Alexsei! Yes!"

"Yes," he groans loud and long and I feel him shuddering, coming inside her.

I let go. I hammer into him, then grip his waist hard, keeping his ass pressed tightly to me as I empty myself.

We're all breathing raggedly. Luna has her arm over her face again, a move that I'm starting to suspect is her way of keeping some distance during sex.

I squeeze Alexsei's waist again, softer now, then pull back, and head directly into the bathroom on shaky legs. I dispose of the condom and clean up.

I pass Alexsei as I come out of the bathroom and he heads in.

"Be nice," he says.

I smirk. I was very nice to her just now, even if she wasn't fully aware of my part in her most recent orgasm.

I walk back to the bed. She's still covering her face.

"Suddenly shy?" I slide between the sheets, naked, on the far side of the mattress from her. My side.

It's no coincidence that we fucked her on the side of the enormous California king that I don't sleep on. This is how it goes. When we bring women here, we use my room. And then Alexsei curls up in the middle, with the woman on the outside. On the side I don't sleep on.

Luna pulls her arm away from her face. "No. Just trying to get my bearings back."

I don't say anything to that. Alexsei has that effect on women. I fluff my pillow behind my head and let my eyes slide shut.

Alexsei is the aftercare guy. The cuddler. The *want to stay over?* guy.

Besides, we've already established she's staying. And making pancakes.

Wait, we did establish that, right?

I roll my head to look at her. "I like lots of chocolate chips in mine."

She looks over at me from where she's still lying, spread out, and bare naked.

She lifts a brow. "Me, too."

"Good. Then you should make pretty good ones."

"Everything I make is good."

Sassy confidence. I can't help it, I like it.

Oh, it's a pain in the ass. I don't want it around a lot. But I admire it.

"You know," I say, closing my eyes again. "People who really are good at everything don't feel the need to tell people they're good at everything."

I hear her breathy little laugh. "Wow, you really excel at being an asshole."

"And I'm also beautiful," I say, making sure she hears the smugness in my tone.

"And grumpy," she says, emphatically.

Yet, I can hear the fucking smile in her voice.

She doesn't deny the beautiful thing, though. And I don't deny the asshole thing.

And we both know she kind of likes me. Or at least me spanking her. Just like I kind of like her. Or at least spanking her.

Fuck, I'm going to keep thinking about that, aren't I?

"We have all the ingredients for pancakes from scratch," I say. Then yawn. On purpose. "If you think you're going to get away with using a mix, you're crazy."

"What happens if I do?" she asks. Because it seems she can't help sassing me.

"Well, I'd say I'd spank you, but we both know you'd like that."

She doesn't say anything to that. But I'm imagining I got an eye roll. Possibly a middle finger.

In fact, I'd be disappointed if I didn't get one of those. Or both.

CHAPTER 5

Alexsei

I LOVE SLEEPING in Cam's bed.

I tell myself it's because he's kind of a diva and has enough money to buy a really amazing mattress and sheets.

The truth is, I have enough money to buy the same mattress and sheets, and I still don't sleep as well in my bed as I do in his, though.

So I like these sleepovers we have every once in a while.

Of course, it might also have to do with the fact that when I'm in his bed, there's always a woman in my arms. A soft, warm, sweet-smelling woman. There's just nothing like them.

The truth is, I don't really like sleeping alone. I love skin-on-skin contact, cuddling, or even just knowing someone is near me. I don't really like being alone at all. I'm a people person.

I roll over, feeling twinges in my body that are not from hockey. Some of those twinges came from someone who is not soft or sweet-smelling like a woman, and I have to admit, I like those touches just as much.

And Cam does smell pretty good, actually…at least compared to hockey players.

We don't really talk much about what happens in the bedroom between us. After the first time we did, and we both agreed we wouldn't be mad if it happened again, but that it wouldn't affect our friendship or be anything serious. It's about sex and what feels good in the moment. It's all about getting caught up in what we're doing. The woman gets us going, and it's a natural progression that adds to everyone having a great fucking time.

It's lust. Everyone's a consenting adult. There's no reason to think it's anything other than that, and Cam agreed with me way back when. Then when we dated Sara, we did talk about that it works because we trust each other and that we could share a woman without jealousy or it getting messy.

But last night... *damn*. That was fucking unreal.

I blink up into the darkness. Why am I awake? I played a hard hockey game and then had hard, hot sex. I should be sleeping like the dead.

And then I hear it. The shuffling of bare feet on Cam's bedroom floor.

Someone's up, and leaving the room. And it isn't Cam. I can hear his slow, steady breathing on the other side of the bed.

That means it's Luna.

And she's sneaking out.

I don't fucking think so.

I wait until she leaves the bedroom to slip out of bed and follow her so we don't wake Cam.

"You gotta give me another chance at a five-star."

Luna whirls around, her hand going to her chest. "You scared me!"

"Not used to men coming up behind you at four a.m.?" I prop a shoulder against the wall, crossing my arms, and watch as she tries to pull her second boot on without falling over.

"Not really," she says.

"Satisfaction guaranteed," I say. "If that wasn't five-stars, I'm willing to keep trying until it is."

She straightens, boot on, and runs a hand through her hair. It cascades around her face, the pale strands falling just past her chin and catching the moonlight from the windows, almost glowing like a damned halo.

She's so fucking beautiful, I ache when I look at her. And now that I've had a taste of her, I'm not getting over this crush.

She's got a mouth like heaven, a pussy that makes me willing to sin in any way necessary to have it again, and I'd do anything to have more of her smiles, her moans, the way she touches me, clings to me as she comes...

Yeah, I can't let this woman walk out the door. I am not done with her yet.

She laughs lightly. "You damned hockey players are so competitive. Always need to be the best at everything."

I nod. "Yep. And we know how to train hard to get there. So come back to bed."

She smiles and shakes her head. "It was ten out of ten stars, I swear."

"People don't sneak out in the middle of the night after a ten out of ten."

"It's actually morning. The start of my day. I own a bakery. We start before the sun comes up."

"You're going to work?" I hadn't even thought of that. We should have let her get more sleep maybe.

She chews on her bottom lip and I wonder for a moment if she's contemplating lying to me. I just wait. This will be interesting.

She finally blows out a breath. "No, I'm actually closed today and tomorrow. I'm open on the weekends, so I take other days off to catch up. But I'm going into a really busy season. I have some recipes I need to test and some designs to finalize. When you own your own business, you kind of work all the time."

I know this. Cam works all the time, it seems. After making his first million, he seems to push even harder. Doing what, I'm not exactly sure. Nerd stuff. But it keeps him busy as hell.

I push off the wall and move toward her. She doesn't step

back. She just tips her head back and looks up at me as I come to stand in front of her.

It strikes me that her boots have at least a three-inch heel and she still only comes up to my chest.

I reach a hand up and thread it through her soft, silky hair. "Stay."

She shakes her head. "I can't. A lot to do. This was really fun. Exactly what I wanted and needed. But I gotta go."

"You're not open today. Stay here. Test your new recipes here. Hell, Cam and I will be wonderful taste testers for you."

She smiles. "Cam said you had all the ingredients for pancakes, but I doubt you have all the ingredients I'm going to need."

"I'll get them." I drag my thumb over her jaw. "I'll call in an order as soon as the places are open. Deliver it straight here. You don't have to do anything but come back and press that sweet ass against me and let me hold you for a few more hours."

She wants that. I can see it in her eyes. I'm not going to make her stay, and I'm not going to make her feel guilty if she leaves, but I am going to do whatever I can to make it easy for her if she chooses to give me more time with her.

Finally, she asks, "Do you even have a stand mixer?"

"Can you buy one of those in Chicago on a Sunday in November?" I ask.

Her smile grows and she nods. "Yes."

"Then I *will have* a stand mixer."

"I have designs to finalize. Everything's on my computer."

I lift a brow. "You don't save things to the cloud?"

Again, she pulls her bottom lip between her teeth, and I think she's contemplating lying.

"Tell me the truth," I say firmly.

I'm not the bossy one. That is most definitely Cam. But I can be firm if I need to be. I need to be here. I want her to stay and I need her to know that.

She nods. "Fine. Yes. I do save it to the cloud."

"So you can access it from here. Despite how he acts in the bedroom, Cam is a huge nerd. He has so much tech and computer equipment I can't even explain it. I promise you he has a computer you can use. Probably some amazing graphic program that you haven't even dreamed of. You'll have the best designs you've ever seen when you walk out of here."

She narrows her eyes. "You want me to stay here and *work*? I'll be busy the whole day. How does that actually get *you* anything?"

I pull her closer. Now her body is up against mine. "I get to see you longer. I get to be around you. Look at you wearing only one of my hoodies and nothing underneath. Flirt with you. Laugh with you."

She's watching me with an expression that's hard to describe.

But she's not saying no.

"And you're going to make a to-do list," I tell her. "Everything you need to get done. And every time you cross something off, I'm going to give you an orgasm."

Her eyes go wide. "*Every* time? I have a lot on my to-do list."

"Then you're going to be very, very relaxed and productive while you're here." I lean down and put my mouth against hers. "Say yes."

"I might be really sore and unable to walk when I leave here," she says. But again, she's not pulling back and she's not saying no.

I smile against her lips. "There are lots of ways to give people orgasms other than with cocks. I promise to be gentle."

She reaches up and wraps her hand behind my neck and pulls me against her mouth more firmly. She kisses me, her tongue stroking deep into my mouth, her body arching against mine.

When she leans back, she says, "You better not be."

I grin as lust and satisfaction rush through me in equal measure.

We had a pretty big win last night, and I don't think I've ever felt more triumphant.

I go down on one knee and tug her boots off. Then I strip her out of the jeans and T-shirt she wore over here from the game.

Then I sweep her up into my arms and carry her back to bed.

"Hey, I have stuff to do," she says. But she doesn't even wiggle. In fact, she loops an arm around my neck.

"To-do lists don't start until at least seven," I tell her softly, laying her down on the mattress and then climbing in beside her.

She snuggles against me and in spite of my now hard cock, I wrap an arm around her and pull her in to spoon.

"I like the way you boss me more than the way grumpy-ass does," she whispers.

I grin.

I don't believe her. I think she liked the way Cam bossed her just fine, and I'd put money on the fact that she's going to be poking at him tomorrow just to see what it takes to get another spanking.

Fuck, that was hot. He's never done that before. But I really fucking want him to do it again.

And now I get to look forward to chocolate chip pancakes, a whole day with Luna and getting creative with doling out orgasms when she's a good girl.

I nuzzle my face into her hair and drift back to sleep with one thought on my mind—this is the start to something really amazing.

CHAPTER 6
Luna

I WAKE UP WITH A START, buried under Alexsei's beefy and very heavy arm. It's like being pinned by a bus. I definitely didn't mean to fall asleep, but instinct has woken me up. I get up five days a week at four a.m. and I've trained my biorhythms after two years of this schedule. My mouth is dry and Alexsei is compromising my ability to breathe, but otherwise, I'm warm and extremely content in this bed.

Cameron's bed. I sneak a glance to my right and see him asleep, on his side, turned away from me. That amuses me. I feel like he is the guy who doesn't want to breathe in someone else's recycled air. He and I have that in common. I'm not big on sleeping all wrapped up in a man, but Alexsei was persistent. I couldn't get away from him once he decided he wanted to cuddle, peppering me with tiny kisses. Eventually, I just fell asleep.

Now I need to get the hell out of here.

It's *Wednesday*.

For the love of all that's holy and cannoli's, it's fucking Wednesday.

I've spent the last two days in a hot boy sandwich, and now I need to get back to reality. As if to punctuate my point, my alarm starts chiming, muffled. It must be buried in my purse or under a pile of clothing that was ripped off of me the night before. The alarm means it's four on the nose and Books and Buns is due to reopen for the week in four hours. By the time I get there, I'll be forty-five minutes behind schedule.

Trying to lift Alexsei's arm is like bench pressing two hundred pounds and I don't work out. Which I don't. I hate the gym. I finally give up and just shimmy down lower and lower until I'm free of his arm. He doesn't even move. He does give one tiny snuffle/snort and rolls over, but now I'm halfway down the bed, buried under the covers with his ass in my face. It's a great ass.

That ass is part of the reason I'm in this mess. Not to mention his tongue, his cock, his big, big hands that slide over my body, making me feel tiny and cherished and so turned on...

Damn it.

I close my eyes and plunge myself out the bottom of the bed, clearing the comforter and landing on the floor with a soft thump. Thank Jesus there is a rug under Cameron's ginormous bed. Breathing hard, I crawl across the floor, grateful that Cameron is a very clean guy. His bedroom is orderly and impeccable. The rug actually smells like it was recently steamed.

I'm actually grateful for a lot of things about Cameron...

I shut those thoughts down immediately.

The room is dim, but I manage to find the pile of my clothes and gather everything up. I uncover my phone, which makes the alarm now much louder in the quiet. Afraid one of them will wake up, I silence it with a hard punch of my finger and keep crawling to the door, which is thankfully open. Once in the hallway, I stand and scramble to the living room. I have to pee, but it's going to have to wait. I drop the pile of clothes on the couch and fish through them. It's a mixture of my clothes and Cameron and Alexsei's.

I spent most of the last two days in nothing but one of Alexsei's sweatshirts or T-shirts over me. I washed the clothes I wore over here yesterday, but I only had them on for about two hours before they were stripped off of me again.

For some reason I don't want to examine it too closely, I lift Cameron's T-shirt to my nose and breathe it in deeply. There's something about his smell. The cologne scent flips my tummy and sends heat to my core. I drop it like it's hot, shaking my head. I'm not even sure how I feel about Cameron, other than he both intrigues me and turns me on. Alexsei is easier to compartmentalize. He's a nice guy, an open book, thoughtful and friendly.

Very friendly.

His tongue...

I'm doing it again.

Crap. I put my bra on with lightning speed and tug my shirt on over my head. I can't find my underwear, so I step into my jeans and jump up and down to get them on as quickly as possible. I only find one sock in the pile, so I ignore it and pull my boots on barefoot, wincing at the sensation of cold faux leather on my feet. I shove my phone in my back pocket and glance back toward the bedroom. All quiet.

With a sigh of relief, I retrieve my coat and purse from the coat tree by the front door. Feeling a little guilty about the state of the kitchen, which is a mess of dirty pans and dishes, I tamp down the urge to stay and clean up, reminding myself this is all their fault. I was supposed to leave *two days* ago. None of these dishes would exist if they weren't so persistent in holding me as a captive in their apartment. Okay, a *very* willing captive, but if they hadn't been so damn sexy and overbearing with their clear desire for me, this wouldn't have happened.

Totally their fault.

Or at least Alexsei's anyway. I have a feeling Cameron would have happily let the door hit me in the butt on my way out two mornings ago. He seemed to enjoy my company during the night but was less interested during the daytime. Did he ever even kiss me? No. But Alexsei kissed me enough for the two of them. The man loves a good kiss and cuddle.

With one last glance back at the bedroom, I open the door and slip out, giving another sigh of relief when the door snicks shut behind me. I'm free of their seductive web. Ordering an Uber, I jog down the stairs to the lobby, running my fingers through my hair.

What the hell had I been thinking, staying so long when I have so much work to do?

I hadn't been thinking. That was the problem.

I'd just been having a string of orgasms.

Nothing I can do about it now except tuck it away in my memory bank as a perfect couple of days of sex and get on with my life.

Fucking hockey players.

Such a pain in my ass.

I'm covered in flour when my first interview of the day texts me.

> This is Lydia, I'm here for my interview but the door is locked.

> Be there in a sec.

Wiping my hands off on a paper towel, I glance around at the disaster my kitchen is in and shake my head. It took me almost thirty minutes to get home from Cameron and Alexsei's in traffic and I *had* to take a shower. Going without one wasn't an option. Yes, I'd showered while I was at their place, but every time I got clean, they didn't waste any time getting me dirty again. And once *while* I was getting clean.

I smelled like sex, men, and bad choices when I finally stumbled into my apartment. So by the time I got to the kitchen I was a solid hour behind schedule and I have customers who will riot if I don't have my signature eclairs in the case. Plus, I always have scones and pain au chocolat, so I'm buried in dough and glazes. It's already seven thirty and I'm in panic mode.

In joggers and sneakers and a T-shirt that says Bake It Til You

Make It, my hair pulled back in a stubby ponytail, I go to the front door and unlock it for a teenage girl who is standing there. She has a boy her age with her.

"Hi," she says with a bright, but shy smile. "I'm Lydia St. Clair. I hope you don't mind my boyfriend being here. He can wait in the bookstore during the interview, if that's okay."

"I'm Brady Phillips," the boy says, sticking out his hand for me to shake it. "I don't like Lydia walking by herself. I can wait outside if you want."

I shake his hand, impressed by both his manners and his chivalrousness toward his girlfriend. "No, no, that's fine, come on in. Do you need a job, too?" I'm half-joking.

They exchange glances. Lydia gives him an encouraging nod.

"I mean, yes?" he says with a smile and a shrug. "But I play hockey, so I don't know if you can work around my schedule."

"Hockey," I say flatly, in a little bit of disbelief. The damn sport follows me around incessantly. "I guess it depends on your schedule. Let's go sit in the bakery and we can all talk."

I lock the front door behind us and gesture for them to come and sit in the cafe side of the shop.

"It's so cute in here," Lydia says, looking around and giving a happy sigh. She's a tall brunette, makeup free, wearing a granny chic brown and orange sweater that looks thrifted. "I come in here all the time to read and do homework."

That's why she looks familiar. "Oh, right. Wednesdays and Saturdays."

She beams at me. "Yes. I'm usually studying my chemistry. I suck at science."

"Babe, don't say that," Brady says, sliding his hand over hers. "You're *so* smart."

Brady looks like a hockey player. Bulky, floppy hair that has a hint of red to it. He's looking at Lydia, who is honestly a little on the plain side, like she's hung the moon. My hidden romantic that I like to pretend doesn't exist, melts a little at his devotion.

I had a boyfriend like that in high school. He used to call me

Luna the Luminous, and he was dead serious. Parker. I wonder what happened to him. We broke up in an appropriately dramatic teenage fashion at prom, with tears and screaming and hateful words to each other. I had ripped off my corsage and thrown it at him.

Relationships are a lot of fucking work. Since then, I've mostly stuck to casual dating and hookups.

Lydia blushes. *"Brady..."*

She draws his name out in a way that has Brady's eyes darkening.

Oh, boy. These two have already seen each other naked. That's pretty obvious. I clear my throat. "So, you don't have any job experience, Lydia?"

She shakes her head, looking crestfallen. "No. I'm sixteen. But I'm very reliable. I'm a straight A student and I'm in the student government. I learn new tasks quickly. Plus, I'm a Virgo, so you know I'm a perfectionist."

I wasn't expecting her to drop her astrological sign, but she's not wrong. I nod. "Very true. Virgos are sticklers. I'm a Pisces so I have great intuition. I'm borderline Capricorn though, so I'm also grounded. And Capricorns work well with Virgos."

Brady is looking at me blankly. Lydia is nodding enthusiastically. "I can tell that about you. You're so creative. Classic Pisces."

"Okay, how many hours a week can you work and when can you start? Next week is Thanksgiving and I'm going to be slammed every day until then. We're closed on Mondays and Tuesdays, but I'm going to be baking orders both of those days for Wednesday pickups."

Lydia sits up straighter. "I can be here after school any of those days."

I study her for a second, curious. "Why do you want a job?"

"The school trip to Paris is next spring and my parents said I have to pay for half. I *have* to go to Paris."

"That's awesome. I've never been." I eye Brady. "Are you saving for Paris, too?"

But he shakes his head. "I'm not in French class. My dad made me take Spanish. You might know my dad, actually."

For a split second, I'm terrified that I've had sex with his dad. I went through a brief daddy phase that was me sexually experimenting. It wasn't really my thing, but that would be awkward.

But before I can properly freak out, he adds, "He's the Racketeers assistant coach."

"Oh!" I say in relief. "No, I've never met him. I mean, I know who he is, but we've never met." Coach Phillips is big and bearded and yells at the players all the time. So, like any other coach. He looks like he's in his late thirties and he gives off married dad energy, which is probably why I've never given him much thought.

"He's, like, so nice," Lydia assures me. "In person, I mean. Not during games."

"What do you mean?" Brady asks.

"He yells a lot at games."

"That's what a coach does."

I nod. "That's been my experience, yes."

"You played hockey?" Brady asks, sounding excited.

But he also eyes me skeptically, which is fair. I'm five foot nothing. "God, no. I just spent half my life at my brother's hockey practices, games, tournaments." Way more than I ever cared to.

I can't get away from hockey. It's my lodestone.

"I can't believe Crew McNeill is your brother. That's so cool."

"Yeah. So cool." If you love playing second fiddle to your sibling your whole life. I glance at my phone. "Well, anyway, you probably need to get to school and I need to get back to the kitchen. Can you start tomorrow?"

"Yes!" Lydia says with enough animation for the both of us.

I'm suddenly aware how tired I am. It's hard to get quality sleep when an eight-inch cock keeps nudging you awake. I've been running on adrenaline since my eyes popped open this morning. Good thing my two employees, Elise and Austin, both come in today.

"Brady, you can literally just show up whenever your schedule allows, and I will find something for you to do," I tell him. "Just text me whenever you're free to come in."

I usher them off and head back to the kitchen right as my phone buzzes with a text. For a heart-stopping second, I think it's Alexsei, wanting me back in his bed. The next heart-stopping second, I wonder if I'm actually going to be able to tell him no. Because I *really* liked being in bed with him. The *next* second, I realize I never gave him my number, and the text is from Dani.

> Did you really just let Alexsei walk you to
> your car?

> Good morning to you, too. Yes, he walked
> me out.

And then to his car and his apartment and then the bed. Well, he *carried* me to the bed...

But I can't tell Dani that, which feels a little gross. I don't keep secrets from my best friend. But if I tell her, two things will happen. One, she'll tell my brother and he'll have opinions I'm not interested in hearing. Two, she'll want me all cozied up in a real relationship with Alexsei like she is with Crew, Michael, and Nathan.

I'm not interested.

I have too much to do right now, as is evidenced by the state of this kitchen. I sigh and pull out my piping bag. These macarons aren't going to pipe themselves.

But the minute I do, I'm reminded of Cameron.

Macarons is your safe word.

I can't believe I let him boss me around like that.

I also can't believe I didn't realize sooner what is now totally obvious to me—Cameron wasn't that into me. The asshole didn't even kiss me. Not even when I begged.

Because he was into Alexsei.

Literally.

And Alexsei didn't seem to notice Cameron wouldn't kiss me. He kept saying Cameron was a guy who likes to watch, but that didn't stop Cameron from touching Alexsei. In the moment, I was aware of it on a certain level, but it didn't totally click because I was drowning in orgasms.

Now it's glaringly obvious to me. Cameron wants Alexsei.

Though he did seem to really enjoy spanking me...

My inner thighs clench.

One more reason to stay the hell away from both of them.

Relationships are complicated.

Elise walks into the kitchen via the backdoor with the key I gave her. "Oh, my God, what happened here?" she asks in shock, reaching for an apron.

"I was sick the last two days," I lie.

Complicated. No, thank you.

I start piping like a madwoman.

CHAPTER 7
Cameron

THE RACKETEERS MASCOT is annoying as fuck.

That damn dog is constantly sniffing around Luna.

I give him my second glare of the night and he gives me a dopey head shake so that his Santa hat, instead of his usual fedora, bounces a little. Granted, Luna doesn't pay much attention to him, and it's not like I'm jealous of a stranger in a furry suit, but it's still annoying because he's always blocking my view and my ability to talk to Luna.

Who is ignoring me. Again.

Sure, she greeted me when she took her seat in front of me, but that's it. It's been that way for a month now. She doesn't look angry or aloof. Just like she could give two shits if I'm there or not. Like she's a fucking champ at having one night—or three nights—stands and doesn't need anything else from me other than pleasantries. Even though we've seen each other naked and my palm was on her ass.

Which is exactly the way it should be. Her attitude, I mean. I should be applauding her ability to handle casual sex. I would be, too, if it was just up to me.

Except Alexsei has been moping around the apartment ever since she disappeared like Cinderella, leaving behind only her pink panties and socks. A naughty Cinderella. Alexsei has posed the rhetorical question, "Why do you think she left?" to me so many times that I don't even bother to respond anymore. At first I gave him very rational explanations. Like that she has a life and a business to run. But then he would follow it up with, "But she didn't leave her number or anything. Do you think she didn't have a good time?"

"She stayed for two and a half fucking days, I think she had fun," as an answer only seemed to send him spinning faster.

"So then why didn't she say goodbye?" he's asked me at least four times.

He keeps asking because he doesn't like my answers.

She didn't want to disturb you.

She wouldn't have disturbed me.

Well, maybe she doesn't want to see you again.

But, why not if she had fun?

Around and around we go and I'm one more question away from moving out of my own apartment. Except I would never do that. Because I want to be around Alexsei. Hell, I *need* to be around Alexsei. Even if he is sulking and eating an offensive amount of Taco Bell, which is weirdly his comfort food. Our whole apartment stinks like old chalupas and it's vile.

More than that, though, it kills me to see Alexsei hurting in any way. He's always upbeat, always the one encouraging me and everyone else in his life to stay positive. He can make me feel better on the worst day with just a few words, a clap on the shoulder, and a grin. I want to do the same for him, but I suck at it.

So I'm at this damn hockey game taking deep breaths and trying not to punch Sammy the Malamute and digging deep to find something akin to charm inside my prickly personality so that I can convince Luna to give Alexsei a chance.

That will make him happy. And if he's happy, I'm happy.

"Luna," I say, leaning over close to her ear.

"Hmm?" she asks, barely glancing over her shoulder at me.

"I need to talk to you."

"I'm busy right now."

Busy being a pain in my ass.

She's not doing anything. For once, she's not even looking at her phone. She's just sitting there, alone. Dani went to the snack bar. Luna can fucking talk to me.

Okay, maybe there's something else bothering me.

She's being *me* in this situation.

I'm usually the one being nonchalant and casual after a hookup.

I don't like being on the receiving end of it.

I pull a page from Alexsei's playbook and climb over the back of the seat next to her and sit down in it. Hard.

She sits up straighter and gawks at me. "What are you doing?"

"I need to ask you why you left without a word to Alexsei."

"I had to work. I didn't want to wake him up."

"And since then?"

"Since then, what?" She fidgets with her earring, which is a little crescent moon. She also shifts her thigh away from mine.

"Alexsei's a great guy. What the fuck is wrong with you?"

She instantly stiffens. "What is that supposed to mean?"

"Why aren't you talking to him?"

Her jaw drops. "He hasn't reached out to me."

I run my hands down the front of my jeans to tug them down. They aren't sitting right now that I've climbed over an arena seat. "Because you left in the middle of the night."

Her eyes narrow. "Did he send you to talk to me? Because that's stupid."

"No, of course not. But he likes you."

"Then he can tell me that himself." She turns resolutely back to the ice and watches the game. She picks up her drink and takes a noisy slurp. "How did the two of you become friends, anyway?"

I let my gaze drift to the ice as well. I seek out Alexsei and find him immediately. He's skating fast, catching up with a Beavers player and stealing the puck from him. He's powerful in his play, passionate. He'll take heat and not get riled up, but if someone goes after his teammates, he's quick to defend them. He's the most loyal guy I know.

"We both were at Ohio State and as part of my grad school scholarship, I had to tutor athletes. For some unfathomable reason, they put Alexsei in Organic Chem his freshman year." I still don't understand the rationale behind that. Especially considering he didn't even graduate. He went pro after two years of college.

The corner of her mouth turns up, but she doesn't look at me. "Ah. He wasn't excelling?"

"He wasn't even on the grading scale. But we hit it off." It wasn't an instant click for me. I thought he was being nice to me so that I would do his work for him so he could stay on the hockey team. But Alexsei genuinely liked me, in spite of my general asshole-ish-ness. "I don't always relate well to people and not everyone… likes me."

Now she does turn to me. She gives me a grin. "You don't say?"

I glare at her, but she's unfazed. "Shocking, I know. But Alexsei just did for whatever reason and he adopted me as his token nerd friend."

"Nerds aren't usually as bossy and annoying as you." Her gaze momentarily drifts to my mouth, then lifts again.

She's still mad I wouldn't kiss her.

Good. Let her stew on that. She's definitely a girl who likes a challenge.

"How did you meet your best friend?" I ask her.

"In college, like you did. Only Dani was the quiet one whose mom told her to find the loudest, chattiest person in the room and talk to her."

I almost grin. "And she picked you? How odd."

"I know, right? I still don't understand it."

"Me either. You're so quiet and reserved. Were you in the same dorm, is that how she approached you?"

"Yes, our rooms were next to each other. I might have been

playing my music very loud and twerking when she knocked on the door." Luna smiles.

I clear my throat, picturing her on a dorm bed in panties and a tight T-shirt, back arched as she shook her ass. I bet she was the girl in college who would have wound up on Alexsei's shoulder at some point during a party. He used to love to pretend to pairs skate after he had a six-pack in him.

Another reason he and Luna are a good fit.

"We were best friends in a matter of days. We threw a Harry party, and that sealed the deal."

I frown. "What's a hairy party? Everyone wears a fake mustache?" I've never understood theme parties.

Luna laughs. "No. Harry. The name. You come dressed as a famous Harry."

"Oh. By the way, you don't have the ass for twerking," I tell her. "It's too small. My hand is bigger than one of your cheeks."

The cheeks on her face get red and her mouth drops open. It takes her a second to speak, and I know the memory of me spanking her is rolling through her mind.

"*Rude*," she finally says. "I absolutely can twerk."

"Prove it to me."

Luna snorts. "I'm not falling for that."

"Come home with us tonight," I murmur.

"No, thank you." She looks away again.

Five minutes pass without her saying anything.

I can't stand how easy it is for her to ignore me. She's such a fucking brat.

I grab a handful of the popcorn that's perched in her lap. She always gets popcorn.

"Hey! Get your own popcorn."

"I won't ask you again," I warn her. "Come home with us. Last chance." I toss a piece of her popcorn in my mouth and stand up.

We stare at each other.

She doesn't blink.

I don't blink.

Then a weird fucking thing starts to happen. As we face off in a staring contest, a classic battle of wills, I start to get turned on.

She does, too.

I see the subtle change. Her eyes widen. Her tongue flicks across her lower lip. Her pale blue eyes darken. She lifts her head, her body leaning toward my thighs.

A slow heat builds inside me, my dick hardening. I'm thinking about cracking my hand on the curve of her tight ass and making her moan in pleasure before I...

"Can you sit down?" an exasperated voice from behind me asks. "We're trying to watch the game!"

The woman's voice breaks the sexual spell that was brewing between me and Luna.

"Sorry." I turn and shift sideways without another word, heading toward the aisle. I don't return to my seat. Instead, I jog up the steps to the exit, needing some air.

I run my hands through my hair.

What the fuck was *that*?

And I'm pretty sure I blinked first on top of it all.

CHAPTER 8
Luna

IT'S my brother's birthday.

That means the whole day is about him. People showing up to shower him with attention, affection, tell him how great he is, and give him gifts.

So it's pretty much like every other day in Crew McNeill's life, except for the gifts.

I love my brother. I really do. He's a great guy. He's funny, charming, mostly laid-back, and, as much as I hate to admit it, he really is good at almost everything he does.

I pick up three cake plates from the table as more people come through the front door of my parent's house, and Crew greets them loudly.

He's standing in the foyer, his arm around my best friend, looking like a king greeting his subjects.

I roll my eyes. Nothing new about any of this.

I head for the kitchen with the plates. I just need a minute without a hockey player in my personal space.

I've felt that way, generally, for most of my life. They're big, loud, and don't always smell very good.

But for the past three months whenever I think of hockey, or hockey is mentioned, or ice is mentioned—and it's winter in

Chicago, so that's a lot—I don't think of my brother as the hockey guy.

Nope. It's a whole other hockey guy.

And his bossy, kind-of-a-dick-but-God-he's-hot best friend.

I'm used to being kind of *ugh* about hockey.

Lately, the whole thing has been making me horny instead.

It is *very* annoying.

It also isn't getting any better, even though it's been *three months* since my hook-up with Alexsei and Cameron.

I still don't like hockey.

I also *really* don't like getting all tingly when I hear the word.

Or the word *stick*. Or the worst one of all...*puck*.

This is all very strange. Awkward even. My family's life has revolved around hockey almost since this day twenty-three years ago that Crew came into the world.

Okay, maybe for the first six or seven years it was just about *him* in general. But then, he became a hockey prodigy.

I mean it. Really young, Crew showed signs of being one of the best hockey players ever.

He took to the ice as if he'd been born on skates.

From then on, my parent's lives revolved around him, and hockey practice, hockey games, travel hockey tournaments, extra hockey coaching, dealing with hockey injuries, hockey, hockey, hockey.

Hockey is a fine game. I'm convinced that I would like it if I was any other person.

But hockey is definitely not *my* favorite pastime.

Hockey basically disrupted my family.

It stole my parents from me.

There I said it.

It wasn't that my parents weren't loving. I always knew they loved and supported me. But my interests were a lot quieter and easier and could be handled by other people. I loved to bake, cook, and read, so my parents found me pretty easy to leave behind.

Thank God.

My younger years were spent in the stands surrounding ice rinks. When I got a little older, they were able to leave me with my grandparents. That was a lot more fun. It's where my love and talent for baking came from. It turned into my career and I can't be upset about that.

Still, I can resent hockey.

"Oh my God, Luna, these are fucking amazing." Blake Wilder bursts into the kitchen and scoops up a huge handful of macarons. He shoves three in his mouth at a time — they're not even all three the same flavor — and gives me a grin. "Crew's a lucky motherfucker."

Then he stomps back out of the kitchen.

He doesn't mean to stomp, but he's a huge hockey player with gigantic feet and that's just how he walks.

It's how they all fucking walk. My parent's house is noisy, crowded, and chaotic today because all of my brother's hockey friends—current and past—are here to celebrate the day of his birth.

Including Alexsei Ryan.

I know he's here. I saw him walk in. And I immediately ducked into the kitchen then, too.

I've seen him, of course, since our wild weekend. But I see him while I sit in the seats in the arena and he skates around the ice. Looking fierce, powerful, cocky, and amazing.

I thought the guy was good-looking before. I thought he seemed fun and easygoing.

But now? Now that I've had his hands and mouth on me? Now that I've had his cock *inside* me? Now that I've had his dirty talk in my ears? Now I can't watch him skate around an ice rink without starting to sweat.

He was also a lot of fun. Sweet, considerate, making me laugh as he cuddled me on the couch and smothered me with kisses. Reminding me that I've been lonely, especially since Dani now spends just about every night with one or all of her men. I can't help but think that maybe, just maybe, it wouldn't be a *bad* thing to date Alexsei Ryan. He's on the road a lot, he's affable, accommodating. Good God, is he accommodating. I fan myself in the stuffy kitchen.

But I haven't actually talked to him since that night. I've been avoiding the back hallway where the WAGS all gather after games.

I haven't been able to avoid Cam, of course. He still sits behind me at the games. But ever since our weird stare down after he told me that was the last time he was asking me to come home with them…well, he meant it. He's behind me, a brooding, smoldering presence that I swear makes the back of my neck actually heat up a few degrees, but we haven't talked. Which is disappointing. Which is confusing.

Still, as soon as I saw Alexsei walk into my parents' house, Cam's voice was in my head.

Alexsei's a great guy. What the fuck is wrong with you?

I don't know what's wrong with me. Maybe I'm trying to run a business. Maybe I'm trying to be a modern, independent woman. Maybe I don't really fucking like hockey and I don't want to date a hockey player. Maybe I'm scared that I do actually want to date Alexsei and what that could mean moving forward in my life.

And by the way, Alexsei hasn't called me. He hasn't sought me out after any games. He hasn't shown up at my apartment or my bakery. None of that information would be hard to get if he really wanted it. My brother might give it to him. Even more likely, my best friend, the sweetest woman on earth and constant presence in that back hallway after games, would give it to him.

But he hasn't pursued me. So I have to assume that our three-day fling was a *one-time* three-day fling. Which is perfect. Just what I wanted.

Then.

Now? I don't know. Having someone respect your space and boundaries is awesome. It says amazing things about Alexsei's character. But… I haven't had sex since I was with those two. I'm still stressed. I'm lonely. And I'm starting to think being a workaholic is slightly overrated.

But I decide to stay in the kitchen, anyway.

I'm not hiding out from Alexsei and my jumbled thoughts and feelings. I'm making sure the desserts that I made for my brother's birthday are perfect.

Of course they are. I'm an amazing baker and baking for my family and a bunch of hungry hockey guys who barely chew macarons before they just swallow them is super easy.

"Hey, Luna."

Well, damn. That didn't really work did it?

Heat and tingles trip down my spine at the sound of his voice behind me.

I'd know that voice anywhere.

It said filthy things to me three months ago. Filthy things that I've thought of over and over. Yes, while using my vibrator. And other times, too.

I take a deep breath, plaster on a smile, and turn to face him.

"Hey, Alexsei."

"You look fucking amazing."

Okay, well, things have changed a little since November. He never used to say things like that to me.

I blow out a breath. "Thanks. You've had a bunch of really great games. Congrats."

"Thanks. It would've been awesome to see you afterwards and hear you tell me that."

He's standing just inside the doorway of the kitchen and has his hands in the pockets of his blue jeans, but it feels like he's taking up all the space in the kitchen even though it's a huge room. And all the oxygen. We're in here alone, and the heat, and the tension, is intense. And my body remembers him. Really well. And wants to be close to him again. My nipples are already hard, my panties are wet, and I have to consciously force myself to look away from his mouth.

"I just thought maybe it was better if we left it alone," I say.

A decision I am definitely regretting.

"Yeah, I got that message when you snuck out."

"I didn't sneak. It was four a.m. I told you that's what time I get up."

He nods. "Right. You did." He just studies me for a moment. Then says, "Anyway, I just wanted to say hi. Tell you that you look amazing. Tell you that I think about you all the time. Tell you that I can still taste you on my tongue, and hear the sounds you make when you come, and how your eyes look when I first thrust into you."

My eyes go wide and my heart starts pounding. "Alexsei!"

"Just needed you to know all of that."

Well...now I do. And I won't be able to stop thinking about that.

I wait for him to ask me to come over. To come home with him tonight. To meet him for a drink. To at least ask what I'm doing after the birthday festivities are over.

But he doesn't.

He just gives me a little smile, then turns and leaves the kitchen.

He's either still respecting my space or... or what? Nothing. He's respecting my space. Which makes me want him even more.

I blow out a breath. "Fucking hockey players," I mutter.

"Is he bothering you?"

I jump and swing around, startled. Another man is in the kitchen. Clearly, he came through the other doorway.

It's Owen Phillips, one of the assistant coaches for the Racketeers.

"Oh my God, I didn't see you there. Hi, Coach."

"Hi. Uh, call me Owen."

"Okay, Owen. Uh, hi." I don't know what to say to him. I don't know what he heard. If he heard Alexsei say he remembers how I taste and look when he...

I shake my head and clear my throat. "Did you ask me something?" I blurt.

Owen's eyes dart in the direction Alexsei disappeared. "Was he bothering you?"

Yes. Very much. I'm going to have to walk around with wet panties for the rest of the day because of him.

I smile. "No, not at all. I mean he won't ask me out, and that kind of bothers me. But it shouldn't. Because I told him I don't want to date anyone right now, anyway. Especially a hockey player. So, no. He's not bothering me."

Owen gives me a look that clearly says *wow more information than I expected.* And *I have no idea what to say now.*

"Can I help you find something?" I ask, realizing that I shouldn't have said *any* of that. Lord, I sound crazy. And needy.

This guy's a hockey coach. He's as used to puck bunnies following his players around with hearts in their eyes as the players themselves. Hell, he was probably a player at one time. That's usually how coaches get into coaching.

"I'm not like stalking him or anything," I say before Owen can answer me about why he's in the kitchen. "I'm Crew's sister. I'm supposed to be here."

Owen nods. "Yeah, I know who you are. I didn't think you were stalking him."

"Good. That whole thing about him not asking me out sounded weird. And pathetic."

"No worries." He shifts his weight. "Hockey players get hit in the head a lot, you know."

I give him a curious frown. "I do know that. Why do you bring it up?"

"Because that's likely why he isn't asking you out."

I smile. "You think so?"

"I can't think of a single other reason that makes any sense."

Oh. Well. I didn't expect that. He doesn't know that Alexsei isn't asking me out because I gave him zero clues that I wanted him to and now regret that for reasons I don't entirely understand. But this feels like a compliment and I'm willing to take it.

"Thank you."

He just shrugs. "Seriously."

I study Owen. He's very good-looking.

He's in faded blue jeans, and a light green Henley with a thick darker green button-down over the top of it. His hair is the same shade as Brady's, his *son*, his *teenage son, who now works for me*. But my brain doesn't linger on that fact. It catalogs the shade of *Owen's* hair–brown with a reddish tint–his full beard, and his green eyes. I also take stock of the fact that he's big. Tall and broad. Built like an athlete, but he's not as rock-solid and bulging-muscles as the guys out in the other room. I wouldn't say he has a dad bod. He's definitely in shape. But he looks solid in a different way than Alexsei does. He's solid in a I-can-change-your-oil–while-dealing-with-the-asshole-hitting-on-you-at-the-bar-after-you-turned-him-down-while-making-you-the-best-lasagna-you've-ever-tasted way.

And that is maybe the weirdest thing I've ever thought about another human being. Ever.

And I'm sure his *wife* thinks he's nice and solid and that I should keep my eyes off of her husband's solid-ness.

Fucking hockey players *and* the coaches.

I need to avoid *all* of them.

CHAPTER 9

Owen

LUNA IS STARING AT ME.

Why is she staring at me?

Actually, she's *studying* me. Like she's trying to figure something out.

Probably why I said such a stupid thing.

I mean, I assume telling her Alexsei wasn't asking her out because of a head injury was not a cool thing to say. Fuck if I know, actually. I'm only thirty-six years old, but I spend all of my time either with my sixteen-year-old son and his friends, or the young, hot, cocky, rich hockey players who can't sneeze without dozens of women falling over as if it's the sexiest thing they've ever seen.

There is no way I'm going to feel cool with a teenage son and hanging out with hockey players.

Not that I give a shit about being cool.

Until this moment with this girl, I haven't really thought about it in a while.

Since Brady, I'm just a dad and a coach. That's all I need to be. I barely date.

Well, that's not true. I spend time with women. I go out for coffee, or even dinner sometimes. I sleep in other beds than my own from time to time. But...I accidentally date.

I get hit on a lot by single moms. Or by friends of single moms.

It took me a while to figure out what was going on when a mom of one of Brady's preschool friends would ask if I could stop over and take a look at a malfunctioning water heater for one of her friends, and then I'd suddenly find myself having dinner at that woman's place and then having a drink on her back patio. And then suddenly my clothes are on her bedroom floor and I'm sneaking out of her house at the crack of dawn.

Or something like that.

Sometimes the women *were* Brady's friends' moms. And it wasn't always a water heater I was checking out.

And sometimes I got hit on at the playground, or the grocery store, or even at Brady's hockey games. It happened often enough that my needs were met and I never had to pursue women or think about it much and years have just slipped by.

I haven't actually asked a woman out on a formal date in a really long time. Longer than I can remember.

Not that I'm complaining, exactly. I'm fine.

But I definitely have no idea how to flirt. And I realized that thinking about flirting, dating, one-night stands, and even relationships while I am five feet away from Luna McNeill, is all very inappropriate.

Luna is the sister of one of my players. She is easily ten years younger than me, if not more. She is wildly out of my league. And she is apparently interested in another one of my players.

Alexsei Ryan is a dumbass, though. This girl wants him to ask her out, and he's not?

She's gorgeous. She's also bold and feisty. We've never actually spoken directly to one another before, but she's around a lot. She's at a lot of the games, it's hard to miss her sitting in the second row behind the glass. I've also seen her in the back hallway. It doesn't surprise me that she's not really ever noticed me, but I've noticed her. She's got this white blonde hair, tipped in purple, a killer body, a bright smile, and some kind of—I guess people call it an *aura*—about her that makes people look. Makes people want to linger. Draws people to her. She has a light laugh, sassy come-backs, and loves to tease.

It's clear that she's been around hockey players all her life. Their locker room talk and stupid jokes don't phase her.

And she definitely knows how to flirt.

It always seems fairly unserious, but she can make more than half of my team of big tough hockey guys blush.

"Well, thank you," she says to my stupid statement about hockey players' head injuries.

I nod. "Alexsei is a good guy." Ryan is probably perfect for her. Young, energetic, earnest. He is one of our best players and is infinitely coachable. He's cocky, but he has reason to be. He always takes direction and critique, and plays his heart out.

Everyone on the team likes him. Hell, I think most of the players on the other teams like him, too.

"Yeah," she nods. "He is a good guy. He's just…a lot."

I study her. She seems a little confused about Alexsei. Which is interesting. Luna gives off a vibe that makes you think she's always in charge.

"Is he?" Yeah, I can see that. If she means it in the way that a brand-new puppy is a lot. Energetic, happy, eager to please. But he wasn't pleasing her a minute ago. "I thought he wasn't even asking you out."

She meets my gaze. "Right. He isn't asking me out." She takes a breath and blows it out. "He's just a lot when we're together."

I feel a jab of disappointment I wasn't expecting. They'd been together. Of course, they had.

Alexsei Ryan isn't quite as stupid as I think he is.

But why the fuck isn't he asking her out? All I'd heard him say as I walked into the kitchen was, *Just needed you to know all of that.*

I don't know what he thought Luna needed to know. But the look on her face was stunned. Her cheeks had been pink, and she'd been staring at him. He'd said something that had surprised her, though.

Then he turned and walked out.

And now she is talking about how she wants him to ask her out, but he isn't.

What the hell?

"Anyway," she says, shaking her head. "Can I help you find something? Geez, I'm being a terrible hostess."

"Are you hosting this party?"

I know Crew McNeill very well. I know who Luna is because of Crew. Crew's family is very close and very supportive, but Luna loves to give her brother a hard time.

I'm sure she would be surprised to find out all of the things I've overheard and witnessed about her. But she's around a lot and, like I said, she draws people like moths to a flame.

Or maybe it's just me.

I would never admit this out loud, but I'm very attracted to her.

It bugs me.

She is far too young, and she is, frankly, a cool girl.

I never could've gotten a girl like Luna. Not even back when I was her age, a young hockey player, coming up the ranks, high scorer, in the best shape of my life.

I just never had the swagger.

Fuck, do people even still say swagger?

I'm only thirty-six, but I feel some days like I'm seventy-six.

Focusing on coaching and raising my son has made me feel out of touch with other people my age. I started off as a dad really young, and I did it as a single dad. His mom and I are on good terms, and we've co-parented since day one, but we've never been together, and we never parented under the same roof. We get along fine, but we each kind of do our own thing.

Worrying about Brady, worrying about if I'm fucking up, worrying about how he's turning out has consumed most of my time and attention.

"Oh, I came in for more cake," I admit. "I snuck into the kitchen because I didn't want everyone to see that it's my third piece."

She looks very pleased. "Well, I might not be hosting the party, but I am the baker. So I consider that a huge compliment."

I'd assumed she'd provided the desserts today. I knew she was a baker even before Brady and Lydia started working for her, but now I know a lot about her bakery and how amazing it is, and how funny she is, and how creative she is, and how caring she is toward her employees, and how hard she works. Brady and Lydia love working for her and think she can do no wrong.

I realize the kids talk about her more than I realized, and I know more about her than I thought.

Speaking of stalkers, I probably shouldn't admit that. I haven't found any of this out intentionally, but all put together it might sound a little creepy.

"You should definitely take it as a compliment, it's all amazing."

"Thanks."

"Yeah, I'm serious." I reach for a plate of cake on the counter. It looks like it's been cut and is waiting to go out to the dessert table. I grab a fork and take a huge bite. It's some layered thing with chocolate and pecans and some other flavor I can't quite place. But I want to eat three *more* pieces. And to sneak some home with me at the end of the party. It is fucking delicious.

I close my eyes for a moment and moan. "I could eat your cake all day."

I open my eyes to find Luna watching me with her brows up and a wide grin. "Oh, really?"

"Yeah, seriously." But then I actually look at how she's looking at me.

I said something wrong. Fuck.

"Well, I think I would take you up on that."

Oh boy. I feel heat arc through me and I don't even know why exactly. Except I must've said something accidentally sexual and my body is reacting instinctively to the tone in her voice.

This is what I get for not being online more.

I clear my throat. "Well, your *cake* is fucking delicious," I say, emphasizing the word. "Best I've ever had."

Her grin grows. "Wow."

Okay, that made it worse, not better. Why did that make it worse?

I swallow and open my mouth to say something that I hope comes out smart when Alexsei strolls back into the kitchen.

He gives me just a nod, but his eyes then immediately go to Luna. I notice how she straightens, and her cheeks immediately get pinker.

"There were two things I forgot to say," he tells her.

Her eyes go wide and she glances at me and then back to him. "Okay."

"I think you're amazing. And I miss you." He takes a deep breath, then nods. "Yeah, there's all the things I needed to say." Then he pivots on his heel again and walks out of the kitchen.

She stares after him, mouth hanging open.

I just wait. I have no idea what to say.

After ten seconds of silence, she snaps her mouth shut and looks at me. "See what I mean?"

I'm actually swallowing another bite of cake, so I cough slightly and nod. "That was nice."

She frowns. "Nice? He came in and said *that*, and then *still* doesn't ask me out? He could have asked me to come home with him after the party if he misses me so fucking much. Even if that's all he wants."

Okay, now we are talking about sex, I'm ninety-nine percent sure. "But isn't it nice that he's not asking you to just come home with him? After what he just said, it seems like he's into you."

She props her hands on her hips. "Then why doesn't he ask me out?"

I honestly can't answer that. "I'm sticking with the head injury excuse."

That takes a little bit of the tension out of her shoulders and she lets out a little breathy laugh. She shakes her head and moves closer to me to start cutting and plating more cake.

I have my hip propped against the center island where the cake, plates, and utensils are all set. She's now close enough that I can smell her light, spicy scent. I can definitely smell the sugar and chocolate from the cake, and the coffee brewing on the counter, but there's an extra spiciness in the air now that Luna's closer.

"Were you still playing hockey when you met your wife?" Then she shakes her head. "I mean, obviously, right? Brady is sixteen. You can't be retired from playing for that long."

I finish off my cake and set the plate down reluctantly. I brush my hands together.

"No, I played 'til I was about twenty-eight. Brady was nine then. But I'm not married. His mom and I never did that. We share custody and get along, but it's never been more."

That was probably way more than she needed to know. I have no idea why I'm feeling so rattled with this girl.

Her eyes fly to mine and she straightens like she did when Alexsei walked into the room. "Oh really? You're single?"

Luna looks very interested in that information and something about that makes my heart kick against my rib cage.

"Yes. Hockey and Brady have taken up a lot of time and energy."

"Brady's a great kid."

"Thank you. I hope I can take some credit for that. But you just never know."

She smiles. "I'm sure you can take some credit for it. He's actually very sweet and affectionate and respectful and protective of Lydia. I think men model their fathers when it comes to relationships."

"Brady hasn't seen me in any relationships. Maybe that's just the person that he is."

"Hmm," she hums softly. "Maybe. But that has to come from somewhere."

"Maybe his stepdad." I don't hate my ex's husband. I actually like Dev a lot. He's a little older than Chelsea, but he adores her, and he's very good to Brady.

"Come on, Owen. You know he gets *some* of his goodness from you," Luna says, looking up at me from what has to be barely over five feet.

She makes me feel gigantic.

And she has a smudge of chocolate frosting on her cheek that I desperately want to wipe away. I fist one hand and brace the other on the counter, leaning onto it to keep from reaching for her.

Of course, I could *lick* it off…

Knock it off.

But goddamn, she's really beautiful.

I'm not sure why that thought hits me suddenly, out of the blue. But it does. And then I can't stop thinking it.

And I don't feel strange studying her. Cataloging details about her.

She's so petite. I swear my hands could encircle her waist. I know both of my hands could totally cover her ass.

Her ass? Really? I am thinking about touching this woman's ass?

But then I look back into her eyes.

Oh yeah, I am thinking about touching her ass.

And I think that maybe she's thinking about me touching her ass. Or other parts of her.

Why? Why are we both suddenly thinking about me touching her?

She's into Alexsei. They've been together, clearly. He thinks she's amazing, and he misses her.

She wants him to ask her out.

I cannot hit on a woman that one of my players is into. Fuck. I can't hit on one of my player's sisters, anyway. She's too young for me. She's too beautiful for me. She's way too cool for me. If I ask her out, she would absolutely say no. She might even laugh. And that would be devastating.

"Thanks for letting me have more of your cake," I say. Then I groan out loud. I have got to let this cake thing go.

She smiles and turns to face me. Then she steps closer. She's almost standing on my toes now. She reaches up toward my face and I freeze.

Her thumb skates over the corner of my mouth. Her touch sends bolts of heat over my lips and straight to my cock. I part my lips. I'm not sure if I'm going to *say* something, or suck her thumb into my mouth. I want to do both. Though I'm not sure what to say other than, "Forget about Alexsei, go out with me."

And that is a terrible idea.

But before I can do anything, she pulls back and shows me there's some frosting on the pad of her thumb. Then, much to my shock and my cock's delight, she slides that thumb into her own mouth and sucks.

"I love when people enjoy my cake."

Jesus. Christ.

"There you are!" Lori McNeill, Crew's mother—I guess she's Luna's mother, too—bustles into the kitchen just then. "Honey, can you help me take more coffee around to everyone?"

Luna doesn't jump back, or seem flustered, or try to make it seem as if we aren't very much in each other's personal space. She slowly removes her eyes from mine. "Sure, Mom. No problem."

"Thank you." Her mother crosses to the refrigerator and removes a carton of cream. She proceeds to pour it into a little creamer pitcher and then sets it along with a sugar bowl on a tray. She adds a bunch of spoons, all the while chattering about... something.

I honestly have no idea.

Because Luna is still standing right there. Right in front of me. Her eyes on mine. That smudge of chocolate icing on her cheek.

I actually really like Lori McNeill. I've met her and her husband several times. They are huge supporters of the team. But right now, I have no idea what she's saying, nor do I care.

"It was nice talking with you," Luna finally says.

"Same." My voice sounds raspy. But that's the truth. Whether or not I *should* enjoy spending time with Luna McNeill, I did.

She finally steps back, crosses to the coffee maker, and removes the glass carafe from the burner. "See you later, Owen," she tosses over her shoulder as she heads out into the living room.

As she leaves, I finally take a big, deep breath. *What just happened?*

Uh, you just got a hard-on for your player's sister. The one who has a thing going with another player. That's what happened.

See, that girl can just suck people into her orbit. It's like she's a sun, and we're all just planets that revolve around her.

I guess I'm the new planet in her galaxy.

Because fuck, I know as soon as I step out into that living room, I will immediately find her wherever she is.

I look down at the empty plate in front of me. What the hell? I grab another and eat it in three bites.

Because honestly? Luna McNeill's cake, the one she baked, is the best thing I've ever put in my mouth.

But I have a feeling that Luna could give me something that would rival even this cake.

When I've gathered myself, and make sure I don't have any more frosting on my face, I head out into the main room with everyone else.

Immediately, I find Luna, just as expected.

Not only because she has some spell over me, but also because she's standing next to Alexsei.

And he just made her laugh.

And that tinkling sound, along with the gorgeous smile on her face, makes hot need clench in my gut.

Then he leans over and says something in her ear and she nods.

Yeah, they look really good together. They're the same age. They have the same contagious energy.

And she really likes him.

I didn't have to have her say a thing to know that. It's very obvious by the way she looks at him.

I sigh.

Well, at least I can always have her cake.

The kind she *bakes*, of course.

"Hey Coach." I feel a big hand land on my shoulder and I look over at Jack Hayes, our right winger.

"Hey."

"Just wanted to tell you that he's pooping fine now."

I nod. "Glad to hear it."

Hayes' dog had been having some constipation issues, and I'd given him a couple of tips my parents had used with their older dog with the same troubles. Yes, I talk to my players about more than hockey. Most of them are young, away from home, just starting out trying to be adults. And they're not always getting it right, in part because they're running into issues for the first time. I don't want them to only look to me for guidance when they've got skates on.

Crew is up on the couch now making a toast, because of course he is, and he calls out his sister's name.

My attention is immediately back on the tiny blonde.

Luna goes over to her brother for a hug and the second she moves away from Alexsei, I say, "See ya' later," to Hayes' and bee-line for my star defenseman.

"Hey, man," I say to Alexsei, quietly so no one else really pays us any attention.

He grins. "Hey, Coach."

"So you're dating Luna?" I ask. I don't have a lot of time before she's probably headed back over here, so I don't bother with small talk.

"Uh." He glances at the woman in question. "Not...exactly."

"I'm just wondering because it could get sticky with McNeill. Crew I mean," I say. That's not *untrue*. But also not the reason I'm here at the moment.

"Yeah. I know." He shoves a hand through his hair. "I like her, but no, we're not dating."

"Why not? Because of Crew?" I hadn't thought of giving Luna that reason, but that would make sense.

But Alexsei shakes his head. "Nah, because of Luna."

"She said no?" Had he finally asked, and she was now going to make him regret making her wait? For some reason that seemed like her style.

"I didn't ask," Alexsei says.

"Don't you think you should?"

"Luna isn't the kind of girl you just take to dinner and the movies and have a little fun with," he says. He's watching her now.

She didn't come straight back to his side after her brother's toast. She's moving through the room, talking and laughing, seemingly having forgotten Alexsei.

"What kind of girl is she?" I ask, following her with my gaze.

I know what he means, but it's more of a feeling than something I can put into words, so I'd love to hear him articulate this.

"She's the kind of girl who will change your life," Alexsei says.

I jerk my head to look at him. He said it with a strange wistfulness.

"So," he goes on. "You have to be damned sure you want your life changed."

"You're serious about her," I say, watching him. "You want more than just dating?"

He's young. Does he really know what he wants? And what's my role here? I definitely play the role of an advisor to the guys on a whole range of topics, but I'm not the best one to talk about relationships.

He shakes his head. "I do. But even a night with her reset every bar and expectation I had. She ruined me for anything less." He meets my eyes. "But I'm letting her figure it out."

"You're waiting for her to come to you," I say. "Isn't that risky?"

"I've gotta be the guy she needs me to be."

"The one who doesn't even ask her out on dates?"

"The one who wants her to be whatever and however she wants to be."

Okay, maybe he doesn't need an advisor. Because that sounded pretty well-adjusted. I look over at Luna again. She's now talking to her brother's girlfriend's other boyfriends—yeah, that's a long story—and smiling at them, too.

She doesn't seem like someone who doesn't know what and how she wants to be.

"How long do you think that will take?" I ask Alexsei.

He shrugs. "Not sure. But I'm not going anywhere."

"No?" He's a hotshot and has women throwing themselves at him constantly. He's really going to wait for one woman?

"Can't. She's got me. Even if she doesn't know it. Even if she thinks she doesn't want that. Yet."

Wow. Her siren song might be even stronger than I thought.

And I should probably just avoid her. I already felt a pull in the kitchen over cake. It is really fucking good cake and yes, I can be won over through my stomach—I'm very cliché—but giving Luna a wide berth might be in my best interest. I don't think I'm ready for Luna McNeill.

"Okay, well, good luck with that." I clap Alexsei on the shoulder. I should tell him that she really does want him to ask her out. But I don't.

He chuckles. "Thanks."

I start to walk away, but turn back after a step. "Hey man."

"Yeah?"

"What's 'cake' mean? In slang? Sexual slang?" I feel like an idiot.

He grins. "A girl's ass. Why?"

Jesus. "No reason."

I am so not ready for Luna McNeill.

CHAPTER 10

Owen

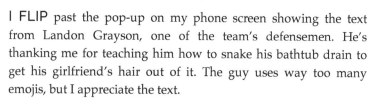

I FLIP past the pop-up on my phone screen showing the text from Landon Grayson, one of the team's defensemen. He's thanking me for teaching him how to snake his bathtub drain to get his girlfriend's hair out of it. The guy uses way too many emojis, but I appreciate the text.

And I love when the guys come to me with questions and problems.

I should probably pull the whole team together annually to teach them about bathtub drains, though. That's an important thing to know if you're going to be having a girl showering at your place regularly, and I teach that to at least four guys a year.

But I can't text him back right now. I need to find my kid.

I check my phone's Find Friends app again. Brady's phone still hasn't moved from Luna McNeill's bakery, Books and Buns. But I know the way his mind works. He could have easily left his backpack with the phone tucked in it in a backroom and taken off with Lydia to God knows where. He thinks he's smarter than me and he's wrong.

I did every stupid and shady thing possible when I was his age, and I know that his brain is consumed by two things these days—hockey and Lydia. Specifically, sex with Lydia. I'd have to be both an idiot and not a man to not recognize the way they look at each other. Plus, there is a lot of rubbing up on each other. So much rubbing. I've even caught him with her in his room, which is against my rules. I understand wanting to get laid.

Hell, I wish I was getting laid, but that's a whole other issue.

I had a one-track mind at his age, too, which is why he exists in the first place. But the last thing he or Lydia, who is genuinely a nice girl, needs right now is to get pregnant. It's the last thing I need, too. The thought of being a grandfather at thirty-six makes me grimace.

Yanking open the door to Books and Buns, I step inside. The bakery is warm and cute and smells like a special kind of heaven, but I don't want to be here. I made an ass out of myself with Luna at Crew's birthday party. She's gorgeous and sexy and *way* out of my league and I think I'm maybe a little afraid of her. Or of the havoc she could wreak in my life, anyway.

I'm the guy who accidentally gets women, not because I have any game. Which maybe isn't even what you're supposed to call it these days. Brady always points out my dated slang, or straight up misuse.

I could eat your cake all day.

Jesus. I'm an idiot.

But Brady told me he's been logging major hours working at the bakery and I think he's straight up full of shit, so I'm here to confirm that. I also am debating if he is actually working this many hours, forcing him to quit because his grades suck. He thinks he can skate by—no pun intended—and go to college based on his hockey skills, but that's no guarantee. He's a good player, but so are a lot of guys and all it takes is one injury and his future is fucked.

I should know.

Nothing like blowing out a knee and knocking up a girl at the age of nineteen to send my life off in a totally different direction.

Not that I have any complaints. I landed in a cake job—I know *that* is one way to use cake—that I love. Working with the guys and our head coach is rewarding as hell and the Racketeers are having a great season.

But now I have to wrangle my horny son.

To my total surprise, he is actually behind the pastry counter, wiping it down. Lydia is collecting coffee mugs from the tables scattered around in front of it. There's no sign of Luna, which is a relief and a disappointment.

"Coach Phillips," Lydia says, looking up at me in surprise. "Hi."

"Hi, Lydia."

Brady's head snaps up, and he groans. "Dad, what are you doing here? This is so embarrassing."

"I just wanted to make sure you're where you said you were going to be."

"When am I ever not where I'm supposed to be?" he demands, looking outraged. "You have control issues."

"Uh, fully thirty percent of the time you're not where you're supposed to be." Brady is a good kid, but he's also a sixteen-year-old boy. I need to keep an eye on him. I stroll up to the counter. Damn, these baked goods look amazing. "Give me an eclair."

"You'll have to pay for it," he warns.

That makes me snort in disbelief. "Why wouldn't I pay for it? And I have three dollars, you know."

"If you want to buy an eclair in two thousand and five," he tells me. "They're six dollars now in modern times. For one."

Damn. Dough has gotten pricey. But I try to pretend like I'm not shocked at skyrocketing prices because my son already thinks I'm a thousand years old. "I'll take three."

The case looks a little empty, like the business isn't doing well. It makes me feel bad for Luna.

"I'm busy. I'll box those up for you later and bring them home. But you have to pay for them now. Then leave because you're embarrassing me at my place of employment because you don't trust me even though I've done nothing to not deserve your trust."

I fight the urge to roll my eyes. "You said this bakery has been slammed, so you're working extra shifts." I glance around. "I'm the only one in here. And how many bakeries have a run on cupcakes for St. Patrick's Day, anyway?"

"My bakery is always busy," Luna says in a light voice, appearing out of nowhere like a sugar goddess in a tight T-shirt that says, "Roll With It" with a picture of a sticky bun. She likes puns. Maybe I'm not such an idiot, after all. Except I just insulted her business.

Definitely still an idiot.

It's unnerving to me how gorgeous Luna is. Her hair is almost white, with those purple tips, and it has the superfine texture of silk. It shifts and flows around her face every time she moves, before settling back down, pin straight. Her eyes are enormous, her lips are pouty, and she's wearing her signature sassy smile.

I want to paint her body with frosting and lick her clean from head to toe. I want to kiss those plump lips and haul her onto my lap and...

"That's why our case is mostly empty."

"What?" I ask, because I've completely lost track of the conversation.

That seems to happen when Luna is anywhere near me.

"Because the bakery is always busy. That's why the case is almost empty. It's six o'clock. We close at seven."

Right. I clear my throat. "Of course. I mean, I tasted your... stuff at your brother's party and it was delicious. As you know. Amazing. So I could see why you'd be almost sold out. Congratulations."

Oh, God. I really said that.

Brady is eyeing me in disbelief. "Dude, did you have a stroke?"

Lydia giggles.

I glare at him. "Don't 'dude' me."

"Nice seeing you, Owen," Luna says, giving me a smile before returning to the kitchen with a wave.

I watch her go, sighing, even as I check out her ass, which is really inappropriate.

"You're being weird," Brady accuses me.

He's right. I don't even bother to deny it.

"Just give me the damn eclairs." I want to say the fucking eclairs, but I restrain myself. "And I expect you home right after the bakery closes so you can study. You have that calculus test tomorrow."

"I know. Now just go before you mess everything up."

Lydia gasps. "Brady…"

That makes me pause. "Mess what up?" I take my wallet out and pull out my debit card for the eclairs. "Ring me up."

The bells over the front door jangle and I turn automatically when both Brady and Lydia cast a fearful glance toward the door.

"That's him," Lydia murmurs.

"Who him?" I ask, narrowing my eyes.

The guy who has just walked is in his mid-twenties, covered in tattoos, sporting long hair and multiple piercings. He pauses, taking in first the bookstore, then the bakery. He hesitates when he sees us and alarm bells go off in my brain.

Are these damn kids buying weed?

I will fucking kill Brady if he fails a drug test for hockey when I'm shelling a ton of money out on his gear and traveling team.

"Dad, just be cool," Brady says.

"Oh, I'll be cool." I shove my wallet back in my pocket so I have both hands if I need to grab this guy by the coat collar and throw him out.

The guy approaches and gives a friendly smile. "Hey, um, is Luna here?"

"Let me go get her." Lydia disappears faster than I've ever seen her move.

I don't understand why and I don't like whatever is happening here.

"Thanks," the guy says and rocks back on his heels, shoving his hands down into the pocket of his jeans.

I give him a friendly smile, determined to make sure this is all on the up and up. "So how do you know Luna?" I ask.

"Dad..." Brady gives me a warning look.

"I, um..." The guy rubs the back of his head. "I'll just wait over there for her." He retreats to the nearest bookshelf.

"What are you doing?" Brady hisses. "Lydia is going to be so pissed at me."

Now I'm totally confused. "Why? Who the hell is that guy?"

Brady sighs and leans forward onto the counter, like he's giving up. "Lydia and me thought Luna is so cool and works too hard and maybe she needs to have some fun. So we might have made her a profile on a dating app."

That's almost worse than buying drugs. "You did *what*? Does she know about it?"

He shakes his head rapidly. "No. And it was mostly Lydia's idea."

"Oh, come on." Now I'm really furious. "You can at least be a man and take the heat for your girlfriend. Not throw her under the bus."

Brady turns red. "Shit. Sorry. We were just trying to do something nice for Luna."

"Doing something nice for her is sweeping the floor or bringing her lunch. Not pimping her out to total strangers online."

"No one says pimping anymore, Dad."

I swear to God. The vein in my temple starts pulsating. "He could be a murderer, he could be a stalker, he could be married with three kids, for all you know. At worst, it's dangerous. At best, it's none of your damn business who Luna does or doesn't date."

"But Lydia said that this guy likes all the same bands Luna does."

I also know for a fact Luna doesn't want to be set up. If anything, she wants Alexsei to ask her out. Alexsei thinks Luna needs to figure some things out. So they're dancing around each other. And she wiped frosting off *my* mouth. She doesn't need Tinder to find men to fall at her feet.

And what the *fuck* am I talking about.

Still…"I'm getting rid of him."

Brady straightens again in alarm. "But—

"But nothing."

"Lydia says…"

I raise an eyebrow and wisely, he clams up.

"Don't be a dick to him," Brady says. "It's not his fault."

"I'm not going to be a dick to him."

Knowing that I have a good seventy-five pounds and four inches on this guy, I stride over to him and give him a friendly smile. "Hey, listen. You're not going on a date with Luna, buddy. Sorry. There's been a misunderstanding."

"Who the hell are you?" he asks, frowning at me.

I point to the door. My words sound cheerful, but my expression is meant to be menacing. "I'm her boyfriend and there's the door."

I'm not sure why I say I'm dating her. Maybe it's wishful thinking. I don't need to pretend to be her significant other in order to get rid of this guy. But it's what comes out of my mouth and I run with it. But hopefully if he thinks I'm around all the time, he won't get any ideas about showing back up. Luna is probably in this place alone sometimes, and the thought of her being vulnerable if a random guy comes sniffing around makes my blood run cold.

"Boyfriend?" He eyes me up and down with a confidence that I have to respect. Even if it's sadly misplaced. I could crush this guy without breaking a sweat. "Then why is she trying to hook up with me?"

"I think there's been a misunderstanding," Luna says, coming across the bakery. She eyes me in amusement.

"Is this guy your boyfriend?" Tinder Fool demands.

Fully expecting her to call out my lie, I still stare down the guy in front of me. Boyfriend or not, I'm not leaving her here with a total stranger.

To my shock, Luna doesn't deny it, though. "Yes, he is. And you've been catfished."

"Ah, fuck," the guy says. "I'm about done with these apps. No one is real."

"I'm sorry," Luna says, looping her arm through mine. She glances up at me and gives me a conspiratorial wink. "Owen and I met through my brother. Dating apps definitely suck."

I barely hear the latter part of what she says because I'm instantly hard from that wink. Damn it, I love it when a woman winks. She makes it worse by leaning her head against my bicep.

"Sorry about your luck," I tell the guy, tugging Luna a little closer to me just because I can. She feels fantastic all snug up against me. Tiny and curvy and like a perfect fit. She smells good, too. Like butter and sugar and that spice that's all her.

Not that any woman wants to hear that.

Tinder Fool leaves with a hard push of the front door and still Luna stays tucked into my side.

"Thanks for that."

"My pleasure." And I really fucking mean that.

She finally lets go and rocks back on her heels. "So… who was that guy?"

"My son and Lydia thought that he seemed like your type, so they invited him to stop by. It was matchmaking gone wrong. I apologize for my son's stupidity." I tap my head. "Remember, I told you hockey players take too many hits to the skull."

"I… wow." She bites her lip. "Do I seem that desperate to teenagers?" She looks half-amused, half-horrified.

"I don't know what anyone looks like to teenagers. I thought they were buying weed from him. The truth was worse."

That makes her snicker softly. "It really is worse. Especially since I said the things I did at the party. You must really think I can't get a date." She puts her hands to her cheeks. "I'm actually embarrassed. I don't like this feeling at all."

"Don't be embarrassed. I'm the one who keeps sticking my foot in my mouth. My very big foot."

"You know what they say about men with big feet."

I do. I cough a little and cover it with my fist. I want her to say it because she looks... flirty? I think. "What do they say?"

"They need big shoes," she says lightly, with a quirky smile.

I laugh softly. "Right. Of course." I want to kiss the corners of her cute little mouth.

She reaches behind me and flicks the lock on the door. "Since my case is almost empty, as you pointed out, I'm going to close up a little early. Brady and Lydia can head out for the night so Brady can study."

"Are you sure?"

She nods. "School is important. And I'm worn out. It's been a long week." She starts walking toward the counter, where Brady and Lydia are furiously whispering to each other, heads together.

"Okay, thanks. And I'll buy whatever you have left." I'll spend a thousand dollars on eclairs if it will make her happy.

"You don't have to do that."

"I want to. I like your stuff." I really do. She's a fantastic baker. I also like her ass. Which I'm staring at.

The jeans she's wearing sit high on her waist and they flow loosely down her legs, but they're snug in the butt, the seam sliding up between her two tight little cheeks, and I want to touch her so damn bad.

"You'll have to tell me what you like the best," she says, turning just in time to catch me checking out her backside. "You have a sugar fetish, don't you?"

"Uh..." I have no idea how to respond to that. She's definitely flirting and I'm way the fuck over my head here. "Yes." I pat my gut. "Obviously."

But Luna gives me a little sexy once-over. "Hmm." Then she turns to Brady. "You can go home with your dad," she tells him. "After we box everything up for him."

"Everything?" Brady shakes his head in disbelief. "Dude. Get a hobby."

"Dude. Get your ass moving if you want to see Lydia in the next month," I snap.

This recent power struggle is really getting on my nerves.

Ten minutes and two hundred and twelve dollars later, I have four bags of pastries and we're heading toward the door. It turns out a mostly empty display case is still a lot of pastries when you crowd them all together in boxes.

"See you Saturday," Lydia says to Luna, who is biting her lip as she waits for us to exit so she can relock the door.

She tried to dissuade me from buying all of this three times, but I persisted. Because I committed and I won't back down from that. Even if I am going to gain ten pounds.

"Goodnight," she says to me, giving me a faint smile.

I want to ask her out. I think she wants me to ask her out.

But she also wants Alexsei to ask her out.

But he's not going to because he wants her to figure some stuff out.

But he's also been hit in the head a lot and I think maybe he's being really stupid about this. He needs to go for this girl.

So maybe I need to not worry about him. It would be a life lesson for him to lose out because he was fucking around.

But maybe I'm reading it *all* wrong.

And Lydia and Brady are hovering. I refuse to embarrass Luna or myself in front of them. More than I already have.

"Goodnight, Luna. Be sure to lock up."

She nods and we exit. I watch to make sure she locks the door and activates her alarm system, then I start down the sidewalk. I shove two bags at Lydia. "Here, take these home for your family." Lydia has four younger siblings.

"You like Luna," Lydia murmurs, looking up at me in awe as she juggles the two pink bags like this is the most romantic thing she's ever witnessed in her entire life.

Brady's jaw drops. "*Dad.* Is that why you bought all these pastries?"

"I did it to apologize for your crappy behavior," I tell him, dryly. I pause on the sidewalk and look around. "Where the hell is my car?"

"It's right here," Miss Helpful says, pointing to my car, which is indeed right here.

"Oh, man, you've got it *bad*," Brady says gleefully.

He's right. I do.

I push my fob to unlock the doors. "Just get in the car."

CHAPTER 11

Luna

"OH MY GOSH, Luna, this order is so huge! You should be so happy."

I look over to where Dani is arranging frosted sugar cookies on one of the glass trays. She is sincere, I know, but she has no idea how much work I've had to put in on this huge order for the after-game party for the Racketeers.

"Yeah, it is a huge order. And it kind of came in last minute." I arrange the macarons by color on another tray and set it up on one of the higher tiers. I should've skipped the macarons. The hockey players don't appreciate them. But the order did specifically include them.

"Well, I'm thrilled you did it. It's been a while since we've been to a game together, and it was so great to sit with you tonight even if it was only a period."

Again, I haven't been to a game because I've been so busy at the bakery. I mean, besides the fact that I can think of ten other things I'd rather do besides go to a hockey game. But I love my best friend. She is truly the sweetest person I know. And she is genuinely happy that this order came in for the bakery. But Dani hasn't been around a whole lot. She's been spending so much time with her boyfriends and with even one, that could take a lot of her time, but she's got *three*. And they're pretty demanding. She hasn't been back to our apartment in two weeks.

Also, we own Books and Buns together, but the books side of the business hasn't done as well. So Dani's work level isn't quite the same. Not that I expect that she would know that.

And I'm not upset with her. I know she really wants this to do well. She thinks I'm an amazing baker, and she's really proud of me.

Then a thought hits me and I turned to face her. "Please tell me that you didn't ask Nathan to place this order."

Dani looks up from where she's now rearranging the cookies she just arranged. She gives me a little frown. "No. I didn't have anything to do with this." Her frown deepens. "Nathan ordered all of this?"

One of her boyfriends is the billionaire owner of the team. I will admit that ordering a bunch of cupcakes and cookies for his players after a game he didn't know they were going to win, doesn't really sound like Nathan. Okay, it doesn't sound like Nathan even if they were going to win for sure.

For that brief moment when I thought maybe Dani had put him up to it to "help the business" I wondered. But I shake my head, confused. "Nathan would do this to help our business anyway, though, right? Have you said anything to him lately about business being slow or the bakery not doing well?"

I swear to God, if someone did this to try to help me out, I'm going to scream.

I've been swamped, and I'm thrilled with that, obviously. I need to pay my dad back. That is going to nag at me until I get it done. I want to just own the bakery flat out. I want that to be mine. I don't want to go down to the bakery every single day and think about how it was paid for with guilt money.

But I don't want other guilt money helping, like guilt money from Nathan Armstrong because he's stolen my friend and roommate.

I definitely don't want my best friend's rich boyfriend giving me handouts.

Especially handouts that kept me in the bakery til midnight making cookies and macarons.

"I guess he would," Dani says. "Nathan would do anything to help me. Us. But I haven't said anything to him about the bakery. Not specifically."

"Who else would place an order like this?" I muse out loud.

This is the first time it's really occurring to me to wonder about this. I was so focused on just getting the order done, getting it over here to the arena and set up, and then worrying about tearing it all down and taking it back to the bakery to clean up, that I honestly didn't give a lot of thought to who was behind the order. It was for the Racketeers, for the team, that was all I really needed to know before now.

"I don't know. It probably could be anyone, right?" Dani asks. "All the guys on the team know what an amazing baker you are. They all love your stuff. Almost all of them tasted it at Crew's birthday party."

And that's when it hits me. Crew's birthday party. Someone who was really a fan of my baked goods. And someone who has enough money to pay for something like this.

It's not like the hockey players couldn't afford it, but they wouldn't think of throwing a big party for the whole team. They'd place an order for just themselves.

But there is someone who might want to celebrate the team, and throw a little business my way.

"Owen did this," I say.

I'm not really sure how to feel about that.

"Who's Owen?" Dani asks.

"Owen Phillips. Coach Phillips. The assistant coach."

Dani straightens and turns to face me. Her eyes were wide with interest.

Oh no. That means she's going to want to know everything

about how I know Owen Phillips. Which also means she's going to think I should give him some more attention. She's going to mention how good-looking he is. And what a nice guy he seems to be. And how Nathan really likes him and respects him. And how Michael really likes and respects him. And the thing is… I'm sure she's right.

And I probably should give him more attention.

And that doesn't help me at all. Because I already want to give him more attention, and I don't have any fucking time to do that when I'm baking until midnight.

"Why would Owen Phillips order a whole bunch of desserts from you for the team? How would he even know to order desserts from you for the team?"

"He was at Crew's birthday. He really liked my…cake." I know she notices how I pause and almost trip over the word 'cake'.

But I'm reminded of how fucking cute it was when he said he could eat my cake all day. And also, how hot I got when he said that. I mean it was dorky and I know he didn't mean it that way, but it's made me blush and want to tease him more and definitely led to me thinking about other things of mine he could eat.

And no, I'm not talking about cakes that I bake.

"You like him," Dani says, pointing at me.

Dani and I have known each other for a very long time. Through a lot of things. Through a lot of guys. Well, I've been through a lot of guys. Her much less so. But if anybody in the world would be able to read on my face about how I feel about some guy, it would be her. And why would I keep these feelings from Dani?

Except that she is madly in love, and would very much like me to be as well.

But I don't want to be in love.

Not that she believes me, no matter how many times I say that.

I don't *object* to love. I just don't have time for it.

And I'm not even sure I believe it myself anymore that I don't want to be in love. Right now, the idea of going home to a partner who would pour me a glass of wine and rub my feet sounds pretty damn pleasant.

"I do like him," I decide to admit because lying would be stupid and she would know anyway. "He seems like a really good guy. Brady is his son." At Dani's blank expression, I sigh. "Brady, the cute, nice kid who's now working for me at the bakery? Lydia's boyfriend."

Dani nods. "Oh, he seems like a great kid."

"Yeah, and Owen's his dad. So, obviously, he's a good guy if he has a son like Brady. And the guys on the team all seem to like him. And Nathan Armstrong has very high standards for the people he spends time with—" I give her a smile and a wink. "So I can assume that Owen is a good guy. And he was sweet and almost a little awkward when we met at Crew's party."

Owen seems like a rub-my-feet kind of guy.

"So he ordered a bunch of stuff for the guys because..." Dani trails off as if she's still not quite sure how that all fits together.

And I'm not either, except for one thing. "He stopped by the bakery to check on Brady and Lydia one day, he made a comment about how he thought the bakery wasn't doing very well."

Dani's eyes widen.

"I corrected him, but maybe he didn't believe me."

"So you think that maybe he placed this huge order to help you out?"

I frown. "Maybe. Which is kind of a dick move, right?"

Dani laughs. "Actually, it's kind of sweet and romantic."

I shake my head. "It's not. It's him one, not believing me and two, thinking that I can't handle my business without a man injecting his help and money."

"Or, maybe it's a guy who likes you and is trying to make your life a little easier."

I sigh. "We are going to see this differently no matter what. So, I think I just need to talk to Owen about it."

Dani looks slightly concerned. "Just don't be mean to him."

I look at her in surprise. "I'm not going to be mean to him."

"If you're insulted by this and you think that he thought you needed help, you might be mean."

I open my mouth. But then close it, thinking. Okay, I might be mean. I won't *try* to be, but I can get very defensive. Especially about the bakery. My mom and dad buying it for me in the first place is hard enough, but I definitely don't want some guy waltzing in and thinking that he needs to keep me afloat.

"I will try really hard not to be mean to him," I say, feeling like that's at least a promise I can keep.

"Would you go out with him?" Dani asks.

I groan. This is exactly what I knew would happen. "Sweetheart, I barely have time to sleep. I can't date anyone."

"But when you date the right person, they make your life easier," she says. "They help you, they make you happier, dating them is better than not dating them."

I would love to argue with her. And six months ago, I absolutely would have. But dammit, she knows more about this than I do. She doesn't just have one relationship, she's technically got three going on. And yes, those guys — including my brother, shockingly enough — seem to make her life easier. They help her out, they support her, and they definitely make her happy.

If I said I wasn't at all jealous and didn't want any of that, I'd be lying. Of course, I want that. Even if I am crawling into bed after midnight, completely exhausted, I would love to be curling up next to someone.

The nights when I barely get a chance to eat because I'm doing books, or inventory, or waiting for something to come out of the oven, would I love to have someone drop by with dinner and keep me company? Absolutely.

I love taking on this bigger business challenge, and when it's done, and I have my dad paid off, and Books and Buns is going full steam ahead, I hope I'll be able to relax a little bit, step back, and look at the rest of my life. As much as I love cupcakes and cookies, I don't want them to be my entire life.

But for right now, it is.

Especially considering that the man I want to ask me out is *not*.

"I just can't focus on that right now. I know what you're saying, and I am thrilled for you. But right now, the idea of adding something else to my plate makes me want to cry."

"Let me know if you need more help from me," Dani says. "I know I've been a little absent and you've been really understanding, but I want this business to succeed, and I love you. You're my best friend. I want to be there for you."

I do need to lean on her more. It is her business, too. But still, it was my father who bought it for us. He did it because of me. I just feel like I'm the one who has to pay this off. But I nod. "I will. In fact, next weekend I could use your help."

She nods. "I'm here for you."

I step back and survey the dessert tables. They look amazing, I have to admit. I'm very proud of the products, all the icing looks amazing, and everything is set up beautifully.

So I guess Owen got his money's worth.

As I think about that, my stomach flips. I am annoyed that he felt like he needed to step in and didn't listen to me when I told him that the bakery was doing well. But Dani's not totally wrong. It is nice that he wanted to help. That he even cares.

Hockey players and members of the staff start filtering into the room. Most of these players are benchwarmers. They were able to get off the ice faster and get cleaned up. But I know the rest of the team isn't too far behind. And that means I'll probably see Alexsei.

I have mixed emotions about that as well. I've missed him.

But I don't know what to do with that. He's a lot. I feel like I lose track of all time when I'm with him. Even just talking to him at my brother's birthday party seemed to suck up all of my attention. I wasn't even with him constantly, but it seemed that every few minutes, he would manage to walk by and say something sweet or flirty. Then I'd look up and suddenly fifteen minutes had flown by.

There's just something about him that makes me want to sink into him, wrap myself around him, just lose myself in him.

That freaks me out.

So does his intensity. I know he likes me. It's never been like this with any other guy. The guy looks at me with heart eyes, I swear. I feel like any second I'm going to see cartoon hearts popping out of his eyes. On one hand, being adored is pretty fucking great. The guy could have any woman in Chicago—and I think he's had several—so the idea that he is suddenly all about me is kind of amazing. I mean, come on, that's pretty great for my ego.

On the other hand, it's a lot. He's going to want me to give him that same kind of attention and energy, right?

"Hey Luna."

The rich, warm, deep voice seems to wash over me and I take a deep breath. Damn, I almost feel calmer.

I turn and smile up at Owen. "Hey coach."

"How are you?" he asks.

I smile in spite of myself. "I'm okay." Then I decide Owen seems like the kind of guy I can be honest with. "Actually, I'm exhausted. But okay." I pause. "The bakery's been really busy. Business is great."

I watch his face closely and his expression brightens as he gives me a big smile. "That's fantastic. Congratulations."

I notice that Dani has moved off. Crew hasn't joined us yet, but of course Nathan and Michael are both already here. I don't have to feel bad about turning all of my attention on Owen. And in this moment I can't seem to help it.

I prop my hands on my hips. "So you didn't have to do this."

"Do what?"

I turn and look at the dessert tables, then gesture with my hand. "This."

"Well, I had to show up. First of all, I assumed that the cupcakes were probably almost as good, if not as good, as the cake from the birthday party. And we both know how I feel about that." He gives me an adorable grin. "And I wanted to see you. I'd hoped you would be here."

"Is that why you did it? You could've just called me."

His brows rise slightly. "What?"

"Ordered all of this stuff. Had me show up here with a van full of baked goods."

He scans the table and looks back at me. "You think I ordered this?"

"Yes. Didn't you?"

He shakes his head. "Honestly? When I want more of your stuff, I intend to just come to the bakery." He looks around the room. "I love these guys, but feeding them is a really big expensive endeavor."

I'm studying him and I can tell he is not lying. I also can't deny that my stomach flips a little when he says that he intends to come back to the bakery.

This is not how I should be reacting to that news.

But then I look back at the tables, completely confused. If Nathan didn't do this, and Owen didn't do this, I have no idea who placed this order. Who else would want to?

"Hang on a second." I move behind one of the tables and crouch to pull out some of the boxes that we've shoved underneath the tables. They're covered by tablecloths so no one will see the mess, but I left all the papers and wrapping with them. I rummage around until I find what I'm looking for.

The order slip.

At the bottom, I notice what I had skipped over before—the name of the person placing the order.

I pull it out, straighten, and cross back to Owen. I thrust it at him. "I'll admit I probably don't appreciate this as much as I should. My friend pointed out that this is kind of a sweet thing to do. She even used the word romantic. But don't worry, I'm not necessarily thinking that. I understand that maybe you think this would be helpful to me? Or maybe helpful to Brady and Lydia indirectly. But it's done. I'm not mad. I'm just saying that I don't need this kind of help. The bakery is doing great. And if you're doing it to get my attention, you can just stop by the bakery or give me a call."

I almost regret saying that because if Owen does stop by or give me a call, then I'm going to have to come up with the answer to a question about if I want to see him or not.

And I honestly don't know what that answer is.

Actually, that's not true.

I do want to see him.

That's my problem.

He's frowning at the order I've put in his hands.

"This's my name and phone number," he says.

"Yeah. Exactly."

"But I did not place this order, Luna." His eyes meet mine directly. "Seriously. If I had, I promise I would tell you. I did not place this order for the team."

I frown. "Why would someone put your name and phone number on the order? How would someone else even know that you work here? Or know your number? Do you think one of the guys is playing a prank or something?" I shoot a glare around the room. "Somebody is paying for this."

He looks around the room, then back to the order in his hand, then up at me. "I wouldn't put it past them exactly," he says slowly. "But I think there might be another explanation."

"Like what?"

"Whose handwriting is this? Who took the order? I assume it wasn't you?"

"No. Obviously, I would've known if I was talking to you."

He nods. "So who took this order?"

It's obvious to me. "That's Lydia's handwriting."

Then our eyes meet and realization dawns.

"No," I say.

He nods. "Yeah. I think so."

I pluck the order form from his fingers. "You're telling me that Lydia and Brady placed this order as a way of...what? Making me think that you were doing something sweet and helping me out?"

"I'm guessing Lydia and Brady know that you would be offended that a guy would step in and try to help you this way."

I shrug. "Probably."

"My guess is this is their way of getting us together and ensuring we run into one another again."

Oh, wow. I really don't think I'm ready for matchmaking teenagers. "This is pretty elaborate."

"They are teenagers in love. Elaborate and over-the-top is kind of the main theme."

I blow out a breath. "I guess that's true." Then I shake my head. Then laugh. "I like them both so much. It's hard to be mad at them. But this is really shoving me in your face."

Owen's grin is a little crooked and he almost looks shy for a moment. Wow. I am really not used to that. The guys I hang out with are fairly confident, even if they shouldn't be.

I find myself taking a step closer to him.

His gaze drops to my mouth and then comes back to my eyes and I feel a surprising arc of heat sizzle through me.

"I wouldn't mind having you shoved anywhere."

I blink at him and can't help a little snort.

He closes his eyes and groans. "Jesus. That sounded terrible."

I laugh louder. "It was cute."

He shakes his head but meets my gaze. "I think I'm a little old to be cute."

I lift my shoulder. "I don't think your cuteness got the memo."

Well fuck, I'm flirting. And I'm not sure I'm doing a very good job of it. That was kind of a dorky thing for me to say. But he doesn't seem to mind.

"The kids went to a lot of work here," he says.

I lift a brow. "Did they? I don't think they paid for any of this. They didn't help me bring it over and set it up. And they only made about half of these cupcakes."

He looks thoughtful for a moment. "You know, we could really torture them for this."

"I'm intrigued. Tell me more."

"You like the idea of torture?"

"Oh, sometimes it's warranted."

"Well, I think, I should ask you out."

"Really?" I'm amazed to feel my heart actually flip over in my chest. And I don't mind it. "And how does that torture them?"

"We go out, and I refuse to tell them anything about it. As do you."

I nod. "Right. So they're trying to kind of get us together, it will kill them if they don't actually get any details."

"Yeah, something like that."

"You know what would be even better?"

He leans in, and I'm not even sure that it's a conscious movement. "What's that?"

"If I spend the night at your place and happen to leave something behind, and Brady finds it, wonders about it, but nobody's dishing any details."

Why the *fuck* did I just say that?

Heat flares in Owen's eyes and I realize oh *that's* why. I wanted a reaction from him.

And yes, there's a part of me that wants to spend the night with him.

I don't know about the dating thing, but sex? Yeah, I think that sounds pretty good. Stress reliever. I could definitely use that.

I can tell I surprised him in spite of the heat. Maybe by the time women hit thirty-six they aren't quite so assertive.

If that's the case I better enjoy myself over the next twelve years or so.

But Owen slowly starts nodding. "And we should eat all of his favorite cereal the next morning."

My smile is quick and wide and—dammit—genuine. "You're okay with your kid knowing I spent the night?"

He shakes his head. "Probably not, but I'm very caught up in this moment and that whole idea of that. I'm probably not thinking straight."

I laugh, stupidly delighted. "We can table that part of the discussion until later."

"Okay."

"So we're going out?"

"Yeah. Let's do it."

Yeah, let's do it. I have no will power when it comes to sexy, but I guess I don't when it comes to cute either. "Great. There's this bar I love. We could meet there on Sunday night. I don't have to work the next day so I can stay out a little later. Or stay out all night."

His eyes darken and I relish his attraction to me. Which is very convenient considering how I'm starting to feel about him.

"Let me take you to dinner," he says.

"Dinner? Um…okay."

"Great. I'll pick you up at eight. We'll go to Rinaldo's."

Now both my brows arch. "Rinaldo's? That place is really nice."

He smiles and there's just a touch of affection in his expression. "Yeah, it is really nice. I'd love to take you there."

I pressed my hand against my stomach. "Wow, like a real date."

"Not like a real date. Actually a real date, Luna."

And now I'm a little breathless. "Honestly, I haven't been on a real date. Like dinner and the guy picks me up and all of that."

"Never?"

"We usually just meet somewhere, have drinks, something like that."

Something like determination crosses his face and he nods. "I am definitely taking you on a real date, Luna. I hope to take you on several."

Yeah, now my whole stomach swoops. And damn, I know I'm going to say yes when he asks me out. Every time.

This is worth carving time out of my schedule. To feel like this.

"So Sunday," he says.

I nod.

"And we *are* going to continue this conversation about how you have to really be sure to clean up all your stuff the morning after you stay over."

Stomach swoop and heart flip at the same time. "I can do that. I guess I'll see you at eight."

CHAPTER 12

Alexsei

I'M in a bad fucking mood.

I'm never in a bad mood.

What do I have to be upset about? I'm young, healthy, get paid a shit-ton to play my favorite game as a job. I have women throwing themselves at me. I live with my best friend in a gorgeous, kick-ass apartment. I also just played a hell of a hockey game. We won huge and everyone is saying this is the year the Racketeers go all the way. I have everything I could possibly want and more.

So what's my problem?

A tiny, blond pixie.

She's my fucking problem, and she has been for four months now.

More than. Four months, two weeks, and five days.

I throw my helmet into my locker, gratified by the loud *bang*. But then I want to throw more things. Maybe punch something.

"Fuck yeah!" Blake Wilder yells, thumping me on the back, clearly thinking I'm heaving my equipment around in celebration. "Racketeers!"

The whole locker room cheers.

I roll my neck. I would typically be leading that cheer. But no. I had to fall for Luna McNeill.

Luna is turning me into a new man.

A man who fucking watches the stands during a game—a huge sin—and notices when she leaves mid-game. And doesn't come back.

A man who hasn't been laid in *four months*.

A man who can't eat a cupcake or a goddamned cookie without getting hard. Seriously, the ones she practiced making in our kitchen the two days she spent with me and Cam were incredible, and I dream about them almost as much as I dream about her pussy. Which is almost every night.

A man who worries about her, and wonders if she's getting enough sleep and if she's making sure she's locking her doors at night, and who wants to make her life easier and better and would do anything if she'd just let me wash her hair in the shower again, or spoon her on the couch while we watched South Park re-runs, or... I don't know, carry heavy boxes for her or something.

Her independence turns me on and makes me nuts at the same time.

"Let's go celebrate boys!" This comes from Jack Hayes, our right winger.

I strip down, not saying anything. I don't want to celebrate. And I'm actually concerned now.

We just had a decisive win over one of our biggest rivals and I don't want to celebrate?

But I don't. I haven't really felt much like going out lately at all.

Interestingly, neither has Cameron.

Not that we've talked about it. Cam and I don't really talk about our "social lives." Otherwise known as who we're fucking when we're not sharing, unless one of us gives the other a heads-up we're having someone over to the apartment.

But I haven't been with anyone since those two days and three nights with Luna. And, if he's been with anyone, it hasn't been at our place.

Cam goes out with guys unless we've got a girl together. I know that. It's always been that way. It's never bothered me. Exactly. I mean, I don't have a problem with my best friend being obviously bi-sexual. The only problem I have is the occasional niggle of jealousy. Which is stupid and I quickly dismiss. I can't tell Cam who to date and I have no right to feel jealous about him being with other guys when I can't give him what he clearly needs.

But I do find myself wondering what Cam sees in the guys he goes out with. Not the sex part—Cam likes *really* good-looking dudes—but just what they're like as people. Are they funny? Do they like the same books or something? They're probably super smart. Cam's practically a fucking genius, so they'd have to be, I figure. But it's not like I ever get to know them. They never stick around and he doesn't introduce us.

Which is fine by me, because I suspect I won't think any of them are good enough for him.

The only time Cam dated anyone for any length of time was when we dated Sara for about six months two years ago. That was the longest relationship either of us has had since we've known each other. I had a high school girlfriend for almost a year, but I haven't been serious about anyone since then.

We had a hell of a good time with Sara, though. Things seemed great.

Then she dumped us. Both of us. At the same time. With a smile and kiss on each of our cheeks and a, "God, I really hope you guys figure out how to be happy."

We didn't know what that meant exactly, but we didn't talk about it much since there wasn't much to say and we haven't repeated that let's-both-date-someone-together thing again either.

I stalk to the shower with my towel slung over my shoulder. I dodge my still celebratory teammates, hoping no one asks me what's wrong because I know exactly what it is and I'm not willing to confess it to anyone but Cam.

And Cam's sick of hearing it.

But he's going to hear it tonight.

Every time I've brought Luna up in the past couple of months, he's the one telling me to leave her alone, that she has to come to me, that I should make her work for it, that she knows exactly where to find me and if she wants me, she'll come get me.

He's starting to really piss me off.

Then again, the one night he and I went out and actually *said* we were going to try to find a girl to take home, he was picky as shit. He rejected every one I pointed out. He never does that. Come to think of it, he almost always lets me pick the girl. But that night, he was grumpy as hell and didn't like anyone. Not that I was all that into it either. I was going through the motions, trying to show him I'm not a pathetic lapdog for Luna.

But when he finally pointed out a gorgeous, petite little blonde, and I brought her over to the table, it only took about ten minutes before he gave me a look and shook his head.

He was right, of course. I wasn't interested in her at all. I didn't want her at all.

But I *should have,* and what the *fuck* was going on?

Then Cameron was a complete dick after that. Grumpy and quiet, and went straight to bed when we got home.

I shut the water off and can hear the team still whooping and laughing out in the locker room. I towel off roughly.

The guys want to go out tonight, and I should go with them. I should get laid. Maybe take two girls home.

Or I should get shit-faced drunk.

I should definitely forget all about Luna McNeill.

I sling my towel around my neck and tip my head back.

But I'm not going to.

I need to see her.

My only debate really is do I tell Cam before I do.

I head back toward my locker, head down, hoping not to attract too much attention.

"There's our guy!" Blake yells out. "Ryan! Let's go!"

The problem is, being one of the stars on the team, playing a fucking great game, and usually being one of the guys leading the party, it's pretty hard for me to keep my head down.

I force myself to grin. "Can't go out tonight guys, sorry."

Blake looks at me as if I just announced I have to go perform open heart surgery. "What the fuck do you mean you can't? We gotta celebrate! You have to come!"

I shake my head. "Not tonight." I start getting dressed, hoping they'll drop it, and knowing they won't.

"You're gonna turn down cupcakes?" Crew asks. "I mean, head home like an old woman if you want to, but at least take some of the cookies or macarons to go."

I freeze with one leg in my pants, oxygen rushing out of my lungs and my body tightening.

Fuck. I cannot have this reaction every time I hear the words cupcakes, cookies, or macarons.

Fucking macarons. Before my time with Luna, I never realized how often those fucking things came up in conversation.

I blow out a breath and pull my pants the rest of the way up, zipping and fastening them as I turn to look at Crew. "What the hell are you talking about?"

Maybe he brought some stuff in from his sister's bakery. Maybe that will make me feel better if I can have a taste of her treats.

I almost groan out loud as that thought goes through my head. This is not the taste of Luna that I need. And honestly, having something in my mouth that I know she touched might kill me.

"Coach ordered an entire spread for us. Luna is in there setting it up. Come on, you gotta come by for a little bit."

I frown at him. "Luna?"

Crew cocks a brow. "My sister? You've met her before. You were drooling all over her at my birthday party." He slaps me on the back. "Lucky for me, she doesn't date hockey players. Otherwise, I might have to keep an eye on you."

That jabs me in the chest. Luna is my teammate's sister. I mean, obviously, this isn't the first time I've thought that. I've known it since the minute I met her. Crew was the reason I met her. But I definitely wasn't thinking about that when I had my face between her thighs, or my dick in her mouth, or had her bent over Cam's expensive couch, or when we had her spread out on the dining room table.

Even at Crew's birthday party, their relationship didn't stop me from flirting with her. Or, let's be honest, laying my heart on the line.

Not that it shook the little blonde sugar magician up.

I don't know what the fuck she puts in the desserts she makes, but I feel like I've been under a spell.

Or what she puts in her pussy.

I'm definitely addicted either way.

I clear my throat as I look at her brother. "Of course, I know who Luna is. I didn't know she was setting up some dessert spread for us."

"Yeah, it's a surprise. I guess from Coach Phillips. That's what the staff is saying, anyway. Luna's team showed up with her van full of stuff saying Coach had ordered a bunch of stuff."

"Really?" Now I flash back to when I walked into the kitchen at Crew's birthday party and found Luna and Coach talking.

I haven't thought much about it, because I had been so focused on Luna and what I needed to say to her. But they had definitely been in there for a while, and they looked pretty friendly.

Was something going on with Coach and Luna? Was that why she wasn't calling me? Was that why she wasn't coming back to me?

Oh fuck that.

I've been giving her space because she didn't want to date. Allegedly. She wants to focus on her business. She has huge plans and dreams and I'm trying to respect that.

But if she can be flirty, go out with other guys, then she fucking has time for me.

Not only did I make that girl come harder than she ever has, she had *fun* with us. Dammit, she did. I know it.

I jerk my shirt off the hanger and ask Crew, "Where is this thing?"

"Down in the conference room."

My heart flips over. She's still here. That was why she left.

I feel a little loosening of the anger and hurt—yes, I can admit that's what I was feeling—that had been tightening my chest all night.

She hadn't left because she didn't want to see the game, or me.

She hasn't been in the back hallway for weeks. Months. But she's been at all of our games. And every once in a while when I look up at her, our eyes meet.

She's watching me.

Cam says they don't talk, but I know my friend well. That's as much because of him as it is because of her.

But I like having her eyes on me. I like just having her there.

Now she's just down the hall, and I am going to fucking see her, and talk to her, and tell her how I'm feeling tonight.

I shrug into my suit jacket and pull my phone out. I text Cam.

> After game thing with the team. I'll find a way home.

I wait just a second for his response, which comes quickly.

> Fine

That's Cam.

I grab my tie, slip it on, but only tie it loosely. I don't button my top button either. We have to wear suits on game days, but after the game we're all a lot more casual.

Thank God tonight Crew was the high scorer and Blake, as our goalie, had an incredible game, so they were the ones the press wanted to talk to and I got to avoid all of that.

I grab my stuff, slam my locker, and head down the hallway.

A bunch of players have already gathered. The room isn't really made for a bunch of hockey guys, and with the tight space and huge bodies, I don't see her right away.

But, like I have a radar built in, I find her within a minute.

She's standing at the front of the room by two long tables arranged in an L shape. They're draped with white tablecloths and have desserts arranged on glass plates and trays on what look like white boxes that put everything on various levels. There's a rainbow of colors on top of cupcakes, cookies, what look like eclairs, and the fucking macarons.

I start toward her and it isn't until I get about halfway there that I take in the whole picture.

She's not standing there alone. She's talking to someone. Smiling up at someone.

No, not just anyone.

Coach Phillips.

And he's standing a lot closer to her than he needs to in order to review his purchase order.

He towers over her, and even though she and I have been as together as two bodies can be, I marvel at how small she is next to him.

She looks gorgeous, wearing black leggings that hug her legs and ass, a long sweater over her Racketeers T-shirt, and the same black boots that she wore to our apartment four months ago.

My body reacts to the whole thing.

Just being within her orbit, but the boots, her standing next to iced cookies, and another man looking at her.

I'm not the kind of guy who won't let any other man even glance in my girl's direction.

No, this is all about *how* this man is looking at her.

Coach Phillips is looking at her like she's the iced dessert that he would very much like to drag his tongue all over.

I shove past two of my teammates without even looking.

"Hey," one of them says.

"What's your problem, Ryan?" the other grumbles.

But I don't even slow down.

And I'm still too late. Because I arrive next to Luna just as I hear her say, "I can do that. I guess I'll see you at eight."

I look from her to Coach and then back to her.

Her eyes go wide and her mouth drops open.

"Ryan," Coach says, extending his hand. "Great game."

The guy has no idea how badly I want to punch him in the face.

Because it's pretty clear that Coach Phillips just asked the woman I'm falling in love with out on a date.

And she said yes.

CHAPTER 13

Cameron

I CAN'T TAKE it anymore.

Alexsei had a great game.

Again.

Yet he's sitting in the passenger seat of my car rubbing his temples and looking and sounding pissed off and miserable.

Again.

It's destroying me to hear him like this.

"Coach Phillips asked her out, and she just said yes, man. Just like that. 'I can do that. I guess I'll see you at eight.'" Alexsei gives a howl of frustration and slams his fist into the dashboard. "What a dick. He pretended at Crew's birthday party to be all concerned about me and do you know what he was doing?"

I have an idea. But Alexsei needs to get this out. "What was he doing?" I ask obediently.

"He was pumping me for information. He wanted to see where I stood, hear if she rejected me or not because the whole time, the whole goddamn time, he wanted to make a play for her himself." Alexsei groans again, like a wounded animal. "All while I was respecting her boundaries. This is your fault. You told me to let her come to me."

I'm driving us home, Alexsei having texted me again after first saying he didn't need a ride, retracting it and saying he needed to get the fuck out of there. *Now.* My hands gripping the steering wheel tightly, as I'm forced to acknowledge what I thought was true, but I was trying to ignore. Alexsei has fallen for Luna *hard.* Like as hard-as-my-cock-when-I'm-in-him-hard. Which means I have to fix this for him, with her, because if I can't make Alexsei fall in love with me—there, I fucking said it—then I want him to be able to be with whoever he *does* fall in love with.

It looks pretty damn clear that someone is Luna. If not fully in love with her yet, he will be with the slightest bit of encouragement.

He's right. I did tell him to hold back and give her space. Let her make the first move. I thought if he pushed too hard, she'd balk. Which was obviously a fuck-up.

It can be fixed, though.

"But that was what, February?" I ask. "It's the middle of March. Maybe he wasn't thinking that then."

Maybe he was. I don't know what the fuck the guy was thinking. But I do know that Alexsei's career could be jeopardized if he suddenly decides to give the Racketeers assistant coach a hard time at practice. If he has attitude about following direction from Coach Phillips. Or if he can't keep his head in the game.

Alexsei's financial security, his identity, his passion, are all dependent on hockey.

He can't be angry with his coach. I *will* fix this.

"If he was interested in her at the party, wouldn't he have asked her out then?" I ask, slowing to a stop at a red light to glance over at him. Alexsei is slumped against the window, smacking it a couple of times with his temple just to express his outrage, his hair still damp from his shower. I want to push the hair that's flopping into his face back out of the way, but I restrain myself.

I always restrain myself.

Always have. Always will. Because I'm not touchy-feeling and I'm not ruled by my emotions and I refuse to ruin my friendship with Alexsei all because I have feelings for him that go beyond what they should or he thinks they do. That's not what he wants from me.

I want him to be happy, damn it.

"Maybe he was just being a pussy," Alexsei grumbles.

"Maybe he's gotten to know her better over the last month since his kid is working at her bakery and he developed feelings for her." I've heard Luna discussing Brady with Dani and she thinks he's a good kid.

"Is that supposed to make me feel better?"

"Yes. It is. I'm just saying that maybe he was sincere when he was talking to you at that party."

"You're the one who is always telling me everyone has an angle and I shouldn't trust people so easily."

I inwardly wince. "Don't listen to me. I'm a jaded asshole."

Alexsei isn't, and it doesn't suit him. He's an optimist, a fun-loving team player, who tears up when sweet girls don't get the final rose on The Bachelor. Nothing about him needs to change, and I'll be damned if it does now because Luna McNeill has double standards for dating.

"Why *are* you so jaded?" he asks, like it's just occurred to him to wonder why I'm the way I am.

"You've met my mother. If you ask her about emotions, she pinches everything she has up so tight she looks like a freeze-dried prune. She thinks hugs are for lower life forms." I love my mother, don't get me wrong. But she's a retired prosecutor and not a warm and fuzzy woman. At forty-two, she'd decided no man was ever going to cut it as a life partner and had gone to the sperm bank with a laundry list of requirements and selected the one with the most potential for producing an intellectual prodigy. Her words, not mine.

The end result was me and a childhood filled with flashcards and rules, but no cuddles and nothing sticky. Chewing gum and Play Doh would just about send her over the edge. The apple didn't fall far from the fucking tree there. I hate sticky anything outside of the bedroom.

My comment distracts Alexsei from his angst. He even cracks a grin. "Do you need a hug, bro?"

"No, but you obviously do." I really don't need hugs. They make me feel incredibly awkward.

That's why I chose the path of science, and ultimately, technology. Minimal human interaction. There's no one to question why I'm so straight-forward. I'm straight-forward because I don't like bullshit. Or games. Or leading questions. Or fishing for compliments. Or needling. Or guessing.

Which is ironic, given my feelings for Alexsei, but I'm not ruining my friendship with him.

Otherwise, say what you mean and let's fucking get on with it.

Which is why when Alexsei grumpily says, "I'd like a hug from Luna," I tell him, "Then let's go get you one."

"Wait. What?"

"Let's go to Luna's." I'm already calculating where we are and how to get there the fastest route possible.

He gapes at me like I've lost my mind. "Why?"

"To tell her how you feel. To call her out. To *ask* her out."

"But she told me no."

"Did she though? Officially? Did you even ask?"

That stops him cold. "I… fuck, I don't know. I guess not. What do I say when we get there?"

"That if she can date the coach, she can date you. That she is denying herself unlimited pleasure at your hands."

That's a little cringe-worthy to my ears, but it sounds like something Alexsei would say and could pull off.

He sits up straighter. "You're right. Damn it, you're right. Let's go."

"On it." I pull into an alley and then back my car up so I can turn around and head east.

"She's not going to turn me down, is she?"

"No." I feel confident she won't. She likes Alexsei. She's just being stubborn because he talked her into staying at our place for two days. "She doesn't trust herself around you. Why is that? Because she can't resist you."

"I can be very persuasive," he says, rolling his head and shaking his hands, like he's warming up for a game.

"Put that tongue to good use," I tell him.

That has him cracking a grin. "Now that's a plan I can get behind."

"I'll be your wingman." I can be persuasive, too, and I know just the right way to handle Luna.

Twenty minutes later, we park in front of the bakery. The bookshop and bakery are dark, but the windows over the front door have lights glowing.

I start to get out but Alexsei grabs my arm.

I look over questioningly.

"What if Phillips is here with her?" he asks.

"She said she'd see him at eight."

He nods.

"The next eight o'clock is tomorrow morning at eight a.m. And he doesn't strike me as the show-up-at-midnight type. He's not here."

He nods again. But he still looks worried.

This woman has him tied up and I hate the idea that she might hurt him.

My voice gets a little firmer. "And it won't matter if he is."

Alexsei looks surprised. I don't blame him. I've never been like this. Not over anyone I've ever gone out with and certainly not because of a girl.

"Don't upset her," he says.

I lift a brow. He's feeling protective of her from me? This is so interesting. But if I have to upset Luna a little bit to get my point across, I will.

She can handle it.

"It's going to be fine," I tell him.

"Should I go up there by myself?"

I open the car door. "No way."

Alexsei gets out and jogs around the car, catching up with me as I stride toward the side of the building. I stop at the door and press the button on the intercom. This building doesn't look as secure as I'd like, but at least she's got this.

Luna's voice comes over the intercom a moment later. "Hello?"

"It's Cameron and Alexsei. Open your door."

She doesn't say anything for a long moment. I'm imagining that she's shocked we're here. Maybe wishing she had a camera down here.

"What do you want?"

"We're here to talk."

"You could've called."

"You didn't leave us your number."

"Maybe you should take that as a hint."

I breathe in through my nose. "Open the fucking door or I'll call Danielle."

Again she pauses.

"Dani doesn't live here anymore."

"But she still has a key," I say, assuming that this is true.

"But she's not here to let you use it, and she's not going to let crazy men into the apartment to accost me anyway," Luna says.

I grind my teeth, then say tightly, "When I tell her that I'm head over heels in love with you and here to sweep you off your feet she'll hurry over to let me in." I pause. I give Alexsei a confident and reassuring nod.

He shakes his head.

Luna snorts. "No one is going to believe you're in love with me. You're not that good of an actor."

"You underestimate how much people want other people to be in love. She's your best friend and *she's* madly in love and she wants *you* to be madly in love. Better yet, madly in love with two guys. Better yet another hockey player who her boyfriend really likes. She'll have visions of double dates and your babies being best friends. Open your fucking door before we have to make this dramatic."

I hear a sigh again, but she doesn't say anything, and a moment later there's a buzz and a click.

I yank the door open and immediately start up the steps, with Alexsei on my heels.

Luna already has the door at the top open. She has her shoulder propped against the doorjamb and her arms crossed as if she's not about to let us across that threshold.

She still has the black leggings on that she wore to the game. But her feet are bare now, and she's changed into an oversized sweatshirt that hits her about mid-thigh. Her hair is down and loose and she looks gorgeous.

Alexsei is staring at her like she's a goddess and he steps forward immediately. "Hi."

"Hi." She gives him a soft smile.

But I jump right in. She has the power to hurt him and I can't let that happen. I also strongly suspect that if I'm not bossy enough, the two of them could easily cut me out of whatever they do going forward. "You need to quit fucking around," I tell her.

She lifts a brow. "Excuse me?"

"If you're ready to date Coach Phillips then you're ready to date Alexsei."

She looks at Alexsei. "You want to date me?"

He nods. "I do."

She looks at me, narrowing her eyes. "And what do you want?"

"I want you to date Alexsei." I do. It will make him happy.

She eyes me for a second, then looks at him again. "You have to *talk* to me. Tell me if you want to see me. Ask me out."

He squares up. "I'm crazy about you. I've thought about those days together every damned day since. I want more. Please let me take you out. All the time."

"I can't do anything all the time," she says quickly.

He nods. "Let me take you out whenever you can and want to."

She studies him. Then wets her lips and asks, "Do you want to come in?"

He nods quickly. "I really do."

She steps to the side, giving him space to pass by. But she steps in front of me when I start to move forward. "I want to go out with *him*. Where do you think you're going?"

I just stare at her for a moment. God she's a pain in the ass. And there are a few things we need to get straight. I look at Alexsei, who's still beside me. "Go on in. I'll just be a minute."

There is electricity between Luna and I and I know Alexsei picks up on it and it concerns him. But I also know that he's not leaving this apartment until she agrees to be with him. So Luna and I need to come to an understanding.

He finally moves past her. I watch as he trails his palm over her stomach as he does, leaning over to press a kiss to the top of her head. I also note how her eyes drift shut, and she makes a sweet humming sound as he touches her.

I really want her to take care of him.

Alexsei heads into the apartment and drops onto her couch.

Then Luna looks up at me.

I stare down at the blonde menace.

This woman has had my friend tangled and twisted up for the past four months. And she has the audacity to look at *me* as if I'm annoying *her*.

"I can't believe that you were going to go out with another guy," I say, trying to keep my voice low and between us.

She lifts a brow. "I *am* going out with another guy. There's no *was going to* about it."

"So now you're going to date a coach and a player?"

She lifts a shoulder. "Guess so."

"You think that's a good idea?"

"If you don't, you shouldn't have brought our player over here."

I narrow my eyes. I'm not sure what it is, but something about her calling Alexsei 'ours' grabs me in the chest.

She starts to step back and close her door. On me. My hand lands flat against the wood and I press. "I don't think so."

"I don't remember inviting you to stay."

"But you want to."

"Do I?"

"You do." I lean in so only she can hear me, and it won't drift to Alexsei. "You play this big independent badass, but I think you're scared of Alexsei, and I think you want me to stay, so it's not just the two of you. So things don't get too serious too fast." I'm not sure I believe any of that, but I don't want to be cut out and left behind.

For more than one reason.

"Scared? Of Alexsei? He's a complete cinnamon roll."

Oh, she's definitely pegged him.

"Yeah. Because you know that he's about two minutes away from wrapping around your heart and not letting you go."

She looks up at me, studying my eyes, and I suddenly realize that I have miscalculated.

I might be able to read her, but she can fucking read me, too.

"You know something about that?" she asks. "About Alexsei getting in under your skin and making you feel warm and safe and loved in a way that's addicting in about half a day?"

I sure as hell do.

"Shut up," I murmur to her.

The corners of her mouth curl slightly.

I lean in until our noses are nearly touching. "I won't let you hurt him. I'm staying so that you don't crush our boy."

I see emotion flicker in her eyes at *my* use of 'our' in referring to Alexsei.

"Fine, you can stay." She pauses. "If you kiss me."

I should have seen something like that coming. Or maybe I did. And maybe I fucking love sparring with this woman.

"I know you think that you're the boss," I tell her. "I know you think you *want* to be the boss." I can't believe how husky my voice is. Or, how hot and hard my body is. "But you're wrong on both counts."

"You're on my turf," she says softly, not moving back away from me.

"When we're together, it's always going to be my turf, Pixie."

She rolls her eyes.

"You're such a pain in the ass," I tell her. Because suddenly I cannot stop looking at her fucking mouth.

"I think you're —"

With a growl, I cup the back of her head and kiss her.

I'm not happy about it, but I do. I kiss the tiny, sweet-smelling, sassy, full-of-herself, blonde fairy who has the potential to fuck up three men very badly.

It's a miscalculation. Because she melts into me, her body pressing into mine, her hands gripping the front of my shirt, her mouth opening under mine almost immediately. My tongue strokes along hers and she meets me, thrust for thrust.

Because, of course, she does.

I pull my mouth away and say against her lips, "Tell us to leave and we'll leave. But it's both of us. Or neither of us."

"I kind of hate you," she says.

But she doesn't tell us to leave.

I smile. Then I say, "I know. But it's kind of fun, right?"

Luna smiles back. "I don't hate it. I hate you, but I don't hate *it*."

Sweeping my gaze over her mouth, I take a read on what I'm feeling. Anger that Alexsei had his heart hurt. Fear that he might have a relationship with Luna that doesn't involve me. And lust. For *Luna*.

It feels out of left field. But it's not. It's been simmering, slowly and steadily since that night four months ago. Every time I sit behind her at a hockey game and watch her watch Alexsei, it simmers. Every time I lean forward and sense her stiffen at my closeness. Every time she dismisses me or spars with me or refuses to acknowledge I exist, the heat turns up another millimeter.

And now, standing in her doorway, I'm shocked to realize that it's burning. I want Luna, too. Not as much as Alexsei does, because he really is head over heels in love with her, or at a bare minimum halfway there, but a whole fucking lot.

But yeah, I want her.

I ease my fingers around the base of her neck and yank her up against me, the hard plane of my body stopping her forward motion. Her soft curves collide with my chest, my thighs. My dick. She gives a gasp in surprise, her eyes widening. Her hair feels like silk beneath my fingers and I marvel at how much I want to explore her body, her feminine and lush hips. I've fingered her pussy before, but now I want to taste her mouth.

I give her time to pull away, reject another kiss from me, but she doesn't. In fact, she tilts her head up and parts her lips in invitation. I lean down and tease my tongue across her bottom lip. She shivers and her hands come to rest on my waist, lithe fingers hooking through the belt loops.

This time when I kiss her, we both dive in. We don't kiss gently. We attack each other, hard, warring for domination in a hot, plunging tangle of tongues and heat. Kissing her is like a sweet, sexy battle of wills, and I want to win. She tightens her grip at the same time she yanks away, panting lightly, staring at me like she doesn't know what to do with me. I tug her hair, forcing her head back so I can bury my nose in the delicate curve of her neck and breathe in her spicy scent. I flick my tongue along the vein that's pulsing below the surface and revel in the hitch to her breath.

Then I lift my gaze, crowding her in the doorway, and pinning her with a hard stare. "Now get inside and suck Alexsei's dick like a good girl. It's the least you can do after tormenting him for months."

She instantly blusters, but I place my palm over the curve of her ass in a slow slide, before giving her a hard smack. *"Now,"* I growl.

My emotions and my lust are tightly coiled, ready to be unleashed at the slightest provocation.

Luna's cheeks turn pink, but to my pure fucking delight, she simply turns, steps into the apartment, and reaches for Alexsei.

I step in behind her and slam the door shut.

Alexsei jumps up off the couch, looking alarmed. "What the fuck, man?" he demands. "Why does Luna look..." he studies Luna.

"What?" I ask as Luna moves toward him. "What does she look like? Like a girl who wants to do what she's told so she can get fucked nice and hard? Because that's what she is."

I pull a condom out of my pocket before stripping off my jacket. Moving behind her, I run my fingers through her silken strands. "Isn't that right, Luna?"

She nods. "Yes," she breathes.

"Then get on your knees." I push her down in front of Alexsei and toss the condom on the coffee table.

His eyes darken, and he's already fumbling with his jeans. He shoots me a look like he thinks maybe I'm being too harsh, but he's clearly not going to stop it if she isn't. And she definitely isn't. She loves it. Reaching forward once she's on her knees, I yank her sweatshirt by the waistband and tug it over her head so Alexsei can see her tits in her purple bra. Luna likes bright colors, and the pop of color against her pale flesh matches the tips of her hair.

Sliding my hands in alongside her jaw, I guide her forward. "Go on. Suck him." I take Alexsei's hard swollen dick and my mouth waters.

"Jesus," Alexsei murmurs, staring down at her hard as she obediently opens her mouth and closes her lips around the swollen tip of him. "Luna. Damn, girl, you are so fucking gorgeous right now. Suck me, baby. I need it."

He drops his hands to her head, too, so that we're both gripping her, crowding her with our thighs. The sight turns me on, not just for Alexsei but for her, too, this newfound need to touch her overwhelming me with greed and lust.

Then Alexsei groans when I ease her head forward to take more of him. Briefly, he looks at me, then closes his eyes. His head tips back and I drop my gaze to Luna's pretty pink lips, taking his length like a fucking champ. Shifting my right hand, I drag my finger through the saliva-soaked path Luna's mouth has left on Alexsei's dick, from just under her lips to his balls.

"*Fuck*," rips from his mouth.

My plan is to grip him hard and follow her mouth with some rough strokes, but Luna bats my hand away. She pulls off of him completely, breathing hard, breasts heaving up and down.

Frustrated, I lightly pinch her bottom lip. "I didn't tell you to stop."

She tilts her head back to look up at me, eyes snapping with both anger and desire. "So punish me."

A bolt of lust shoots through me like an electrical jolt. I smile, slowly. "You'd like that, wouldn't you?" I ask, even as we both know the answer. "Switch with me," I tell Alexsei.

He looks a little surprised, but he doesn't protest. I release her head so I can undo my jeans and pull my hard dick out and tease it at her lips. "My turn, sassy girl. And this time, you don't stop until I tell you to stop."

She nods, her cheeks stained pink from arousal.

Then she's around me with her hot, wet mouth and I'm drowning in her touch. She cups the base of my dick, brushing her fingertips lower and lower as she finds a hard, driving rhythm. I grip her head to hold it still, staring down so I can take in the sight of her soft blonde hair cascading over her cheeks like a curtain, my swollen cock disappearing between her shiny lips.

"Very impressive," I tell her, managing to sound cool and collected even as I can feel the force of each suck all the way down deep into my balls. "You can take it all."

Alexsei has his hand on his own cock, stroking himself with

quick jerks, his eyes glazed over. He's shifted to the side, so he can see the action better, and that gives me an undeniable thrill.

"You like that?" I ask him.

He nods, and sinks down on the couch so he's at eye-level with Luna's mouth. And me. For once, I don't wish it was Alexsei taking me like this. This time it's different. I like this exactly the way it is, little Luna sucking me dry and Alexsei watching. She's a greedy little thing, filling her mouth over and over like she can't get enough, and that has me giving a hard, low groan.

"I'm coming," I warn her, through gritted teeth.

She gives an excited nod, her fist wrapping around me tighter as she buries me to the hilt. I break, giving a low angry, "*Fuck*," as I grip her head hard, exploding in the back of her throat. It rolls on in low waves of ecstasy, before I'm finally able to pause, suddenly aware I've been thrusting into her, hard.

"Holy shit," Alexsei says. "Damn, Luna." His eyes are trained on her.

Damn Luna is right. My thighs are shaking and as I pull back, some of my cum trails out over her swollen lips. She's straight up breathtaking, looking aroused and eager and ready for more dick. She wipes her mouth, then sucks my cum off of her finger.

It nearly undoes me. This fucking woman…

"Have you been punished enough?" I demand, stepping back.

She shakes her head. "No. I don't think so."

I toss the condom to Alexsei and sink down into the nearest chair. "Show her who's boss."

For a second, I think he's going to tell me I've gone too far, as he helps her rise to her feet. But then my boy makes me proud. He kisses her, hard, before bending over and stripping her leggings and panties right to the floor in one smooth, rough yank of his big hands. Luna quickly grabs his arms for balance and breathes his name. "*Alexsei*."

I'm still half-hard, so I pump myself in easy strokes as I take in the sight of Luna bare-assed and getting shoved against the nearest wall by my best friend. His finger drags across her slit, and I can see the sheen of moisture on her inner thigh.

She's ready for him, and he doesn't hesitate. Once he has the condom on, he hitches up her hip and drives into her. Luna slams into the wall.

"Yes," she cries out. "I need you so much."

He's fully dressed, but I can still see the hard muscles of his thighs, his ass, his back as he thrusts up into her pussy. "That's it," I say. "Take that little pussy. Own it."

Luna locks eyes with me briefly, something passing between us that I've never felt before. I freeze, hand on my dick. I can hear her sharp pant each time he shoves inside her and it's so damn sexy.

"Good girl," I tell her. "You're so damn good at taking that cock."

Her eyes roll back in her head in ecstasy, breaking our connection.

I'm a little disappointed, but at the same time, I'm enjoying her pleasure, because now she's coming all over him with soft little cries, chanting his name like a prayer.

"I missed this," Alexsei growls. "I've missed you. God, baby, you feel so fucking good."

Her orgasm sends him over the edge. He plows into her faster, before pausing and letting go with a low groan.

Then they're breathing hard, kissing, hands tenderly stroking over each other and I feel an undeniable burst of jealousy that neither of them is giving that affection to me.

Which stuns me.

I don't need or seek affection.

Standing up quickly, I shove my dick back into my pants. "Ask her out."

"What?" Alexsei glances back at me, easing out of her body as he still cradles her gently.

"Ask her out on a date. That's what we came here to do. Then we're leaving."

"You're leaving?" Luna gapes at me.

I nod. "Yes. You're very busy, remember? We're giving you space."

"Cam," Alexsei says, shaking his head. "Don't be an asshole."

"He's good at that," Luna says, but she doesn't look mad. She drops her feet back fully onto the floor and shakes her hair out of her eyes.

"Say goodnight to Alexsei."

She very prettily obeys me. "Goodnight, Alexsei."

"See, that's not so hard, is it? To listen to me. Now it's your turn, Alexsei. Ask Luna out."

He looks torn between wanting to tell me to fuck off and wanting to scoop her up and carry her to the bedroom. In the end, he seems to read her intention to allow me to be the one in charge, because he cups her cheeks and says, "Will you go out with me? I would love to see you again."

She nods. "Yes. I'd like that."

"Great. Thank you." He kisses the top of her head. "Goodnight, Luna."

He tucks his dick and zips up. I grab my jacket off of the floor. Luna is still naked except for her bra and she makes no move to cover herself up or get dressed. I rake my gaze over her, wondering how exactly she's managed to get under my skin so thoroughly.

Because she has.

She's under so deep I can barely stand still.

I'm going to be thinking about her sucking my dick for days.

"Goodnight, Cam," she says, padding over to me and placing her hand on my chest. "May I please have a kiss?"

Those words threaten to rock my world.

She sounds sweet, but with fire.

And she's giving control over to me.

She's making that clear.

It's the hottest fucking thing ever.

"Since you asked so nicely." I brush my lips over hers in a

barely-there kiss, as I reach between her thighs and give her clit a pinch. When she gasps, I release and step back. "Sweet dreams, Pixie."

Then we're out the door and Alexsei is dragging his hands through his hair. "What the fuck was *that*?" he asks.

"That was me making everybody happy," I say, jogging down the stairs. "You're welcome."

CHAPTER 14

Alexsei

WHISTLING, I put six bottles of the sparkling water I know Luna likes in my shopping cart, anticipating she'll need to be well-hydrated for what I have planned for her. I add a jug of iced tea and six different kinds of pop because I don't know what she likes.

"What is all this?" Cam asks as he turns from pulling a single can of an energy drink off the shelf. "Are you having a party or donating to a local food bank? Or maybe planning for the apocalypse?"

"I just want to be prepared for when Luna comes over Sunday."

His eyebrows shoot up. "Prepared for what? To hold her hostage for a month and force feed her liquids?"

I grin. "That's not a bad idea. Can you imagine spending twenty-four-seven with her for thirty days? Man, that sounds like heaven."

"That sounds like a felony." Cam flicks non-existent lint off of his coat. "She was very clear in her texts with us that this is a date with you and some sex with us, and then she's going home. Don't get your hopes up that you can charm her into staying for days on end like the first time."

"Too late." I already have my hopes up. Hell, it's not even a hope. It's pure determination. I can't get enough of this girl and I want to steal every second I can with her between our busy schedules. Soon we'll be heading to the playoffs and I'm going to be training hard.

I move down the aisle to the snack foods. "What munchies do you think she likes? I see her as a tortilla chips and salsa kind of girl." I don't know why, given she always smells like sugar and something else I can't quite put my finger on. It's just her. She always smells amazing and I am so fucking looking forward to easing my tongue between her thighs and lapping at her pussy until she draws out my name on a moan.

"Popcorn. She eats it at almost every game."

"Oh. Okay." But it makes me jealous Cam knows that, which is stupid. I'm on the ice. There's no way I can get a great visual on her snack foods. But it makes me wonder if Cam is being totally honest about not talking to her at games. Which is also stupid, because why would he lie about that?

Cam is an honest guy. He's actually brutally honest.

"Butter or no butter?"

"Extra butter."

I'm scanning all the options.

Cam gives a huff of impatience. "I'm going to grab condoms so we don't have to be here all damn day."

"Why, do you have somewhere to be?"

"You know I hate the grocery store."

He does. He much prefers ordering food online and getting it delivered to our doorstep. But I like to browse, which irritates him to no end.

With that, he strides down the aisle at a fast clip. I'm still debating between popcorn brands when I hear my name.

"Alexsei Ryan?" a woman asks.

Turning, I put a polite smile on my face, assuming it's a Racketeers fan.

Instead, I see Sara, mine and Cam's ex-girlfriend. "Sara," I say, surprised to see her. "I thought you moved to L.A.."

"I did, but I'm back in town to visit my parents." She holds her arms out for a hug. "It's great to see you."

Tossing the popcorn boxes in the cart, I reach out to embrace her, because she clearly wants me to, and I have no ill will toward her. Mostly just confusion as to why she dumped us. But as I pull Sara up against me in a loose hug, I have no lingering romantic feelings for her at all. I feel nothing. No pangs of regret. Not nostalgia. Just acknowledgement that we shared some nice time together, nothing more.

A certain blonde pixie is to thank for that.

"How have you been?" I ask her, pulling away almost immediately.

"Great. Good." She holds her hand up and wiggles her fingers. "I'm engaged."

There is a diamond ring on her hand. "Wow. Congratulations. I'm happy for you." I mean that. "I'm glad you found what you were looking for."

Her lips purse. She looks around and tucks her dark hair behind her ear. "Listen, I should explain about what happened... about us..."

While a little curious as to what went wrong, I have no interest in making her feel uncomfortable. "You don't need to explain anything," I tell her, truthfully. "It didn't work for you. It's cool, seriously."

Water under the bridge. She's moved on and so have I.

She continues anyway.

"It's just that I thought I would like being in a throuple, and I did enjoy the sex. We had a lot of fun. But I always felt like I was an afterthought. A prop or something."

My jaw actually drops. "*What*? I had feelings for you, Sara. I never thought of you that way. And an afterthought to *what*?"

I'm fucking offended. I was a good boyfriend. I texted her

good morning, I said good night every night even when I was exhausted. We took her to Florida for her birthday. I listened to her complain about her job. I was never late picking her up. And I always made sure she came before me or Cam.

A fucking prop? Savage. And total bullshit.

But she just shakes her head. "Maybe that sounded wrong. You treated me well, Alexsei. I'm not saying otherwise. But I still felt like a third wheel."

I want to point out just because she felt that way doesn't make it reality, but there's no point.

Especially when Cam reappears in the aisle, carrying a box of condoms and a bottle of lube.

"Sara," he says, surprised. "Hey, how's it going?"

She glances at him and gives him a polite smile. "Good, thanks."

She doesn't invite him to hug her, and he doesn't offer.

Her gaze drops to take in his haul as he tosses the items into the cart.

She gives a small smile. "I'm glad to see you two have finally figured this out." She points from me to Cam and back again and then to the cart. "Take care."

"Yeah, you, too. And seriously, congrats." I say it sincerely, but a little absently. She carries her basket down the aisle and disappears around the turn.

Was she thinking…

I eye the condoms and the lube.

Oh, yeah. She was thinking.

"I think she thinks we're in a relationship," I tell Cam, astonished.

He freezes in the act of putting back two of the six boxes of popcorn I've put in the cart. "What?"

I repeat it, because now I'm sure of it. "I think she thinks we're in a relationship. She said when the three of us were together, she felt like a third wheel."

Cam just shrugs. "Okay. Does it matter?"

"What do you mean, okay? Doesn't that bother you? I thought things were good between all of us."

"They were. Until she dumped you."

"Because we made her feel like a third wheel, apparently." I don't know why this is bothering me so much, but it does. I never want to hear that I made a woman I'm dating feel less than important. If I did something wrong, I want to be aware of it so I can make sure I don't repeat the behavior.

"That's not what we did." He puts the boxes back on the shelf and I'm so caught off guard, I let him.

"Yeah, but, why would she say that?"

"I don't know. Maybe because we live together, and she was only with us a few times a week. Neither one of us took her on solo dates. It could be anything. Don't let it get to you."

I realize he excluded himself from the dumping part. "Wait. What did you mean when you said she didn't dump you? Did you keep dating her?" The very idea has me flabbergasted.

"*What*? No. Of course not. I mean, she wasn't really there for *me*. She wanted you. I was just the side dish. She just put up with me to be with you."

Understanding dawns. "And you put up with her to…"

Be with me.

Holy shit.

It feels like the foundation of everything I've ever understood about my friendship with Cam has just shifted. My palms are sweating and my mouth feels hot. I don't know how to feel. Or what I feel.

Not upset.

Just… floored.

I care about Cam. A lot. He's my best friend. I'd go to bat for him any day of the week and he's loyal to me, too. And I like waking up in his bed with a woman. I like when we get caught up in the moment with a girl and… things happen between us.

I'm a sexually open guy. I believe anyone should do what and who they want. But I'm not attracted to any other men but Cam. I'm Cam-sexual. I enjoy it when he touches me in the heat of a threesome. He obviously enjoys it, too, because he keeps doing it.

I didn't think it meant anything other than sex is sex and we have a good thing going.

But now I'm starting to wonder if it means more than I realized.

On both our ends.

Cam doesn't react, though. He just says calmly, "I wasn't putting up with her. We were having fun. I just think she wasn't as open to actually dating as a threesome as she was into it in the bedroom. That's all."

I'm caught up in a tornado of thoughts and feelings that I don't know what to do with. I just nod, absently.

Cam takes over pushing the cart. "Come on. Luna awaits."

That snaps me out of it.

"Yeah," I say gruffly, my mouth as dry as the desert and just as hot.

Luna. Who doesn't want a relationship.

I sigh and grab the boxes off the shelf that Cam put back. "Don't make Luna feel like a third wheel," I say to Cam's back. "You need to fuck her, do you understand?"

Cam stops and turns. He stares at me. Hard. "You're telling me what I have to do?"

"Yes," I say. "Or you're not invited to join us."

Maybe it's a dick thing to say, but there is no way I'm risking losing Luna like we did Sara.

I expect push back. For him to say something hurtful, like maybe Luna won't want just me. But he doesn't, because Cam would never purposefully hurt my feelings.

Instead, he gives me a slow smile that kind of scares me. "I'm fucking her instead of you?"

He's never said it like that. So bluntly.

I suck in a breath, my cock suddenly throbbing.

That is *not* really what I meant or want. I would love to see Cam buried in Luna, but not at the expense of him touching me. Because I'm starting to think I *need* Cam touching me. But I'm in it now. I have to stand my ground. "Yes."

"Done."

CHAPTER 15

Luna

How old do I look right now?

I SEND the full body photo through text to Dani.

I'm wearing a simple black dress and black heels. The dress nips in at my waist, has a scoop neckline, and hits me just above the knee. It's very basic, not sexy, but I'm trying for sophisticated. I'm also wearing a necklace with a purple pendant, and I've curled my hair and done my makeup a lot less boldly than I usually do. I'm hoping it's what my mother would call "tasteful".

But black isn't really my style. And curled or not, my hair still has purple tips.

I'm going on a real date for the first time in my life. I'm going out with a guy who is twelve years older than me. He's got a kid. A *teenage* kid. And I'm nervous.

I didn't expect that.

But as I was perusing my closet, I realized that Owen has probably taken dozens of women out. I refuse to think that the number might be in the hundreds. The guy is really good looking, and he was a hockey player, which I know ninety-five percent of women think they're hot just because of that. He's also nice. Like really nice. And lots of women go for that.

We all should go for that, by the way.

But he's also a little awkward and sweet and while I find that cute, I don't see him as a smooth-talking ladies' man.

Still, he has a lot more experience than I do. At least with dating.

He's taking me to Rinaldo's. None of the guys I've dated in the past couple of years probably even know what Rinaldo's is, not to mention being able to afford so much as an appetizer there.

I get a text back from Dani.

> You look gorgeous! Where are you going?

> > You didn't answer my question.

I can't tell her where I'm going. She'll think I'm on my way to being Brady's stepmom.

Oh my God, I'm going out with a guy who has a kid and if things got serious, I'd be a stepmom...

I stop *those* thoughts *immediately*.

Dani replies.

> I feel like it's a trick question

I laugh lightly. Dani is so sweet she'd rather avoid the question than answer incorrectly. Especially when she has no idea what I want to hear.

> > I'm trying to look sophisticated.

> Well, you do. You're perfect.

That makes me smile. And then I realize that I can't trust Dani. She's too sweet and would never tell me that I look ridiculous.

I hear a knock on my door, and I suck in a breath. He's here. I can't change, anyway. Okay, so this is what I'm wearing.

Ugh. I hate black.

I go to my door, take another breath, and pull it open.

I don't hate the look on Owen's face, though, when he first takes me in.

"Um, hi. Um, Luna, I'm—" Owen clears his throat. "Hi."

I smile. I always feel a little rattled by Owen, but I think I do the same to him. "Hi."

"You look absolutely amazing."

"Thank you." I let my gaze run over him from head to toe. He's wearing a dark gray suit with a light blue button-down. No tie, but he does have a jacket on. "You do, too."

"I'm really glad we're doing this."

"Me, too. Thanks for asking me."

He gives a soft chuckle. "I barely resisted the first time we ever spoke."

I really like this guy. "Well, I'm glad you didn't resist any longer."

"Can I ask you a question?"

"Of course."

"As gorgeous as you look...why are you wearing black?"

I look down. "Is this not okay for tonight?"

"Well, it's perfect. It's just not what I pictured you in."

I look up with a frown. "What do you mean?"

He gives me a soft smile. "You can wear whatever you want, but... it doesn't seem like your usual choice. Do you wear a lot of black?"

I have no idea how he knows to question this, but I shake my head. "This is literally the only black thing I own."

"That's what I thought. You should change into something more you."

"But black is sophisticated."

He nods. "It can be. But I want to go out with *Luna*. You don't have to dress up or act any certain way tonight. Just be you." He pauses. "Unless you don't want to change."

I study him. It's strange that he knows this about me, but I love that he's this insightful. Is that an older man thing? A dad thing? Just an Owen thing? I'm not sure, but it makes me feel warm. Like he's been paying attention and really thinking about me.

"I would really like to change."

He smiles. "I'll wait."

I only take five minutes to shed the black dress and pull on a dress that's a lot more me. It's a multicolor, Boho style that ties at the waist. I pair it with strappy sandals, add some bangle bracelets and a couple more rings, but I leave my pendant necklace on. I smile into the mirror. Much better.

When I step out into the living room, his smile is wide and sincere. "Seriously gorgeous."

"Thank you."

"I'm surprised you even have a black dress."

"I got it for my grandma's funeral."

He stops. "You were going to go out with me in a funeral dress?"

I laugh. Then wince. "Yeah."

He shakes his head. "This is much better."

And I agree.

Thirty minutes later, Owen pulls the restaurant door open, and escorts me inside.

"Right this way, Mr. Phillips," the hostess says, and I'm hit by a terrible thought that causes me to giggle.

He has his hand on my lower back as he leads me to our table. He looks down at me with a brow up. "What?"

I shake my head.

At the table, he pulls my chair out for me, and I watch as he rounds the table, taking his seat.

I feel a little more at ease now that we're at the table. I've had nice dinners before. I know how to put the white cloth napkin in my lap, I know which fork to use, and I'm very much looking forward to the salmon they have here.

The hostess tells us that our waiter, Stephen, will be right over.

As soon as she's gone, Owen leans in. "What were you laughing about?"

I lean in, too. "It's just that the only times I've ever been here, I've been with my parents."

He narrows his eyes. "And you are thinking about how much older I am than you?"

My smile gets wider. "Yes. And how you definitely seemed at ease with the hostess calling you Mr. Phillips. None of the guys I date are ever called Mr. anything except maybe by the high school principal when they've gotten caught sneaking in late to class."

Now he grins. "You will not be calling me Mr. Phillips tonight," he warns. "I am older than you. But I'm not *old*."

I nod. "Okay. I'll just stick with Sir then."

I can see that I've shocked him, but he's unable to answer because the waiter arrives just then.

I feel Owen watching me the entire time the waiter tells us the specials, fills our water glasses, takes our wine order, and then leaves.

I pick up my water and take a sip as my eyes finally meet Owen's across the table.

"What?" I ask after I swallow.

"Just thinking that I'm pretty sure I'll like that."

Heat arrows from my stomach down into my panties. I know that we're talking about my use of 'Sir' with him. And I'm not only surprised that he said that, but also that he said I'll, as in I *will*, rather than I *would*, as if it was some kind of hypothetical.

I set my glass down and say, "Duly noted."

The waiter returns and pours our wine and asks if we have any questions. I don't because I know exactly what I want. It seems Owen does as well, so we place our orders.

I take a sip of my wine and close my eyes to appreciate it. I don't get to spend money on this kind of wine very often.

When I open my eyes, I find Owen leaning onto the table on both forearms, just watching me.

"Did I spill down the front of me?" I ask, looking down.

He shakes his head. "No. I'm just kind of in awe that you're here with me."

Surprised, I lean back in my chair. "In awe?"

"I've never dated anyone like you before."

"What about me makes me different? Besides the age?"

He gives me a quick, stern look, that I'll admit I kind of like. Owen seems very easy going for the most part. I know that he has a more aggressive side. I've seen him coach. But he's more mature than all of the guys I've dated, and with that just comes a confidence that means he doesn't get worked up about little things.

"I actually don't think I've dated someone who doesn't have kids in years," he says. "For one thing."

"What else?" I'm fascinated to learn more about him. And I would say dating history and type say a lot about someone.

In my case, maybe not super complimentary things. Still, I want to know more about him.

"I don't think I've ever dated anyone who has been as involved in hockey as you probably are."

Before I can help myself, I roll my eyes.

"Oh, does that mean you don't know a lot about hockey?"

"I know a lot about hockey. And all of it, I've learned under duress."

He chuckles lightly. "Elaborate on that."

"Well, being Crew McNeill's sister isn't always a picnic."

Owen nods. "I can imagine that."

"Really? Usually the guys I date think being Crew's sister has to be amazing. And when can they meet him?"

"Well, I've already met him. And a hundred guys like him. You don't have to worry about that with me."

I think about that. That's actually really nice. There's no way in hell Owen is interested in me in an attempt to get closer to Crew.

"I have a confession," I tell him.

"Oh, juicy stuff already. I can't wait," Owen says, leaning in further.

I smile. "You want to hear all my dark, dirty secrets, Owen?"

He nodded slowly. "I really do, Luna."

There's something in his tone of voice when he says my name that makes my stomach flip. And I want to tell him *all* of my dirty, dark secrets. But he's a dad. He's thirty-six. He's a responsible, mature adult. He's probably not into some of the dirty things I like. Oh well. He's a really nice guy, he brought me to Rinaldo's on a date for the first time ever, and he actually seems interested in me. That makes up for a lot.

"Okay, confession secret number one, I don't really like hockey."

His hand goes over his chest. "Ouch. That's a big one."

I nod. "I know. It's a fine game. And I do know a lot about it. But, I'd literally been forced to watch it since Crew was old enough to skate."

"Can *you* skate?"

I give him a mock insulted look. "Almost better than Crew."

"That doesn't surprise me. You have a competitive streak."

"Yeah, for a lot of years, the best way to keep me from being super bored was to strap skates on me and let me loose on the other end of the rink during his private lessons."

"But you run into a lot of people who only think of you as Crew's sister?"

"Yep. Including my parents."

Wow, I can't believe I said that.

Owen doesn't seem shocked. And he doesn't rush to reassure me that can't be true. "I'm sorry," he says instead. "I can imagine he throws a pretty big shadow."

"He does." I sigh. "And my parents are great. They love me. I don't doubt that. It's not like they forget my birthday or things like that. But Crew was the center of their universe."

Owen smiles. "Does it make you feel any better that the moment you walk into a room, all I can see is *your* light and energy and Crew could literally hit me over the head with a hockey stick and I wouldn't be able to look away from *you*?"

It's cheesy and over the top but...it does make me feel better. Just that he'd say something like that to *try* to make me feel better.

"Thank you."

I'm going to sleep with this guy tonight.

I probably was going to before, but that just cinched it.

"What made you feel that way when you were kids?" he asks. "With your parents?"

"Well, he was always loud and getting into things, so he took up a lot of their attention and energy from day one. But when he started playing hockey, everything in our family started revolving around his schedule. Practices, games, private lessons. When he got old enough to be on travel teams, my parents would drop me off at grandma's house and I wouldn't see them again for days."

"Lucky for your grandparents."

I smile in spite of myself. This guy is sweet. And do I want a little more of that? Some fucking attention and adoration? Yeah. I'm not too proud to admit that. It's what's so fun about Alexsei, too. He thinks *I'm* amazing. And he knows my brother, too. He doesn't need me to get close to Crew. If he wants to be with me, it's really about me.

"My grandparents were great," I say, feeling the warmth in my chest I always do when I think of them. "I was very close to them. My grandmother was the one who taught me to bake. About half of the recipes in the bakery are hers. She wasn't that into French baking. So the pain au chocolate, macarons, and éclairs are all mine. But the cookies and a lot of the cakes are hers."

"I'm a huge fan of hers then."

"I was, too."

"Was?" he asks. "Was she why you have a black funeral dress?"

"Yes. I miss her every day."

He reaches across the table and takes my hand. He makes it seem like the most natural thing in the world. He strokes his big thumb across the back of my knuckles and I feel my whole body warming. But it's not with the heat of desire, or a desire to take my clothes off like some of the other actions he's done. This is a warmth, like a hug.

I study him for a moment and cannot avoid the thought that hits me–*I bet Owen gives really great hugs.*

I want to sleep with him. For sure. But I also want to know what his hugs are like.

Wow.

"I'm sorry you were lonely growing up. I suppose that's how you became so independent, though."

"So, I'm not really that independent, that's the thing. But I'm working on it."

"What do you mean? You own your own business. Getting a chance to see you is difficult because you're so busy. You live alone. You don't even have a dog."

"Well, I only live alone because my roommate recently fell in love. And I only have a business because my dad feels guilty."

"Guilty for what?"

"For giving all of his time, money, and attention to Crew. It occurred to them when Crew got recruited that everything they put into him had paid off and given him this amazing career. And they realized they hadn't really done that for me, so my dad bought the bakery and completely furnished it. There is nothing in there that he doesn't own. Except for one set of china. My grandmother's. I got it after she passed. I use it for these really special high teas that I host."

Owen doesn't say anything, he just keeps stroking my hand.

He only pulls away when the waiter arrives with our food.

We're quiet for a few moments, starting with our meal.

But after a few bites, Owen says, "Speaking as a dad, I don't think your dad bought you the bakery because he felt guilty."

I look up. "What?"

"I mean, yeah, maybe that was part of it. But that's not the whole story." He sets down his fork and looks at me. "Parents feel guilty, constantly, Luna. We never know if we're getting it right.

And the truth is, we're *not* getting it right a lot of the time. I've only got Brady, and I still feel like I'm not always meeting all of his needs. And then if I do, I wonder if I should. Like, should I make him work for some things? Shouldn't I make him go without, so he appreciates what he has? Like I need to give him food and stuff, of course, but I mean, I give him a lot of opportunities, and I make things easier for him. Maybe I should make him work a little harder. But then when I do that, I feel guilty about that. Like, isn't my job as his dad to make things easier for him? I'm fortunate enough to have a great job, so I have plenty of money, so why shouldn't I give him every opportunity and convenience?" He finally stops and takes a breath. "So all I'm saying is maybe yeah, your dad's probably feeling guilty, but he would be anyway. So just let him take care of you a little bit. It's really all he wants. And that's not such a bad thing."

I'm staring at him. He seems so sincere. *Earnest* almost. Like me, understanding this is really important to him. And he is a dad. And he has a pretty great kid.

I swallow. "I don't mean to make it sound like I don't love him. We're close. And I know that everything he's done has been to try to help me. I do appreciate him and my mom."

"I know you do. And your brother, right? Because you do go to a lot of hockey games for someone who *claims* not to like it."

I appreciate him trying to lighten the mood. I smile. "Eighty percent of the time."

He chuckles. "Hell, that's a lot more than most siblings can say."

I take a small bite of salmon. "Do you have siblings?" I would love to know more about him, I realize.

He nods. "Two sisters." He takes a bite of his steak. "One is back in Minnesota, close to my folks. The other is out in Seattle. Both married with kids. My parents are great. Very normal family. Very little drama. In fact, I'm the one with the most drama."

Oh, and here we are, at the subject I most want to ask about but wasn't sure I could. Or how to bring it up. I cut off a little piece of my asparagus and chew for a moment, then ask, "Is it dramatic with your ex?"

"You mean Brady's mom?"

I nod. "Yes. Obviously. Wait, do you have another ex? Do you have an ex-wife? I guess just because you didn't marry Brady's mom doesn't mean you've never been married." Why did that not occur to me before? He's definitely old enough to have been married and divorced.

He gives me a *really?* look. "You're thinking that I'm definitely old enough to have been married and divorced, even with a kid, aren't you?"

I feel my cheeks get pink. But I nod. "Yeah."

He shakes his head, but he's smiling. "Never married. No ex-wives. But Brady's mom isn't really more of an ex than any of the other women I've dated. Hell, I've dated a couple of other women longer than I did her."

"You didn't even date very long?"

"She was a one-night stand. At least until she came around with a positive pregnancy test."

I reach for my wine and take a sip. "Wow. So that is kind of dramatic."

He swallows his bite of potato and then says, "Honestly? It's not. Chelsea is great. We hung out a little bit while she was pregnant. I went to appointments with her. She called me when she went into labor, so I was there. And we've shared custody ever since. But she met Dev when Brady was about eight. He's a fantastic guy, so I was thrilled when he proposed to her, and he's a great stepdad. He and Brady are close. And their daughter Amara is great, too. She hangs out at my place with me and Brady sometimes. I don't try to be her dad. I don't discipline her or anything like that, but if they ever need a last-minute babysitter or someone to swing by and pick her up after school, I'll do that if I can. She's totally comfortable with me and we get along great."

I'm watching him as he talks about all of this and he is so at ease, so genuine, and clearly feels affection for all of these people. I set my fork down. "Who are you?"

He tips his head and smiles. "What do you mean?"

"Are all thirty-six-year-old men this well-adjusted? Because I definitely need to start dating older."

Something flickers in his eyes, and he sets his fork down. "How about if you're interested in dating well-adjusted, mature men, you just stick with me?"

My heart does a little swoop in my chest. "Are you interested in *dating* someone like me? Like more than a couple of times?"

He looks at me for a long moment, then says, "More so every minute."

And dang, there goes my heart, my stomach, and my panties. If I hadn't already decided to sleep with him, that would have totally done it. "Well, in that case, I will take that under advisement."

For the first time tonight, his gaze drops to my mouth before coming back to my eyes. "Yeah, you take that under advisement."

I am not going to be able to think about anything else, I realize. So this is what it's like to date a real man? I have obviously had a lot of fun with the guys I've gone out with and that was all I thought I wanted. The guys I've dated have given me exactly what I've been looking for—companionship, some laughs, some hot sex, and nothing I felt bad about breaking off in the end.

What about Alexsei and Cam?

I can't help the thought that goes through my head.

They feel different, too.

I'm not sure that Alexsei is all that much more grown-up than any of the other guys I've dated, but he makes me feel different. Special. He pays attention to me. He makes me feel amazing in a way no other guy has.

And what about Cam?

I could chalk Cam up to just being a necessary evil. It's clear that if I get involved with Alexsei, Cam comes along with that. I don't know how, exactly, that will work. I don't know if Cam is going to be there all the time or what, but I don't think I'd mind if he was. Yes, we fight. He pushes my buttons. And I find it exhilarating.

But now, looking across the table at Owen, I feel something else. It's like I can breathe easier when he's around. He's steady. He clearly has his shit together, and that is so fucking attractive.

And worth finding the time to fit into my life.

"What are you thinking about?" He asks me and I realize he's been watching me this whole time, as all of these thoughts have spun through my mind.

"Just that if this is dad energy or something, it's really working for me," I tell him, honestly.

Again, something I can't quite place just flickered through his gaze.

Then he asks, "Dad energy?"

"I just feel good around you. Safe. Like I don't have to worry about anything."

He nods. "That's true. I will take care of you, Luna."

I bite back the *Oh, I bet you will* that I almost say out loud. That would not be mature.

But I believe him. "I like that," I tell him.

"Good," he says simply. Then he looks down at my plate. "Eat. Everything is delicious." Then he looks back at me. "But I am hoping maybe we can go somewhere else for dessert."

"I happen to know the owner of the best bakery in the city."

"Are you asking me back to your place for some *cake*?" he asks.

And I like him so much more in that moment. Because that wasn't exactly mature, but he delivered it perfectly.

I laugh. "Yes, Owen I am."

CHAPTER 16

Owen

AN HOUR LATER, I stand behind Luna as she unlocks the bakery. She has two locks and a security keypad.

"I like how much security there is here," I tell her.

She laughs lightly as she pushes the door open.

I step in behind her and shut the door, turning to relock it.

She sets her purse and keys on one of the little bistro tables.

"Let me guess," I say. "You're thinking that was a very 'dad' thing to say."

She gives me a smile. "Maybe."

I can't decide if she thinks all of this 'dad energy' stuff is a good thing or a bad thing. I get the impression it's good.

Luna seems to like that I care and am competent. Yes, I'm older, but that doesn't really seem to bother her. Now that I know more about her, I realize that yes, she has a very strong independent streak, but she was also kind of forced into that. She's been alone a lot and had to rely on herself. She seems to want to prove that she doesn't need anyone. I admire that. But it also makes protective instincts that I've not felt for anyone other than Brady surge to the surface.

I want to take care of her. Not because she needs it, but

because I want to show her that she deserves it. And because if she lets me, that means she's allowing me close and trusts me.

I move further into the bakery. "You know, I feel like maybe I could show you some reasons that dating an older guy is a really good thing."

"Really? Like you could install another lock on my door?"

I stop in front of her. "As a matter of fact, I could. And if you ever need anything like that, I hope you'll call me. But there are other things, too."

I lift my hand and cup her cheek. Her hair is so soft and silky that I just want to bury my face in it. I want to run my hands through it. I want to feel it spread out over my chest.

I'm incredibly attracted to this woman, but I also want to worship her.

That's a new one for me. I've had sex. I had really good sex. I've learned a lot about women over the years. But as long as everyone has a good time, I'm happy. With Luna, it has to be *mind-blowing.*

Luna might not have been out on a "real" date before, but I feel like she's going to be the first for me. And in new ways as well.

"I'd love to hear all about the benefits to dating an older guy," she says.

I swear I feel her press her cheek into my palm slightly, like she's enjoying the touch and wants more.

"Okay, for one, I've had a lot of practice in things that other guys think are just normal and nothing to be lingered over."

"Things like what?"

"Things like kissing." I lower my head until our lips are almost touching. "Kissing is definitely something that gets better with practice."

"I don't —"

Before she can finish that thought, I press my mouth to hers.

In spite of the sweet little gasp that sends heat streaking to my cock, I take my time with the kiss. I slide my tongue over her lower lip, I press and release, then press again, taking the kiss slowly deeper. I touch her tongue, then I stroke deeper, then I tip her head, open my mouth, and drink her in.

She lets me. She participates, of course, but it's almost as if she's wanting me to show her something.

And oh, I'm going to show her something.

I kiss her for several long, slow, sweet moments. Then lift my head.

"We also know that women are stimulated differently than men. And we respect that. And we love to *give* pleasure as much as we like to get it. Maybe more."

She's looking up at me with those huge blue eyes, heat and curiosity in them.

"Even more?"

"Oh, definitely. Giving pleasure to a beautiful woman who could have any other man but chooses to be in the moment with *you*? Nothing hotter."

"I'd love to hear more about that." Her voice is breathless.

"Well, for instance, I would love to eat your pussy so well and for so long that you can barely remember your own name. I'd love to make you come so hard that you're begging for my cock. And then I'd love to do it again, until you're practically out of your mind. And then I'd love to do it *again*, feeling you come all over my cock the third time."

Her eyes were wide, her lips parted as she nearly pants.

"Wow." She swallows. "I thought you were shy and a little awkward talking about sex."

I almost laugh at that. "Just because I don't know all the slang and got a little tongue-tied around the hot, younger woman at first doesn't mean I don't know how to talk dirty."

She wet her lips, then nods. "Good."

Yeah, it is good. I want her out of her mind. For me. Because of me.

I honestly didn't think I would be saying things like this to

Luna tonight. It's our first date. I was going to make it nice, romantic, sophisticated.

And now here I am talking about eating her pussy.

But I'm not sorry.

I want that.

And the look on her face tells me that she wants it, too.

I also don't know where I'm getting off bragging about three orgasms in a row. I do really love to eat pussy. And I've been told I'm good at it. I also do love to give multiple orgasms. But I probably shouldn't be quite this cocky before I even get her naked.

Still, as I look down at her, stroke my thumb over her cheek, and feel the heat building between us, I think that if any woman can come multiple times, be fully free and open, and let me just worship her from head to toe, it's this woman. She's bold, knows herself, and won't have any trouble taking what she needs in the bedroom.

And I am so fucking hot and hard for her, I can barely breathe.

Finally, she says. "I thought we came here for dessert."

"Oh, I definitely want my mouth on the sweetest thing in this bakery."

She pulls in a long breath. "Should we go upstairs?"

I look around at all the small bistro tables, the bakery case, and think about her prep tables and counters that are likely in the kitchen. I nod. "A big horizontal surface that is soft would probably be best, since you're gonna be lying on your back for a while."

Finally, she laughs and lifts a hand to cover her face. "I had no idea you would be like this."

I stroke my thumb over her jaw. "Too much?"

Her hand drops away and she quickly shakes her head. "Oh, no. Definitely not."

"Good." I lean in and kiss her softly again, then pull back. "Take me upstairs, Luna."

She just takes another deep breath as she grabs my hand and starts toward the bookstore. I'm nearly on her heels as she leads me up the stairs at the back of the bookshop and to the door of her apartment. This one also has two locks, and she gives me a little grin over her shoulder as she unlocks them.

I put my hands on her hips and squeeze. "I'm glad you're safe."

I feel a little shiver go through her. "That's really sweet," she tells me.

I hate that she thinks it's sweet that someone cares if she's safe. Everyone should want her to be safe. The guys she dates should give that much of a shit about her. This is driving me nuts.

I can't help but wonder about her and Alexsei Ryan. I don't know if they're dating, hooking up, just flirting, or what. I do know that I don't have a claim on her. But if they are doing any of those things, I also know that he better be fucking treating her right and keeping her safe.

I also know that I cannot have a conversation with him about that.

I also know that I might not be able to help myself and that gives me a trickle of trepidation down my spine.

This woman cannot become a problem between me and one of my players.

But as Luna pushes the door to her apartment open, steps inside, and then turns to face me, walking backward, I take her in. I realize that she could become a problem for me in a lot of ways. I could fall ass over heels in love with her, and she'd shake my life up in every single way.

I still step across the threshold, though. I'm not staying away from her.

I shut the door behind me, again locking it securely. Then I start walking toward her. "Take your clothes off."

No reason to tease or drag this out. We both want this and I need her naked five minutes ago.

She kicks her shoes off, and they tumble somewhere near the sofa.

"You, too," she says.

I shake my head. I do shrug out of my suit jacket and toss it to the couch, but that's it. This is all about her for a little bit. It's not that I don't trust myself without my clothes on, but it's hotter thinking about being fully dressed while she's completely bare to me.

"Just you. For right now."

Her brows rise, but she reaches behind her and unties the tie at her waist.

When it's loose, the dress hangs in one straight line and she reaches to pull it over her head. I just watch.

She tosses it onto the sofa on top of my jacket.

I can't take my eyes off of her.

Because she's now only wearing a thong. A tiny little peach colored thong. No bra. Nothing else but the pendant necklace around her neck.

"That stays on," I tell her, pointing at the necklace. "Only that."

She hooks her thumbs in the top of it and pushes it down her legs, bending to step out of. She drops it on the carpet.

And I just stare.

I zero in, first, on the cupcake tattoo on her left hip.

That is so fucking perfect.

Then my gaze sweeps over her, slowly.

She has perfect, small, sweet tits. Her nipples are already hard, and her body is small and tight and perfect.

I know that I could lift her by the waist, pin her against the wall, and thrust deep. I wouldn't even break a sweat.

Except that the heat she stokes inside me has me already sweating.

She's built like a dancer. Graceful, subtle curves, perfectly proportioned from head to toe. Her skin is smooth and pale and she almost looks delicate. Except for the look on her face. There she is bold and determined, and there's even a flash of challenge in her eyes.

She is letting me stare at her. She knows she's gorgeous. She's just waiting to see what I'm going to do.

Or maybe waiting to see me crack. Because she can tell that I'm already on edge.

I haven't gotten undressed yet, and she wants to see how long I can last.

She has no idea.

I have a fuck ton of willpower.

"Where's the bedroom?" I ask. I unbutton the cuffs of my shirt and start rolling them up my forearms. I went without a tie tonight, but think for a moment about undoing my belt.

She watches.

"Luna?" I ask, when she doesn't answer me. "Bedroom?"

She wets her lips. "Through here." She starts down the short hallway, turning into the first door on the left.

I follow behind far enough to admire the sway of her hips and the sweet curve of her ass.

When I step into the bedroom, she's standing at the foot of the bed waiting for me.

"Lay back, legs spread."

There's no reason to say anything else, is there? We both know what's going to happen.

What she doesn't know is how much time I'm going to take with her.

So fucking much.

My mouth, tongue, and hands are going to be all over her before my cock even sees the lamplight in her bedroom.

The bedroom is very Luna. The walls are a soft mint green, the quilt on the bed is multicolored, and the Papasan chair in the corner has a bright pink cushion, the rug is yellow, green, blue, and white. Everywhere I look is a different color.

She has bedside tables that don't match on either side of her queen-sized mattress, and they look like she picked them up at a flea market. The lampshades are covered by multicolored scarves, which cast the room in a rosy glow.

She also has jewelry, clothes, photographs, make-up and knickknacks strewn everywhere on the top of her dresser, bedside tables, on the tiny desk next to her window and on the chair. It's not really messy. It's colorfully chaotic. It looks like a fucking kaleidoscope, to be honest.

And the room smells sweet, with just a hint of spice. Just like her. It reminds me of a Snickerdoodle cookie—sugar with a touch of cinnamon—my favorite.

"Just like this?" She sits down on the bed and leans back, propping herself on her elbows. Then she lifts one heel to the edge of the mattress, letting the other leg dangle, and spreads her thighs.

She looks like a damned goddess, and though I'm the one giving the orders, who's fully dressed, who is about to make her crazy with lust, it looks very much like she knows she's in charge.

"That will do. To start."

I step up to the foot of the bed, standing between her legs, and let my gaze rake over her. From the purple tips of her light hair and the sweet little nose on her face to those kissable lips, down her slender throat, to the sweet tits that are begging to be sucked on, over her flat stomach to her trim hips to her toned thighs, and all the way down to her dainty feet.

But then I come back up to the place my mouth is watering for. Her pussy is perfect. She is pink, and clearly already wet, and I cannot wait to be right there for the next hour or so.

"You're exquisite," I tell her honestly.

"Older guys use fancier words, too," she teases me softly.

I can tell she's completely turned on now. Her nipples are hard, her face is flushed, and despite her fairly casual position, her fingers are curling into the quilt.

"Yeah, we know words with more than two syllables," I tell her as I sink to my knees. "But if you want to hear that you are so goddamned gorgeous that I'm about to lose it, and I cannot wait to fuck you all night long, I can do that, too."

Her breath hitches, and she stares at me.

I put both my hands on her knees, and even that makes her suck in a quick breath.

With my eyes on hers, I slide my palms slowly up her thighs. But I stop before I get to her pussy.

"I intend to do some very dirty, wonderful things to you. Is that okay?"

She pulls her bottom lip between her teeth, but nods.

"If there's anything you don't like, just tell me. It's that simple."

She nods again. But she lets go of her lip and asks, "Do I get to do dirty, wonderful things to you, too?"

I chuckle. "Woman, you just lying here like this is pretty fucking wonderful."

Her smile widens. "Awesome. But I would really like to touch you, too."

"That can be arranged. But I've got some stuff to do first."

My gaze drops to her pussy again. I notice how her stomach sucks in and she says, "You can do whatever you want to me."

Lust hits me hard and my cock literally throbs.

I drag in a ragged breath. "Just keep talking to me so I know you're okay."

"Owen, I cannot imagine not being okay with you."

And I know she has no idea, but those words probably turn me on more than any others could.

I lift up, brace my hands on either side of her hips, and lean in and kiss her.

This is not a soft, teasing, tasting kiss. This is a carnal, I'm-going-to-fuck-you-hard-so-get-ready kiss.

Her hands go to the back of my head, her fingers digging into my skull, as she returns every single tongue stroke and angle change. I kiss her and kiss her, one hand running up and down her side over her soft, silky skin. Finally, I moved to one breast, no longer able to stop and drag it out any longer.

The way she arches closer and gasps against my mouth is incredible. Her hard little nipple presses into my palm and my tongue tingles with the need to taste it.

I drag my mouth from hers, down her neck, nipping gently. "I'm going to fucking eat you up," I tell her gruffly.

She moans. "Yes, please."

I kiss my way down her chest to her breast, sucking her nipple into my mouth, hard.

She groans and arches even closer, so I suck even harder. She clearly loves that.

I switch to the other side, taking the wet nipple between my finger and thumb, tugging and pinching.

That causes her hips to start to writhe against me.

And from there, things pick up quickly.

I kiss my way down her stomach, pausing to nip and lick the sweet skin as I go. I swirl my tongue over the cupcake tattoo, looking up to find her neck arched and her eyes closed.

When my knees hit the floor, I nip her inner thigh. "Eyes on me, Luna."

As soon as her beautiful blue eyes fasten on mine, I waste no time. I lean in and lick up one side of her pussy to her clit, stop and give it just a little kiss, then lick down the other side. I relish her little gasp and moan, and then I do it again. I swirl my tongue around her clit this time, before teasing down to her slick, hot opening. I tongue her there for just a moment before licking up to that pretty little clit and sucking on it harder this time.

"My God, Owen!"

"Yes, let me hear you, Luna," I praise, my voice rough.

I want nothing more than to see and hear this woman come apart for me. I want to take care of her in every way, and in this moment, I want to make her lose her mind with physical pleasure.

"Give me everything. I want to feel you pressing this sweet pussy against my face hard. Use me to get off."

"*God*," she says raggedly.

Then my girl does exactly as I asked. She presses closer to me and lifts slightly. I reward her with a harder lick and suck.

We repeat this, me responding to the lifts of her hips with hard, long licks and sucks on her clit as she cries out my name.

"Please, Owen! *More*!"

"That's my girl," I praise. "Tell me what you need. I'll give you anything."

"More. Harder," she pants.

I suck on her clit and then slide a finger into her. She gasps and presses against my hand. I give her another finger, fucking deep into her, curling against that spot that I want to undo her with.

"Yes! There!"

I finger fuck her as I suck hard and I feel her pussy start tightening around my fingers.

"There you go, give it up. Come for me, sweetheart."

"Oh, God! Owen!" she cries out as she comes.

And the feel of her pussy clenching around my fingers has my cock aching.

"I cannot wait to be buried inside this sweet cunt," I tell her.

I lick her release from my fingers and crawl up her body. I kiss her deeply, stroking my tongue and her taste into her mouth.

She clings to me, her hips pressing up into my pelvis. My cock settles against the sweet apex of her thighs and I press, knowing that her sensitive clit will feel how hard I am and it will make her needy again.

"You're right," she says against my mouth. "You are really good at that."

"*You're* really good at that. I love how you come apart."

"I want you. Please get naked with me," she says, running her hands down my back to my ass and pressing me into her.

I rock my cock against her, but I say, "Not until you give me one more."

"Maybe it will happen with you inside me."

"It will," I promise her. "But you'll have another before that."

It is now my mission in life to make this woman orgasm as much as possible. To be the best she's ever had. To wring every drop of pleasure out of her. I want her legs shaking, her pussy throbbing, and every other inch of her feeling me when I roll out of this bed.

"I've never had three in a row."

"That's because you've never been with me."

I slide my hands under her ass and roll us so I'm on my back, and she's splayed across my chest. I palm her ass, noting that I was right about how big my hands are on her. I kiss her again, then start to slide her up my body.

When those perfect tits are right in front of my face, I stop and suck on each nipple, playing with the other with my fingers.

She's straddling my stomach, and she grinds her pussy into me.

"You're good at that, too."

"Worshiping you? I hope so. It's already one of my favorite things to do, and I'm just getting started." Then I continue sliding her up my body. "Hands on the headboard."

"Owen, I —"

I squeeze her ass. "Don't argue with me. I want you to sit on my face. Grab that headboard and put your pussy on my mouth.

She sucks in a shaky breath, but she doesn't fight me anymore. She lets me move her into position. She grips the headboard with both hands.

"I had no idea you'd be this dirty."

"Yeah, well, I had a pretty good idea you'd taste this good. I'm addicted." I give her a long lick, loving the way she almost immediately starts grinding against my face as I lick her pussy, tonguing that sweet opening that's so hot and wet from her first orgasm, then finding her clit and sucking hard. My hands hold her ass and I don't give her any space.

"I'm so sensitive. It's almost too much."

I squeeze her. "You'll take it. All of it. You're gonna come again."

Her head is hanging forward, her silky hair cascading over her face as she looks down at me. She's watching what I'm doing, and that fucking turns me on.

"I don't know. It's so much."

"Luna, give me another," I growl against her. "If you want to be fucked, you're gonna come again like this," I say firmly.

She grinds against me, and I suck hard on her clit.

"You're so damn sexy. I will never get over the taste of you. I'm going to want to bury my face in your pussy every time I see you."

She whimpers.

"I want you to know the next time I see you, the next time we make eye contact, know for a fact that I'm thinking about this right here—" I suck hard. "Right now."

Another whimper and a shaky breath, and she grinds down harder.

"Fucking, come on my face, Luna. Do it."

And she does. This sweet, sexy, gorgeous woman, comes again, coating my tongue and crying out my name.

I'm so fucking hard that I know it's going to take about three pumps to be done.

"Oh my God, oh my God, oh my God," she's chanting over and over.

I slide her down my body until our mouths meet. I kiss her hard and deep. "You are fucking fantastic," I tell her, my voice gruff.

"I think that should be my line," she says, breathing hard. She drops her forehead to mine. "Holy shit, Owen. I've never come twice like that."

"Just one more to go."

She shakes her head, lifting to look at me. "No. I can't."

"You will. With my big thick cock buried deep inside this sweet, hot, very wet pussy. You definitely will."

She swallows hard. "I want that."

"You'll get it. Every fucking inch."

Suddenly she sits up and starts working the buttons of my shirt.

I laugh at her eagerness.

She grins at me. "Are you kidding? I've been dying to get you naked."

"Liar. You've been way too busy thinking about your pussy.

And my mouth. You haven't thought about my chest or even my cock."

She bites her bottom lip as she finishes my buttons and spreads the shirt open, running her hands over my chest and then down over my abs. "Okay. That's true. But now? I'm *all* about your cock."

Even hearing her say that, makes it throb.

"This might not take all that long."

Her eyes snap up to mine. "Good. Fuck me hard and fast."

"Jesus," I breathe out. "You're a fucking dream girl, you know that?"

She gives me a sly grin. "Easy to say when I'm straddling you, completely naked."

I reach up and settle my hands on her waist. "Always easy to say. This body? That sassy mouth? Your quick sense of humor? Your drive and determination? The fact that you *bake*? Fucking. Dream. Girl."

She grins and shimmies down my body until she's straddling my thighs. She makes quick work of my belt and my fly and I lift my hips so that she can drag my pants and boxers down.

Her eyes go wide when my cock springs free. "Oh my God, *yes*."

I chuckle. "You're happy?"

"That I get to have that huge thing inside me? Yes, sir, very happy."

She wraps one small hand around my shaft, stroking up and down, and I nearly lose it. I reach for her wrist, encircling it and squeezing.

"Yeah, about that sir thing," I say, my voice tight but trying to make the moment light and sexy instead of ordering her to her knees to suck me off. Which also would take about three strokes of her tongue. "We haven't really done that."

She looks up at me. "What do you want, Sir?"

"You, on your back, legs spread. Then you begging me for my

cock. And then you taking every inch of me and crying out *'thank you, Sir,'* when I make you come *again*."

Her eyes widen. "Yes," is her simple response.

And I think I fell just a little bit in love with her.

I have never had dirty, fun sex like this. I've been fortunate enough to date a few women who liked things a little more gritty, but I was always aware that I was going to run into them at the elementary school art fair, or that they were going to have coffee or yoga or a PTA meeting with other moms who I was going to see at park clean-up day, or that I was going to run into them, and/or their friends, at Little League practice where I was coaching their kids. I couldn't just let loose. They'd talk. They'd remember. And it would be awkward as fuck.

With Luna, I can be freer. I can just be Owen. I can be myself.

Plus, she seems to like it. I've definitely dated some women who, regardless of their parental status, would not have liked hearing some of the things I've already said to Luna.

"Get on your back," I command.

"Yes, Sir." She climbs off of me, lays back, and spreads her thighs.

Fucking perfect. She's so Goddamned gorgeous, willing, eager, and I am literally never going to get over her.

And it's not just the gorgeous body. It's all of the light and energy she brings. The way she makes me smile. The way she makes me want to hug her and hold her. The way I want to know what she looks like first thing in the morning, and how she takes her coffee, and what row she likes to sit in at the movie theater, and what songs she sings along to in the car, and what book she reads when she's feeling nostalgic.

But as she says, "I need your cock, Sir. *Please* fill me up and make me come," I'll admit it's her body right at this moment.

I move over her. "Condom?"

"Left side table."

"My left or yours?"

She giggles. "Mine."

Her giggle makes me just as hard as hearing her beg for my cock.

I reach into the drawer and find what we need. I tear it open, roll it on, and then kneel between her thighs.

"You ready?"

Her eyes are on my cock and I swear it gets even harder.

She licks her lips. "Oh God, I'm so ready for you."

Yeah, the thing is, I'm not sure I'm ready for her.

I grip her hips and lift her slightly, then position my cock in her entrance. I know this is going to be a tight fit and fuck, it's gonna feel so amazing. I circle my thumb over her clit and she shivers.

"Really sensitive," she tells me.

"I know." I give her a cocky grin.

"Yeah, you're amazing," she teases. Then I start easing into her and she gasps. "And so big."

"Hence, the reason you need to come a couple of times before I take you. Gotta get you hot and wet and ready."

"You didn't just do all of that to prove you could?" she asks.

I grin at her. "Oh, I totally did that just to prove I could. But it's also very helpful when you have such a tight little cunt and I need to fuck you hard."

"Yes, *God*, please."

I grit my teeth and slide in a couple more inches. "Oh, I'm going to."

"It's okay if you hurt me a little."

I groan. "No." I could never hurt her. Not even in the sexy way. This all has to be good and pleasurable.

"Seriously, Owen. *More*."

I'm still easing in. I circle her clit as I go.

"Owen," she pleads.

"But I like you begging. I like you needy."

"I *am* needy."

She reaches up and starts playing with her nipples and I swear I almost come.

"Did I tell you to play with your tits?" I ask her, trying for cross and commanding.

"I need *something*."

I circle harder on her clit. "*I* will take care of you."

"Then fuck me," she begs.

"I'm trying to make it last more than thirty seconds," I tell her, my jaw tight.

"If it doesn't, we'll just do it again later."

I chuckle in spite of myself. Then I look down and really take her in. That blonde hair tousled, her cheeks flushed, her lips pink and swollen from my kisses, nipples hard, whisker burn all over her pretty smooth skin, and that sweet pussy stretched around my cock.

What the fuck am I doing?

I pull back and I thrust hard.

"Yes!" she cries out.

And that's what does it. That sound. I want to hear that over and over again. Of course, her pussy's tight grip on me is part of it as well, but I want Luna to have whatever she needs.

I thrust again and again and again and I feel my orgasm start tightening. She's right there with me. She's gasping, holding onto the quilt, her eyes locked on me, urging me on.

"Yes, Owen. Like that. That's perfect. Oh, my God!"

"Come for me," I tell her. I'm circling her clit again.

"I'm close," she tells me.

I can tell. I need her over that edge. "Need you to come on my cock, Luna. I want to feel that."

I feel her tightening, and she's biting her bottom lip.

I keep one finger on her clit, and with the other hand I reach up to her nipple and squeeze.

"Yes!"

"Tell me what you need."

"Just you," she said breathlessly. "Harder. More."

I pick up the pace, hammering into her, and the next thing I know her pussy is clamping around me and she's shouting, "Yes! Owen! Thank you, Sir!"

Jesus Christ. I let go, my orgasm hitting hard, her name roaring from my chest.

I feel like I come for a full minute before I finally slump forward, bracing my hands on the mattress on either side of her and just breathing in and out.

I stare at her. "Holy shit."

She nods. "Yeah."

We just look at each other as we catch our breaths for several long moments, then I lean over and kiss her on the forehead before rolling to my side, bringing her with me.

I stare at her ceiling, taking a huge deep breath in and out.

Well, it's official.

I am dating one of my player's sisters. And potentially one of my other player's crushes.

But there's no getting over this girl. And I'm not even gonna try.

CHAPTER 17
Luna

OWEN PHILLIPS IS the Orgasm King.

I wake up with his big arm slung across my stomach and I just lie thinking about that for a moment. Okay, several moments.

My pussy is tingling even now. Not in a bad way. In a thanks-for-bringing-the-new-guy-home way. He not only gave me three orgasms when we first got back here, but he woke me up about two hours ago and gave me two more. He couldn't quite wait long enough to fuck me to give me two before thrusting inside, thank God. He's a magician with his mouth, but damn I love his cock, too.

I almost laugh out loud. I have been very spoiled lately. Between him and Alexsei and Cam…

Well, I haven't had Cam's cock yet. And for a moment I think about that. Am I ever going to get Cam's cock? Because he seems to like giving it to Alexsei.

And that is something I would really like to have a further conversation with him about.

I think it's cute he thought that I wouldn't notice. Not just how much he likes giving it to Alexsei, but the fact that I think Cam's *in love* with that sweet little cinnamon roll.

Okay, he's a *big* cinnamon roll.

Who Cam's madly in love with.

The guy thinks he is so mysterious. Please.

My stomach rumbles and I realize what woke me up. I'm a little tempted to wake Owen up, because I don't think he'd mind, and I think he would make it worth being tired tomorrow.

But I want to be fed. And I kind of want to impress him with more of my baked goods.

I have a guy in my bed for the first time in a while who really appreciates me.

Sure, he appreciates what we did for the last few hours, but he really likes my business. Not just the products I make, but the fact that I *have* my own business. And it doesn't matter to him that my dad bought it and got me started.

In fact, he helped me see that in a whole different light last night.

I don't remember the last guy I hung out with who actually wanted to talk about my business, not to mention being impressed with me because of it.

He's big, hot, and heavy. He reminds me of sleeping up against Alexsei, except Owen's a little softer. Not in a bad way. He's just not hard ripped muscles the way Alexsei is.

I really like them both. For just a second, I think about what it would feel like to be sandwiched between them.

Then I shake my head.

That is not a conversation that any of us are going to be having, so I need to put that little fantasy out of my mind.

I slip out from underneath Owen's arm, stretch my foot until I feel the floor, and then slide off the edge of my mattress.

This is different from sneaking around in Cam and Alexsei's apartment. I know every creaky floorboard, every piece of furniture, and exactly where I left my big fluffy robe that I can wear down to the bakery to grab us treats.

I walk into the kitchen, flip on the lights, and head for the back-up fridge for some extra cream puffs that I made yesterday.

I pull the door open and...suck in a breath.

No.

No, no, no.

No.

The tears start immediately.

Which makes me cry even harder. Because I fucking hate when I cry.

Fuck my life.

Seriously.

I was upstairs having amazing, blow-my-mind sex, and my refrigerator—thank God it's just the back-up—was down here dying.

If Owen and I had come in here for dessert before getting all frisky upstairs, I would've known about this hours ago. I could've saved at least some of these items.

But now, as I stare at the shelves in front of me, I realize I can't save any of this.

I don't know how long it's been off, but judging by the temperature of the foods, maybe most of yesterday.

I haven't had to open it. It's my backup fridge, and once I store things inside of it, like the icing, cream filling, and the dough that I was going to use for the desserts for the high tea I'm hosting tomorrow, I don't need to open it again until it's time to prepare the items.

What am I going to do?

It's not just a matter of replacing all of these things. I need to replace the refrigerator. Because I need a place to put all this stuff. Once I remake it.

"Hey, what are you doing?"

I startle, and spin to find Owen standing in the kitchen doorway. He's pulled his dress pants back on, but he's down here with no shirt and no shoes.

"I'm…"

He notices the tears on my face, and he immediately moves toward me. He stops right in front of me and cups my face in both hands. "What's wrong?"

I gesture to the refrigerator. "I came down to get us something to snack on. It's broken."

He looks at the refrigerator back to me. "Okay. What do you need?"

I laugh. "A new refrigerator. And all of that stuff replaced. Like eight hours ago."

His thumbs are stroking over my cheeks, drying my tears.

He gives me a smile. "Okay. We can't do that. So what can we do?"

His low voice is calming, and I find myself taking a deep breath.

"Remember I told you how I use my grandma's china for high teas once in a while?"

He nods.

"Tomorrow I'm hosting one of those. For a woman named Sandra Wilcox. She is very rich. And very picky. She also brings her very rich, very picky friends to these teas. But she pays me a lot of money and she really likes my stuff."

His hands are still stroking over my cheeks and I feel his body heat, and the comforting scent of him wrapping around me.

"Of course she does," he says.

I appreciate that. "This will be our fourth one. And just last month, one of her friends hired me for a party because she had been to a tea. So it is really an excellent promotional opportunity besides the fact that she pays really well. But all of these items are specially made for her. And I had everything prepped so that tonight I could get them all done, so everything is fresh and ready to go tomorrow. And now..." I hear my voice wobble. "It's all ruined."

He looks at the refrigerator and then back to me again.

"Okay, then we'll fix this."

I sniff. "And now you're going to tell me that you're a refrigerator repairman on the side?"

He smiles. "Part of me really wants to tell you that. I'd love to be the big hero coming in here with a toolbox. But no. However, I do know one."

"You know a refrigerator repairman?"

"Yes. I have owned a home for ten years. I know repair guys of all kinds. This one happens to be the dad of the kid who played hockey with Brady. Nice guy. And I know he'll do me a favor."

I feel my eyes filling with tears again. "What kind of favor?"

"Like coming over here to fix your refrigerator, even if he's really busy."

I sniff again. "Really?"

"Yes, really. So if you have a working refrigerator, what else do you need?"

"To redo everything."

"Okay, how long will that take?"

I swallow hard and think about it. "Three hours."

"Okay, so we can get that down to at least one."

My eyes widen. "How are we getting it down to an hour?"

"You by yourself can do it in three. Then you, me, Brady, and Lydia can do it in one, don't you think?"

"You would help me redo all of this?"

"I assume you can teach a guy like me to do some of it. I can stir, mix, and follow directions."

God, this guy. "I can't pay Brady and Lydia to do it," I shake my head. "I can't afford the overtime."

"You don't have to pay them."

"Yes, I do. They're my employees. I can't make them work for free."

"When he's off the clock, he's my kid. Actually, he's my kid even when he's on the clock. She's his girlfriend. And they're both currently in trouble because they missed curfew by two hours the other night. Which means they are working that time off. Which means I can tell them what to do during those hours. That time does not get paid for."

I frown. "But making him come here and work doesn't feel fair."

He laughs. "It's not about whether it's fair or not. He broke a rule and now he has consequences for it."

"He'll be mad at me," I say softly.

"No. He thinks you're amazing. And he'll much prefer this to any of the yardwork or repairs at home I had planned for him. And this will be a really good lesson for him."

"What do you mean, a good lesson?"

"I want my kid to understand this is what we do when our friends need help. We step up."

He leans in and kisses me on top of the head. Then he looks me in the eye. "I think that's a lesson I want *you* to learn, too. We're your friends. You have people who *want* to help you. You don't have to always do everything on your own, hot shot."

Dammit, I think I just fell a little bit in love with Owen Phillips.

And then I correct myself.

I just fell a little bit *more* in love with Owen Phillips.

CHAPTER 18
Alexsei

HOCKEY HAS ALWAYS BEEN my escape. Where my focus is. Everything in the outside world disappears when I'm on the ice.

All I'm thinking about is the game.

Where the puck is.

And how to keep the other team away from the goal.

I work out my problems on the ice during practice and I don't bring them to the games. The puck drop kicks my adrenaline into high gear and my head is clear.

Except for tonight.

The last few days have been chaotic and awesome and confusing as fuck.

I've had the high of getting to be buried inside Luna again. To watch her suck Cam off and have her willingly let him boss her around. Have her agree to go on an honest-to-God date with me.

Then there's Coach Phillips, who is also dating her, which is a little weird. In fact, my date with her has been delayed almost an entire week because he got there first. Between my schedule and hers, we can't see each other until Sunday.

And added to all of that, there's Cam.

He's half the reason I didn't ask Luna out sooner. I was just trying to respect her boundaries, but he also thought I should let her come to me. That aside, my head has been spinning over Cam ever since we ran into Sara at the grocery store yesterday.

I'm glad to see you two have finally figured this out.

Until that moment, I didn't think there was anything to figure out. Sara clearly thinks me and Cam are together though. A couple. That she felt like a third wheel for that reason.

Last night I lay in bed and rewound through all the times we had shared a woman and those six months we were dating Sara together, my cock growing hard. I thought about how it felt to have Cam's hand on my dick, stroking me with a firm grip. I had laid there and closed my eyes and jerked off, remembering all the times he had done this to me and how much I enjoyed it. I let myself wander into a headspace where I could see clearly there might be more to Cam's feelings for me than just friendship or sex.

And that mine might be more, too.

Cam actually went out last night with his buddy from work, Rodan, but came home around midnight. When I heard him in the living room and headed down the hallway to his bedroom, I had breathed a sigh of relief that he wasn't spending the night in some guy's bed. Which made me even more confused. There was a time when that wouldn't have bothered me. When the hell had that changed? Not recently, if I'm honest with myself. Jealousy over who he hooks up with has been brewing inside me for a while.

Maybe my feelings are even more complicated than I realized. Maybe it's not just sex when Cam slips a finger in my ass during the heat of the moment. Maybe it's more than physical or friends sharing some fun. Like... something real.

Like... *love.*

I had tossed and turned all fucking night, which probably isn't helping my game play tonight.

The fans are loud in the stands, gearing up for a potential playoff run, and there's a palpable energy and excitement. Only my fucking feet feel like lead and my brain seems to be moving as slow as my skates. I've failed to steal the puck twice, and I got two minutes in the box for tripping.

The only good thing about tonight is neither Luna nor Cam are at the game to distract me even further. Yet their absence also bothers me. I've gotten used to glancing up and seeing them in their regular seats, Luna decked out in Racketeers gear. Even when she and I weren't communicating with each other, I had that. I could always see her in the stands. But I've been texting with her and she said she was going to catch up on her laundry since she's been so busy lately. Cam is at dinner with his mother. My own mother and stepfather are on a spring break Disney cruise with my little sister, which right now only adds to my loneliness.

I hate feeling alone.

The weight of the stick in my hand feels heavy and my left skate is rubbing my heel in a way that is pissing me the fuck off. The Gators have already scored, and it's on me. I'm moving too slow and their center smoked me. Now I take a shoulder to the wall and wince from the impact. I turn around and shove the big hulking guy everyone calls the Swede. He barely moves when I jostle with him, which pisses me off even more.

Coach Phillips calls me out when the ref blows the whistle a few seconds later and I put my hand on my hip, breathing harder than I would like, and glide over to the bench.

"What's going on?" he demands, frowning.

I plunk myself down on the bench and tap my stick on the floor, edgy and impatient. "Nothing."

"It's something. You're skating like you've got goddamn hemorrhoids." He rubs his beard and gives me a look of concern. "If this is something personal, we can talk it through later."

I give him an are-you-fucking-kidding-me look. "I don't have anything to say."

I don't. Luna can date him if she wants. That's what I assume he's referring to. I may be on the damn edge of falling in love with her, but she's free to do whatever the hell she wants, even if it's starting to get under my skin.

Because Coach is relationship material. And Luna doesn't

want a serious relationship. But if anyone can weasel his way into achieving one with her, it's more likely to be him than me, and that pisses me off. Mostly, though, I'm pissed that he pretended to be concerned when he was actually pumping me for information about if I was dating Luna or not.

It's tempting to tell him I just wall-banged her a few days ago, but this isn't the time or the place. I also like to think I'm cooler than that.

He stares at me hard. "I don't buy that."

I actually groan then and stand, too keyed up to sit still. I adjust my helmet. "Put me back in."

If he wants to have some kind of heart-to-heart later where he tries to be my dad, we can, but right now I want to get back out there and redeem myself from a shitty beginning to this game.

He gives a nod and I don't wait for him to say anything else. I go over the board and slide my feet back and forth, ready to go when the action starts again.

I take my last glance at the empty seats before the puck drops.

When I get home tonight, I need to talk to Cam.

Clear the air. See where his head's really at.

The Swede slams into me. Hard.

While my teeth are rattling, he gives me a grin.

It's all I need to take a swing at him. I make contact with his helmet.

The crowd roars its approval.

I rip off my glove to really go at him.

But then I'm being yanked backward by Hayes and I refocus on the puck, swiping my glove back up off of the ice.

We lose 3-2 and I'm fucking exhausted by the time I get home.

"Hey," Cam says, lounging on the couch in a white T-shirt and dark gray sweats, feet on the coffee table. He has a jar of cherries in his hand and he's sucking on one, which is very fucking distracting and not helping my confused thoughts. He's the only person I know who eats cherries from a jar. But Cam is like that. He does whatever he wants, confidently and with no concern for anyone's opinion.

"Hey." I drop my bag and kick off my shoes, tired as fuck. "How was your mom?" Cam's mother has always scared me a little. She's thin and has delicate features, yet her gaze is sharp and her words are shrewd. I don't think she means to, but she makes me feel big and dumb. Then again, maybe she does mean to. I suspect she thinks Cam could have a smarter best friend. Which he could. But for whatever reason, he wants it to be me. Which is what I want to talk to him about.

"She was Miriam in full form. She wanted to tell me what's wrong with our generation."

"What's wrong with our generation?" I peel my jacket off and toss it on the club chair across from the couch. I don't feel like hanging it up.

"School of resentment. It's a whole theory." Cam fishes out another cherry and flicks his tongue over it.

Heat swirls in my gut. "I don't know what that means," I tell him.

"I'm not going to explain it because I don't actually care." He sucks the cherry. "And you look tired."

"I am." I drop into the chair, leaning back against my jacket and close my eyes briefly, trying to figure out how to have this conversation. "Why do we live together?" I ask, lids still shut.

People have asked me why Cam and I are still roommates. I always shrug and say because I'm on the road half the time. It's cost effective. It's practical. Food doesn't go bad in the fridge because Cam doesn't travel. We're best friends.

With most people, I don't add that it makes it easy to do our threesome thing, picking up a girl and bringing her home to share.

But now I'm second-guessing our living arrangement motives —on both our ends—and why we've never actually really discussed it.

"What? Because we've always lived together, and it works. Do you want to move out?" he asks.

When I open my eyes, his feet have dropped to the floor. He's staring at me, frowning.

"No. I don't. I just wondered if maybe... I don't know."

It means something more.

I want to say it, but scared to because I value my friendship with Cam so damn much. I don't want to ruin it by pissing him off or making him uncomfortable. Maybe I'm wrong.

"You wondered what?" he demands. "You can tell me. You know you can tell me anything."

Running my hand over my jaw, I stare at him, willing him to understand. "What Sara said. About feeling like a third wheel. It's got to me."

"You don't want to share women anymore? Is that what you're saying?"

"No, I'm not saying that." I don't know what the fuck I'm saying. "You know I like doing that. It's hot."

Cam's forearms rest on his thighs and he just watches me. When I don't say anything else, he narrows his eyes. "I know you want to take Luna out by yourself. You're falling hard for her. It's different with her than other girls you've dated."

I nod. "Yes, but this isn't about Luna. This is about you and me."

His expression goes blank. "I don't understand." His voice has cooled.

"You're my best friend," I tell him. My tone is pleading. "You know me better than anyone."

He relaxes a hair. He goes for another cherry. "You're my best friend, too, you know that. I'm not close to a lot of people."

The damn cherry goes to his lips and this time when he sucks, I have to shift in the chair. My dick is getting hard. "Will you stop doing that?" I demand, exasperated.

"Doing what?"

"Sucking that cherry. It's distracting. I'm trying to have a serious conversation here."

Cam goes still. He lowers the cherry, rolling it between his fingers, tongue flicking over his bottom lip to lap up the juice. "What are we talking about exactly, Alexsei?" he asks in a low voice.

He sounds sensual. Sexy. I need to hear it out loud. From him. "There has to be a girl, right? With you and me. That's what you like?"

A heartbeat passes and then he just says, "Come here. You're too far away."

When Cam uses that voice, I always just automatically obey. I trust that he knows what's best. I rise to my feet and stroll toward him, feeling the air shift and crackle between us. We're about to do something that will change the dynamic of our friendship. I can feel it.

Hell, maybe we already have.

We're just acknowledging it now.

I don't want to shy away from it. I want to embrace it.

Cam stands, too, so that when I reach him we're almost eye-to-eye. "Does there have to be a girl?" I ask again.

He places his hand on my jaw and I realize I'm trembling a little, body tense with desire and with fear, that I'm wrong, and that we'll change everything between us and regret it.

His touch is firm, yet soothing, as he slides the pad of his thumb along my jaw and over my bottom lip. I suck in a breath.

"Not for me," he murmurs, gaze dropping to my mouth. "I just like you. I just need *you*."

Then he kisses me.

We've never kissed.

He's touched my body everywhere. He's been inside me.

But we've never kissed.

My heart is pounding, but the second his lips cover mine, all my fears melt away. He feels and tastes amazing, and his kiss is confident and skilled. His hand slides up into my hair and I kiss him back without hesitation, gripping the waistband of his sweats. I know his scent, I know his breathing, I knew him in all ways, but this... this is different. This is intimate and hot and I want to taste him thoroughly.

When he teases my lips apart with his tongue, I let him, then give myself over to what I'm feeling. I pull him against me, letting our hips collide as the sweetness of those damn cherries floods my mouth. "Cam," I pull back briefly and groan, before going in again. I need more. We're engulfed in a hot, demanding kiss that turns into another and another until I'm lost to him.

I'm grinding my throbbing dick against his, and I want more. I grip his ass for the first time ever, enjoying the growl that radiates from him at my touch. I've never really touched him like this and I slip my palms inside his sweats so I can feel his heated skin. He has a tight ass and I squeeze, thrusting him forward onto me as we make out.

His head falls back as he says, "Yes. Fuck, Alexsei. Yes."

It gives me confidence to hear those words.

I take the opportunity to nip at his earlobe, to brush my lips over his neck and revel in the satisfaction of feeling him shudder at my touch. He is always the cool one, in total control. The one driving me wild. Now I'm rattling him and it's turning me the fuck on. His hand slips between us and he rubs my cock with the heel of his palm.

Driven by a sharp need, I kiss him again, but my nose bumps against his glasses, tipping them askew. I laugh softly. "Sorry." I pull my hands out of his sweats and reach up to remove the glasses.

Without them, Cam looks vulnerable. Softer. He blinks and his gaze drops to my mouth. I sense hesitation.

But then he shocks me by saying, "I love you."

There it is. What's been knocking at the back of my subconscious for a while and took Sara to force me to admit.

Him saying it makes everything less scary and confusing. Peace settles over me when the last piece of the puzzle clicks into place for me. I smile, understanding that his view of me being blurry without his glasses on gave him the courage to admit what he feels. He looks fucking cute as hell right now, and I want him with everything inside me.

"Did you hear what I said?" he demands, sounding more like the grumpy Cam I know and love.

Because yes, I love him, too.

Somewhere along the way, friendship deepened and became more and I didn't even understand it or recognize it. Or maybe I did. I don't know. All I know is that there is only one guy who can turn me on physically and also make me feel this safe and light and loved.

Cam.

"I heard you."

I fold the glasses closed and set them on the coffee table, fishing one of his stupid cherries out of the jar and popping it into my mouth, the tart sweetness bursting over my tongue.

I do it on purpose, to get a reaction from him, and he doesn't disappoint. His eyes darken and his hands ball into fists. His cock jumps in his sweatpants.

With a swagger in my step, I return to him. I stop inches from him. Slipping my finger between his lips, I watch him suck the tip as I swallow the cherry.

"I love you, too," I tell him.

His eyes widen, and then the vulnerability instantly disappears as he registers my words. He bites down on my finger and then he yanks it out, before gripping both of my cheeks with ferocity, and kissing me with a passion I didn't even know he was capable of. He always holds back. But this? It's a wild, reckless kiss and I want to feel him, touch him in a way I never have before. In every way I possibly can. I race my hands under his T-shirt, across his abs, before slipping into his sweats. His cock is thick and hard and I explore the feel of him beneath my hand.

There's a bead of moisture already on the head and I stroke, up and down, enjoying the way his breath hitches against my mouth.

Cam drops his fingers to the buttons of my shirt and quickly undoes them. Then he shoves it off at the shoulders. When I step back to peel it off completely, he yanks his shirt off over his head. I've seen Cam without a shirt many times, but I've never really taken it in, and I want that now. I admire the view of his lean torso, his tan skin. He shaves everywhere, so he's smooth and I tease over his nipples, goosebumps following in my wake. I like the hard plane of his chest, the firm abs, how different he feels from a woman.

"Take your pants off," I tell him. I yank my undershirt off. When the fabric clears, Cam is standing there fully naked, his dick hard as a fucking rock and ready for me. He's squeezing it at the base and watching me through hooded eyes.

For a second, I hesitate, fingers on the button of my pants. I don't know how this works between us. Cam's always the one telling me what to do.

He must sense that, because he steps forward and puts his hand over mine. He helps me with the button and runs his lips over my jawline, up to my ear. "Are you sure?" he murmurs, his breath tickling me.

He's asking me about more than this, about sex. I nod. "Yes." My voice is low. But steady. "I want you. I can't ever be without you, you know that, right?"

Cam shudders, then he kisses down my chest, hot presses that have my balls tightening. Rocking back on my heels, I twine my fingers in his dark hair and watch him descend down to my waist, the zipper slipping down. Then he has my dick out and the first feel of his tongue flickering over my head makes me shiver.

"Jesus," I mutter, as he takes me fully into his mouth.

I've had his hands on my dick many times, but never the wet stroke of his tongue and it's fucking unreal. He isn't gentle, but commanding, skilled. He knows just how to take it all the way in, then release, his palm massaging my balls. His free hand comes around to grip my ass, guiding me to thrust harder and faster.

I'm lost to the sensation of Cam sucking me, my eyes drifting closed. I'm climbing fast, drowning, unable to hold back. "I'm going to come," I spit out, gripping his head tightly. "Oh, shit. Cam. Don't stop."

He doesn't. He just works me harder and then I'm exploding deep in the back of his throat with a string of curse words, emptying my balls and marveling at how fucking good it all feels.

When he pulls back, he gives me a very Cam smirk. He wipes his bottom lip. "Damn, you're easy to get off."

That makes me give a burst of laughter. "Fuck you." I shove my pants to the floor. "Let's see how long you last, asshole."

"Longer than you."

I reach out and put my hand on the back of his neck and haul him up against me, hard. I kiss him. "Let's find out."

His eyes are dark. "Get in the bedroom."

When I strut past him, knowing he'll be staring at my ass, he crowds up behind me. "Walk faster."

Anticipation makes me do just that.

I know to go to his room, not mine. His is always clean and has fresh sheets. Besides, it's a control thing. He prefers his space. Plus, he keeps lube and condoms in the nightstand.

But I can't resist shoving my pants and briefs to the floor and purposely climbing on his bedding. He always pulls the comforter off first before he lets anyone on his bed for sex, but he doesn't say a word about it now. He just digs in the nightstand and rips open a condom and sheaths himself. He tosses the lube on the bed next to me. I lay down on my back, heart racing with both anticipation and a minor case of nerves.

I really have no idea what to do with my hands. I stick them behind my head. I cross my ankles, but then immediately uncross them because that's dumb. He's fucked me before. But never with this level of intention.

And we've never admitted we have feelings for each other.

That we love each other.

God, it feels amazing to know that truth.

He isn't smiling. He's looking over my naked body with a greedy gaze that makes my dick swell. It calms my nerves, so that when he climbs on the bed, over me, hands on either side of me, it feels natural and good to spread my legs for him as he kisses me.

His dick is nudging at my rim, teasing me. I arch my back, questing more. He squeezes lube onto his fingers and then he's pressing into me, stretching the tight channel. Lust shoots through my body as I close my eyes.

"Look at me," he demands.

He's right. I need to see him. We've never made eye contact when he fucks me. I want that. I want him. My eyes fly open.

Without thinking, I drop my hand to my dick, pumping it up and down a few times in rhythm with his fingers as he thrusts them into me. He kisses me again, and it feels so good, so natural, that I lose the last of my nervousness and let his tongue and his fingers ground me in pleasure. Once we're both panting and desperate, me lifting my hips up in urgent need for him, he eases his fingers out and lifts my knees up and apart. Then he lubes up the condom and replaces his fingers with his cock, rubbing against my entrance.

"More," I beg. "Cam. Please."

"More?" He's watching me the entire time he enters me, slowly, his arms shaking as he struggles to stay in control. "I'd fucking love to take more. You feel so damn good, Alexsei. It's killing me to hold back."

I squeeze my cock harder, his words sending a jolt of desire through me. "So don't."

"Are you—

"Don't ask me again if I'm sure," I tell him, smacking his ass with a hard crack. "I wouldn't say it if I wasn't sure. If I didn't trust you."

"Damn," he murmurs at my demanding tone. "Okay, then."

"Now please," I say, through gritted teeth as he strokes

painfully slow in and out of me. "Fuck me for real. Like *you*. I want *you*."

He hitches me up higher without warning. Then he slams into me.

"Holy fuck…"

That spot he's hitting…

My eyes roll back in my head as he pumps harder and deeper, his expression fierce and determined.

I can't speak. My mind empties.

Then his hand reaches between us and gives my dick tight, hard strokes.

He's right.

He lasts longer than me.

CHAPTER 19
Cameron

ALEXSEI EXPLODES all over my hand with a sharp cry, a hot burst of cum that nearly makes me blow my own load. But I fight for control, sweat beading on the back of my neck. I want this to last. Fucking forever. I want to enjoy every second of being buried inside him, his body milking my cock as he shudders through his orgasm.

He loves me, too.

I never thought I would hear those words. It's everything.

As is the fact that he wants me to be me. For him. With him.

He feels so fucking good I almost can't stand it.

"Damn it, I fucking hate that you're always right," he growls, as he lifts his hips higher and meets me thrust for thrust.

My hand falls away from his dick so I can have more leverage. I want all of him, balls deep. "Oh, yeah? You hate that I'm right about this being good, you and me?"

"I hate this so much," he says, his large hands palming my ass. "I hate everything."

That makes me laugh softly in spite of the circumstances. Alexsei doesn't hate *anything*. He's the toughest softie I've ever met in my life. He cares more about other people than he does himself, and I love that about him.

"I can stop." I slow down and pretend like I'm going to pull out. I'm not going to. There's no fucking way I can leave him without finishing this. But I want to see his reaction.

He grips my ass harder. "The fuck you can," he says fiercely. "Fuck me, Cam. I want to see you come." He reaches up and brushes his fingers over my lips, startling me. "I never get to see you come."

That nearly does me in.

But I want, no *need*, to savor this moment. Where I get to be fully inside him, staring into his eyes, braced over his rock-solid athletic body. There's just me and him, and I never thought this would happen. Ever. I've seen him naked more times than I can count, and I love the view. All those hard muscles and his large shoulder tattoo. I love the feel of his rough skin, his powerful thighs, his tight ass when we're with a woman and I can glide my hands over him. Never with this kind of freedom. Never with him acknowledging that it's more than just sex for sex's sake.

Never with him saying *"Fuck me, Cam."*

He wants this. He wants me.

"Yes," he groans. "Don't hold back. That feels so fucking good."

It does. It feels like nothing I've ever experienced before. I'm losing control, in the best way possible, gripped by him. I pick up speed again and in seconds, I'm giving him everything I've got, calling out his name as I explode, wave after wave of pulsating ecstasy ripping through me.

"That's it," he's coaxing. "Show me how I make you feel."

With a final shudder, I ease back and press my forehead to his, half-collapsing onto his chest. "I love you." It comes out of my mouth comfortably, a relief to be able to share it. "That's how you make me feel."

"I love you, too." His voice is raw, gravely. He cups my cheek.

My throat is tight with emotion and I can't speak.

So I kiss him.

After a second, where my heart rate attempts to return to normal, he says, "Now get off of me. You're heavier than a girl."

I shake my head and peel myself off his slick skin. "And you're sweatier than a girl."

But I leave the bed and go to the bathroom to get rid of the condom, thinking he might need space. Hell, maybe I need space for a second. That was... amazing.

Everything I've ever wanted all at once.

The room is slightly blurry without my glasses and I misjudge the corner of the bed on the way back, stubbing my toe. "Fuck."

"That's why your mother didn't name you Grace," he says with a grin. "And why I refuse to let you put on a pair of skates. You'd break a bone."

I climb onto the bed beside him. "It's your fault. You took my glasses off."

"You look hot without them." Alexsei shifts his arm, inviting me into his space. "Hot with them, too."

Our thighs are touching, and I'm about as content as I've ever been. I wish I could appreciate the view of his nakedness with a little more clarity. But I'll just have to enjoy the feel of his hard, muscular frame.

He yawns.

"Tired?" I ask, kissing the side of his head. I'm in awe that I'm allowed to do that now. After years of wanting that, it's happening, and I fucking love it.

I love *him*.

"Yeah. I slept like shit last night. I'll sleep good tonight, though."

I smirk. "You're welcome."

He rolls his eyes. "It's because your bed is more comfortable than mine. I always sleep great here."

I don't point out that he could have bought himself the same mattress at any point. Instead, I just tell him, "Then you should sleep here from now on."

With me.

A thrill rolls through me.

His eyes don't meet mine. But he does nod. "I think I will."

My heart almost bursts out of my damn chest. I know this is all new to Alexsei. I don't want to be greedy and scare him off. But I need him to know where I'm at. "I'll be here every night. Even if you're not."

Now his gaze does flick over to meet mine. He studies me. "No other guys?"

I shake my head. "No other guys."

Just you.

"Why would I want another guy when I have a hot hockey player in my bed? I'm not an idiot," I add, wanting to keep things light so he doesn't freak out and think I'm rushing him.

"Good," he says, gruffly. "Because last night I was jealous when I thought you might be with a guy."

"Really?" I can't quite keep the glee out of my voice.

He nods. "Yes. It's how I knew for sure what was what." He frowns. "Don't fucking gloat."

I try to wipe the smile off my face, but I don't succeed. "Sorry. Not sorry."

Alexsei gives me a shove that makes me laugh. "You're an asshole."

"It's one of my many charms."

"Hardly."

"So you just put up with me? Is that what you're saying?" I ask.

"Something like that." But he pulls up onto his elbow and studies me. "Why didn't you say anything? About how you felt?"

My throat constricts again. "I didn't want to risk losing our friendship. I didn't want to make you uncomfortable."

"So you just slid in when you could?" Alexsei makes a face. "Jesus. I don't mean that literally."

I laugh and reach forward and kiss him. He's adorable when he's awkward. "What *do* you mean?"

"I mean, you were with women with me, so you could be *with* me."

I nod. "The first time wasn't intentional. You know that. But then, I liked you and you seemed to like it. Then you told me it wasn't serious, it was just sex, so I accepted that. Better to share you than not have you at all."

"It might have started out that way for me, not serious, but somewhere along the way it changed without me knowing it. But you know I haven't even dated anyone without you."

"To be clear, I didn't want to date women without you ever, but they do add to the fun. I was attracted to how attracted to you they were." It's probably more complicated than that, but I just choose to let it be what it was. "And like you, I liked some of those women more than others. I really did like Sara as a person."

"What about Luna?"

That makes me shake my head, genuinely bewildered. "She's different. I am honestly attracted to her. I want to shake her and fuck her all at the same time. She's something special, she really is."

"So you want to keep seeing her?" He rubs his mouth. "Because I don't think I can quit her."

"I don't want you to quit seeing her. I know you have feelings for her. Strong feelings for her." He actually loves her. I can see it in the way he looks at her and I'm always going to be happy that he's happy. "Like I said, Luna is different. I like her, too."

"Good. We'll just feel our way through this?"

"I'm definitely going to do a lot of feeling my way through this. And I do mean that literally."

He snorts. "That was bad."

I don't even try to deny it. But I'm feeling uncharacteristically goofy right now. I'm not even sure who the fuck I am right now, because I'm so damn happy I could easily be jump-on-the-bed guy in about two seconds.

Then Alexsei drops down on the mattress and rolls on his side.

His rough, masculine hand lands on my stomach, which makes my muscles tense. "So, how long have you been in love with me?"

I turn and take in the sharp angles of his jaw, his long nose, those eyelashes that would make a woman jealous. The little scar above his brow that he told me was from falling off his bike as a toddler. "Not that long. Just since the first day I met you."

His expression softens. "God, you've been hiding a romantic guy under that grumpy-ass face all these years and I never even knew it."

"You want me to keep hiding him?" I ask, partly teasing, partly serious.

But Alexsei shakes his head. "No. I like him, too, right along with grumpy Cam."

That means everything to me.

"Will you still like him if he doesn't let you sleep yet?" I ask, reaching my hand down and lightly stroking over his half-hard cock. I don't want this to end yet.

Alexsei moans. "I'll like him even more. But babe, I don't know if I can. It's already been twice."

He's never called me 'babe' before. It feels as monumental as him saying he loves me. I shift down, easing the comforter off of him. "You can. I believe in you."

I flick my tongue over him, then take him deep without any preamble.

His fingers fist in the pillow. "I believe in your mouth. *Fuck,* Cam."

Pulling back, I tell him, "I can't see what I'm doing. Go get my glasses."

Alexsei groans in disappointment. "Shut the fuck up." He pushes me back down onto him.

God, he's so easy to mess with. I laugh softly and get back to business.

CHAPTER 20

Luna

WHY IS Alexsei different from other hockey players?

That's the question I'm asking myself as I sit across from him at a tapas bar.

Because he is. Something about him, the way I am when I am with him, gives me different energy than every other hockey player I've ever met. Which is a lot. So many damn hockey players.

I think he's hot. I've always thought he was hot. That's why when Cam suggested I go home with them, I was interested. I saw Alexsei as a hockey fuck boy. If anything, I was more curious about Cam, whose asshole-ish behavior was a total relationship red flag, but was something of an intriguing challenge when it came to a one-night stand.

I had meant it when I'd said I didn't want a relationship and I had thought that was true, but it hadn't stopped me from letting Alexsei talk me into an entire weekend of sex, movies, and couch cuddling. He'd been easy-going, quick to tease and laugh, and had ordered me everything I needed to work on my recipes while I was at their apartment. I will bet money that stand mixer has been collecting dust ever since.

He doesn't need to be the center of attention either. It was immediately clear to me that he takes direction from Cam—which is easy to do—but I've watched him in a dozen hockey games since then. He doesn't need to be the star. He excels at assisting, and unlike my brother, the Racketeers Prince Charming, he doesn't drop his stats every chance he gets.

Confident, sure. Arrogant, no.

Definitely not a fuck boy.

I can see why Cameron is in love with him.

It will take very little for me to be in love with him, and I realize I want that. I want to be in love. I want to stop falling into bed exhausted every night alone, fretting over the bakery. I love my business and fretting isn't going to go away, so why can't I allow myself some happiness along with it?

Alexsei shoves the appetizer fork around with his huge hand, probably unaware that he's making a face at the buttermilk fried quail with baby turnips. This restaurant was his idea and not only does the fork look absurd in his hand, so does the size of the plate and the food portion itself. He also looks like he would give his left arm for a burger.

I purse my lips together and try not to smile.

But he glances up and catches me. "What?"

"You look like a little kid whose parents make him try a bite of everything on the plate."

Alexsei grimaces. "Well, so much for trying to look sophisticated."

That surprises me, and instantly makes me feel compassion for him. I had just done the same thing with Owen. Tried to be something I'm not. "Is that why you picked this place? You didn't have to do that. Just be yourself, Alexsei, seriously."

"But you don't like hockey players."

"But I like *you*."

He nods, and tugs at the neck of his button-up shirt. "I like you, too. A lot. That's why I'm trying to impress you."

Vulnerability can be pretty damn hot. "You do impress me. Otherwise, I wouldn't be here trying to choke down chicken liver pate." I gesture to my own plate and shudder. "It looks like what my mom feeds Snickers, her cat."

Alexsei laughs. "It does seem like we're in a Fancy Feast commercial, doesn't it?"

"Yes, it does. Insert pussy joke here."

"I'll pet your pussy anytime." He sets his fork down. "I have a confession. I ate before I left home because I was worried I wouldn't get enough to eat. I smashed on BBQ ribs."

That makes me snort loud enough that I clap my hand over my mouth when a couple of diners turn and stare at me. "That's sad. Brilliant, but sad. But here's my confession. This is Dani's sweater that she left behind at our apartment. I was trying to not be sexual." I shake my head, amused. I had gotten Alexsei's text with the name of this restaurant, and I'd been determined to make this be a "real date." "I didn't want you to be distracted by thoughts of sex when we're trying to get to know each other."

His jaw drops. "Um, well, I'm always distracted by thoughts of sex when I'm with you. A pink sweater isn't going to change that, gorgeous. I've seen you naked already."

My nipples tighten beneath the conservative sweater. "So, basically, neither one of us knows what we're doing."

He nods. "Seems that way." He pauses, like he isn't sure he should say something, but then reaches for my hand. "I know you said you don't want a relationship. That's why I didn't reach out to you sooner. But I've thought about you nonstop since we spent those days together. I like you, Luna. So damn much. I think you're amazing and I want whatever you can give me."

My heart squeezes. I love his honesty, his willingness to take anything I have to offer. "I've thought about you, too. Constantly. And me saying that was months ago. Maybe I don't feel as strongly about not wanting to be with someone as I did then. I'm more open to it now."

Very open.

Wide fucking open.

For a second, he seems to mull over my words. Alexsei's

emotions are always on full display on his face. He's not a hard man to read. Hope is warring with confusion for him.

For me, I just feel hope. That this can be something that I'm missing in my life. That I can relax and allow myself to enjoy his company, his genuine affection.

"Is that a general statement or about me, specifically?" he asks.

I squeeze his fingers. "You. I want to try this, with me and you because you make me feel... lighter. I love to laugh with you."

"That's good. That's really fucking good. I love to laugh with you, too. But... why didn't you say anything? Reach out? Cam says you never talk to him."

I ease my fingers out of his and sit back in my chair. "Cam never talks to me either. And we're not talking about Cam, are we?" It's my way of trying to uncover the truth of his feelings for Cam, but he doesn't take the bait.

"Well, no, but I have to admit that I would have reached out to you if he hadn't insisted that I let you make the first move. I wanted to be respectful of what you wanted, but it nearly killed me."

"You should trust your gut more. Because I'm not a girl who chases."

Alexsei sits back, blowing out his breath while rubbing his jaw. "Yeah. I can see that."

"But maybe I'm ready to be caught," I tell him with a flirty smile.

He sits straight up, and his voice is low, gravelly. "Yeah?"

"Yeah. So let's try this. We'll grab the check and go somewhere else while we talk more." I glance around. "If we can get the server. I feel like we're being blown off."

"Oh, we totally are. But I think that's the point of this place," he says with a smile. "To be treated poorly enough that you feel like you're lucky they even *let* you dine here."

"That's exactly it! Like we should be grateful they're giving us thirty-dollar cat food."

"Nailed it." Alexsei tries to get the passing server's attention and is completely ignored. He stabs a sardine. "I do like these, though. Reminds me of my childhood."

"You ate sardines as a kid?"

He nods. "I grew up in Ukraine until I was eight. My mom was a single mom, working hard as a waitress to make ends meet, and these were a delicacy at my grandparents' house, believe it or not."

"I had no idea you grew up in Ukraine. Is that what your tattoo is? The Ukrainian flag?"

He nods.

"How did you end up in the States?"

"My stepfather was on a business trip and my mother was his waitress. He fell instantly for her, because she was beautiful, and she fell for his bank account." He grins. "And I don't mean that in a bad way. Patrick is honestly a really good man, but he was fifty and she was twenty-six. He adored her, and she fell in love with him because of how much he just genuinely wanted to take care of her, and not in a controlling way. A protective way."

"Are they still married?"

"Yes. I have a little sister who's twelve. My mom is still beautiful and Patrick is still spending every minute making sure she's happy. He was, is, a good stepfather. He treated me like his own son and he adopted me when I was ten."

"So your last name came from him?"

"Yes. I was born Alexsei Bondarenko. We added the Ryan to the end. How's that for a mouthful?"

A little sizzle rolls through me. "I think it's sexy. Do you still speak Ukrainian?"

"Yes, and no. I can, but I don't often enough anymore to feel completely comfortable. I talk to my grandparents in Ukrainian and that's about it."

"That's very cool." I eye him. "Maybe you can whisper something in my ear later."

"How about now?" He lowers his voice and says something that sounds amazingly sexy.

"What did you say?" I murmur, assuming it was a sexual innuendo.

But he grins. "Pass the salt."

I laugh. "There's no salt on this table. The chef would be insulted if you dared to season his masterpiece."

"It's all I could think of off the top of my head." He winks at me.

"I'll give you suggestions later. So, do your parents live in Chicago?"

"No. Ohio."

"So, how did you get into hockey? Did you play in Ukraine?"

"A little. But with English not being my first language and it clear pretty quickly that I wasn't the sharpest kid in school, Patrick wisely realized that keeping up with my peers academically was going to be a challenge for me. He thought hockey would be my ticket to college. Which it was."

"Cam told me you went to Ohio State."

He frowns. "When did Cam tell you that?"

"At a hockey game. He said you needed tutoring. And I think learning a whole new language and culture at eight-years-old is quite an accomplishment."

"It was. I still remember the first time we pulled into the driveway at Patrick's house. I thought we were moving into a mansion." He gives a grin. "Man, I thought I'd hit the lotto. Hell, I did."

That's when I realize what makes Alexsei different.

It's appreciation.

He appreciates everything he's been given. What he has. His family. Who he is.

I appreciate who he is, too.

"I think I've hit the lotto, too," I tell him, softly. "Because I met you."

His eyes darken, and his hand snakes across the table. "I think you're amazing, Luna. I feel so fucking lucky you're even giving me the time of day."

I'm about to tell him we should just go back to my place and have hot sex and cuddle until the sun comes up when the server picks this moment to insert himself into our space. "Was everything not to your liking?" he drawls, like he had assumed our palates weren't sophisticated enough to appreciate it, anyway.

"It was fantastic," Alexsei says. "We'll take the check."

The server turns on his heel without a word and goes to print our bill.

He tips the server way more than I would have.

"Want to go to a bar?" Alexsei says as we exit the restaurant. "I could use a beer to get rid of the taste of pretentious douchebag from my mouth."

I nod. We can go to my place afterwards. "I love craft beer. We could go to McGinty's."

"I love craft beer, too," he says, sounding as delighted as if we've both discovered we share everything that has ever existed in common.

"I've been meaning to ask you... do you and Cam share girls a lot?" It's yet again my not-so-subtle way of trying to root out what's going on with him and Cam. Mostly because I'm curious, partly because I half-expected Cam to be with him tonight.

"We have. We shared a girlfriend for about six months." Alexsei looks up from his phone where he's been ordering us a rideshare. "But I should tell you that Cam and I... well, he told me he's in love with me."

I nod, not at all surprised. "I figured as much."

He looks shocked. "How did you know that?"

"It took me a minute, but then it was so obvious I didn't know how I didn't see it right away. How do you feel about him?"

"I love him, too," he admits. "With Cam, it's just... I love him. I do. Maybe I always have. Does it bother you that I want to date you even if he and I are together? I wasn't trying to hide that from you. Back in the fall, when we all hooked up, I didn't know I was in love with Cam. It's new, with him and me."

Shaking my head, I reach out and lace my fingers through his again. Touching Alexsei is something I can't believe I've been denying myself for all these months. It feels... *right*. "It doesn't bother me at all. I think you can love more than one person at the same time, in totally different ways. Not that I'm saying that you're in love with me."

Though I realize I want him to be.

"It won't take much," he murmurs. "I'm falling hard for you, Luna."

My heart starts to race with excitement and understanding that I want more, much more with Alexsei. "I feel the same way, I really do. I can date you while you're in a relationship with Cam, if it's okay with both of you. I don't want him to be jealous."

"I don't think he is. He's attracted to you, too. But you should ask him. We should all be open and honest about all of this."

That makes my inner thighs heat. "He drives me insane, but I think another way to describe that is sexual chemistry. I would love to be with *both* of you again."

"Damn," Alexsei says, leaning over and giving me a hard, passionate kiss. "You're fucking perfect."

"I love what's happening between us." I bury my fingers in his hair and drag him back for another kiss. "All of us. Text Cam to meet us at the bar."

"On it." He shoots off a text.

We make out in the car, and I don't even care that the driver keeps glancing at us in the rearview mirror. I work my ass off. I'm entitled to a little fun. I'm entitled to happiness. I'm entitled to a relationship with a man who is willing to meet me where I need to be met.

I'm entitled to *relationships*. Plural.

In the back of my mind, I know I need to tell Alexsei that I'm seeing Owen, which I think he knows, but I want to make it clear. But it's impossible to talk when his tongue is teasing over mine.

Later. I'll tell him later before our clothes come off, I vow.

Only when we get to McGinty's—a Racketeers hangout—Owen is there.

CHAPTER 21

Alexsei

IF I HAD any question about how Luna's date with Coach went the other night, it's answered when we walked into McGinty's and she sees him.

She lights up.

Well, fuck.

The grin he gives her–and the frown he gives me–tells me that he really likes her, too. So...here we are. Me, the girl I'm falling for, and the other guy she's dating.

And the guy I'm in love with and sleeping with if not actually dating–can Cam and I be dating if we already live together?–is on his way down here to join us.

It's gonna be a fucking party.

Coach Phillips heads straight for us. I try my best to be cool. He's a good guy. He's my Coach.

But then Luna says, "Hi, Owen!" and he wraps her up in a big hug that's a lot friendlier than just 'I coach your brother' and I want to punch him.

This isn't good.

"You look gorgeous," he tells her, his voice husky as he lets her go and sweeps his gaze over her.

"Thank you," she says, smiling up at him.

Why does that annoy me? She does look gorgeous. Probably twenty other guys in the bar think so, too.

I sigh. I need to get okay with this or I'm going to piss Luna off. And she's being *very* cool about me and Cam. I can be cool about her dating Owen.

I think.

But their body language is telling me they've seen each other naked and, well… that doesn't make me feel so cool.

"Hey, Alexsei," he says, shifting his attention to me.

"Hey, Coach."

"We just came in for a drink. Didn't think about the team being here," Luna says.

I believe that she didn't choose McGinty's because she knew Owen would be here. And so what if she did? I texted Cam to join us. And *we're* taking her home later. I need to relax.

I'm getting what I want.

Luna.

For more than I even expected. She wants to *be* with me. I can be happy with that.

"Do you want to join us for a minute?" I ask Coach, thinking I'll be the bigger man here. I don't need to be jealous. Luna *just* told me that she feels like she could fall for me and that she wants to be with both Cam and me again tonight.

His gaze goes back to Luna, and she gives him a smile. He nods, "Yeah, sure."

We choose a round high top table along the wall, so Luna ends up sitting between us. We seem to instinctively leave the open fourth stool between us on the other side. Cam can sit there. Even though we all seem fine with this, there is a weird tension around the table as the waitress comes to take our order and we're left alone.

Then Owen puts his hand on Luna's leg, and she covers it with her hand.

He squeezes her thigh and gives her a look that's a mix of

affection and I-want-you and I do feel a little jab of jealousy, but I also...don't mind. Because it makes Luna look all glowy.

I don't know if that's a word, but that's how she looks. She looks happy and hot and like she really loves having his hand on her and his attention. There's a crackle of electricity between them and it makes a tingle go down my spine.

What the fuck is that?

It feels a lot like how I feel when Cam touches her. When he kissed her in the doorway of her apartment the night we went over there, I felt this tingle. It was stronger then, but I knew what it was. Desire.

I loved watching them together. I loved how he made her hot, how he made her respond, how he made her feel good.

It's different with Owen. Luna and Owen have a different connection, a different chemistry than Luna and Cam do, but watching them gives me a similar jolt.

Because she clearly likes what he does to her and how he makes her feel.

Okay. So I can actually work with this. I have to work with this. Because I'm not going anywhere.

I lean in and decide to broach the subject and get it out into the open.

"I take it your date the other night went well?"

Luna's gaze snaps to mine. "Uh..." She wets her lips.

I suddenly have the weird urge to see Owen kiss her. Her and Cam kissing was really hot. He kisses her differently than I do. I wonder how Owen kisses her.

I put my elbow on the table and turn to face her, moving one leg behind her stool, and leaning into her space. "I know you and Owen went out. Is that what you're surprised about?"

"I was going to tell you."

I tuck her hair behind her ear. I'm aware that Owens's hand is still on her leg. But he's not saying anything.

"Do you feel like you needed to tell me?"

"Yes. I feel like we're in a relationship. My dating someone else is probably something you should know."

I am thrilled that she's officially calling what we're doing a relationship. "I appreciate that. And I'll admit I'm a little jealous." My gaze flicks to Owen. He's just watching and listening. I look at Luna again. "But considering everything between Cam and me, I can't really say anything."

She nods. "We should still be open and honest with each other, like you said."

"What you said just earlier tonight about being able to love more than one person is true, though."

She smiles. "Yes."

I study her beautiful face. I'm still feeling conflicted, so I decide to roll with the open and honest thing. That's probably mature and shit. "I'll be honest then, in spite of me and Cam, I still feel jealous as hell thinking about you with Owen." I stubbornly refuse to look at him this time.

She takes a deep breath, then turns to look at Owen. "And how are you feeling?"

He lifts a brow. "Jealous as fuck. A little confused."

She squeezes his hand. "Those both make sense."

He looks from her to me. "So, you two are dating?"

"Actually, tonight is our first date," I tell him. "But we have been hooking up."

Luna gives a little groan.

"Hey, open and honest, right?"

She sighs and nods. "I've been seeing Alexsei, too," she says to Owen. "But you're not shocked by that."

He shakes his head. "No. Though I'll admit I was hoping the other night with me would make you want to be monogamous."

My heart kicks in my chest. If Owen wants that from her and they had a great time together, there's a chance I might have a challenge on my hands.

"I really don't want to have to choose between you," Luna tells him.

Thank God.

Just then, Cam strolls up to the table.

"Well, this is a cozy little group."

I'm so relieved to see him. Cam always knows how to handle any situation. Or at least he seems to. He never lets anything fluster him.

"Hey, man. You remember Luna," I say dryly. "And you know Coach Phillips. Her other boyfriend."

Cam's brows both rise as he looks from me to Luna to Coach.

"Okay, then," he says. "Nice to see you all."

"Owen," Luna says. "This is Cam. Alexsei 's best friend and roommate."

"And the other guy Luna's been sleeping with," Cam adds.

Luna sighs, Owen straightens on his stool, and I grin.

"And my boyfriend," I say.

Cam looks at me in shock, which is replaced a second later by heat.

We haven't talked about if we are going to tell anyone, and if we do come out as a couple, who we tell. But in that moment, I realize I want to claim him. I don't care who knows. I love him. And after everything, all the years that he waited around for me, it feels like I need to be the one to take this first public step.

We're just staring at each other, heat zinging between us, when Luna grasps my hand and reaches across the table to grab Cam's.

She squeezes both of us, smiling widely. "That was awesome. I'm really happy for you guys."

I grin at her and Cam gives her an I-don't-know-what-to-do-with-you look, but a smile tugs up at one corner of his mouth. I think he's not sure what to do with her, because he's surprised by the way she makes him feel.

Owen finally says, "What the hell is going on?"

Luna squeezes our hands again before turning to him. "It's not that hard to keep up with. Alexsei and Cam are in love. They're in a relationship."

"But you've been sleeping with both of them."

"Yeah. But together. They both knew about it. I mean we all did it at the same time."

Owen stares at her. "Together."

And then the feisty little blonde who we're all falling too hard and too fast for says, "Yes. Together. Though, Alexsei has actually been the one getting the most benefits. Cam has been very stingy with his cock and his mouth when it comes to me." She delivers that while looking directly at my best friend.

I choke on my drink of beer. Owen just sits with his mouth hanging open. Cam simply gives her a smirk.

"All you asked me for was a kiss, Pixie," he says.

"Oh, I have to ask for the rest?"

He leans in and pins her with a hot gaze. "No, you have to *beg*."

The temperature ratchets up around the table. And it isn't entirely sexual.

She leans in, too, with a grin. "Well, you might have noticed that I have two other big, handsome, happy-to-oblige-me men, so don't hold your breath waiting for that."

Cam grins at her. A full, wide, genuine grin.

Which makes me grin. I love these two people so damned much.

"So, Mr. Phillips," Cam says, looking at Owen.

But Luna breaks in. "Not Mr. Phillips. Owen, or —" she looks at Owen. "I call him sir."

Cam reaches over and takes her beer, lifts it to his lips for a drink, and sets it down, nodding. "Okay, Owen, are you joining us tonight, then?"

"Looks like I am," Owen says, but he gestures at the table in front of us.

"Oh, I don't mean here. Luna is coming home with us tonight."

Owen looks down at her. "Is that right?"

She seems a little hesitant, but she nods. "That's the plan. Alexsei and I went out and then we decided to go home and end the evening with Cam."

"Alexsei 's boyfriend," Owen says.

"And the guy I really like spending time with, too," Luna says, looking across the table at Cam.

"I don't know why you'd want to invite me then," Owen says to Cam. Tersely. Very tersely.

"Because it could be fun. Luna likes all of us, we all like her. And it actually can help with jealousy and questions about relationships."

"Really? To watch two other guys with my girlfriend?" Owen asks.

I feel Luna give a little jerk of surprise at his use of the word girlfriend, as if they haven't talked about how to define their relationship yet.

Cam nods. "I much preferred the nights when Alexsei and I fucked someone together to the nights when he was off with someone by himself. I was a lot less jealous those nights. I got to be a part of it, and actually appreciated the other person because of how they were making him feel."

"Seems like that could complicate a relationship." Owen seems angry. Or something. He's gripping his bottle of beer tightly.

But is also not getting up and stomping away.

So maybe it's not just anger. Or jealousy. Maybe there's some lust in there.

I know exactly how that feels.

It's exactly how I felt the nights with Cam and someone else.

I preferred the nights we were together to the nights he was off with other people alone, too, but sure there was a bit of jealousy mixed in.

Now that I know why, it makes complete sense.

"But we're living proof that it actually made us closer. We've shared the most intimate thing—our fantasies. We know exactly what makes the other person tick. We know every single thing the other person needs. And we care enough about each other to make sure that they have that."

Luna is watching him, her cheeks a little pink, but seemingly fascinated.

I decide to try an experiment. I lean in and put my hand on the back of her neck, stroking my thumb up and down the side of her throat. She gives a little shiver of pleasure.

Then I put my mouth just below her ear, and kiss the soft skin before saying, "Do you think it would be hot to have Owen join us?"

Her eyes drift shut, and she gives a little sigh before she says, "Yes."

I continue, "Does he fuck you differently than I do?"

She swallows hard, but nods. "It's all so good. But yes, different."

"I can't decide if I want him to come over because I want to see how he fucks you, or because I want him to see how well I can make you come apart."

This shiver of desire is more like a shudder.

I run my hand from the back of her neck down her spine to her ass. "You like that? The idea of two guys competing over who can treat this pussy the best?"

"God," she says, but it's more of a moan than an actual word.

I lift my head and look past her to Owen. I know he heard every word I just said.

I don't know him super well, but he was an athlete, he's a coach, there has to be a competitive streak in there somewhere.

But before I can issue any kind of challenge to him out loud, Luna says, "Owen made me come three times in a row. Twice before he came once. Before he even fucked me."

Her voice is soft enough that no one else in the bar can hear, but the three men she's sitting with definitely heard every word.

I sit back, realizing that I should feel a much stronger stab of jealousy. But I know what she's doing.

She's playing my own game.

Because I don't know Owen that well, but *I* for sure have a competitive streak.

I look from Owen to Cam — who is sitting back watching this whole thing with a knowing look on his face and a stupid smirk on his gorgeous mouth — then to Luna. I put a finger under her chin and turn her to face me.

I meet her gaze, and say simply, "Game. On."

CHAPTER 22

Cameron

I MAKE note of several things on our way from the bar to our apartment.

One, Alexsei never lets go of Luna's hand. Two, Owen never stops touching her, either. In the car—we all share an Uber because, of course, no one was going to get into a vehicle without Luna—the two hockey guys put her in between them in the back while I take the passenger seat. Owen keeps his hand on her thigh while Alexsei holds her hand.

On our way up to the apartment, Alexsei continues to hang onto her as if he's afraid of getting lost in a crowd, and Owen's hand rests on her lower back.

I bring up the rear, partly amused, partly exasperated.

This might be a terrible idea.

It also might be brilliant.

For her part, Luna seems content, slightly befuddled, and because she's kind of a brat, mildly amused as well.

She knows these two guys are trying to stake their claim on her and she's enjoying every fucking minute.

All of these observations have combined to help me figure out exactly how this is going to go.

And yes, I'm going to be in charge.

Owen definitely gives off an in-charge vibe. He's a coach. He's a dad. He's the oldest of us. But he's never done this group thing before. And he's also the third guy to come into Luna's life. Alexsei and I were here first. And we're not going anywhere.

Coach Phillips needs to figure that out. He needs to understand how a group like this works and he needs to quickly get over seeing two other men with his girl.

He's either going to be in or out, and the sooner he makes that decision, the better for all of us.

Alexsei unlocks our door and pushes it open, ushering Luna through it. Because he refuses to take his hand off of her, Owen steps through the doorway behind her, brushing past Alexsei.

Alexsei glowers at him.

Yeah, we need to establish some ground rules here quickly.

I let the door shut behind me and stop, hands in my pockets.

"Luna," I say, firmly.

She looks back at me.

"Come here."

The three of them are well into the living area.

She stops and turns to face me. The guys turn, too. Alexsei just watches me, but Owen has a definite *what the hell do you think you're doing* look on his face.

I focus on the tiny blonde who has done a fucking number on the three of us.

I take in her little smile and think, *yeah, tonight is definitely going to be payback.* We're going to make her forget she could ever be satisfied without all three of us.

She wets her lips. Then walks toward me, without saying a word.

She stops directly in front of me and then just waits for me to tell her what happens next.

I give her a little smile. Then I look up at the other men over her shoulder. Alexsei's arms are crossed, waiting. He doesn't look happy exactly, but he is not grinding his teeth and glaring at me the way Owen is.

I focus on Luna. I step closer, reach up and run my fingers through her hair, sweeping it to the side, then lean in and put my lips against her neck. I kiss her there, then drag my mouth to her ear. "Are you ready to make your men crazy?"

"Yes," she breathes softly.

"And you'll do as I say?"

"Yes."

"Good girl," I say gruffly, just for her. There will be plenty of praise coming up, I'm sure. But right now, I want her to know that I'm very pleased with her and that she's letting me lead this. And I love knowing that she trusts that I have big plans that will make her very happy.

I pull back, but keep our faces close. "Tonight is all about you," I tell her loud enough for the others to hear. "You're the whole reason we're here. The three of us would never be in the same room naked, hard, crazy with lust, vulnerable if it wasn't because of you."

I lift my eyes to look at the other men. "Everything is about Luna. She's chosen the three of us all for different reasons. And together we're all going to give her everything she needs and wants."

I run my hand from her face, over her shoulder, and down her arm. I settle my hand on her hip and squeeze. "On your knees, Pixie."

She kneels immediately, and when she looks up at me, I see the heat in her eyes. "Unbuckle me."

I hear a little growl from Owen. I glance. "Got a question, Coach?"

"I thought you said this is all about *her*," he says, his voice tight.

"It is."

"Having her suck you off is about her?"

I put my hand against her cheek and run my thumb over her jaw. "Oh yeah, this is for her."

"Bullshit," Owen says.

I focus on him again. What Owen is about to discover—something Alexsei is about to discover as well—is that one of the hottest things you can possibly witness is someone you care about, someone you want desperately, being absolutely worshiped and pleasured by someone *they* care about and want desperately.

I've been fortunate enough to see it before with Alexsei. It's always been about the women with him. But seeing him get that pleasure, even when it's not coming directly from me, is such a fucking turn-on. I love the guy, and seeing him get everything he possibly needs and wants, does things to me that nothing else can.

I know that Owen and Alexsei both care about Luna. I know they both want her, but they also care. And tonight they're going to see her brought to heights that they cannot give her by themselves.

This isn't for everyone but gazing down into the big blue eyes of the sweet little blonde in front of me, I know it is for her. Luna is exactly the kind of woman that needs three men like us. She has plenty of light and energy and heart for all of us, and watching her be worshiped by other men who want to give her the ultimate pleasure will be the hottest fucking thing any of us have experienced.

I can't wait for that to happen to Alexsei. This is going to be amazing for him. And that matters to me because of how *I* feel about *him*.

And yeah, okay, I really like Luna, too, and seeing this will be hot as fuck.

But Owen is about to experience something that he can't even imagine. And he'll be really fucking grateful in the end.

I just need to get him through these next few minutes.

For all our sakes.

"The door's right there," I tell him. "You're in or you're out. But this is happening. And if you leave, you're leaving alone. Luna's staying."

"She's not fucking staying if she doesn't want to."

Now I smile, and I look down at her. "Of course not. But I don't think you're going to be able to tear her away."

I do notice a brief flicker of worry in Luna's eyes. And that's how I know she cares about Owen. She doesn't want him to walk out. She worries if he does, things are over between the two of them.

But I run my thumb over her cheek again reassuringly. He's not going to be able to walk away from her for good. No way. The man is as addicted to her as Alexsei and I are. He's already been with her. He's tasted her. He's seen her come apart. There's no way he's ever going to really get over her. Sure, he might be angry tonight. Jealous. Resentful. Confused. But he'll get over it.

He might not like this, at least at first, but he's also way too protective of her to walk out of here and leave her with two other men.

"Unbuckle me," I repeat, looking at Luna.

She hesitates.

I grip her chin to keep her from looking over at Alexsei or Owen. "Just me and you for a minute here, Pixie."

She nods, then unbuckles my belt, opens my fly and takes my cock out. She gives a little moan when she finds how hard I am. Her fingernails are a deep navy blue, and they scrape along my flesh, teasingly. She strokes up and down and looks up at me and the look in her eyes, that sexy, knowing look, I swear, makes my legs wobble. She knows she's completely in control here. She loves seeing what she does to me. She loves knowing that she can drive me absolutely insane.

I thread my fingers through her hair. "She loves knowing that she's the siren and we are all just the fools who will do anything to be near her," I say.

She hums as she licks over my tip, and I swear. "*Fuck.*"

That was unintentional. Everything else I've said has been calculated, but now that she's touching me, licking me, I'm going to be as out of my mind as Alexsei and Owen are just watching.

"Suck on me," I command.

She does, and I lift my eyes and meet Owen's gaze. For two reasons. One, to gauge his reaction to me ordering his girlfriend around. Two, to show him that I have no trouble being naked and very intimate with Luna in front of him.

He's going to have to get used to it. And if he wants *his* dick sucked? He's going to have to be willing to do the same in front of me.

He looks like he really wants to punch me. But the bulge in the front of his pants says that he's not completely pissed off by this.

Plus, he's still here.

Stroking my fingers through Luna's hair, I say to him, "Luna isn't going to do anything she doesn't want to do. She knows how to stop it. We're all here for pleasure and fun. *Her* pleasure, and fun. She knows that. She loves being the center of our attention. And now she's got three of us. This is her fantasy." I looked down at her. "Even if she didn't realize it until just now."

She hums around my cock, and I grip her hair a little tighter. She looks up at me and I know that she knows she's making me crazy.

Brat.

I let her suck and lick for another few seconds before I pull her off.

"Stand up."

She does, so obedient and sweet that I shake my head when our eyes meet. She smirks. She's messing with me. She's being obedient because we both get off on it, because she's putting on a show for Owen, not because she actually thinks I'm in charge.

I like her so damn much.

I turn her to face the other men. "So we're going to treat Luna like our sexy little plaything. A pretty little slut who's here for three men to use and fuck and enjoy all night. But we all know that she's the one who's getting off, who's going to be coming so fucking hard she sees stars, and no one rests until *she* says so."

Alexsei sucks in a long, deep breath through his nose and then blows out. "Holy fuck."

Owen doesn't say anything. His hot gaze is locked on Luna. It looks for a moment as if he's battling with himself. Is he going to stay or leave? Then I realize that he's reading her face, her body language, thinking over what he knows about her, trying to figure out what she's feeling.

I lean in and put my mouth against her ear again, but say loud enough for him to hear, "Assure Owen that you're fine. That you want this. Tell him you want him to stay and help Alexsei and me fuck you hard and well, exactly the way you deserve. Because you're greedy and need *three* men to really satisfy you."

Her breath hitches, and she leans back into me. I splay my hand over her stomach, again making sure that Owen is absorbing the look of another man touching her.

She wets her lips and nods. "I want this, Owen. I want you to stay. Please."

"You really want this? All of us together? At once?"

She nods. "So much."

Then he glances at Alexsei. "You're seriously into this?"

Alexsei meets his gaze directly, and it hits me again that this is a player and his coach. There are all kinds of scenarios where this could get really messy. But at the moment, Alexsei just lifts his chin and says, "Yeah. I'm all in. No matter who else stays, as long as Luna is here, I'm here."

"So even if I stay?" Owen reiterates.

"Yeah."

"This could be really fucking complicated," Owen says.

Alexsei lifts a shoulder and looks at Luna. "She's worth it."

I feel her breath hitch again, but then Owen's gaze finds hers as well. And it seems that he finally makes his decision.

"I'm not going anywhere," he says.

I feel some of the tension leave Luna's body and I can sense her wanting to step forward.

I tighten my hold on her. "Oh, I'm not done here," I tell her, my voice husky against her ear. "We have a lot more to show, Coach."

She stops and relaxes into me again. "Whatever you say."

Yeah, right. Still, I'm going to take this moment.

I grip the hem of her sweater and strip it up over her head, tossing it behind me. Now she's only in her little bra, but I make quick work of that as well. She's got awesome tits and we all deserve to see this woman bare, not a single stitch of clothing between us and her.

I run my hands to the fly of her jeans, unbuttoning and then pushing the denim and the silk panties underneath to her ankles.

I hear the other two men give low groans. I squat behind her, helping her out of her shoes, and pulling her jeans and panties free. Then I skim my hands up her smooth legs to her hips, where I grip her, holding her on display for the two men in front of us.

"So it's going to be a long night. For all of us. Luna needs to lose her mind. Owen needs to get used to watching two other men with her. So we're going to start right here."

I'm not exactly a breast guy, but I do love the way Alexsei's eyes burn when I cup Luna's breasts and tweak her nipples. I also like the way she arches into my touch and moans.

Then I run my hand down to her pussy and circle her clit. Alexsei's breathing hard, clenching his fists at his sides. Owen actually takes a step forward. I slide a finger lower, through her very slick, hot folds. Then I slide it deep. She reaches to grasp my wrist, gasping my name.

"Seems our girl is really into everything so far, boys," I tell them, my finger sliding in and out.

"Fucking killing me," Alexsei says.

"Come here and help me."

He immediately moves towards us, and Owen adjusts his fly as he clears his throat.

"Feel free to get more comfortable," I tell him.

He tears his eyes away from Luna to glare at me.

"The only rule right now is Alexsei and I are getting her ready. But you do whatever you need to do. Undress, jerk off, whatever you need."

I'm not going to lie, I'm a little eager to see Coach Phillips in the buff. The guy's built. He's not a hockey player anymore, so he's not as ripped as Alexsei, but he's big and broad and I'm guessing he's hung well.

"I'm good," he says gruffly, pulling his hand away from his crotch.

"Okay. Just saying, can't really be shy anymore."

He glares at me, but then immediately returns his gaze to where Alexsei has dropped to his knees in front of Luna. I grasp her thigh and lift it, spreading her open for him.

He dives right in.

"Oh my God, Alexsei," she moans as he starts licking her pussy.

I continue to play with her nipples as he sucks and licks.

"Damn baby, you taste so fucking good. God, I need you so much," he says against her.

"Yes, like that!" she exclaims as he sucks harder.

"Keep going," I tell him. But against her ear I say, "Don't you come yet,"

She sucks in a breath. "*What*? That's so mean."

I pinch her nipple. "Don't get sassy. You're going to come so many times tonight you're going to lose count. But right now, we're going to drag this out. You need to be hot and dripping and begging before anybody starts fucking you. Because we are going to do our best to ruin this pussy for any other man."

She gives a choked laugh. "Like I could ever want or need another man."

And I like that a lot more than I should.

I don't need to be this woman's man. Or even one of them. This is fun. It's fucking hot. But we're not talking long-term here, are we?

But in the next second, I know that, of course, we are.

The other two men in the room are, at least. I know that well enough. And I'm planning on Alexsei for a very long time. Judging by the way Luna got under my skin so fast, in a way no woman ever has before, I need to get resigned to my fate.

These people are probably my future.

So tonight is really important.

And those are probably not the feelings and thoughts I should be having right now as my best friend/boyfriend eats out our new girlfriend while her other boyfriend watches for the first time.

CHAPTER 23

Owen

WHAT THE HELL is even happening?

I don't know how I ended up here, about to engage in group sex for the first time in my life.

Scratch that.

I know exactly how I ended up here.

Luna.

This girl has me wrapped around her tiny finger so tightly I am about to get naked in front of a dude I've never met and one of my players. Because I am, obviously, or I would have left already.

Such a bad idea. Such a fucking bad idea.

That's what this is.

Like, in the hall of fame of Bad Fucking Ideas, this is top five.

And about to engage in group sex might be understating it. Luna is currently getting her pussy lapped at by Alexsei while Cameron—who I can't decide if I admire or hate—is playing with her nipples. Group sex has already started.

And Luna? She's loving every second of it.

She's making the most incredible little mewling sounds of pleasure. Her head is thrown back and her eyes are half-closed.

It's already started without me and I hate that, but... I'm not hating how Luna is reacting.

Luna is moaning and gripping Alexsei's hair. He's groaning her name and saying things like, "Fuck, you're so delicious. I love your pussy."

Taking another step closer, wanting to be in her orbit, I marvel that I can feel this level of pain and lust simultaneously. My jaw is so tight I'm going to have a major migraine by tomorrow if I don't lighten up.

But I don't know how to do this. How to process what the fuck I'm looking at and feeling. How to jump in, or even if I truly want to.

"Come here, Coach," Cam says.

I glare at him. This fucking guy. I was prepared for the fact that Luna was into Alexsei. But I wasn't aware that Alexsei had a boyfriend who is a bossy prick.

Or the swirl of conflicting emotions it would create in me to see Luna obeying him without question. See her mouth wrapped around another man's cock... hell, yeah, that made me jealous.

I want her mouth on *my* cock.

Common sense tells me I should walk out of this apartment and go back to my regularly scheduled life.

There's no way I can do that.

"Get over here and help make our girl feel good," Cameron tells me, clearly reminding me what this is about–Luna and *all of us*.

It's all or none. I have to be all in or all out. I'm torn, agonizing over how she's writhing under the dual attention of Alexsei and Cam.

Luna decides to help. "Come here, Owen. Come touch me," she pleads softly.

Nothing will draw me forward faster than Luna reaching out for me. If she wants me, I have to be there for her.

"*Fuck.*" But I stomp forward. I don't mean to stomp, but I do, because fucking hell, this is confusing and *hot*.

Maybe that will change when I'm hemmed in on all sides by a couple of naked guys fucking my girl, but for right now, I have to admit, it's fascinating to see how aroused Luna is. Cam moves out of the way for me, and I slide in behind Luna, hands immediately cupping her breasts.

Luna sighs against me, her hips undulating, restlessly trying to get more from Alexsei. She loops one arm up around my neck, leaning into me fully, moaning louder as Alexsei slides a finger into her pussy.

"Yes," she begs. "More, Alexsei."

Part of my brain is insisting it should be my name on her lips, but another part is reminding me that Cam is right—this is about her. What she wants. What she *craves.*

Human beings have complex physical and emotional needs. It's arrogant as fuck to assume I could be all things for her at all times. If they can give her greater pleasure, I need to be man enough to let them.

If one of the hockey moms I had hooked up with over the years had asked to bring along a female friend, I have no doubt I would have jumped at the chance. Because sex is fun. It wasn't something I would have sought out, but I would have been open to it. The more the fucking merrier, right?

Alexsei pulls back and Luna moans in disappointment. "Don't stop."

He says something in Ukrainian. I've only heard him speak in his native language a few times, so he's either really into it or they have a private joke. Or both.

"What did you just say?"

"This is the best I've ever tasted. Five star dining."

She laughs softly.

Then he buries his face in her hot pink folds again.

She moans.

Cam sucks in his breath. He's next to Luna, and he taps the inside of her foot with his. "Spread your legs further."

Obediently, she shifts outward, while Cam slides his palm along the inside of her thigh and tugs her soft fold open so Alexsei can have better access. It gives both me and Cam a better view of the strong thrusts of Alexsei's tongue inside her glistening channel.

I'm staring, hard, mouth hot with desire. "You like that, don't you, sweet girl?" I murmur in her ear.

"Yes, sir," she breathes, rubbing her ass back against my desperately-wants-in-the-game-hard-as-fucking-steel dick.

"Quit wiggling," Alexsei reprimands, pulling back to take his palm and give her pussy a little slap.

Luna gasps, shuddering against me. I pinch her nipples, and she presses her face into my neck.

I can see how wet her pussy is. Alexsei's fingers are shining with moisture as he lifts them to his mouth and draws them between his lips and sucks all her essence off. "Mmm."

Her lips seek mine and I kiss her, squeezing her breasts harder. Her fingers on the back of my neck are trembling and I feel a wave of tenderness along with the lust. I'll give this woman anything she wants. And fucking love doing it.

"What do you need, baby?" I ask her.

"She needs us to decide," Cam says firmly. "Luna spends every day being a strong, independent woman and here, with us, she needs us to just let her enjoy being worshipped."

Alexsei is casually toying with her clit and feathering kisses along her inner thigh. "That's exactly right," he confirms.

"Is that what you need?" I ask her, wanting verbal confirmation.

She nods, her lids heavy as she meets my gaze. "I don't want to think. Just *feel*."

"You cool with that, Coach?" Alexsei asks me.

My big hands cover the entirety of Luna's breasts, her nipples hard pebbles beneath my palms. She's subtly rubbing against me everywhere she can, and I'm not sure she's even aware of it. I'm grasping all of this now.

Luna practically raised herself. She's been barreling down this side of college with fierce determination to be a successful businesswoman and creative, to not be beholden to her father and to prove she can do this on her own.

She's fierce and self-reliant.

And so when it comes to sex, just like it was one-on-one with me, she needs to relinquish control.

I nod.

"Let's sweep this amazing and fucking irresistible woman off of her feet, boys." I tip her chin and give her a hard kiss. "Alexsei, carry her to the bedroom."

Luna sags against me and I see relief and desire in her blue eyes. She wants me here willingly, not reluctantly.

"Great idea, Coach." He slips a hand around the back of her thighs, making contact with my thigh, too, and it doesn't bother me. I've played hockey my whole life. Male contact doesn't unnerve me.

Alexsei hauls her up in the air and I get an incredible view of her tight ass passing right in front of me as he puts her over his shoulder. Luna gives a shriek of protest, but also delight. His arm is between her legs as he settles her against his back and it only takes a second because her hips are rocking her little bare pussy against all that muscle, her hair cascading forward over her face.

Cam shakes his head at the maneuver, but then he's ripping his shirt off over his head. I use his distraction as a chance to indulge my own need to touch her. I trail my palm over her tight ass cheek and up her spine. I bury my fingers in her hair as I come around Alexsei's back before yanking her hair, hard, wanting her to understand what the fuck she's done to me.

She gasps and runs the tip of her tongue along her bottom lip.

"I'm eating you next," I tell her. "And you're going to come so fucking hard on my tongue, baby."

She nods eagerly. "Yes, sir."

I have to adjust myself in my pants at her words even as Alexsei groans.

"Fuck, Coach. You just made her even wetter. She's fucking *dripping* on my arm."

He doesn't sound jealous of that. He sounds excited.

I'm starting to understand how that's possible as he carries her down the hallway with little effort, Cam leading the way, me taking in the contours of Luna's sexy little body draped over Alexsei's muscular frame. My own shirt comes off and I'm barely aware I'm doing it. I just know that when I'm nudged up in between this girl's pretty thighs, I need my skin on hers.

"We need to tie her down," Cam says firmly, pulling restraints out from under the mattress. "Or she's going to fucking levitate."

I come to a full stop in the doorway, kicked in the gut with lust at the thought of Luna pinned to the mattress, being touched and fucked *everywhere*. I have to drag in a deep breath.

She's nodding eagerly even as Alexsei deposits her on the bed. "Yes, Cam. Tie me up."

The way she wants this so desperately is making me come apart.

"Alexsei, you get behind her and hold her hands while Coach goes down on her. I'm going to secure her feet."

I watch in fascination as Luna spreads her legs without hesitation and lets Cam slip cuffs around them. She is compliant, giving an excited gasp when he jerks the restraints tight.

"That's it," he tells her. "No escaping for you." He glances over at me. "Her safe word is macaron."

I almost laugh at that, but I'm too fucking turned on to do anything but nod.

Because she's now secured to the bed frame, open wide for us to take turns plundering her body. Alexsei is behind her, cradling her upper body in his lap, holding her arms firmly as I shift in closer at the foot of the bed, studying her from head to toe as I shove my jeans down to the floor.

She preens beneath my gaze, arching her back to show off her tits and rocking her hips up as if to make sure I really admire her. "You are fucking gorgeous," I tell her. "Look at you, showing off that pretty pussy for us. I appreciate the view so much."

Her cheeks are pink, her eyes already glassy.

And we've barely started on her.

I can't wait to see what heights we can take her to.

"Do you really like it?" she asks.

I pull my thick, throbbing dick out of my pants and show her. "See what you do to me?"

Luna licks her lips. "God, you're so hard."

"Damn right I am." I stroke myself a couple of times, hard pumps to try to contain my need to just shove inside her slick body.

Cam gets on his knees next to her and spreads her folds apart. She gasps. He plunges two fingers into her without hesitation and strokes in and out for several seconds before pulling out and lifting his hand to Alexsei's mouth.

"Taste our girl, babe."

Alexsei sucks his fingers, drawing them in deep with a soft moan. Luna is whimpering and Cam's cock is pressing forward against the open fly of his jeans, straining against his briefs.

The sexual vibe between them is palpable.

Cam yanks his fingers back quickly, as if he remembers Luna is the star here.

"Get in there," he tells me, harshly.

I want to bristle and tell him to fuck right off, but I don't.

Because I want to taste Luna so bad my shoulders are tense, and my hands are shaking. Besides, she lifts her hands in a plea for me.

"Owen, I need you."

Alexsei is massaging her tits as Cam leans in and takes her mouth, interrupting my view of her pleading blue eyes. That has me down on the bed between her knees and reaching up to brush a thumb over the swollen bud of her clit. Her thighs tense but if she moans, Cam captures it with his mouth.

I can smell Luna's tangy scent and see that Alexsei was right. She's dripping wet. "I can't believe how wet you are," I muse, fascinated by how confident she is, how sexual. How damn delightfully sexy.

"Owen," she breathes.

I glance up to see she's ripped her mouth away from Cam, who doesn't miss a beat. He's now kissing Alexsei.

"*Please*," Luna begs, before Cam breaks off the kiss with Alexsei and tips her chin back to face him.

I have to give the guy credit. He has smooth choreography.

He's got all three of them panting and rubbing on each other.

Then there's me. Just staring at Luna like I've never seen a pussy before.

I may not know a damn thing about having a foursome, but this? This I know. I've proved it to her before. I'm competitive enough that I'm going to be the first one to make her come. Plus, I can already taste her on my tongue. I know how much she loves this.

Using my thumbs, I massage up and down her soft fold, blowing gently on her clit. She tries to move her legs, but the restraints and the boys hold her still. Which is hot. Really fucking hot.

I can hear them murmuring to her, but not specifically what they're saying as I drag my tongue up into her pussy, closing my eyes so I can fully experience her taste. Damn, she's so sweet and perfect. I take my time, sucking one fold, then the other, easing my tongue over her clit, before stroking deep inside her over and over. Her thighs are trembling under my grip and I'm gripped by a cry of pleasure that flies out of her mouth before being cut off.

Eyeing her over the flat plane of her stomach, I see Alexsei's hands splayed out, his thumbs brushing right above her pubic bone, and Cam's hands on her nipples, pinching them between his thumb and forefinger. So much of her bare flesh is covered with hard male hands, mine included, that Cam's words ring in my ears.

We're going to treat Luna like our sexy little plaything. A pretty little slut who's here for three men to use and fuck and enjoy all night.

When he spoke them, it both turned me on and unnerved me.

I wasn't sure if I should be offended on her behalf or if I was on board.

But now seeing hands all over her, stroking her, teasing her, dominating her, I know where I stand. Because she *loves* it. She's whimpering and bucking, thrusting her hips up to take more of my tongue, turning her head from side to side, seeking a tongue in her mouth as well.

Alexsei obliges her and a hot rush of moisture greets my mouth as her arousal kicks up higher and higher. I slip a finger into all that wet heat as I shift my tongue to her clit to toy with it. I suck gently before returning my tongue to fill her alongside my finger. It only takes a second before she's coming hard on my tongue, my name ripping from her lips.

"Owen!"

Yes.

That's what I want.

My name, absolutely.

But even more?

Her pleasure. Her wild, unrestrained pleasure.

If one of these other guy's names gets called out because they made her come?

I'm actually fucking cool with that.

Because Luna is our focus.

"That's it," I say as I pull back, wiping my bottom lip. "Cam was right. You are a pretty little slut."

I shuck my jeans and boxer briefs off, well aware I'm the first guy in the room totally naked. But I need to be. My dick is so hard it hurts.

Luna is breathing hard, her head buried in Alexsei's neck.

But Cam's eyes rake over my body as I kick my clothes across the floor. They darken, as if he likes what he sees, and I'm not weirded out. Hell, I'll take it as flattery. I stroke myself again, knowing there is only one way to ease this ache, and that's Luna, but needing the distraction.

I strongly sense Cam isn't going to think it's my turn.

He eases back and reaches into his nightstand. He pulls out three condoms and tosses me one. "Suit up, Coach. But I'm going first."

He expects me to challenge him. I can see it on his face as he stands up to remove his own pants and briefs.

The instinct to tell him we should let Luna decide is strong, but I can see by the way she's breathing, her chest rising rapidly up and down, her hand reaching behind her to stroke Alexsei's dick, that Cam is right. She doesn't want to make decisions. She moistens her lips and looks at me with pleading eyes.

"It's only fair to take turns," I tell him. "Why don't you go down on Luna?"

But he shakes his head. "Not my thing."

"Cam!" Luna protests. "I want you to lick my pussy."

But he just gives her a slow smile and pushes his glasses up. "No, you don't. I'll leave that to Alexsei and Coach." But he does casually reach his hand between Luna's legs and strokes her as he looks at Alexsei. "I did promise Alexsei I'd fuck you and not him. That was his personal request."

Alexsei makes a sound in the back of his throat.

"Is that true?" Luna asks Alexsei, rolling her hips to encourage Cam's touch.

I'm toying with the condom packet and I toss it on the nightstand. Alexsei's hand has appeared out of nowhere and he's giving Cam a hand job. I feel out of my element again, so I tell Alexsei, "Move. I'm holding Luna for this."

One, because I want to touch her. Two, because I get the sense he's going to want to see Cam disappearing into her pussy.

We change positions and I'm behind her shoulders, on my knees, encouraging her to lie down, her head in my lap. The silken strands of hair tickle my balls and my mouth is hot, thick with desire. Cam moves in between her legs. He releases her ankles from the restraints, which is disappointing, but then I realize he has to or he'll be just about on top of me. I don't know about him, but I'm not ready for that. I focus solely on Luna's face, running my hands over her lips, her nose, her jaw.

With her legs free, Cam hitches them way up on either side of his shoulders. He's sheathed in a condom and is nudging the tip of his dick between her legs. "This is what you want, right?" he asks her. "Me to fuck you?"

"Yes, I want that so much," she breathes.

I ease my finger between her lips, and she sucks on it.

Cam surges into her with one powerful thrust, and she bites down on my finger with a cry. My dick surges beneath her head. I know what Cam is feeling right now as he pauses on a moan. How he's holding, savoring the tight clamp of her cunt on his dick.

I should be jealous.

Instead, I'm fascinated by how exciting it can be to watch Luna get off on another man's dick, but also how it can heighten my own anticipation.

"Luna," Cam spits out. "This fucking *pussy.*"

"You like?" she asks around my finger, her breath tickling my flesh.

"I *love.* Only pussy I've ever wanted to own with my cock."

Then he settles into fucking her and I watch him so I can watch his rhythm with my finger, pushing between her swollen lips. She licks and sucks on my finger, her hands flying up to grip Cam's forearms. Alexsei is standing next to the bed, naked now too, squeezing the base of his dick as he watches with rapt attention Cam shoving into Luna.

I shock myself by telling him in a gruff voice, "Get over here. Luna needs something better to suck."

She does. She's sucking hard on my finger and she needs more. I turn her head toward him and ease my finger out of her. Alexsei doesn't hesitate. He presses between her damp lips with his swollen head and lets out a curse.

"That's it," I tell her. Or him. Or me. Fuck if I know at this point.

"Don't fucking come," Cam orders Alexsei, his hips pistoning as he furiously fucks Luna. "We're all taking a turn in this pussy. This pussy needs three men fucking it."

Luna is being rocked back into me, and I hold her shoulders down. "You're not going anywhere, little girl. We've got you."

She nods, even as she desperately sucks Alexsei's dick, like she needs her mouth wrapped around him to stay grounded. There are goosebumps running up her arms and her eyes are closed as she gets pounded.

I'm in fucking awe of how sexy she is.

It's obvious when an orgasm sweeps over her. She tenses, briefly, then gives a choked cry from around Alexsei's dick, her body bucking up and down on the bed. I press her harder to the mattress, wanting her to feel every ripple of that cascading wave of pleasure.

Cam keeps going and going, his head thrown back. He's lost in the magic of Luna, and I get it.

I'm lost, too.

For good.

I'm never coming back from this.

I have never met a woman as fully in her own body as Luna is, and it's beautiful. Thrilling. Incredible.

My balls are tight, my dick hard on her back.

Alexsei pulls out of her mouth quickly. "Need to stop," he grunts. "It's too good, baby."

She falls back with a moan, lifting her hips higher. "Come inside me, Cam. It's so good, so good."

She almost sounds drunk, her words thick.

But then Alexsei reaches in between her body and Cam's and flicks over her clit. She screams. Literally screams. Then she's coming again, her body shuddering from head to toe.

"My God..." Cam groans. "You're soaking me, Luna. You perfect little slut, you're fucking killing me."

Then he pauses briefly, teeth grinding, as he finally releases.

She loves it. She spirals again, her legs tensing on either side of him.

When Cam shifts out of her, her hands fling out, reaching for him, trying to bring him back inside of her.

But he strokes her thigh gently and eases her legs down. He looks rattled as he rips the condom off. I understand exactly how he feels. He tilts his head toward Luna as he orders Alexsei, "Go. *Now*."

I ease her head down onto the bed and shift to the edge, as Alexsei takes Cam's spot and strokes his cock over her clit. Luna whimpers. Cam squeezes Alexsei's ass and looks around him down at Luna.

"Look at that throbbing, begging pussy," he breathes. "*Luna*."

Luna has gone slack, her eyes closed. She keeps lifting her hips lightly, but she looks spent. "You want more?" I ask her, taking her chin and turning her head toward me.

She nods quickly. "Yes."

"Then you have to beg for it. Alexsei doesn't know how much you want him, gorgeous. Tell him you need him."

I don't even know where the fuck those words come from, but it feels right. It feels necessary. She wants more. She *needs* more. Alexsei continues to tease at her clit and her opening with his dick, his jaw tense, his concentration fierce.

She nods again, eyes locked on mine. "Yes, sir."

"Then beg."

"Please, Alexsei," Luna whispers. "Please fuck me. So hard. I want you inside me."

"Now suck my cock," I tell her. I turn to Cameron. "You tell her to suck my cock, too, since she listens to you so well."

"You heard the man," Cam said, a little looser now, a little more relaxed since he's already exploded inside her. "Suck him." He cracks the curve of her ass right as Alexsei crams his cock into her.

Luna gives a shout before turning to me and opening her

mouth eagerly, her hands easing down my length, squeezing and pulling me toward her.

After that it's a blur, just her wet mouth sucking me in, her fingers tickling at my balls, her tits bouncing from the onslaught of Alexsei pumping into her. Cam has shifted around back onto the bed on her opposite side and he pulls the same move as Alexsei, rolling her clit between his fingers, hand wedged between the slap of their bodies colliding.

I feel like I can't breathe with the effort it's taking to hold back, to resist the urge to spill my whole load into Luna's open mouth, especially when she comes again.

"Holy fuck, Luna," I tell her. "Look at you. Coming like a fucking champ."

"She's so wet," Alexsei moans. "Baby, I'm going to come."

She pulls off of me to encourage him the way she did Cam. "*Yes.* Please. Come inside me."

Everything seems to speed up. Alexsei thrusts faster. Luna pants with each push of him inside her. I fist my dick and pump up and down. Cam does the same, coaxing his dick back to full erection.

"Get ready," he tells me. "No down time for her. She wants dick, she's getting dick."

I nod, not needing any encouragement. I want my turn.

It's a blur of anticipation when Alexsei explodes and yanks himself out hard, stumbling backward like he's drunk on Luna.

"Fuck, fuck, fuck," he says. "Wreck her, Coach. Just destroy her."

Luna is almost sobbing now, reaching for me. I've never seen anything like it, or her. She's a goddess, legs spread wide.

I don't even think. I just sink into her heat, wanting to give her everything I've got. "So tight, baby," I manage to say, before I lose myself in her.

She's clamping onto me, milking me with every thrust, and I lose myself in the feel of her. I'm vaguely aware of hands on her, of her own fingers reaching out to stroke up and down Cam's hard shaft, her dark fingernails in striking contrast to his flesh.

Never in a million fucking years did I think that the sight of the woman I love scratching her nails down some other guy's dick would get me off, but it does.

And oh, yeah, I love her.

She's *unreal.*

Pure perfection.

I'm drowning in her sweetness, her body's tug on mine.

Her eyes are lit with unshed tears.

Cam tangles his fingers in her hair. "Tell me how Coach makes you feel."

"Alive," she breathes. "Loved. Fucked so good."

I'm buried in her, seeking that special spot I know drives her wild. I know when I've hit it, because she arches into another orgasm, her eyes rolling back into her head.

I'm wound too tight. That's all I need to go balls deep and pour myself into her.

"*Luna.*"

I collapse onto her and we all pant, shattered.

At least I am anyway.

Totally one hundred percent fucking shattered.

Alexsei told me to destroy her, but I think she's just destroyed me.

CHAPTER 24

Cameron

I WAKE UP SLOWLY, enjoying the feeling of contentment. I know exactly where I am and who I'm with.

There is a dainty foot resting against my calf and I don't have an instinct to pull away. Which is weird. But I acknowledge it for what it is—I like Luna McNeill.

Normally I don't like people touching me while I sleep, but Luna has been the exception to several rules and I'm not at all surprised that this is one of them.

I slowly open my eyes and my gaze traces its way from her foot—seriously, this woman is tiny all over—up the pretty curve of her calf, over her knee, and along the expanse of her bare thigh. The sheet is draped over her hip, hiding everything else. And though 'everything else' isn't typically a focus of my attention, I find myself smiling and wondering what she would do if I slid my hand up her thigh to her ass and started to warm her up for Alexsei.

I swear, she's been a surprise since minute one.

But damn, last night was good. Not just the sex, though, of course, that was amazing, but just the way we all came together.

It was awesome. I want to do it again.

I think Alexsei and I have finally found our third.

I frown at that thought. It wasn't just the three of us, though.

I lift my head and look across the mattress. Instinctively, I know that there are only three of us in the bed, even before my mind actually registers it.

Owen is not here with us.

I'm not surprised. Disappointed, but not surprised.

It's not that I'm disappointed that another man didn't spend the night in my bed. I'm disappointed that he bailed, though. Because that's going to hurt Luna. It might even hurt Alexsei a little. I know my friend thinks that we've worked everything out. That we've got a happily ever after coming at us.

So the fact that Owen snuck out in the night is a middle finger to all of us.

I really thought he'd turned a corner. Sure, the whole thing was a big surprise to him and it took him a little while to warm up.

But when he got warm, he got hot.

He was there with us every second after he walked into the bedroom. I really thought he was in for the long haul.

My frown deepens. The long haul. What the fuck do I mean by that? Last night the idea of these three people being my future had flitted through my head. I hadn't had time to really dwell on it, but that's the problem with waking up before everybody else the morning after. Lots of time to think.

I throw back the covers and ease off of my side of the mattress. I'm awake now, for sure. Might as well have some coffee with these deep thoughts. Because not only do I need to figure out what Luna, Alexsei, and I are going to do going forward — and that actually feels like a pretty easy answer, to be honest — I now have to figure out what to do about Owen.

Because it's clear that Luna is not Owen's problem.

I walk past the couch toward the kitchen, then do a double-take.

I look at my couch and blink.

Owen is sprawled across the cushions, snoring softly.

Okay.

So he didn't sneak out in the middle of the night. He didn't bail. Not entirely anyway. But he's not into sharing a bed with two other guys.

Well, I get that. I guess.

Maybe he just needed space.

I go into the kitchen, trying to decide how to handle this. I go for opening and closing the cupboards and drawers loudly.

Sure enough, five minutes later, Owen strolls into the kitchen. He takes a seat at the breakfast bar that divides the living area from the kitchen.

I glance over and see that he's pulled his jeans and shirt back on. But he's barefoot. His hair is mussed as if he's just run his hand through it a few times. He still looks a little sleepy, and very wary.

"Morning," I greet.

"Morning."

"How'd you sleep?" I turn and lean back against the counter, bracing my hands on the edge as the coffee percolates.

"Not great," he admits.

"Is that because of the couch or because you were tossing and turning over how you felt about having a foursome?"

He sighs. I'm not sure if it's in resignation because he knew we were going to broach the topic immediately or if it's annoyance because he'd hoped we wouldn't.

I remind myself that he doesn't know me very well.

But he needs to.

"The second," he says.

"And was that just the general angst about liking it, or was it because two other guys were fucking your woman?"

He nods. "Both. Probably more the second."

I appreciate his honesty. "She's our woman, too," I say simply. "And that's what you're going to have to come to terms with."

He narrows his eyes. "I guess I thought maybe there was some discussion to be had there."

"Discussion between you and me? Or discussion between you and Luna?"

"Me and Luna," he says, meeting my gaze directly.

I appreciate that. Obviously, this is all about Luna and her choices. But I do feel like there are some things Owen needs to understand from my point of view.

"Coffee?" I ask him.

"Yeah. I'm gonna need it."

I pour him a cup and cross to set it in front of him. Then I pour myself one. "Cream or sugar?"

He shakes his head. "Black."

I lift my own cup for a sip and give him a minute to figure out what he wants to say.

Finally, he takes a breath. "There's something you should know if we're going to discuss what happened last night," Owen says.

"I thought you were going to talk to Luna," I say.

"I am. But I think you and Alexsei probably need to know what I'm going to say to her."

I shrug. "Okay."

"I'm in love with her," he says. "And I want something serious. Long-term. I'm ready to tell her that."

I take another sip and swallow. "Okay. How do you think that affects us?" I ask. It does. Obviously. But I'm not sure it affects us the way he thinks it does.

"You guys are great. And obviously she likes you a lot. Last night was pretty hot. And I'm very glad she had a good time. But, I want to pursue something serious with her." He pauses. "Just her and me."

Yeah, that was pretty much what I thought he was going to say. "And what are you gonna do when she says no?" I ask.

His jaw tightens. "I don't know that she will say no. We have a connection. I think she might be ready to be more serious than she realizes."

I actually agree with him on that. Luna's been so focused on her business that she's told herself she doesn't have room or time for anything else. But we're proving her wrong. We're showing her she can have it all. And I think she's starting to not only believe that but want it.

But instead of that, I say, "But what if she does say no?"

"Then I'm okay with her dating you guys until she's ready to be serious."

I'm surprised to feel my jaw tighten. My shoulders, too. I like Luna. And I realize what I'm feeling is more than just the potential loss of the hot sex or even protective of Alexsei losing the woman he's falling for.

I don't want to lose her. I want her in our lives. She's the perfect fit for us.

And I'm feeling protective of her. She needs us. She needs more than Owen can give her. I'm not saying he shouldn't be a part of this. I think he should. But we should be…a *we*.

I'm worried Owen is going to make her make a choice that she shouldn't have to make.

"Well, there's something that you should probably know then, too," I tell him, setting my coffee down and crossing my arms.

He straightens. "Okay."

"Luna is the girl that Alexsei and I have been looking for."

He frowns. "What does that mean?"

"Alexsei and I are in love with one another. We will be together long term. But Alexsei needs a woman to be fully fulfilled, relationship-wise, sexually. And because I love him, I need him to be fully fulfilled. We've been looking for a woman to fill that role in our relationship for a long time. We've actually been with a few women in the time we've been together. But we've never found the right one.

"Until Luna. Not only can she fully accept Alexsei and I the way we are together and understand and support our relationship, but I can have a relationship with her, too.

"In the past, the woman has always been…extra for me. She's had a relationship with Alexsei, but not me. So it's always felt empty. For her and for me both, though I didn't really realize it. With Luna it's not like that. She and I actually have a dynamic together. One that we both need and like." I shrug, feeling a warmth spread in my chest as I think about the blond pixie that's turned everything upside down.

Or maybe she's turned it right-side up.

"She's our unicorn," I tell Owen. "The one that fits with us and actually needs our threesome, too. So that means we're not letting her go."

Owen just stares at me for several ticks. Then he blows out a breath and shakes his head. "I don't totally get that. But I'm trying to."

I nod. "I know. Some straight guys have a hard time with sexual fluidity."

He chuckles. "Is that what this is?"

"And some jealousy, and possessiveness."

"So we have to make her choose?"

"The exact opposite of that, actually," I tell him.

"You said she needs your threesome."

"The choice is *yours*, Owen. She's already made hers."

He looks very unhappy, but thoughtful. I think he's actually letting these words roll around in his mind.

I hear footsteps coming to the hall and I know they're not Alexsei's. I've lived with the guy long enough to know what it sounds like when he's walking around.

"She's coming," I say softly. "Do not ruin this morning after for her."

I realize with him sitting out here having coffee with me, Luna doesn't even need to know that Owen got out of bed and slept on the couch.

He gives me a short nod and I realize that we're on the same page about protecting her.

At least that's a start.

"Good morning," Luna says brightly as she steps into the room.

She gives us both big smiles, but her cheeks are a little pink as if she's feeling a bit shy this morning.

So I do the only thing I can.

I cross the room to her, pull her into my body, cupping her ass in both hands, and kiss her.

I know it totally shocks her because we don't kiss. At least we didn't use to.

But as she melts into me, and lets me sweep her mouth with my tongue, I think that there might be a lot of things changing this morning in this kitchen.

I let her go and say, "Remember, I like a lot of chocolate chips in my pancakes."

She grins up at me. "Okay, but for the record, I was already planning on making pancakes."

I tuck a strand of hair behind her ear, and just say, "Good girl."

She snorts and says, "I'll try really hard not to sneeze in yours."

I grin. "No, I won't spank you this early in the morning. I haven't had enough coffee yet. So stop being naughty."

I don't miss the tiny flare of heat in her eyes, but there's a part of me that thinks it comes from our banter even more than the mention of spanking. I really like this girl.

I pinch her ass, then I turn her and nudge her toward Owen, who opens his arms and pulls her into a hug.

Looking at them together, I find myself hoping that this guy can pull his shit together.

Because he makes her happy, and, dammit, I'm going to have to be pissed at him if he doesn't stick around.

Because, as surprised as I am that it happened, Luna's happiness really fucking matters to me.

CHAPTER 25

Owen

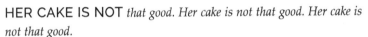

HER CAKE IS NOT *that good. Her cake is not that good. Her cake is not that good.*

I'm lying to myself, of course. Luna McNeill's cake is absolutely that good. Both the literal cake she makes and her... metaphorical cake.

Her cake is not worth it.

Maybe I should try that mantra.

But that's also a lie.

I think that Luna McNeill is worth every single bit of awkwardness I'm feeling during the first time in the locker room with Alexsei Ryan after we fucked Luna together two nights ago.

I'm pretty sure.

Cam called her a unicorn.

Absolutely accurate. And she's not just their unicorn. She's mine, too.

He said that maybe I haven't been with as many women as I need to in order to understand that she's special.

I maybe haven't been with as many as he and Alexsei have, and maybe I haven't been looking for something specific the way they have, but it would take a blind, very stupid man not to understand that Luna is special.

I knew it that first moment I spoke to her in her mother's kitchen.

And I shouldn't be surprised that the other two don't want to let her go.

That night with the four of us was explosive. But it was more than incredibly hot and sexy. There was something else there. And even though it was my first group experience, even in the midst of it, I sensed that there was something more.

It wasn't just about the sex.

Even watching her with the other guys, I realized there was a connection, something that went deeper than just the sex or even the chemistry.

There were real feelings there, and not just from the guys.

Luna is falling for them, too. If she's not *already* in love. That was why it could be as incredible as it was.

And there's been something else haunting me ever since my "talk" with Cam the next morning — he said she's already made her choice. I was assuming he meant that the four of us together would be the ultimate relationship for her. Because we all bring her something different.

But maybe he meant she would choose them over me.

It feels like a punch right in the chest.

I recognize the truth of all of it. That I have to be cool with all four of us or nothing at all.

But I'm still hesitating.

This is all strange. Brand-new. Something I never imagined myself being a part of.

So I guess I'm wondering—do I love her?

At least, do I love her the way I need to love to let her have this? To be a part of something like this so that she can have what she wants and needs?

That's what I've been trying to figure out.

And now I am in the Racketeers locker room, preparing for practice, and feeling like Alexsei Ryan is everywhere I turn.

He's a big dude, but the locker room is filled with big dudes.

Hell, I'm a big dude. Why does it feel like Alexsei is taking up more than his fair share of the space? Why does it feel like he is in front of me every time I turn around? Why can I hear his voice above everyone else's?

"Hey coach, have a good day off?" he asks, slapping me on the back as he walks past.

He's half-naked. He's getting dressed for practice but is being fucking slow as hell about it.

Again, the locker room is full of half-naked guys, but Alexsei is the only one I can focus on.

Which sounds weird.

Or it would have before the other night.

Now I know exactly why his nakedness is such a focus for me.

Because when the naked guy in the room is railing your girlfriend, and she's coming apart as if she's never been fucked that good before…yeah, some things make an impression.

I grit my teeth. "Fine," I say shortly.

He grins and fucking winks at me.

I want to shove him back. He's standing way too fucking close.

The thing is, if I shoved Alexsei Ryan, the entire team would turn and stare.

Everyone loves him. He's a fucking lovable guy. He's an eternal optimist, always nice and fun to be around, friendly, constantly smiling, seemingly just enjoying life.

Okay, maybe not *constantly* smiling. When he's on the ice, he's serious as fuck. And if you're playing on the other side of the puck, you don't think he's such a nice guy.

He plays to win, and he's really fucking good.

I'm pretty sure most of the other teams in the league hate him, as a matter of fact. Maybe not as much as they hate Crew McNeill, because Crew's mouthy as shit. Alexsei mostly lets his play speak for itself.

But he's a good guy. He's a fucking ray of sunshine.

I know exactly why Luna likes him. Hell, why she's *falling in love* with him. He's a perfect balance for her. She's a little stress ball. She's driven, sassy, feels like she has to do it all by herself.

Alexsei can make her laugh, make her relax, tease her out of a bad mood, I'm sure.

I don't even have to be around that much to know that he thinks she fucking hung the moon and constantly makes her feel important and special.

I think I do that for her, too, but in a different way.

The three of us treat her differently. We're three different men for three different sides of her as a woman.

And I do like how Alexsei treats her. How she clearly feels when she's around him.

"You ready?" I ask him. "I'm gonna work your asses off tonight. You have to be ready. We have to obliterate the Dragons."

He grins. "Always ready for anything."

Again, I feel like he's giving me a knowing look, and I don't appreciate it.

But there's no way the rest of the team is going to pick up on anything. There is no way anyone else would possibly guess what Alexsei and I got up to two nights ago.

"What's with the two of you?" Crew asks as he walks by.

Fuck.

Maybe there *is* a way someone would pick up on something.

And, of course, it would have to be the brother of the woman we're sharing.

I groan inwardly.

I'm fucking one of my player's sisters. *With* one of my other players.

This is so fucking complicated.

"Hey, Ryan!" someone calls. "You need your ribs taped?"

I look over to see Doc Hughes leaning out of his office.

"Nah, I'm good," Alexsei tells him.

"You sure?" Hughes asks. "You hit the wall pretty hard the other night."

Alexsei rubs his hands over his ribs. "Perfect shape. Not a twinge."

I realize that he didn't so much as wince the other night with Luna and if he had something serious going on with his ribs, he would have felt it the way he was pounding into her. And again, I groan. Not exactly the way I should be clearing my players for practice and games.

But Hughes nods. "Okay. Let me know if you change your mind."

And it occurs to me that Michael Hughes and Crew are dating —and sleeping with—the same woman while on the same hockey team (the hockey team owned by their girlfriend's other boyfriend), so maybe Alexsei and I don't need to worry.

And am I seriously thinking that we should both date Luna? Really? In an actual relationship?

My eyes slide shut as I take a deep breath.

I hear Alexsei chuckle.

"I was just asking Coach how his date went the other night."

My eyes snap open.

"You had a date the other night?" Crew asks with a grin. "No way. I didn't think you dated."

I frown, but I'm not sure which of them I'm more irritated with. Of course I date. But I don't talk about it with my players.

Which makes me even more irritated.

Because the date wasn't a date to start with. Because she was on a date *with* one of my players.

Jesus.

Alexsei nods. "Oh yeah, he dates. *Really* hot girl the other night."

Alexsei. I'm definitely more irritated with Alexsei.

Crew's brows are up. "Yeah? Nice. Good for you."

"Get dressed," I tell them both. "Need you on the ice in five minutes."

"Did you have fun?" Alexsei asks me. In front of Crew. "You never said."

No, I didn't say. We all had breakfast together. We all made small talk as if we hadn't just had the hottest sexual experience of my life. As if I hadn't awakened with Luna lying on my chest, but my leg wedged up against Alexsei's and Cam's breathing on the other side of the two bodies between us and I hadn't freaked out. As if I hadn't contemplated just getting the hell out of there for about thirty minutes, pacing in front of the huge living room windows. As if I hadn't been unable to leave, but I hadn't been able to go back to bed, so I'd slept on the couch and felt just as fucking awkward about that as I would have waking up next to Alexsei and Cam.

Okay, *almost* as awkward as I would have felt waking up next to them.

I don't have a problem with those two guys being together. In fact, they seem great for each other.

I didn't have a problem with Luna being with them, either. Which had shocked me.

After Cam had dropped everything on me, I'd watched Luna with them both during breakfast.

They do make her happy.

And they have a different dynamic with her than I do. Each of their dynamics with her is different.

Cam teases and bickers with her. But I can tell her snarky comebacks and sassiness are completely natural for her.

Alexsei dotes on her. He touches her constantly, rubbing her back, and kissing the top of her head whenever he passes by. He tells her she's amazing and gorgeous and she practically preens for him.

I don't think I could do any of those things with her if I tried. I don't have the sharp sense of humor Cam does. And I can't treat her like a porcelain doll the way Alexsei does.

I want to hold the door open for her and then whisper something dirty in her ear as she passes by me. I want to just sit at her bakery counter and go over game plans while she finishes up her own work.

Fuck me, I want to take her home to meet my mom.

So, with the realization that Cam was right about everything and that if I want a relationship with her long-term, I'm going to have to be okay being a part of a *foursome* and then realizing that I'm probably not a foursome guy, I decided to get the hell out of there. When Alexsei started making out with her while they were doing the dishes and she reached out, trying to pull me into it, I almost let the door hit my ass on the way out.

"I don't think we need to discuss my personal life in the locker room," I tell him. "Get dressed."

"Oh, come on," Alexsei says. "I'll tell you about my date. She was *amazing*."

Crew looks from him to me and back. "Damn, boys. Way to go. Glad you're both out there having fun."

"So much fun," Alexsei agrees. "I actually think I'm falling in love."

I suck in a sharp breath.

He's going to tell Crew that?

He and Crew are buddies. McNeill isn't going to let that go.

"No shit?" Crew asks. He narrows his eyes. "Are you fucking with me?"

Alexsei shakes his head. "Nope. I'm feeling it. Actually, some kind of big serious shit is going on."

Crew's eyes widen. "That's awesome. You'll have to tell me about it."

Alexsei nods. "I need to. We should grab a beer."

Jesus Christ. Alexsei's going to tell Crew about him and Luna? Or is he going to tell him about Luna, Alexsei *and Cam*? What about me?

"Ice. *Now*," I bark.

Alexsei looks at me with a frown. "Alright already."

"Stop fucking around," I tell him, giving him a look that means *in all the ways*.

His frown deepens. "Relax."

"*Move*," I order.

"Guess maybe your date didn't go as well as Ryan's?" Crew asks, but then he makes a very good decision and quickly moves off toward his locker.

Alexsei starts toward his but I say, quietly, "You need to watch it, Ryan."

"Watch what? Telling my friend about my life?"

"It's not just *your* life."

"But it *is* my life, and I should get to talk about how happy and in love I am."

"Just…make sure you're only talking about *you*."

He stares at me for a long moment, then nods. "Got it." He does not look happy.

Then I say, "And remember who Crew is. Do not cause problems on this team."

"Right," he says. "Wouldn't want to cause any tension between me and anyone in this locker room."

And *finally*, he goes to get dressed.

The rest of practice really sucks.

And I have a feeling that's just the start of things that are really going to suck.

CHAPTER 26

Alexsei

LIFE IS SO FUCKING GOOD.

Honestly, I feel this way about ninety-five percent of the time. And I'm aware that most people who know me, feel like being Alexsei Ryan is a pretty great gig most days. Or maybe all days.

I'm a professional hockey player who lives with his best friend in a kick-ass penthouse apartment in the best city in the world, and I'm now dating the hottest, funniest, brightest, sexiest, best woman I have ever met. I truly believe that nine out of ten guys would trade places with me in a heartbeat.

The thing is, most people don't even know about Luna.

And I'm done keeping her a secret.

I watch as Crew crosses the bar to order a round of drinks for the team.

He's the first person I need to tell.

We're just back from Houston, having kicked ass in that playoff series, winning in four, and we are on our way to winning the whole fucking thing.

We're home, out at the bar celebrating getting to the place we've all been working for since day one. Yes, since day one of the season, but really for most of us since day one of putting on our hockey skates and picking up a stick.

Every kid who plays hockey dreams of being a champion. Every player who gets drafted dreams of the Championship. Hell, the reason Crew McNeill came to Chicago in the first place was for this chance.

I could feel it in my bones the first time this particular group of Racketeers took the ice together. The cup is going to be ours.

And here we are, on the precipice.

On top of that, I'm totally, madly in love. And not just with Luna. I've got Cam, too. We finally figured our shit out—okay, *I* figured *my* shit out—and we're living our life and love out loud.

Some of the team knows. Crew cornered me on the plane on the way to Houston and wanted to follow up on our conversation in the locker room a few days ago. He wanted to know all about the big things going on in my life. Because of Owen's reaction to everything that day, I found myself holding back about Luna, but I did tell Crew about me and Cam.

My friend was happy for me. And not surprised. He accepted everything with a huge grin and a, "That's amazing, man".

Crew's a true friend. Which means I have to tell him about Luna.

Not just because he's her brother, but because I want her to be a part of me and Cam for good.

I'm already tired of hiding it.

So tonight's the night. I'm on top of the world, and coming out about having Luna McNeill in my life will just be the sprinkles on top of the very pretty, sweet cupcake she is in my life.

Plus, I want to do it when Crew's in a good mood and tonight definitely qualifies.

Cam strolls through the door, looks around, and spots Owen and I sitting at a high top. He comes toward us with a huge grin.

He catches me in a big hug, thumping my back, and says against my ear, "I'm so fucking proud of you."

He has said those words to me before, several times over the years, but it feels different this time. I didn't know that he loved me before and I hadn't acknowledged that I love him. Now that we have, his words sink deep into my chest. I pull back and give him a smile. "Thanks." Then I add, "Missed you."

I did. There was one thing missing from the huge win against Houston and that was having him and Luna in the stands.

It's just a truth of the hockey life that our loved ones are not going to be at every game. Especially the road games. I found myself looking up into the stands behind our bench out of habit.

That will be different for our run for the championship. Even when we're out of town. I'm going to make sure they're there with us.

"Me, too. But of course, I watched." He takes a seat and grins at Owen. "Congrats, Coach."

Owen returns the smile. "Thanks. We're in a really good place."

I know he's referring to the team, but the words, at least to me, summarize even more than hockey.

"Hey guys, I'm telling Crew tonight," I say without preamble.

Cam looks over at me, an eyebrow up. He knows instantly what I mean.

Owen, on the other hand, asks, "Telling Crew what?"

I look at him for a second, wondering if he'll figure it out. When he doesn't say anything more, I say, "About Luna. That I'm in love with her. That we've been seeing each other."

Owen slowly sets his beer down. "Do you really think that's a good idea?"

I nod. "I think it's a great idea. I told him about me and Cam. He was so happy for us. He's my friend, and he needs to know."

"Sure. But you and Cam are different than you and Luna."

"Not really." I shrug. Really, not at all in my mind. "I'm in love with her. It's the real thing. She's a part of my life, and I want that to be long term. I'd want to tell him even if he wasn't her brother, but he is. He needs to know." I look around the bar. "Fuck man, I want everyone to know. I am madly, head over heels for her. I want to stand up on this table and yell about it. I want to be *with* *her* in public. I want to hug her and grab her ass and tell her I love her and not worry about who's around to hear it. In fact, I want *everyone* to hear it. I want my parents to know, I want *her* parents to know."

"Okay, slow down," Owen says, frowning. "You're hopped up on adrenaline, I get it. You're flying high from the games. Don't let that make you make rash decisions."

"Luna is not a rash decision," I tell him. "She's one of the loves of my life."

I glance at Cam. He reaches over and squeezes my arm, but he's frowning at Owen, too.

Owen sighs. "Well…fuck. Just…wait until after the season, okay?"

I shake my head. "What? No. That's what I'm telling you. I'm not waiting anymore for anything."

"Just wait until after a few more games," he insists. "That way, if there are any problems with Crew, they won't affect your play."

"You think hockey is more important than this?" I demand.

He rolls his eyes. "No, I don't think it's more important. But your *job* needs to be your priority right now."

"I can do both. I can be a hell of a hockey player *and* an amazing boyfriend."

"This isn't about that," he argues. "This is about you and Crew being in sync out on the ice. Think about the team. If he gets annoyed or awkward with you, that could affect everything. You have a whole team to think about. Hell, a whole *city*."

"Luna comes first," I say stubbornly.

"Alexsei—"

"Owen, take a breath," Cam says.

Surprisingly, Owen does.

Then Cam looks at me and says, "Crew will know about me, too. You and I are a unit. If he knows about you and Luna, he'll know I'm involved."

"Yeah. I figured you were fine with that," I say.

He nods. "I am. Just pointing it out." He looks at Owen. "For everyone."

Owen places his hands flat on the table and takes a breath. "What about me?"

Cam leans in. "I was about to ask you that."

I lean in, too, my heart suddenly pounding. "Crew's going to be surprised. But he's going to be okay. We love her. That's what he'll care about." I pause when Owen doesn't say anything. "We're in this, right? Don't you want the world to know how you feel about her?"

Owen looks up at me. "Yes."

"Then let's tell him. He needs to know before anyone else hears and tells him. He needs to hear it from us."

Owen nods. "The thing is, it's not just me telling Crew that I'm dating his sister."

And then I realize what he's not saying. "You'll have to tell everyone that you're with us, too," I say flatly.

Owen doesn't answer.

Cam blows out a breath.

"So what?" I ask, looking back and forth between them. "You're worried about homophobic bullshit? Jokes? People talking about you behind your back? What people will say to you to your face?" I ask.

Owen shakes head emphatically. "No. I don't care about that. We all know what's going on between us. I don't care what people outside of us think."

"What's really the problem?" Cam asks.

"It means that this is all requiring an adjustment to what I thought a long-term relationship would look like in my life," he says. "I'm trying to figure out how this works for me. *If* it works for me."

I'm surprised by how hard the pain jabs me with his words. "I'm telling Crew tonight," I repeat firmly.

"And I'm not ready," Owen says.

Cam swears under his breath.

And suddenly I don't feel angry. I feel sad. Because we have a really great thing going, and I don't know if it's going to keep going.

"I'm telling Crew about me, Cam, and Luna," I say. "But I won't say anything about you."

Owen nods. "Okay."

"But you need to leave," I tell him. My voice is firm and I can tell when he looks in my eyes he knows I am very unhappy.

Yup, happy-go-lucky, everything-is-always-sunshine, Alexsei Ryan is pissed off.

"Why?"

"Because Luna is on her way down here to join us. And I want her to hear two men tell her brother that they love her and want to be with her and that they're *in*. All in. I want her to *feel* that. And if you're here, but not saying those things, it'll hurt her. And I don't like to see her hurt. When she's hurt, it makes me want to punch people. Especially the people who hurt her." I stop and take a breath and make myself say calmly, "And I don't think the team is going to think it's very cool if I start punching our coach the night after a big win. They'll want to know what's going on and you don't want to answer those questions."

Owen looks down at his beer, takes a deep breath, lifts his mug and drains it, then sets it down hard on the table. "Fine." Then he gets up, and stalks toward the door.

I watch him go, watch the door slam behind him, then look at Cam. "Well...fuck."

Cam nods. "Yeah."

CHAPTER 27
Owen

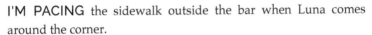

I'M PACING the sidewalk outside the bar when Luna comes around the corner.

I had to wait for her. I couldn't leave and have Cam and Alexsei tell her why I left. Or have them lie for me. She and I need to have this conversation.

It's probably overdue.

I've just been putting it off because I don't want to lose her. So, I've been stalling.

She walks up, giving me a bright smile, and my heart clenches in my chest. How can I let her go? I love her so fucking much. Why can't I just do this thing?

But committing to one person, bringing one person into my life, trying to be everything that *one* person needs me to be is a big step. Bringing *three* people into my life, and trying to be everything they need me to be? How the fuck am I going to do that?

They asked me if I'm worried about what people will say. If I'm worried that people will think I'm gay, or will make homophobic comments or jokes. I don't care about any of that. The people who really know me know the truth, and honestly, if someone thinks I'm in love with, or in a romantic or sexual relationship with Cam or Alexsei, I don't care. They're both amazing men. Fuck what other people think.

No, it's all about the fact that being what someone needs, being there for them, not letting them down, is a big deal.

I mess up with Brady on a regular basis. I've let Chelsea down over the years, and we're not even committed to one another. Except that we are, right? We *are* in a relationship. It's not romantic or sexual, but she needs me to be there for her and our kid at times. We need to communicate. We need to trust each other. And I fall short in that sometimes. Of course, other women have, obviously, found me unable to commit the way they needed me to.

How the hell can I go from being unable to handle *one* relationship to juggling a relationship with three people? Especially these three? Luna, Cam, and Alexsei would expect me to be an equal fourth of this relationship and...if I'm completely honest, I'm not really sure what I bring to this dynamic.

It's clear what they all give one another. It's clear why they all need each other.

I don't know why any of them need me.

And I don't want to be a fourth wheel.

Luna sees me and starts running toward me. "Oh my God! I am so happy for you!"

She throws her arms around me as she jumps, and I have no choice but to catch her in my arms. My hands instinctively cup her ass and I clutch her against me. Her legs wrap around my waist, her arms wrap around my neck, and she hugs me tightly.

I selfishly take a moment to breathe her in, to hug her tightly, to just absorb the feel of her in my arms, loving me.

She pulls back from the hug and smiles at me. "I'm so proud of you."

"I missed you," I tell her, honestly. I *ached* with missing her. And now I get to miss her every day for the rest of my life. Because I know if I walk away from Cam and Alexsei, I walk away from her, too.

At least I'm leaving her in good hands.

"I missed you, too, but I think I've worked out a way that I can go with you guys on the road when you go to the championship!" Her eyes are sparkling and she's practically giddy as she tells me.

I feel like my breath is jammed in my lungs as she says *when* we go to the championship. She believes we'll make it.

"Elise and Austin have already said that they can cover while I'm gone. And I actually turned down an order today." She beams as she delivers the news.

I have to chuckle. "You're kidding."

She shakes her head, her grin growing. "Nope. It was a huge order, too. It was actually for a hockey party for the first game of the championship series. They're planning ahead, too. And I said no. I said the bakery was going to be closed because we were going to be out of town at that time. And you know what?"

I can't help but squeeze her. I'm actually proud of her for this. "What?"

"The woman laughed and said she should've expected that!"

Her laugh jabs me in the gut. I'm gonna miss that so fucking much.

"That's amazing," I tell her sincerely. "I'm glad you figured out that you don't have to work your ass off all the time."

Her smile softens. "Turns out, that as much as I love my job and as much of a part of my identity as it is, I have found other things that I love even more, other things I want to spend my time on, and other things—okay, *people*—who have become as much part of my identity as being a baker and a businesswoman. I want to be there with you guys."

She's killing me. Seeing her blossoming like this, seeing her becoming the woman that she's becoming, I fucking want to be a part of that.

Dammit, I *have been* a part of that. How can I walk away?

"Hey, we need to talk," I say before I can chicken out. "I was waiting out here for you."

There's something in my tone that catches her attention. Her expression grows serious. "Is everything okay?"

I take a deep breath and let her slide down my body. "Not really."

She steps back fully, her arms across her stomach. "You're scaring me."

I wish I could reassure her. But this is just gonna suck. "Alexsei and I were talking and we feel like Crew needs to know what's going on. Alexsei is tired of hiding how he feels about you from your brother."

Her eyes widen, but then she nods. "I've been thinking about that, too. It feels weird to keep this from him. I'm so happy. And it's with a friend of his and his coach. He loves you both. He's going to be fine."

I swallow hard and tuck my hands in my pockets to keep from reaching for her. "The thing is, I can't do that."

She frowns. "You can't do what?"

"This. With you and the guys."

"Oh, Owen," she said softly, and I can already see the tears shimmering in her eyes. "Don't do this."

"It's not what you think," I say. "I really like the guys. I care about them. And I love you. And, I don't care what people think or say. It is not that."

"Then what?"

"Cam and Alexsei are really good for you. Like really good. And they're really good for each other." I blow out a breath. "And you're really good for them."

She's just watching me. She doesn't even try to help me out with words. She's going to make me articulate all of this.

"This just isn't in my…plans. My wheelhouse. I kind of suck at one-on-one relationships and I can't do three, baby. I'll fuck it up."

She studies me. She doesn't protest that, she doesn't argue, she just stands watching me.

"And I don't really add anything that any of you need," I go on. "Those two are going to love you, really well. They can give you whatever you need. All I bring to the mix is an older guy, with some kind of stupid ideas about sex, a teenage kid, an ex, and a not-great relationship track record. None of you need that."

She takes a deep breath and blinks rapidly. "So we're just done?"

"Yeah. I'm going to step aside. You and Cam and Alexsei are going to be great. I'm not even going to say something stupid like, give me a call if it doesn't work out with them, even though I want to. Because I know it's going to work out with those guys. You're going to be really happy."

She swallows, lifts her chin, and nods. "It *is* going to work out with those guys, and I *am* going to be really happy."

It feels like she punched me in the stomach, but that's stupid because she's right. I nod. "You're amazing. And I don't think I'm ever going to get over you."

"Good, I hope not, because that's what you're choosing. It's a *choice*." She steps past me and walks to the door of the bar, but as her hand touches the handle, she turns back. "You know, Owen, there's something really great about being able to fuck up and be loved, anyway. About just being *wanted*, instead of needed." Then she pulls the door open and steps inside.

I watch until it bumps shut behind her.

And I realize that half of my heart just walked into that bar. And I'm not getting it back.

CHAPTER 28

Luna

"CREW, THIS COUCH IS AMAZING," I tell my brother as I lean back on the huge-assed sofa in his, Dani, Michael, and Nathan's new brownstone.

My brother is lounging on the other end and despite his over-six-foot frame, we're not even close to touching. He grins. "I know, right? But can you say that a little louder for Nathan to hear?"

I chuckle. "Nathan's not going to hear anything I say. He is very much avoiding me."

I don't blame him. I'd be avoiding me, too, if I showed up on my doorstep in sweatpants, sunglasses, and a cloth grocery bag of provisions—i.e., wine, potato chips, and ice cream. Michael was the one who opened the door, but he brought me inside, pointed to the couch, and immediately called for Dani.

Yes, I'm here to wallow. I'm madly in love, and only two-thirds of the men are cooperating. The other is very much not, and I miss him more every day. The worst part is that I believe Owen loves me. And I know that he knows that I love him. He even likes Alexsei and Cam. He's not jealous of them. It all just comes down to him not thinking the foursome fits into his "life plan."

God, have I ever dated a guy who even had a life plan before?

They're overrated as far as I can tell.

Business plans are great. Planning for love? It doesn't work. Look at me, trying desperately to avoid dating a hockey player and insisting I don't need a relationship because of the bakery.

Love found me anyway.

And unlike Owen, I was open to accepting it. So were Cam and Alexsei.

Now I can't imagine not having them in my life.

Alexsei is my sunshine. He makes me smile, he makes me feel loved and like I can do anything. He thinks I'm amazing. Everyone needs a little of that–or a lot of that–in their life.

Cam just gets me. It's like he knows what I need sometimes before I do. And it's not always the worshiping I get from Alexsei, strange as that sounds. Sometimes I need to be left alone. Sometimes I need someone to roll their eyes at me and tell me I'm being dramatic. Sometimes I need a funny GIF or a dirty text. Cam always delivers. He never treats me like I'm precious, but I know I'm wanted and appreciated.

And then there's Owen. He makes me feel loved. Safe. Protected. Like I'm a puzzle piece he was missing and I make him feel complete.

That's what hurts right now. I miss him so much. And I know he misses me. Why is he staying away?

Coming to Dani's was a knee-jerk reaction. She's my best friend, and I knew that she would welcome me in, give me a fuzzy blanket, and let me cry, rant, and stuff myself with junk food.

However, she is living in a happy foursome, and that is blatantly on display as I wallow on her couch.

One of the men who adores her and wants to spend his life with her—i.e., my brother—is on the couch with us.

Another, the sophisticated, brilliant Dr. Michael Hughes, is in the kitchen making us "real" snacks. He's actually making us mini quiches, baked brie with toasted baguette slices, and something with bacon. I love him best.

I know he's mostly concerned about Dani not eating crap food just because her best friend is in an emotional spiral, but I'll happily benefit from his caretaking of my bestie.

Her third guy, the grumpy billionaire, is upstairs, trying to avoid too many emotions. Especially crying-woman-that-he-isn't-sleeping-with emotions.

That's fine with me. I like Nathan for Dani, but he's intimidating as hell.

It was actually funny to see him come halfway down the steps, spot me on the couch with a carton of ice cream in my lap, saying something about how stupid men are, and watch him freeze, turn around without a word, and head straight back upstairs. He doesn't even try to pretend.

"Thanks for letting me come over," I say, more to Crew than Dani. Crew used to be the tag-along when Dani and I hung out. It's taken a minute to get used to the fact that *I'm* the extra now.

"Of course. I'm not thrilled that my *coach* is the reason you're here being all sad and depressing, though," he says.

So, yeah, Alexsei and I told Crew about us. And Cam. And he was happy for us after he got over the initial surprise. It's not like he can be too judgmental about foursomes. Or dating his sibling's friend.

But then I showed up here with my support bag of junk food and had to confess about Owen.

Crew was not only surprised by that but also confused. Not that I'd want to date Owen or that he'd want to date me, but that he broke things off.

"You mean sad and depressed?" I ask.

"No, you're being *depressing*," he says. "I like the happy, in-love everything-is-great bubble we've got going here." He strokes his finger down Dani's cheek and she gives him a soft smile.

I roll my eyes.

"You're kind of a downer, sis," he says. But I can tell he's teasing me.

"I know." I sigh.

"Just call him," Crew says. "Like right now. From here. We can be your moral support."

"No. Fucking. Way." I stab at my ice cream. "He made his choice. If he changes his mind, he can come to me."

"This just doesn't sound like Coach, is all I'm saying." Crew's frowning as he says it.

I shove a spoonful of chocolate peanut butter passion in my mouth. "Why not?" I ask around the creamy peanut buttery bliss. "I mean, he's a man. And men are stupid."

Crew rolls his eyes and throws a pretzel at me. "Not Coach. I mean, he's old."

"Watch yourself," Michael calls from the kitchen.

So he *can* hear us, and he *is* listening. That answers that unspoken question I had.

Crew chuckles softly but goes on, "I mean, he's a dad."

I sigh. "So? Tons of men are dads and trust me, percentage-wise, that means lots of dads are stupid."

"It doesn't fit," Crew insists. "I mean, he's not just a dad to Brady. Who is actually an awesome kid, and I have to think Owen has something to do with that. But he's kind of a dad to every-body. I mean, all the guys on the team go to him if they have any problem. Anything from having a tax question to what to get their mom for Mother's Day to which truck they should buy. The guy knows everything. He loves to give advice. He's competent in everything, I swear."

Yeah, yeah, I know. Good lord, I *know*. Competence porn is a real thing and Owen's confidence and ability to be comfortable in an expensive black-tie restaurant or a sweaty, smelly locker room or a dainty pink and white bakery is one of the things I find most attractive.

"Well, I hope he's not giving relationship advice to anyone." I shove more ice cream in my face. I want to get through at least part of this pint before Michael brings me any of his amazing, savory food. I mean I'm going to eat everything that man puts in front of me. He's an amazing cook, and I'll always find room for bacon. But sometimes a girl just needs junk.

I regret what I say about Owen, though. He's not stupid. He's not cruel. And I know he wasn't with me just for a hookup. I believe that he really has feelings for me. I just can't figure out why he's panicking about this relationship.

"Actually, he has given advice about women," Crew says.

I scoff. "I assume they all ended up disasters. He probably told the men to run the second things got a little serious." I'm being a bitch on purpose. It makes me feel better and I know that neither my brother nor Dani actually believe a word I'm saying.

Dani is sitting next to me, letting me rest my feet in her lap. She rubs the top of my foot comfortingly.

"One of them is married with a kid," Crew says. "I wasn't here when he started dating her, but I've heard the stories. Coach kept him from fucking it up."

I roll my eyes.

Crew notices. "What?"

"I'm just shocked that Owen Phillips talked some guy into marrying a girl and having a baby," I say, the sarcasm dripping. "That's so traditional and sweet it makes me sick."

Crew frowns at me. "Did it ever occur to you, that you just caught him off guard?"

I frown back. I did not expect to come over here and have someone defend Owen. That's not how girlfriend-time-with-ice-cream goes. Crew needs to understand the rules.

"What's that supposed to mean?"

"That Owen had an idea of what a serious relationship would look like and then you come barreling into his life with purple hair, and an independent-sassy-I-don't-need-you attitude, and two bi-sexual boyfriends in tow, and maybe Owen needs a second to adjust?"

"First of all," I say, trying to sit up straighter, but finding that this huge, very comfortable couch is too soft to really move quickly on. "They're not bi-sexual."

Not that it matters, but I kind of feel like I don't have an argument here and that seriously irritates me.

"They both fuck guys and girls, right?"

"They both fuck *me* and each other," I shoot back. "Because we all love each other. It's not a wide-open thing. It's about how we all feel about one another and…" I frown. "It's none of your business."

Crew sighs. "Fine. You're right. Whatever. But maybe that's part of what Owen's trying to figure out, too."

See? Him defending Owen *and* making sense is really annoying. "It's not like I planned on falling in love with three people either," I say.

"I don't think anybody does." Crew reaches out to tug on a strand of Dani's hair. She gives him an adorable smile, and he winks at her.

And I realize my best friend hasn't done anything but hug me and hand me a spoon. Crew's been handling this.

"But it's unconventional no matter how you look at it," Crew goes on.

"Yeah, well, some of us adjusted to it easily because we realize what a gift love is," I say. "And we realized that we want to be fucking happy. If he doesn't, that's his problem."

I stab the ice cream with my spoon again.

"Yeah, and some people just need a little more time, Luna. He's been doing the single dad thing for *a while*. Maybe he's been avoiding relationships. And then the one that comes along that he can't avoid consists of three people? Come on. Give the guy a minute."

"Cam and Alexsei didn't need a minute. Falling in love with me was easy for them. Deciding to be with me was easy for them. Don't you think I should go for the guys who want to be in love with me? Who find the idea of forever with me easy to wrap their minds around?"

"Yeah, well, Cam and Alexsei have probably found a lot of things easier. Cam's a billionaire. He works for himself. Lives with and is in love with his best friend. He's gay or bisexual or whatever."

I open my mouth to protest, but he holds up his hand.

"I mean, it doesn't matter. He's comfortable with his sexuality, and I'm guessing he didn't have the wife, two-point-five kids, and white picket fence in mind, you know? And Alexsei is a hot, young hockey player with puck bunnies everywhere he turns. He probably hadn't thought about mortgages and dogs and PTA meetings at all. Owen, on the other hand, has imagined life and the future. Homeowner's insurance and shared custody and shit for like seventeen years."

"Sixteen," I mumble. Almost seventeen.

But...fuck...I hate when my brother's right.

I take a deep breath and look up from my melting ice cream.

"So what should I do?"

This time it's Dani who answers. "The thing you can't help doing anyway...just love him."

My heart squeezes. Dammit. I'm definitely already doing that.

But I let myself really think about Crew's words.

Owen has a bigger life, at least one with more people who are leaning on him and looking to him for guidance and advice than Cam, Alexsei, and I do. That makes it easier for us to fall into a new relationship without thinking as hard about how it impacts everything else going on around us.

I do believe that Owen isn't ashamed of me, or the guys. I know he cares about us. But *any* new relationship has to fit into his already established life. Brady, the team, Chelsea and her family–none of that is going to change, so he has to be sure he can bring someone new into that life. Or, in this case, *three* more people.

And Owen, being Owen, is going to want to be sure he can do it successfully, and truly be what *we* need him to be while not changing what he is to everyone else.

Ugh. I couldn't just fall in love with a bossy, full-of-himself billionaire who is super independent and just somehow understands me, and a sweet, loving, accepts-me-just-as-I-am hockey player could I?

No, I had to also fall for a responsible, puts-everyone-else-first guy who would walk away before he'd make our relationship anything less than perfect.

"Thanks," I tell my brother. "That was all pretty insightful."

He grins and looks at Dani. "Thank *you*. It makes Dani want me even more when I'm mature and a good brother and stuff."

Dani blushes, but she nods. "Sometimes."

"Only sometimes?" he asks, brows up.

"Well, I really like your playful side, too," she says.

I can't see her full expression but my brother looks like he'd like to get *playful* suddenly.

I groan. "God, can you *please* not flaunt your sexy happiness in front of me for like one more hour? Just until I eat a bunch of Michael's food?"

The house smells amazing.

"Hughes! Hurry up and feed my sister so she'll leave!" Crew calls.

"It's ready!" Michael calls back. "I'm just setting the table."

I shake my head. "Snacks at the *table*? When you have this amazing couch?"

"Nathan says he hates this couch, but he bitches if we eat on it," Crew says with a grin as he pushes up from the deep cushions and then tugs Dani to her feet.

"Too bad Nathan didn't overhear you being all mature and wise with the advice," I say, also getting to my feet.

"Oh, don't worry," Crew says, holding up his phone. "I recorded it. I'll play it back for him if he doesn't believe me."

I laugh and follow them into their gorgeous, newly remodeled kitchen, and tamp down the stab of jealousy I feel.

But I can't help the thought—*I would love to see Cam, Alexsei, and Owen in a friendship like these guys have.*

Dani looks down at her phone as Michael and Crew settle her between them at the table.

"Nathan wants me to bring some food up to him," she says.

"No fucking way," Michael says, passing me the plate of bacon-wrapped dates.

Did I mention he's my favorite?

"No?" Dani asks with a giggle that says she's not surprised by his answer.

"You take food up to the bedroom with Nathan?" Michael asks. "We won't see you for the rest of the night. If he's hungry—for *anything*—" The gorgeous doctor gives her a sexy grin. "He can come down here."

I sigh, losing the battle to tamp this wave of jealousy down. Yes, I would also love to be the center of three men's worlds the way my best friend is.

Instead, I spear two more bacon-wrapped dates with my fork.

If I can't have three men, I can at least have three of these.

Sure. That's the same thing.

CHAPTER 29

Luna

"THAT'S IT THEN," Elise says to me, taking off her apron and giving me a smile. "You're all set for tomorrow."

"Thank you so much, seriously," I tell her, giving a happy sigh as I give one last look at the fridge filled with macarons, pain au chocolat, eclairs, cupcakes, and a cake for a wedding tomorrow. I close the fridge and put my hands on my hips.

The last three days have been crazy busy preparing for this wedding and several other events and I'm a mess, covered in frosting and flour, hair up in a tight ponytail. Elise has worked two ten hour days back-to-back and somehow still looks like a pin-up model. I've always been just a little jealous of her curves and her glossy black hair, but never more so than right now when I look like a twelve-year-old let loose in the kitchen and she looks photo-shoot ready in tight jeans and a blouse with cherries on it. Her lipstick isn't even smudged.

She even pulls out her giant handbag and steps into cherry-red heels in place of her work sneakers. "It was fun," she says. "And the cake turned out beautifully. The bride is going to love it, Luna."

I blow my bangs out of my eyes. "I hope so."

Even though I'm tired, it's a good exhaustion. I feel accomplished and ahead of the game for the first time in months. There's literally nothing left to do until Wednesday except make sure Brady delivers the macarons to a birthday party while I take the cake to the wedding reception.

I want to celebrate. But it occurs to me that once Elise walks out the door, I'll be alone with nothing to do. Alexsei is in Seattle. It's the second round of the playoffs and the Racketeers have won two of the first three games already. Dani is there, too, watching Crew play with my parents.

Owen is obviously in Seattle as well, though I'm trying not to think too much about him. I refuse to allow him to ruin my budding relationship with Alexsei and Cam.

"Want to grab a drink?" I ask Elise. "My treat for all your Books and Buns hard work?"

Elise's face falls. "Oh my God, girl, I'd love to, but I have a date tonight." She gives me a grin. "You should grab a bottle of wine, go upstairs and watch your man on the ice while you rub one out."

That makes me laugh. I told Elise I've been dating Alexsei because I've been getting quirky gifts from him every day while he's been gone and she's been witness to the deliveries. It was impossible to explain getting a box of Fancy Feast cat food with a note that said, "Missing you and your pussy," without explaining it.

After her initial skepticism that I'm dating a hockey player—okay, she laughed her ass off at that—she's been very supportive of my gushing and didn't blink when I told her he's also in love with Cam and we're all dating. Now she's just been enjoying teasing me, which I deserve. I did not tell her about Owen initially, because I wasn't sure if he wanted Brady to know or not and now, well, it seems like a moot point to tell anyone about something that is no longer going on.

It makes me miss him and Alexsei even more. And yes, I'm horny, too. I have not been able to get our night together out of my head.

"That does sound like a great plan," I tell her. "And basically my only option. Who's your hot date with? Those heels are giving a vibe."

She kicks her foot up. "Thanks! He's probably a massive douchebag, but he has a beard, so I'm willing to give it a shot. Unless want me to ghost him and hang out instead."

"Oh, no, of course not!" I wave my hand. "Pfft. I'll be fine. I'm an independent woman, remember?"

I am. Accomplished, successful, confident.

And a little deflated that I'm going to be alone tonight.

That's ironic. The guys have been so respectful of my space and now I just want a big man fest. But that's what's cool about being in a relationship, right? Celebrating accomplishments, big and small, together. We're so newly together that I just wish they were all here right now.

"You are an amazingly independent woman dating a couple of very sexy dudes. You have a life I can only dream of. Plus, you know lots of hockey players you could introduce me to." She lifts her perfect eyebrows up and down. "Do hockey players like big tits because I've got a pair they can rest their weary post-game heads on." She grabs her boobs and jiggles them up and down.

"You really do have a great pair," I tell her honestly. "Plus, you're smart as hell and a creative genius who keeps me calm in times of crisis. Any man would be lucky to have you, but unless you want to date a nineteen-year-old hockey player, I think the rest are all taken. At least on the Racketeers."

"Boo." She pouts. "I would break a nineteen-year-old. If there are any breakups among the older guys and they need a vagina to lean on, let me know. I can be very comforting."

I laugh again. "I bet." Then I can't resist a pun because I know she'll love it. "I'll keep you *abreast* if anything happens."

She gives a cackle. "Was that a boob pun? I love it. You really are more relaxed these days." She blows me a kiss. "Have fun with your wine. Bye!"

"Bye. Be safe," I tell her. "Share your location with a friend."

When she leaves out the back door, I lock it behind her and stand in total silence for ten seconds before picking up my phone and flipping through it, looking for anything to entertain me.

Then I realize there is one person I can text. I type quickly and hit send.

> What's up?

Cam responds immediately.

> Who dis?

That makes me chuckle.

> Haha. You're hilarious.

> You send a dumb text, you get a dumb one in return.

God, he's brutal. I love it.

> That's fair. Are you at the game?

> No. Still in Chicago. Had a work issue pop up.

That's good news. I mean, not the work issue. But that he's still in town. Because now I have someone to interact with.

> Want to talk about it?

> Not even a little.

That's so very Cam that I shake my head in amusement as I head through the shop to the stairs that lead up to my apartment. I can't text going up the steps. I've learned that the hard way.

So by the time I'm in my apartment, he's texted again.

> What are you doing? All set for tomorrow?

The guys know about my jam-packed day of orders.

> Yep. Feeling very accomplished.

The dots appear on my screen, then disappear. I shut the door of my apartment behind me and toss the phone on the bench placed in the entryway. I unlace my shoes and glance back up to see the text dots appear, then disappear, which makes me curious. Cam is a confident texter. He's always short and to the point.

Finally, a text comes through.

> Want to watch the game together?

A warm rush goes through me. Cam wants to spend time with me.

He's probably feeling lonely, too, with Alexsei gone.

> I would love to. Let me change before I head out.

> I'll come to your place.

Even better. I don't really feel like taking the bus and I don't want to spend the money on a car. At this time of day on a Friday, the rates surge. I could take the bakery van, but then there's parking…

> That would be great.

Twenty minutes later I'm showered and in sweats and a Racketeers hoodie, with no bra on because I want to be comfortable. I also want to see if I can inspire Cam to touch me, if I'm being honest.

When he comes into the apartment, he holds up an unopened microwave bag of popcorn. "In case you didn't have any."

I love that he knows my snack food of choice for games. I take it from him. "Thanks."

Then he eyes my outfit. "I see you pulled out the stops for me."

I roll my eyes. "It's a hockey game. Not a five-star restaurant in Paris."

The corner of his mouth turns up. "Do you want to go to Paris?" He toes his shoes off.

Cam is very no-shoes-in-the-house. He values cleanliness like I value real butter. It's a must in my kitchen.

"I would love to go to Paris. Lydia, who works for me, you know, Brady's girlfriend? She's saving for a school trip and I'm a little jealous. I would love to visit as many patisseries in Paris as is humanly possible." I shut the door behind Cam.

He surprises me by stroking my cheek with the pad of his thumb and giving me a soft kiss. "Then we'll go to Paris. My treat."

A shiver rolls through me at his touch. "Are you serious?"

"Do I look like a guy who just talks shit?" He looks offended by the thought. "Or jokes all the time?"

That makes me giggle. "No. Funny guy isn't how I'd describe you."

"So to answer your question, yes, I'm serious. Name the dates and we'll go to Paris." He murmurs in my ear. "Ma cherie."

His breath tickles my flesh. "Oh, you're angling for a blowjob, aren't you?" I ask, not at all opposed to the idea. Except for one little issue that we need to clear up.

"I don't have to angle for anything. If I want one, I'll tell you," he says. "And you'll give it to me."

I suck in a sharp breath. His commanding voice makes me instantly wet. I want him to take my hair, hard, and push me to my knees. But he casually exits my personal space as if he didn't just lay down the law.

He looks around the apartment as he steps further inside. "I love your apartment, Luna. This is so you. Colorful and creative."

"Thanks. It's cozy. But a little lonely now that Dani has moved out."

Cam sits down on my couch and fishes the remote out from between two couch cushions. "I thought you wanted your own space."

"I do. But not all the time."

"Good thing you have multiple boyfriends, then." He pats the couch. "Come sit with me."

I love that he uses that term so casually. I decide not to comment, but I can't contain my smile.

"So we can plan a trip to Paris?" I ask, coyly, dropping onto the cushion beside him.

"Yes. Just tell me when and I'll clear my work schedule. How about May? Hockey is over by then. Everyone always says Paris in May is unreal."

He really is serious. "I would love that," I tell him. "Can you picture Alexsei in Paris? He would be adorable. He would one hundred percent want to take a picture to make it look like he's holding the Eiffel Tower in his hands."

Cam nods. "He definitely would do that. And everything would be the best. The best wine he's ever tasted! The best boat on a river he's ever taken! The best French bread in the history of French bread!"

That makes me laugh. I love that we both love Alexsei and can share that with each other. "That is so true, and I would love to see that. I can't afford it, though."

"I told you, it's on me." He turns the TV on and scrolls through the menu to find the Racketeers game. They're doing opening commentary.

He says it so casually. *It's on me.* Like a trip to Paris for three is drinks at McGinty's.

"How do you make your money exactly?" Cam's wealth and employment are still a mystery to me.

"Legally, don't worry."

"I wasn't worried about that. I'm curious."

"I develop software for scientists to use in their research. Plus, I sold a few things along the way."

"Things?"

"Tech things."

"That's impressive."

He doesn't add anything further and I'm not sure what to ask because tech is not my arena. I study his profile. His long Grecian nose, his sharp jawline. The frame of his glasses. His full lips.

He turns to meet my stare. "Grumpy, but beautiful, aren't I?"

That makes me laugh. Cam is entertaining. He's my snarky counterpart and I love going head-to-head with him. "Yes. Very."

We settle in to watch the puck drop. Crew gets the puck and my brother is off, weaving in and out of Seattle's guys with relative ease.

"Your brother is what this team needed," Cam says.

"Yes, he is. They really have a shot at the championship this year. I'm excited for the guys."

"Alexsei would be thrilled."

I love the way Cam's voice changes when he talks about Alexsei. It softens around the edges and it's absolutely adorable. "Do you want some wine?"

"Sure." He follows me into the kitchen and while I pull a bottle of chardonnay from the fridge, he opens cabinets looking for glasses. "Was it hard?" he asks. "Growing up with a brother like Crew?"

His question makes me pause, briefly, before I tell him simply, "Yes. I love my brother. He's a caring person. But he was the sun and my parents were the planets, you know? Drawn into his orbit."

"And you?"

I shrug. "I don't know. Different solar system?"

But Cam sets the wine glasses he's retrieved down on the countertop and tucks my hair behind my ear, gently. "You're Luna. Goddess of the moon, brave and independent."

My heart swells. Cam gets me. He can be prickly and stand-offish, but he truly understands me and his friendship, this connection between us, means so damn much to me.

Going on my tiptoes, I kiss him, briefly.

"What's your middle name?" I ask.

"I don't have one."

"Everyone has a middle name."

"Not me. My mother considers them redundant."

I raise my eyebrows. "Is your mother practical?"

"Very. She got me from a sperm bank. Well, not me. But the sperm used to create me. She didn't want a husband, but she wanted a child. The epitome of practical."

That is…different. But cool in a way. "Really? Wow. I admire a woman who goes after what she wants. What criteria did she use to pick the donor?"

"Education, IQ mostly. It was practical, but also a gamble. I could have been the product of a sociopath for all she knew."

"Are you sure you weren't?" I tease.

Cam lets out a loud laugh. It just might be the loudest I've ever heard him laugh ever. "You're a little brat." He spins me and gives me a hard smack on the ass.

It sends a jolt of desire pinging through my pussy.

Then he murmurs in my ear. "I really, really like you, goddess of the moon."

It makes me shiver as I glance back at him over my shoulder. "I really like you, too, crooked nose."

"You looked up the meaning of my name?" he asks.

"Of course."

"My mother doesn't believe in names giving attributes to infants. She believes in DNA."

I push the wine bottle in his hand. "Open this. And put that popcorn in the microwave."

He grimaces. "Wine with popcorn?"

"Yes. Wine goes with everything. So does popcorn."

"Weirdo."

"Takes one to know one."

When the popcorn is ready, I pour it into a bowl and we head back to the couch and settle in to watch the game. It's stressful sitting here, unable to do anything other than shove popcorn into my mouth and watch Alexsei on the screen, defending the puck and setting up shot after shot for Crew to take.

Cam must feel the same way because he's refilled his wine glass twice and asked me if I have another bottle. I go and retrieve it for him to open.

"They have to win," I say, tucking my feet under my legs and leaning forward, like getting closer to the TV will change the outcome. The Racketeers are up by three, but you can't count Seattle out until the final buzzer.

"They will." Cam is more relaxed, whether it's the wine or the score, I can't tell.

At some point, his hand falls onto my knee and he's stroking it absently. When a commercial comes on, he turns to me. "You'll have to guide me."

I have no idea what he's talking about. "What?"

"How to eat your pussy. I've never done it before. To any woman."

I'm so stunned, I just stare at him. I feel like he's been having a conversation about this in his head without me. That seems like a very Cam thing to do. "Okay. Do you want to eat my pussy?"

"Yes." He nods, firmly.

I have the sudden realization that he needed the wine to make this confession. I feel a wave of tenderness toward Cam. I know how he feels. It's hard to show pieces of yourself. "Are you sure?"

"Of course I'm fucking sure." His hand shifts higher, teasing at the seam of my sweats. "I want to taste you, Luna. I want to make you come."

Heat blooms between my legs. "Then I would love to guide

you." I shouldn't say anything, but I do anyway. "Too bad Owen isn't here. He could give you some amazing oral sex instructions."

"Fuck that guy," Cam says. The commercial break is over and he turns back to the TV.

I *do* want to fuck that guy. I'm even glancing at the bench to see if I can spot Owen. But instead, because it's not fair to lament one man when another is offering to give me pleasure, I lift my wine glass. "Should we wait to see who wins the game?"

"We probably should. Alexsei will be disappointed if we don't."

So we settle in to watch the rest of the game. I put my feet on Cam's thighs in a hint for him to massage them. He blatantly ignores them.

"Rub my feet," I finally say in the third period, wiggling my toes up and down.

"No, thank you." He continues to stare at the game, his hands six inches from my feet.

That makes me laugh. "Cam, please? I've been on my feet all day. Pretty please?"

"That cute girl shit doesn't work with me. You'll have to wait until Alexsei gets home. I don't rub feet."

That does not surprise me, but I enjoy teasing him. "You've never rubbed Alexsei's feet?" I lift my glass to my lips.

"God, no." He turns and gives me a look of horror. "Have you really looked at his feet? They're all mangled from hockey. His toenails look like snail shells. Disgusting."

I choke on my wine, coughing and wiping my chin as it dribbles down my bottom lip and below. "Oh, my God, warn me before you say stuff like that."

The corner of his mouth turns up. "What's the fun in that?"

I'm going to give him the smart ass response he deserves when I see number seventeen, my brother, blow past a defender and take the puck down the ice. "Oh, oh, Crew is going to score, I can feel it!"

Cam leans forward. "He's got it." He grips my feet, and I don't think he even realizes he's doing it.

A tingle shoots up my legs. Cam's touch is special because he doesn't give it readily. But I'm distracted from that because Crew takes the shot. The goalie misses and it hits the back of the net. We cheer as the light flashes to indicate a goal. Crew lifts his stick in triumph and skates around the back of the net.

"Only two minutes left. I think they have this."

Cam drains his wine glass and refills it again. "Alexsei's going to be happy."

I finish my wine and smile. Cam's hands are still on my feet. Between that and the chardonnay, I'm getting warm in all the right places.

This game can't end fast enough.

Two minutes seems to take twenty, but finally the game is over and the Racketeers have secured the victory. We watch Alexsei raise his gloved fist and shake it, a big grin on his face. He's also chewing on his mouth guard, which I find oddly adorable, which I instantly realize is absurd.

It just confirms that I love him.

And his mangled feet. They can be in my bed every night of the week, as far as I'm concerned.

"Well, that's good news for us. No grumpy boyfriend to deal with tomorrow when he gets home," Cam says.

"Yeah, no grumpy boyfriend," I say, with raised eyebrows.

"Brat," Cam says, before shifting my feet and easing my legs apart.

He goes on his knees and gives me a hard kiss before shifting down between my thighs. He pushes my sweatshirt up and kisses my navel, teasing down the waistband of my sweats. I lay back on the couch, a pillow behind my head, and relax under his touch.

"That feels good," I tell him, trying to sound reassuring.

Cam pauses and drills me with a look.

"What?"

But he shakes his head and tugs my sweats down, panties

included. Cool air drifts over my thighs and my pussy. He stares at me so long I start to squirm a little. Eventually, he runs his thumbs down over me and I give a little gasp of encouragement.

"Yes, that's good. Touch me."

Cam flicks his tongue over my clit, and it's definitely experimental. Then he moves his tongue down over my slit and deep inside me. Then he shifts again, right when it was getting good. I can't tell if he's trying to tease me, or if he's just getting the lay of the land.

"Just pick a spot and hang out there," I tell him.

"So I'm at the beach?" he asks, gruffly.

I fight the urge to laugh. "Just move your tongue slowly, up and down. And repeat."

He does, but he's off center.

"A little to the left, no, that's too far, and just a smidge up." He goes down. I sigh in frustration as he just misses the perfect position. "Up, Cameron. Your other up. The opposite of down."

"What am I hanging a fucking picture on the wall?" he asks, his voice muffled.

"No!" Now I have the giggles. "You're not listening."

"So stop talking."

"What? Cam! You told me to give you instructions."

"I didn't realize how fucking annoying that would be."

I smack the top of his head lightly, then run my fingers through his dark hair. "Do you also realize that if *you* don't stop being annoying, I could crush your head like a cantaloupe with my thighs?"

"Your thighs are not that strong."

"You have no idea how strong my thighs are. I can stay on a mechanical bull."

"When did you ride a mechanical bull?"

"College. Townie bar. Four-for-one beer night."

"Where is there a townie bar in downtown Chicago?" he asks me, staring up at me from between my thighs.

His glasses are smudged. I start giggling again. "It wasn't at my college. I visited my high school friend. Why are we talking about this now?"

"We're not. You are. I told you to stop talking. And surprise, surprise, you're being disobedient." He squeezes one of my folds.

That robs me of the giggles. "Oh, yeah? What are you going to do about it?" My voice is breathless.

"I'm taking you off this couch. It feels like we're in fucking high school."

"Well, that is usually when guys learn to eat pussy."

I know I'm pushing his buttons and now it's intentional. I want Cam to go to that place where he's in control. Where he bosses me around and we both love it. I want him to take charge.

He doesn't disappoint.

"That's it." He stands up and points to the bedroom. "Get your ass in that bed. Now."

My nipples tighten, and I nod, eagerly. I start to pull my sweats back into place, but he reaches out and yanks them clean off my legs.

"No pants."

"No pants," I agree and stand up.

When I move past him, he cracks his palm on my bare ass and I gasp, my pussy growing wet immediately. Oh, yeah. This is better.

A glance over my shoulder shows he's ripping off his shirt, revealing the hard plane of his lean, but muscular, chest. Way better.

Once I'm on the bed, Cam takes off my sweatshirt and kisses me until we're both panting, and his cock is hard against my thigh. He rolls over onto the bed on his back.

"Get on my face."

"That's like skipping a few levels," I tell him.

His expression brooks no arguments. "Sit. On. My. Face." He palms my ass in both hands and hauls me up onto him.

"Oh, God!" I say when my pussy collides with his mouth and he sucks my clit.

I grab the headboard.

"You taste so fucking good," he says, digging his fingers into my ass and grinding me down on him. "Give me more, baby. Ride my tongue."

I'm already twisting and rolling my hips, wanting more as I drive him deeper up into me.

"You're so wet," he murmurs.

"You did that." I'm getting frantic now, fucking his tongue toward an orgasm. "*Cam.*"

He slaps my ass, hard, once, twice. A third time.

Then I'm exploding all over him, tossing my head back as the pleasure rips through me like a tornado. "Fuck, yes!"

Then I ease back onto my haunches, breathing hard. I shove my hair back out of my face and watch him wipe his mouth with his thumb. "Class is over. You passed. Accelerated course."

"Practice makes perfect," he says. "On your back. I haven't earned my diploma yet."

My legs are wobbling as I collapse onto the bed beside him. "We don't have to do the whole program in one night."

"We do if I say so." He strokes between my thighs and gets on his knees.

"Okay," I say, because I'm generous that way.

He bends down.

My last coherent thought is that Cam is a *really* fast learner.

CHAPTER 30
Cameron

I LEAN against the bakery counter and watch Luna instructing Brady Phillips as he hauls boxes of baked goods out to her delivery van. I had tried to help carry boxes, but she had asked me to look at her accounting system. Having Luna ask me for help feels like a major step forward in our relationship, so I sip my coffee contentedly as I open her laptop.

Waking up next to her was… peaceful. Even after we both agreed that we hate cuddling during sleep, this morning she was draped over me, her ankle intertwined with mine.

And I liked it.

Because I like Luna.

Or love her. That's seeming more and more like the reality of the situation.

I swear, I can still taste her on my tongue.

I never thought I would get off getting a woman off, but making Luna grip the bedsheets with her fingertips was deeply satisfying. I'm looking forward to repeating it again and again.

A woman enters the bakery, the chimes above the door jingling. She looks familiar and I realize immediately why. It's Crew and Luna's mother. I've seen her in interviews with Crew and at games. For the first time, I wonder why Luna doesn't sit with her at games. Mrs. McNeill is always in the front row, whereas Luna and Dani sit three rows up.

"Mom, what are you doing here?" Luna exclaims, pushing her hair behind her ears as she heads to the door with Brady. She passes off the box to him and lets her mother hug her.

"Do I need a reason to see my beautiful daughter?"

"I just thought you were still in Seattle." Luna turns and heads back toward me and the rest of the deliveries.

"We had to get back. We flew out right after the game." Her mother approaches the counter. "Hi, I'm Lori McNeill. Are you one of Luna's new hires?"

"Mom, he's not one of my employees. This is Cameron Bach. Cam, my mother."

I reach out over the counter and offer her my hand. "I'm her boyfriend."

Lori McNeill's jaw drops before she gives me a wide grin, shaking my hand lightly. "Oh, *really*?"

"Really."

Luna glares at me. I smile back at her.

"Luna never tells me anything. How lovely you two are together." She turns to Luna and says, "He's very cute. I like the glasses," as if I can't hear her.

Luna groans. "Mom. Stop."

Lori still hasn't let go of my hand.

Now I'm regretting my words because I'm stuck with my arm outstretched and Lori McNeill stroking my hand tenderly, like she's afraid if she lets go I'll disappear.

"What? You never have a boyfriend. I'm just excited. How did you meet?"

"At a Racketeers game. Alexsei Ryan is my roommate." I leave it at that.

The door jingles as Brady comes back in for another box. Lori finally lets go of my hand, which is a massive relief.

I know Luna. She's about to brush her mother off with an excuse about work.

Lori seems to sense that, too. "I know you're busy—

"I am," Luna interrupts her.

Her mother is undeterred. "But I just wanted to let you know how proud your father and I are of you. It's because of you the bakery is thriving."

Luna sighs, her shoulders drooping. It's a nice thing to say, but I understand the context behind it. "Thanks, Mom."

"You've always been so capable, so independent." She smiles at me. "She practically raised herself. She was just so easy."

"Well, I didn't really have a choice, did I?" Luna says, brightly.

Her smile doesn't reach her eyes.

"I know and I'm sorry." Lori tries to pet Luna's arm, but Luna shifts away. "I just wanted to come here today to let you know that we're just as proud of your accomplishments as we are your brother's."

"I appreciate that."

Lori sighs. "Luna. We made mistakes. We were juggling Crew's schedule, and you were always so *fine* that we let that be our guide. Parents make mistakes and time flies by and, well, we're sorry if you ever felt left behind."

There are tears in her mother's eyes.

Luna crumples a little at the sight of them. "Mom. It's fine. I had Grandma and Grandpa as a bonus, and I always knew you loved me. I'm good. I turned out okay."

I hide my face with my coffee mug so I don't interrupt when it's none of my damn business.

"You turned out better than okay."

My mouth opens and I add, before contemplating whether it's wise or not, "She turned out fucking amazing."

"*Cam!*"

But she looks pleased.

Lori doesn't look offended by my swearing. She smiles at me. "She did. And I like that you want to champion my daughter. She's very special."

I nod, firmly. "She is."

She's my person. Just like Alexsei is my person. After last night, and after hearing this conversation, I know it deep down in the pit of my gut.

"Oh God, both of you stop. You're embarrassing me." Luna's cheeks are pink. "Mom, do you want some coffee?"

"Can I take a peek at the wedding cake you did?" Lori asks. "I've been dying to see what you created."

"Sure."

Brady is holding the last box. "I'm ready to head out."

"Okay, thanks, be careful with everything."

He nods and heads toward the front door.

"If anyone comes in, just call for me, okay?" Luna says to me.

"I can handle it." I tip her chin up and stare into those brilliant blue eyes. "I love you."

Those blue eyes widen. Her jaws drops. I use my finger to push it closed.

Then I kiss her briefly before turning back to her computer. "This software is really antiquated. I'm installing something better."

I've made her speechless and I'm very proud of that. She just stands there for a few seconds before whirling around and going into the kitchen. I don't need her to say it back. I know I caught her off-guard. That's kind of my thing. Smash and grab when it comes to emotions. I'll let the words sink in for a minute.

As Luna and Lori head into the kitchen, I hear a stage whisper from Lori. *"Did he just say he loves you?"*

"Mom," Luna says firmly. "Do not listen to that and then look at this wedding cake and start planning a wedding for me. I'm serious."

That gives me pause.

I've never given a lot of thought to marriage, but...

"Shit, shit, shit," Brady says, stumbling in the front door, his hand pressed to his forehead.

"What's wrong?"

"I..." He swallows hard. "I wrecked Luna's van."

Shit, shit, shit is right.

I slam the laptop closed and stride over to him. "Are you okay?"

"I hit my head on the dashboard, but I'm okay." He lifts his hand and shows me a cut above his eyebrow that's weeping blood.

It looks deep, but not life threatening, but if he hit his head, he might have a concussion. "We need to take you in to be checked out. Where is the van?"

"I don't need to see anyone. I'm fine, I swear. I've taken harder hits in hockey. The van is wrapped around a pole." Brady looks like he's on the verge of tears. "Some guy just appeared out of nowhere on a bike and I had to swerve hard."

Grabbing napkins from the bakery counter, I roll them into a tight band so they don't stick to his skin and hand it to him. "Press this against it and sit down. I'll be right back."

Brady groans. "We need to get that stuff delivered and Luna's going to freak out. She's so stressed right now."

"I'll deal with the delivery." I'm already pulling my phone out. "And Luna. Just give me a second."

When I step out onto the busy sidewalk, I see the van immediately. Brady didn't even get fifty feet down the street. That helps with the time crunch, at least. I study the damage. It's not as bad as he made it sound. Wrapped around a pole was a gross exaggeration, thank God. He tapped the pole and dented the bumper. But the rim is caught on the curb.

The real concern is that if he hit the dash, he obviously wasn't wearing his seatbelt. I push my glasses up on my nose and use the tow truck app to arrange for the van to be taken to a garage. Then I start transferring the baked goods to my car. Luna needs to deliver a wedding cake. Brady and I can drop off this stuff, and then I'll take him to the ER. A few people are glancing at the van, but for the most part, everyone is going about their day. This is a thriving neighborhood with lots of couples, tourists, and parents jogging with their babies in strollers.

Five minutes later, I'm back in the shop and Brady is shaking his head miserably as Luna and Lori fuss over him. Lori has removed the napkin from his forehead and is inspecting his cut.

"How's the van?" Luna asks nervously when she sees me.

"It's fine," I assure her. "Just a dented fender. The tow truck will be here in thirty minutes, according to this app. I'll deliver the stuff that was in the van if you give me the addresses."

Luna looks worried. "Brady should be seen in the ER."

"I'll take him if you can wait for the tow truck. What time does the cake need to be delivered?"

"Not until two." Luna bites her lip. "Are you sure, Cam? I can probably take Brady and still have time…"

She doesn't have time to do both and we know that. I take her hand. "You don't always have to be the capable one, you know. It's not a flaw to accept help, sweetheart. It actually shows you're strong enough to admit when you need it."

Her gaze softens. "Okay. You're right."

Brady protests. "I'm fine. It's barely anything."

"Hush," Lori tells him.

My thoughts exactly. "Come on," I tell him. "If you're fine, you can sit in the car for an hour while I make deliveries."

"Thank you," Luna says, going on her tiptoes to give me a kiss. "I hope you didn't have plans today."

I actually have plans to hit the gym and meet my friend Rodan for lunch, but he'll understand. I shake my head. "No plans."

Luna tilts her head and studies me. "You're lying," she says, thoughtfully. "I can read you."

"No one can read me," I tell her, flatly. "I'm a stone wall."

It's true. Normally. But *she* can see through me.

And I find that incredibly satisfying.

Luna laughs softly and whispers in my ear, "I love you, too, you big liar. You had plans."

Right then and there, I know I would do anything for this girl. She both challenges me and she accepts me. Exactly as I am.

Cameron no-middle-name Bach, flawed and perpetually pragmatic.

There are no walls with her.

And there doesn't have to be.

"I'll text you the tow truck information." I brush her hair back behind her ear. "I'll let you know when we're at the ER. And I'll call Owen."

Even though I'm pissed at him for hurting Luna.

She makes a face. "He's going to freak out."

"Do *not* tell my dad," Brady says, looking panicked. "He'll call my mom and it will be a whole thing."

"We'll call Owen," I assure Luna.

Brady rolls his eyes.

We leave with assurances we'll get the deliveries done and then we're in the car, Brady grumbling.

"You don't have to tell my dad."

"I'm not going to take you to the ER and not tell your father." I glance in the rearview mirror before I pull away from the curb.

"You don't have to take me to the ER."

I don't bother responding. I was a sixteen-year-old boy once. Arguing is futile.

"I feel so bad about Luna's van. She's going to have to pay for those repairs." He groans and tips his head back against the seat.

"No, she's not."

He looks over. "What?"

"I'll take care of it. She won't pay for anything. Don't worry."

I feel him studying me. "That's really cool of you. Thanks."

I'm not doing it for him. Well, I'm not doing it *just* for him. He's a good kid, and it was an accident and I've got the resources to make this into a non-problem for everyone. Of course I'm going to do that. "It's not a big deal," I say.

After a minute, he says, "This is a cool car." He's glancing around and touching random things. He sends the seat gliding backward. "A Mercedes. Need me one of these."

"Thanks. I bought it for my twenty-eighth birthday."

"So, you and Luna, huh?" Brady asks. "What's up with that?"

"Don't worry about me and Luna."

"I am worried. She's a cool human. Don't be a dick to her."

I appreciate his willingness to defend Luna. "I will not be a dick." Then I reach out and hit a button on the screen. "Call Owen Phillips."

"Dude." Brady reaches out like he's going to end the call.

"Do not touch that," I tell him, trying to be stern, but not threatening. It's hard as hell. I decide to go for another tactic. "I'll be cool about it, you know. If Luna tells him, it will be worse."

That makes his hand drop. But he says, "He's going to freak out no matter what."

"Hey, Cam, what's up?" Owen says, sounding surprised.

He should be surprised. If it was up to me, I'd never speak to him ever again.

"There's nothing to worry about, everything is fine, but—

"What's wrong?" Owen demands. "Is Luna sick? Did she have a car accident?"

Brady shrugs. "Told you."

"Brady?" Owen asks, voice confused.

"It's not Luna. Brady had a minor fender bender in Luna's bakery van. He's fine, but I'm taking him to the ER just to make sure he doesn't have a concussion."

"Holy shit. You sure he's okay? I can't come home. Aw, Christ."

"He seems fine. I just want to make sure since he kissed the windshield."

"He wasn't wearing a seat belt," Owen says grimly. "What a dumb ass."

"I can hear you, Dad," Brady announces loudly. "We're on speaker."

"Why weren't you wearing a seat belt, you dumb ass?"

Brady gives me a told-you-so look. "I just forgot. I was in a hurry."

"No one needs to be in a hurry when they're driving a four thousand pound vehicle."

"Okay. Sorry."

I almost snort at that but restrain myself.

"Call me after you've been seen by the doctor. I need to call your mother."

"Don't call Mom."

"I have to call your mother. I'm in Seattle, and you're supposed to be leaving with her in two hours for her college reunion."

"I don't even want to go to that."

"What, so you wrecked a van to get out of it?"

"Yes, that's exactly what I did," Brady says, sarcastically. He looks at me. "See?"

"See what? Let me talk to Cam again."

"He's still here, Dad. That's what a speaker phone does. It allows you to talk to multiple people at the same time."

Now I'm really entertained. Brady is at peak smart-ass.

Owen sighs heavily. There's a long pause, like he's struggling to maintain patience.

"I promised Luna I would help her at the wedding reception," Brady says.

"Why would you do that when you're supposed to be going to Pittsburgh with your mother?"

"Because Mom thought you'd be home."

"Your mother thought we wouldn't make the playoffs?"

"Yep."

"Oh." Owen sounds stunned and offended.

"She doesn't want me in Pittsburgh, either. She's going to want to drink wine with her sorority sisters and talk shit."

"Then why can't you stay with Dev?" Owen sounds confused.

I'm very confused. I don't even know who the hell Dev is.

"Because he's going with her. Amara is with Grandma and Grandpa."

"Then you'll have to fly to Seattle if you don't want to go to Pittsburgh."

"For one night? That's stupid."

"So is leaving you alone in my house."

This seems to be spiraling with no solution. "Brady can stay with Luna," I offer.

I haven't asked her, but I know she won't mind. She'll want to keep an eye on Brady. Knowing her, she feels somehow responsible for his crash. "And me."

There's a pause. "I mean... I guess... I'd have to run it past his mom."

Brady looks relieved. "It's the perfect solution. I'll be helping with this wedding anyway and then I'll be right there at the bakery to help Luna clean up. Plus, it gives me time to study tomorrow for my math test on Monday."

Nice one. The kid is working all the angles.

"That's okay with you, Cam, if Chelsea is fine with it?"

We pull up in front of the restaurant where the first delivery is. "Yes. We've got it all covered, Owen," I say. "Just focus on hockey. Everything is under control here."

"Thanks," he says gruffly. "I owe you."

"No, you don't."

I want him to understand that this is how it could have been if he hadn't bailed. Yes, a complex relationship with each other. But we would have had each other's backs. He just walked away without even trying.

I assure him I can handle everything and end the call.

Brady shakes his head. "Dude needs to get laid."

That makes me laugh out loud. "No arguments there."

CHAPTER 31

Owen

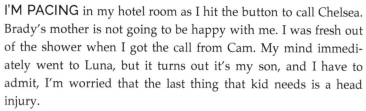

I'M PACING in my hotel room as I hit the button to call Chelsea. Brady's mother is not going to be happy with me. I was fresh out of the shower when I got the call from Cam. My mind immediately went to Luna, but it turns out it's my son, and I have to admit, I'm worried that the last thing that kid needs is a head injury.

"Owen, hi, what's up? I'm in a rush. I need to leave soon for the airport."

"So, about that. It's not serious, I've been assured, but Brady's en route to the ER. I don't think he's going to make the flight with you to Pittsburgh."

"*What?* What happened?"

"He had a minor car accident and hit his head." I run my hand through my wet hair and set the phone down—which I do know how to use, thank you, Brady—so I can adjust my towel.

"He's okay? You're sure?"

"Yes. The ER is just a precaution. Concussion protocol."

"Aren't you in Seattle?"

"Yes. For the playoffs. Which my team deserves to be at." I'm super annoyed she was so sure the Racketeers wouldn't make the playoffs.

"What is that supposed to mean?" she sounds baffled. "And why do you sound salty with me when I'm the one who has to cancel my trip? Again."

I rub my beard and wince. "Okay, we're getting off track here. Don't cancel your trip. Brady can stay in Chicago."

"He's not staying with Lydia. I already told him that."

"Are you okay with him staying with Luna McNeill?" It was a huge relief to me when Cam offered.

It's actually a huge relief in general to have him calmly handling the car accident and taking Brady to the ER. Luna has a big day with her first wedding cake delivery and I know she's been stressed about it. Plus, I know Chelsea sometimes gets frustrated with how much I'm on the road and shuttling Brady back and forth between us. It's even harder now that he's older because it can be tempting to leave him on his own, which I know would be a mistake.

It's also reassuring to know that Cam is there with Luna when Alexsei isn't.

Further proving I am not needed in any sort of relationship with them.

Not that she *needs* anyone to be with her. It just makes me feel better. She was left alone a lot as a kid because of hockey, and I hate the idea that being with Alexsei would set her up for that all over again.

"His boss? Or your girlfriend?"

That's a kick in the teeth. Not my girlfriend. I fight the urge to sigh.

"His boss. Her boyfriend Cameron is taking Brady to the ER right now. He's a… good guy." I wouldn't call Cam 'nice' exactly, but he's competent, responsible, and not easy to rattle. I trust him to handle an ER visit.

If I make it clear Cam is Luna's boyfriend, maybe Chelsea will drop any ideas she might have about me and her.

"I thought you went on a date with Luna. Brady told me. You screwed that up, huh?"

Well, that was a fail. "Wow," I say. "I'm on your hit list today. That one stung, I'm not going to lie. Yes, we went on a date. No, I'm not going to see her anymore."

Chelsea sighs. "Sorry. It's just that I'm frustrated that you're in Seattle. What's the point of having a baby daddy if I can't get Brady-free time?" she says, lightly.

"So this is all about wine with the sorority sisters, isn't it?" I ask, finally getting a read on her mood.

"Yes. Obviously."

"I heard you thought we wouldn't make the playoffs."

"That was just wishful thinking. Again, wine with sorority sisters. I just wanted a weekend away with me and Dev."

"I'm sorry," I say, and I mean that sincerely. "I know my job can be hard on the people in my life. I appreciate you, Chelsea."

"I know. You're a good father, Owen. Even if your job sucks."

That makes me laugh. "So, you're cool with Brady staying with Luna?"

"Oh, God, yeah. I don't want his grumpy butt with me, that's for damn sure."

"Okay, good." I pick the phone back up and put it to my ear. "And what if I had been dating Luna? Would that have been cool?"

"I thought you said she has a boyfriend, but you can date whoever you want as long as she's not a drug dealer or user."

"She does have a boyfriend. Two, actually."

"An open relationship?"

"No. They're in a relationship together. The three of them."

"Oh." She pauses as if taking that all in. Then she says, "Yeah, I don't see that being your thing."

She may be right, but I'm still annoyed and a little offended. "Why is that?"

"You like to be needed."

The mother of my child with the truth bombs today. "That's ironic, because I feel like I'm failing at being there for everyone."

"Hey, no you're not. Don't say that. You've always been there for me and Dev, with Brady and Amara. I'm sorry for saying I didn't want the Racketeers to make the playoffs to Brady. That was bitchy."

"Just honest." I'm not trying to make Chelsea feel bad. I've done enough of that lately.

"And bitchy."

"A little," I relent. "But you have every right."

She laughs.

"Seriously, Chels. God, Brady is so full of attitude right now. Jump on a plane and drink as much wine in Pittsburgh as you can."

"I plan to. I'll call Brady now."

"Sounds good. We'll keep each other updated."

"Of course. Good luck tonight. And I mean that."

"Thank you. I appreciate that."

We end the call after goodbyes and I sit down on the end of the bed.

I'm a little overwhelmed with all my conflicting feelings.

I'm not needed back in Chicago.

I have to admit, it's nice to not have to be *the* man in charge all the time.

But I want to be needed, what's so wrong with that? Luna's words echo in my head.

There's something really great about being able to fuck up and be loved, anyway. About just being wanted, instead of needed.

I toy with the idea of calling her. Though what the hell would I say?

But my phone lights up right then, and it's her, which makes my palms sweat.

"Hello?"

"I'm so sorry about Brady," she blurts out. "I shouldn't have sent him alone."

I'm happy to hear her voice, but upset that she's upset. And that she didn't call because she misses me. She called about Brady.

"No, no, it's fine. Don't feel guilty. There was no reason he couldn't go alone. You hired him to do a job and he should have been more careful. Cam seems to have everything under control. I just wish I was there. I'm sorry."

"I don't want you to worry," she says, sounding worried herself. "Did you talk to Chelsea? Cam told me about Brady staying here and I'm good with that if you and Chelsea are okay with it."

"Chelsea was fine with it. She trusts my judgment, and I trust you."

Her voice softens. "Thank you."

"Thank *you*."

There's a pause. She doesn't say anything.

It grows uncomfortably long. I clench my fist closed and open it again. I need to say something.

"Well—" I start to say.

"So, okay, bye—" she says at the exact same time.

We both pause.

I start to talk again. She also starts to talk.

Luna laughs softly.

I'm not laughing. I wait this time for her to speak.

"Bye, Owen."

"Bye, Luna."

Two hours later, I'm staring at my lunch in the hotel restaurant without eating it. There is activity all around, with several of the players talking and joking. Small favors, Alexsei isn't here. I have no idea where he is, but both him and McNeill are absent.

Hearing Luna's voice was torture.

I'm going through everything I said and wondering if I should have said more.

"Hey, Coach, you on a diet?" Wilder asks me, strolling past me and snagging a sticky bun off of my plate. He takes a tearing bite of the bun. "I didn't want to say anything, but you are getting a little thick in the middle."

"The buffet's right there. Go get your own food," I say grumpily.

Wilder is usually more reserved than this, but the guys are all pumped for the game. Normally, I would be, too, but I'm questioning what the hell I'm doing. Did I fuck up by walking away from Luna?

"Leave Coach alone," Hayes says. "He has a sweet tooth."

I do have a sweet tooth. Cake, cookies, macarons… I love them all and now every single damn dessert in existence reminds me of Luna and her sugary sweet scent. I shove my plate away. I can't eat. I may never eat again.

"Did you see all those girls outside the arena when we rolled up?" Hayes says.

Wilder takes another bite of the bun and talks with his mouth full. "One had a sign that said 'Marry Me Blake Wilder.'"

"That's because you're a goalie and she's never seen your ugly face," Hayes tells him.

"Fuck you. She was too skinny for me anyway. You know I like curvy girls."

Hayes laughs and mimics spanking someone. "That's why."

Wilder laughs along with him. "Damn right. I'm an ass-man. What do you like, Coach?"

"Eating my lunch in fucking peace."

They cackle like I'm hilarious.

My phone buzzes and I see it's Cam. "See you on the ice." I shove my chair back and abandon my lunch to go out into the hallway. "Hello? How's Brady?"

"He's fine. No concussion. They glued his cut, and he's fine. He just needs observation."

I sigh in relief. "Good. Thanks again, Cam. I really appreciate it."

"You're welcome. Now, can we talk about how pointless this is?"

That makes my shoulders tense. "What?"

"You pretending this is what you want—flying solo instead of being with us."

"I'm working."

"That's not what I meant and you fucking know it. I saw her with you. And you with her. I think she needs all three of us. She's conflicted. Happy with us, but missing you."

I miss her, too. So damn much. "But..."

"But what? Luna is so fucking special. If you don't know that, you haven't been around much in your thirty-six years."

Glancing around to make sure no one is listening, I tell him, "I fucking know that."

Cam goes on like I didn't say anything.

"She has so much fire, so much personality, and passion and, just emotion, that she needs lots of outlets. And if you don't want to share, Alexsei and I will probably have to find someone else."

"*What?*" That has never even entered my head, and it makes me feel like I can't breathe. Another guy that isn't me? I swear, my vision actually goes black for a second. It's like taking a puck to the face.

"Because as much as we can give her, I don't think we can give her everything she needs. We all see her differently, fulfill different things for her. She and I need Alexsei because he gives us the softness, the affection, the cuddling, the hugs. She and I push each other and spar. We both need that, but we don't get that from Alexsei. She and I are...like best friends with benefits."

"That's great for you," I say, even though I think it sucks. Not because they have that, but because Cam and Alexsei offer her something I can't. I can't offer her anything. That's why I exited before my emotions were any deeper.

Which is a total joke. My emotions are already deep and permanent.

"We like fucking and we like fucking Alexsei together," I say. "But Alexsei worships her. And that's different from how he treats me."

Rubbing my beard, I interject. "I just said that's great." I feel like I might break a tooth if I grind my molars down any harder. "Drop it, Cam."

Cam ignores me. Of course.

"You take care of her. You make her feel steady and safe. She needs that, too. But she's not going to get that in the same way, with the confidence and solidness, from me and Alexsei. We're all pieces of the whole for her. She feels like something's missing without you.

"If you do love her, then think about this, and think about how Alexsei and I fit in. How much happier she can be with all of us."

I don't even know what to say.

Is he right?

I have no fucking clue.

All I know is I'm miserable.

"Don't replace me," is what I say.

"Then get your fucking head in the game," Cam says. "Now I have to go and feed your garbage disposal of a kid. He eats nonstop."

That pulls a half-laugh from me. "Tell me about it. Thanks. Again. For…"

"Just think about it."

Then Cam hangs up on me.

The guy can be a real asshole. But I'm actually fond of him.

Rowdy shouts come from the restaurant.

And all I can think is that I feel lonely as hell.

CHAPTER 32

Owen

USUALLY I LIKE a few days off after a series, especially a hard-fought one.

I should be on cloud nine. We're going to the championship series. I haven't done that. Not as a coach and not as a player.

This is the best team I've ever been a part of.

The trophy should be ours.

But instead of thinking about any of that and enjoying basking in the afterglow of the victory, I am sitting on my couch, in my sweatpants, eating my third bowl of Cap'n Crunch, and flipping through the channels.

My teenage son comes practically galloping down the stairs. But he draws up short when he sees me.

"Are you sick?"

I shake my head. "No. I'm fine."

"Seriously, did somebody die?"

Just my heart. "No, no one died. Everything's fine."

I really try not to lie to my son as much as possible, but this is necessary.

"Seriously, why do you look like—" His phone pings with a text, and of course, that immediately pulls his attention off of me.

For maybe the first time since he got the fucking phone three years ago, I'm glad that he would rather text with his friends than talk to me. I shovel another spoonful of cereal into my mouth and stare at the TV screen. I don't even know what I'm watching right now. Is this a documentary or a home improvement show? Maybe it's a crime drama? I'm not really sure why we're crawling through the basement of this rundown house in the woods.

"Wait...you broke up with Luna?"

Brady's shocked question jerks my attention to him again.

I frown. "How do you know that?"

"Lydia's at the bakery with Luna. Dani's there, too. So are Alexsei and Cam and Crew. Everybody's pissed at you."

Well, so much for keeping this all from Crew.

My chest feels tight thinking about them all, though.

I miss them.

And not just Luna.

Though the thought of her makes me feel like someone has a fist around my heart, squeezing hard. I can't breathe, it's not beating right, and...I don't care about it beating again if I'm not going to see her, anyway.

Yes, I'm aware that's all very dramatic. I live with a teenager.

I hate the idea that Luna's pissed at me. But I would rather she be pissed than hurt.

But I do hate the idea that Cam and Alexsei are mad at me.

I mean, I'm not surprised. Obviously they are. I'd be pissed at them if they had done this to Luna.

But now Lydia and Dani and Crew are all involved, too?

Of course they are. Everyone loves Luna. As they should.

"Dad, what did you do?"

"Nothing." Then I sigh. He's not going to let it go if I keep that up. "The right thing. I stepped aside so she can date Alexsei and Cam."

"I guess..."

I look up to find Brady rubbing the back of his neck, looking a little uncomfortable.

Then he sighs. "I thought you were all dating each other."

I shrug. "She doesn't need me."

"You're jealous of Alexsei and Cam?"

I look up at him. "Don't worry about it. Don't you need to go somewhere?"

My son gives me a *really?* look. The same one I've given to him about four million times in his life. Then he shrugs out of his jacket, tosses it on the chair, and comes over to sit on the edge of the coffee table, blocking my view of the television. He takes my bowl out of my hands and sets it on the table next to him. Then he leans forward, bracing his forearms on his thighs and levels me with a serious look. "What is going on?"

I'm shocked by the role reversal for a moment. I just blink at him.

"I swear to God, Dad. If this is some kind of homophobic thing, we are going to have a *long* talk."

"Why do people keep thinking that's my problem?"

"Why else would you walk away?"

Okay, maybe that's a fair point. "I like the guys a lot," I say. "If I was gay, I'd totally go for one of them. Hell, I'd be flattered if Cam gave me a second look."

The corner of Brady's mouth curls up. "Okay, that's better. So if it's not a problem with the guys, did you suddenly realize you don't like Luna? Because she is amazing. You are never going to find someone better than her."

I scowl at him. "Of course I know that. I'm in love with her."

"Then none of this makes any sense."

I cross my arms over my chest. Now I completely understand the times when he just wanted me to leave him alone. Sometimes you know exactly what you did wrong and you just don't want to hash it all out.

"Dad, talk to me. I want to help if I can."

Yeah, this role reversal is surreal. Especially considering he has a long-term healthy relationship with Lydia and I'm...an idiot.

"Fine. You know what it is?" I ask. "They are fantastic together.

The three of them. The guys are incredibly supportive of Luna. Since they came along, she's figured out that she can have the work-life balance that she desperately needed. They think she's amazing. She practically walks on water as far as they're concerned. They make her laugh. They help her with everything. The three of them are best friends, but they're also really..."

"Hot together?" he asks.

I lift a brow.

He shrugs. "Come on. The sex has to be great, right? They're all incredibly attractive, confident people." He says it so matter-of-factly, I just find myself nodding.

"So, are you jealous?" he asks.

That is a fair question. But I shake my head. "No. I know that sounds weird. I actually really like the way they are with her. They treat her well, they make her feel good. And vice versa."

"So you felt left out?"

This is a strange conversation to be having with Brady, but I suppose it's also a chance for me to expose him to being open-minded about relationships and sex in a healthy, positive way. I can't let him think any of this is too embarrassing or awkward to discuss.

I shake my head. "Not that, either. Everyone was equally involved and respected and considered." I clear my throat. "In the bedroom and out," I say. "In any good relationship, it should be that way in all aspects. Like how Cam and Luna stepped in to help you out with the accident."

"And you would have totally done the same for them."

"Of course."

"I don't understand the problem," he says. "Honestly. Help me understand."

"They don't really need me for anything. In a relationship, it has to be give-and-take," I say. "You have to be part of the two-way street. Or the four-way street if that's the street you're on. Everyone needs to contribute."

Brady stares at me for a moment. Then he starts to laugh. "Are you trying to tell me that you think you don't contribute? You? The guy who does everything for everyone? The dad to everyone around him?"

"I'm the *actual* dad for you. You see a different side of me."

He shakes his head. "You're the dad for everybody. You're the dad to all the guys on the team. Do you remember when Jack couldn't get home for Christmas last year because his entire family got sick? You practically tied him up and threw him in your car to bring him home with us. And then there was the time Trey got really sick, high fevers and everything and you insisted he stay here, so he had someone looking out for him.

"And that time Wilder bought a bed that was too big to get into his apartment and you went over and took that huge-assed thing apart, helped him get it up three flights, and reassembled it.

"You've taught at least two guys to snake their drains. You taught a bunch to change their oil. You made the entire team volunteer to do yard work in the park last summer because a bunch of them told you they'd never mowed a lawn and you thought that was pathetic. You're the dad to everybody on the team."

He grins at me. But he's also not done. "And what about Amara? She's your ex's daughter. But the other day she told Dev, her actual father, that she wanted to go see her second dad."

I swallow hard. "That's just things you do," I say. "Those guys are all away from home and their own dads. I'm a coach. I can't let my players just flounder. And Amara is your little sister. Of course, I'm good to her. It's not her fault her mom is my ex."

"First of all, your players are all grown men who make millions of dollars. They don't need to change their own oil or snake their drains, or ever mow a lawn probably," he says, laughing. "But you think it's important they know these things and they respect you enough to listen. Plus, I think they like having someone treat them like a dad sometimes. They probably miss their own dads. And some of them didn't have dads. You caring about how they're turning out as men and not just players makes them feel good." He gives me an affectionate smile. "And you love it. Because that's who you are. You take care of people, Dad. You let people lean on you. You want people to have what they need and be the best they can be. You're there for people and if you can't get something done, you know someone who can. And I guarantee that Luna, Cam, and Alexsei see it and feel it and *want* it in their lives."

I feel my chest tighten again and I have to actually blink fast because this is making me a little emotional. Not just the words, but that my son, the kid I've been worrying about and praying over and hoping, is turning out okay for almost seventeen years now, is telling me all of this.

I clear my throat. "So I'm a nice guy."

"You take care of people. And I don't care what Cam and Alexsei do for Luna, they don't take care of her like you do. Because you're you. *Of course* you have something to contribute."

I look at him, my throat tight. "That's kinda sappy."

"Yeah, I know. I have this really great mom and dad who get kinda sappy on me sometimes. I guess it's rubbed off."

I take a big, deep breath. "Well, brace yourself. I'm going to be sappy right back."

He grips the edge of the coffee table.

"I love you. A lot. And I'm proud of you. You treat Lydia with a lot of respect. And you're a really good person."

He shakes his head, but he's smiling. "Thanks."

"Now, aren't you going to be late for work?"

"Maybe five minutes. But, this is kind of important," Brady says. "I want you to be happy. And I want you to know that you're a great guy. People love you. You don't have to do anything special for that to be true."

I finally reach out and grab the front of his T-shirt, pulling him into a hug. He falls onto me on the couch, a tangle of gangly teenage boy limbs, laughing. But he hugs me around the neck before he pushes himself off of me.

"Okay, okay. I gotta go to work."

I listen to him leave, thinking about everything he said.

And I think about all of the people he's going to see when he gets to the bakery.

I let myself miss them all.

And, finally, I let myself admit that I might've made a mistake.

CHAPTER 33

Luna

FUCK, I hate hockey.

I always have. The whole it-stole-my-family thing. But now I *really* hate it for sure.

Because it's ripping my heart out.

I can't imagine being anywhere else tonight. This is where I *have* to be. I want to be here.

And this is the last place I want to be at the same time.

I'm descending the steps that I have walked down seemingly a hundred times to get to the seats where I will sit next to my best friend and her boyfriend, who owns the team. As I've done at least a dozen times now.

But tonight I'm wearing my boyfriend's jersey. I'll be sitting *next* to my other boyfriend instead of in front of him. I'll hold Cam's hand. I'll jump up and hug and kiss him whenever the Racketeers score. I get to watch my brother and my boyfriend play one of the biggest games of their lives, surrounded by other people I love.

And I feel this tightness in my throat because I want to cry.

This isn't just a big night and a big game for Alexsei and Crew. It's huge for Owen, too.

I want to share this with him.

I want to send him a good luck text. Moreover, I wanted to call him earlier and see how he's feeling, tell him I'll be there cheering him on, tell him I'll be waiting after the game no matter what happens.

But that's not my place.

He walked away. I need to let him go.

I've got Cam and Alexsei. I've got what I need.

Mostly.

That's the thing—every time I think 'I have everything I could need or want', there's a niggle in the back of my mind that adds 'almost' or 'not quite'.

I love Cam and Alexsei. I'm so happy with them. They are exactly who I need them to be. And I know they feel the same way.

But something's missing.

No.

Someone is missing.

And now tonight I have to sit in this arena for the next two and a half to three hours with the Racketeers bench, and the coaching staff, *right there*.

I've avoided Owen successfully. There's no reason for us to run into each other.

I've, of course, thought of him constantly. His son works for me. Alexsei goes to practice with him. I'm freaking *in love with him*. So no, I can't escape the reminders and thoughts of him.

But I haven't had to see him.

Now there's no way for me not to see him.

I slide into the aisle, smiling at and hugging Dani and saying hi to Nathan. I respect that the owner of the team sits down here in the stands with the fans. He has a private box, and he's entertained my parents there before games in the past, but Dani likes sitting down here, closer to the action, where Crew and Michael can more easily see her, and Nathan would rather be with her than away from the crowd.

"Hi, Dani," Cam greets, giving her a wave.

"Hi, Cam." She smiles at him.

He and Nathan shake hands and my heart squeezes.

I love that all of these people are mixing and getting along and it's so easy to imagine dinner parties and celebrations all together for years to come.

"Hey everyone!"

I look up to find Brady and Lydia taking the seats right behind us. The one Cam used to sit in and the one beside it.

"Hi, guys," I greet. I turn a questioning look on Dani.

She smiles and shrugs. "I know someone who can get me any tickets in here that I want." She looks over her shoulder at Nathan. "And I think his prices are *very* fair."

He leans in to say something in her ear that makes her blush and I just roll my eyes, but I'm grinning.

"I think Armstrong and I might share a love for tough negotiations," Cam says huskily to me.

I look up at him. "You think so? I've actually found you pretty *accommodating,* for the most part."

"You just haven't asked me for anything I haven't wanted to give you," he says, running the tip of his finger down my cheek.

I let my voice drop a little lower and am gratified by the way his gaze goes to my mouth. "Oh really? How about the kiss I wanted that first night?"

There's a flare of heat in his eyes and he leans in. "I gave you exactly what we both wanted, Pixie...you begging me."

In that moment, I'm hit by the craziest mix of joy and love and *rightness.* I can so easily imagine being with this man and Alexsei forever.

"I love you," I say, emphatically.

I can see I surprised him, but he smiles. "I love you, too."

There's a ripple in the crowd around us just then that distracts me from staring into Cam's eyes.

"Kiss Cam!" someone shouts.

"Um, Luna," I hear Dani say behind me.

"It's Kiss Cam!" someone else shouts.

I frown. It's pre-game. They don't do the KissCam before the game.

But Cam sighs. "For fuck's sake," he mutters. Then he leans around me. "Armstrong," he snaps.

And I love that because no one ever snaps at Nathan Armstrong.

"I thought we talked about that fucking KissCam."

I look over at Nathan.

"And I told you that you needed to up your advertising spend in the arena or make a donation before anything could be done," Nathan tells him.

I look back at Cam. What are they talking about?

"You hate that thing as much as I do," Cam says.

"More," Nathan nods. "But the fans love it and Danielle and Val keep reminding me that I have to care about that."

Cam's sigh is even heavier now. "Damned social media."

"What are you talking about?" I ask him. This seems more than his usual annoyance.

"Haven't you seen? Everyone is calling Cameron 'Kiss Cam' online," Dani says with a giggle. "Ever since he caught you from falling and laid that kiss on you a while back. Once they found out who he is, and his name, it's blown up."

I turn wide eyes on Cam, trying really hard to hide my smile. "Oh. My. God."

"Please don't tell Owen."

I laugh. "But–"

I'm cut off by the crowd around us starting to applaud and cheer.

"Oh, great," Cam mutters.

I follow his gaze to the aisle.

Where Sammy the Malamute is descending the steps.

Oh…no.

"Kiss Cam! Kiss Cam!" The arena is far from full and many people are still milling about on the concourse, getting food, drink, and souvenirs, but the people already inside the arena are making some noise.

"Luna." Dani tugs on the back of my Alexsei Ryan jersey.

I look down at her. She points up at the jumbotron.

I don't want to look.

But I do. Sure enough, it's me, Cam, and Sammy.

Nathan even stands up to let Sammy pass into our row.

Sammy lifts a paw, points at me, then at himself, then at the jumbotron.

I...laugh.

This is all so bonkers. And so familiar.

"You know, Sammy," I say, "Maybe after all this time we should finally–"

"Do *not* finish that sentence," Cam mutters.

Then I'm being dipped back by my boyfriend and kissed, in front of the Racketeers fans, in front of Sammy, on the jumbotron.

Again.

I'm laughing when Cam finally rights me.

"She's *taken*," Cam tells Sammy. "Keep your paws off of her."

Sammy drops his head, shaking it sadly, then puts his hand over his heart and starts back up the stairs.

The crowd gives him a collective, "*Awww.*"

But then the camera pans back to me and Cam, and the crowd cheers.

I grin and, stupidly, wave.

What? I'm happy. I can't help it.

"They're here!" Brady exclaims behind us.

I turn and watch him wave to a beautiful woman who is standing on the steps with a little girl who is talking to Sammy. The little girl is also holding a man's hand.

After a quick interaction with Sammy that involves a hug and a high-five, they continue down the stairs to Brady's row.

"Hi, Mom," Brady greets. "Hey, Dev."

"Brady!" the little girl squeals, shaking her parents off and lunging for him.

He scoops her up, giving her a big hug. "Hey, kid!"

She squeezes him but then pulls back and leans toward Lydia. "Hi, Lydia!"

"Hi, Amara." Lydia accepts the little girl climbing into her arms but hugs her and then quickly lets her slide to the floor as Amara is really too big to be held.

Brady gives the woman—who is obviously Chelsea—a hug, and then hugs his stepdad.

I'm suddenly nervous, but also so fascinated. I so want to meet these people.

I feel Cam squeeze my waist. "Breathe, goddess."

I do, then I look up at him.

He's watching me with such clear affection in his eyes that I can't do anything but take a deep breath and smile.

Then Brady says, "Mom, Dev, this is Luna."

I look up.

"Oh my god! Hi!" Chelsea says. "I'm so glad to meet you!"

Dev gives me a smile. "Hi." He extends a hand. "Brady never stops talking about you. Unless he's talking about Lydia, of course. And thanks for all the leftovers you've sent home with him. Your cupcakes are amazing."

And just like that, we're all friends.

"Hi. It's great to meet you all, too," I tell them honestly. "Brady and Lydia are wonderful. Thanks for letting them work at the bakery."

Chelsea laughs. "Are you kidding? Thanks for hiring them."

"Mom, you make us sound like we're huge problems," Brady says with an eye roll.

"No, not when you have a job that keeps you busy," she says, but she gives him a loving smile and a hip bump.

And stupidly, my heart aches. I know that I'll continue to see Brady and Lydia for a while, but they'll eventually go to college and I'll lose touch with them. I feel a sharp pang of sadness at the sudden realization.

I'd love to see them grow up. I'd love to see where they end up, what careers they choose, and if they stay together. Even if they don't. Sure, they'll say that they'll stop into the bakery when they're home from college visiting, and maybe they will the first couple of times, but eventually, I'll just be some lady they worked for when they were kids.

"Hey." Cam's deep voice rumbles by my ear. "You okay?"

I realize that I'm just staring at Brady and Lydia. I swallow and nod, focusing on him instead. "Yeah. Sure. Of course." I don't even try to force a smile. He can read me, so what's the point?

"You're acting weirder than usual," he tells me, giving me a half-smile. But I can tell he's a little concerned.

"It's just a big night," I tell him.

A big night of trying to keep my shit together while I'm happy and sad and filled with love and despair in equal measures.

Yes, that sounds dramatic. I don't care.

"Will you tell me about whatever this is later?" he asks.

If you'd told me back when I first turned around and he informed me that he and Alexsei both liked chocolate chip pancakes that this man would turn out to be one of my best friends, I would have laughed right in your face.

But now, I nod. I can tell him that I miss Owen and everything having him in my life meant. He'll understand. And he'll make me feel better about it.

Not as good as having Owen back would, but Cam and Alexsei will remind me what I do have and…that's a lot.

"Oh my God, hot hockey players right up close! Thank you, thank you."

I see Elise and Austin both coming down the aisle to join Brady and his family. Delighted by that surprise, too, I'm able to actually laugh as I look at Dani.

She shrugs. "I wanted the whole family here."

Tears sting my eyes, but they're happy, sappy tears. My parents are here, of course. I know Michael Hughes' parents and a couple of his sisters are as well. Dani told me earlier that her dad called to ask about finding the game on TV. Alexsei told me his parents will be at the next game in person but are watching tonight, and Cam said his mom is even tuning in tonight.

I grab Cam's hand and squeeze as I turn around and face the ice.

And then he's there.

Owen.

He's behind the bench, in his suit.

He should probably be watching the players warm-up, or conferring with the other coaches, but he's not.

He's standing there, staring up into the stands at all of us.

But when I turn, his eyes lock on mine.

Not Brady.

Me.

I feel the connection rock through me and I don't even think twice as I mouth to him, *I love you.*

I can see even from here the way he straightens, and that he wants to say something back. Or maybe *do* something.

But he can't.

And maybe I should feel bad about that.

I don't.

Cam always says I'm a brat. And he's not wrong.

Yeah, Coach, just try to get over me.

I'll just be up here in the stands, cheering you on, and *not* being over you.

CHAPTER 34
Cameron

"I HAD a great game tonight and Luna is in the kitchen stomping around making cupcakes at midnight," Alexsei says under his breath, putting his feet on the coffee table. "She's trying to hide it, but our girl really sucks at hiding her feelings."

"You think?" I ask wryly, sitting on the couch beside him. "At least we'll know when we're in trouble with her."

"Are you sure we're *not* in trouble with her?" Alexsei asks, casting a wary glance Luna's way when she smacks the top of her stand mixer with the palm of her hand and calls it a motherfucker.

It's definitely not us. It's Owen.

The last few weeks have been amazing. We've settled into a routine of date nights and sleepovers here at our place when Alexsei's in town, and then when he's not, Luna stays at her apartment to catch up on laundry and work. Sometimes I go over to her place without Alexsei, sometimes I don't. It just depends on Luna and what her needs are that day and I'm flexible. I'm a guy who likes a little space, too, so it works out.

It's all working out with the *three* of us.

We're in love, and we're having a great time.

What's not working out is that Luna misses Owen.

And it's making her angry that she still misses him.

Which makes me angry at Owen.

"I'm sure. She saw Owen at the game, obviously, and it upset her. Brady and Lydia being there was great and everything, but she saw clearly what Owen chose to give up and her heart is hurt." I reach over and give Alexsei a kiss. "You did have a great game. I'm proud of you, babe."

He gives me a bright smile. Alexsei is easy to perk up. It's one of the many things I love about him. He rolls his shoulders and flexes his outstretched legs. "Thanks. I think I'm getting old though. My whole body hurts from head to toe."

"You're twenty-fucking-four."

"In hockey terms, this is my prime."

"You are definitely in your prime." I lean over and murmur in his ear. "You should take a hot shower while Luna finishes up whatever the hell she's doing in there. Then I'll give you a massage."

"A real massage or one that is just a fake-out one so you can get me naked?"

I rub the inside of his thigh. "It's a real one, I promise, but with a happy ending."

"Sold." Alexsei drops his feet to the floor and starts to stand up. "Is she going to be okay in there?" he asks, giving another nervous glance in her direction. "I feel like we should talk to her."

"I think she just needs to work this out in her own way. Our girl likes space, remember?"

He nods. But he does stroll over to Luna and kisses the side of her head. "I'm taking a shower."

"Okay." She blows her hair out of her face. "I'm sorry, I don't know what got into me tonight. I'll be done in a bit."

Alexsei runs his thumb over her cheek. "Sounds good. I love you."

"I love you, too. You were awesome tonight, sweetheart. I'm so proud of you."

"Thanks." Then he turns and mouths *"Phew,"* to me while miming wiping his brow.

I grin at him. He's not known for his subtlety. I'm reaching out to give his ass a smack as he passes by the couch when my phone rings. Pissed off that I'm getting a call this late, I grab my phone off the end table, ready to chew someone out. The number on the screen is the apartment building concierge.

Frowning, I swipe to answer it. "Hello?"

It's the front desk manager, Rob. It's one of the things I love about this building. We have an attendant twenty-four/seven.

"Sorry to disturb you, Mr. Bach, but Mr. Phillips is down here in the lobby. I let him in because he's been a guest before, but now I'm concerned…"

I glance over at Luna. This could be good or bad. I'm not sure yet. "No, no, it's fine that you let him in. Is there a problem? Why isn't he coming up?"

"He's been pacing in the lobby for twenty minutes muttering to himself. With a bouquet of *very* unattractive flowers."

That has me walking over to the door and sliding my feet into what Alexsei calls my lobby sandals. I keep them by the front door for picking up packages, mail, and any other reason I might need to head to the lobby on a moment's notice.

Rob is somewhat of a snarky apartment manager, probably because he works nights and sees some unusual activity, but even if he's exaggerating about how long Owen has been there, I clearly need to intervene. "Thanks, Rob. I will come down and retrieve him."

"Thank you, sir. He's triggering my fear of rejection. Turn him down gently."

That makes me roll my eyes. "Thank you for the head's up." I put my phone in my pocket and call out to Luna, "I'll be right back. I have to run down to the lobby for a package."

"Now?"

"Yes. I'll be two minutes." I don't wait for her response.

The second the elevator doors open, I see Owen, exactly as Rob described him. He's pacing by the leather sofa that no one ever sits on and looking disheveled in jeans and a T-shirt, his hair sticking up a little. Rob even gives me a fucking-told-you-so look while gesturing toward Owen with his index finger.

I see what he means about the flowers. They're blue carnations. Like dishwashing detergent blue. The blue of high school spirit colors and the Smurfs. There might be a party or occasion these would be perfect for, but this is not it.

"Owen."

He pauses in front of the electric fireplace and glances up at me in surprise, as if this isn't my apartment building. "Cam?"

"You okay?" I ask. "I got a phone call that you've been hanging around the lobby."

"I came to talk to Luna." He sighs. "I guess all of you, really. And I figured she was here."

"Good." The guy looks tormented. "Can I ask what you want to say to her? Or to all of us?" Because I'm taking the flowers as a good sign, but if he's not one hundred percent sure of his feelings and what comes next, there's no way he's getting on that elevator.

"I'm not sure what to say," he admits. "That's why I'm still down here."

"Owen, you have to figure your shit out," I say bluntly. "I'm not letting you up if you're not sure."

He shakes his head. "I'm sure of *her*. I want her back. I want to do this thing with all of you. But I've been trying to come up with a grand gesture, something to prove it. And I don't know what to do."

Thank God. He's here for the right reason.

But there are a few things I need to be sure he understands before I let him upstairs.

I take a step forward. "You know that you don't have to always have the answers, right?" I ask. "You do not have to be the one that fixes things all the time. I know people come to you for that. I know you pride yourself on being the guy everyone leans on. You're really fucking good at it." I pause, because I really want this part to sink in. "But if you come upstairs, you have to be okay with *not* always having the answers and with leaning on the three of us sometimes."

He straightens to his full height. He takes a deep breath. And he meets my gaze directly. "I do know that. I'm actually looking forward to having you three to lean on when I need to."

Studying him, I believe him. I can sense his relief and acceptance.

This is going to work out.

I can't believe the surge of happiness I feel.

"You don't really seem like a grand gesture kind of guy," I tell him.

He blows out a breath. "I'm not. But I'm willing to try for her."

That makes me smile. "You don't actually need to do anything other than be honest."

He puts his hands up like he's going to gesticulate, then realizes he's holding the flowers. "I don't know why I brought these."

"I don't either. Where did you get those?"

"The gas station. It was a desperate impulse."

That's a hell no. I reach for the flowers. "You're not taking those upstairs. Luna doesn't need those." *I* don't fucking need those in my apartment. "She just needs you to apologize and tell her how you feel."

Owen lets me take the flowers from him. "Do you think she'll listen?"

"Of course she'll listen." I toss the bouquet on the coffee table in front of the sofa. "She loves you, Owen. She's been miserable without you."

"But she has you and Alexsei."

I sigh and turn to face him. "*Really*? How the fuck are you still not getting this?" I shake my head. "Yes, she's been happy with me and Alexsei. But she's been unhappy without *you*. She wants *all* of us. Together."

Owen groans. "I know, I know. I don't know why I said that. That's why I'm here. I love her. I get it. I want to be a part of the big picture, Luna and you and Alexsei and my kid and the

McNeill's and everyone and everything else that comes with being part of a family, in a loving relationship." Owen takes a deep breath. "I'm all in. For life."

"Then that's what you need to tell her." I clap him on the shoulder. "And maybe grovel, just a little at the end. It can't hurt."

Owen winces. "Grovel. Got it." Then he seems to pull himself together. "Hey," he says as we walk toward the elevator.

"Yeah?"

"You're a good friend. I appreciate you."

It makes me feel more than I would have expected. But I respect Owen, as a man, as a father, as a coach. My chest tightens. "I appreciate you, too." I smack the button for the elevator.

Then because I figure he needs a confidence booster and a bit of levity going into this, I add, "Though I did *not* appreciate having to fill your oral-sex shoes. You're a hard act to follow, Coach."

That makes Owen grin. "Well, no worries. I'm back now. To stay."

CHAPTER 35

Luna

I HEAR the door to the apartment open and close and assume Cam is already back. He said he needed to run downstairs to grab a package. I didn't ask what was being delivered this late. I'm too focused on my cupcakes.

"She's rage baking," I hear Cam say. "We got her a stand mixer and a bunch of pans and bowls and utensils a while back. She's using the hell out of them tonight."

I frown. Who is with Cam? He went down for a package and came back with a person? Maybe it's Rob. He's funny. Maybe the package was so big, Cam needed an extra pair of hands to bring it up. I'll definitely give Rob some cupcakes.

And it's not rage baking. Exactly. It's just baking. I just happen to be doing it while I'm mad. And hurt. And upset. And wound up from the game, from the win, from the excitement, from being with everyone I love for such a big night...which just made me miss Owen even more.

Which pisses me off.

Okay, maybe it's a little ragey.

Why doesn't he want everything we had tonight? Why doesn't he want that group of people with him for all the big moments?

The small moments, too, but tonight should have shown him how awesome it is to have that group there, with him, behind him.

Owen should want all of these awesome people in Brady's life.

In *his* life.

And he can have them. We can all be a family.

He just has to get over himself and...

I stop stirring and take a deep breath.

Okay, I'm rage baking.

This is what I do when I have big emotions.

I hate working out. Excessive drinking isn't a good idea. At least not every time I feel big emotions because...that kind of happens a lot, I'll admit. And until recently I didn't have anyone I could anger bang.

Growing up, I always had a lot of emotions going on when I baked with my grandmother. The love and fun and feelings of home and family were mixed up with some sadness in missing my parents, probably a little anger at being an afterthought, a little resentment that hockey was more important than I was...

Yeah, baking, especially cupcakes, makes me emotional.

But it also makes me feel better.

I can beat the hell out of a bunch of ingredients and it turns into something sweet and colorful.

I can take a bunch of ingredients that, on their own, are nothing special, and combine them into something that is delicious and makes people happy.

Baking is messy. But the final product is awesome.

Because of all of those things, baking comforts me.

It's something I can control completely and that I'm really fucking good at and sometimes I just need to do something that I know will turn out in the end, no matter how messy it looks in the process.

I finish filling a piping bag with blue icing and set it next to the bags with pink and yellow.

I have no idea what I'm going to use these cupcakes for, but

I'm still going to decorate the hell out of them. Rob will have to take some home with him, too, I guess.

I put the bowls and spoons in the sink and fill it with water and soap.

When I turn back...my piping bags are gone.

I frown.

"Hey, Luna?" Cam calls from the other room.

"Cam, did you take my icing?" It'd be just like him to steal it, so I'd stop working and come get naked.

Given that Alexsei is probably out of the shower by now and damp and sexy, Cam is going to want me naked, too.

Not that I'd protest too hard...I am feeling better. More relaxed now that the cupcakes are out of the oven and cooled.

But I could ice the cupcakes and *then* get naked.

And I can think of a few uses for the leftover icing...

"Can you come in here?" he calls.

I blow out a breath and wipe my hands on my apron, starting for the living room. He had to have taken the icing. But if he thinks he's going to just squirt my gourmet homemade icing straight into his mouth or use it on graham crackers or something...

Though that's more of an Alexsei move than a Cam one.

I take one step into the room and stop.

Owen's here.

My brain tells me that fact before it really sinks in.

All three men are standing in the living room.

Each of them is holding a piping bag. Cam's is blue, Owen's is pink, and Alexsei's is sunshine yellow.

Of course it is. Alexsei is also only wearing a towel, which normally would be very distracting, but it's overshadowed by the fact that he's standing next to Owen.

Then the fact that they are *all three* here really sinks in.

My heart starts pounding. "What's going on?"

"Owen came by with a grand gesture to convince you that he loves you and he wants you back," Cam says.

Owen is just staring at me, his jaw set firmly, not saying a word.

I swallow hard and cross my arms. I can't just run into his arms or fall at his feet. He walked away. He *stayed* away.

"Okay, what's the grand gesture?" I ask. This should be good. Owen's not really a big lay-his-heart-out-in-front-of-everyone kind of guy.

"Well, that's the problem," Cam says. "He's not very good at this stuff."

Owen sighs. "I've been told I'm not a grand gesture kind of guy and that isn't wrong. I'm a show-you-how-I-feel-by-fixing-things-guy. So I'm here to fix things, Luna."

And my heart melts. My arms drop to my sides and I feel my eyes fill with tears. He looks vulnerable, but also determined.

"I'm listening."

"Luna…" Owen starts, his voice gruff. "I was trying really hard to come up with a plan. Something I could *do* to show you that I'm sorry and that I love you and that I really do want all of this–you, the guys, the friendship, the love, the life. But…I guess I finally ran into something that I don't know how to fix. At least not alone. I need all of you to help me. I realized that maybe you all don't need me, but *I* fucking need *you*."

He swallows, and I can feel the sob stuck in my throat. But I don't dare even breathe, because the second I start crying, these guys will all gather around and try to make me feel better and I really want to hear the rest of what he has to say.

That will make me feel better.

Just him being here and trying.

That's all I need.

"And," he continues. "I've also realized that for the first time I want to be selfish and just take something I want and worry about deserving it as I go along."

Jesus. This guy. He's just so…good. Alexsei is so easy to love. I need him to brighten absolutely every single moment. Cam is also easy to love. I wouldn't have believed that in the beginning, but the fact that he pushes me and loves my bratty side is what makes him perfect for me. But Owen is more of a challenge. He is real and knows life and relationships can be messy and he's been hurt before. He *does* need me. And he will make me step up and be a better, braver, more open version of myself.

I can't wait.

I step toward him. "Well, it's a really good thing that you fell in love with me then," I tell him. "Because you don't need grand gestures. I accept people just as they are. I understand that people aren't perfect and that they can love each other and still mess up sometimes. And I love you just the way you are."

Owen's gaze is hot on mine, and he clears his throat.

His voice is still gravelly, "I love you so damned much. Being away from you has been the hardest thing I've ever done. I can't not be with you anymore. I want to do this thing with you." He glances at Cam and Alexsei. "With all of you." He looks at me again. "I'm sorry it took me so long to figure out that the things in my life that have been the most unexpected and the most out of my control—my son, and you three—are the best things to happen to me."

I want to leap into his arms and kiss him like there's no tomorrow, but I need to be sure he understands where I'm at. "You hurt me, Owen. You just walked away without even trying. You can't do that again. Things are going to be messy sometimes. You have to stick it out with us when that happens."

He nods. "I'm sorry. I thought if I just nipped it in the bud, I wouldn't get hurt. Or hurt you. That was a bad plan."

"That wasn't a plan. That was fear."

He swallows hard. "I know. I'm asking you to forgive me." He takes a step forward. "And I swear to you, Luna McNeill, I will love you day in and day out the way that you deserve to be loved as long as I'm alive and breathing on this earth."

My throat is tight and I'm nodding, needing this so much. Needing *him*.

"I need you, too, Owen. I can be happy without you, but I'd rather be happy with you."

He reaches me, and he brushes his thumb over my lip. His green eyes are warm, filled with love and contrition and desire. "I can't be happy without you. If you don't take me back, I'll be doomed to live a miserable and lonely life of bachelorhood. Babies will cry when they see me. Dogs will growl. I'll eat grocery store baked goods."

That makes me give a watery laugh. "That is a very tragic picture you paint."

"It's no good without you, baby." He turns and gestures with his shoulder. "It's no good without these guys in my life, either. I love the way they love you, I truly do. We're a team. Team Macaron."

Now I'm laughing and crying at the same time. But I shake my head. "No."

His face falls. "No?"

"No, we can't be Team Macaron. That's my safe word, remember? That stops everything. And the things we're all going to do together need to never stop."

He smiles. "So true."

"We need to brainstorm something else for us." I gesture to the piping bag in his hand. "Something with icing. A nod to baking and hockey."

He gives a sigh of relief. "So… you forgive me?"

"I forgive you. I could use a few more compliments and a little bit of guilt gifting, but I do forgive you. I'm in, but only if Cam and Alexsei agree. This is a decision all of us make together."

I lace my fingers through Owen's because I've missed the feel of him. His warm, callused hands, and his protective frame. I look over at Alexsei and Cam. "I love you both so much. But we can only do this if you both want it."

They deserve to have a say.

Alexsei gives me a smile. "I'm in. Whatever makes you happy, baby." He gives Owen a little shake on the shoulders from behind. "I've missed you, big guy. It's not the same without you."

I never doubted that Alexsei would be agreeable to whatever I want. He's my easygoing, appreciative, golden retriever of a boyfriend. I give him a grateful smile. He winks at me.

Cam is my wild card. He's been angry with Owen for hurting me. It's been simmering under the surface ever since that night at the bar. It will take him longer to forgive and I understand his perspective.

But Cam nods firmly, with no hesitation. "I'm in. This is the way it should be. The four of us."

My tears fall now. I'm overwhelmed with joy and love for my men.

I let myself throw my arms around Owen's neck and he pulls me right off the floor up into a tight, loving hug.

"I'm never letting you go ever again," he murmurs against the side of my head as he peppers me with kisses. "God, I love you so much."

"I love you, too."

Then he kisses me, and everything that's been wrong is made right again.

After several long, deep sweeps of his tongue against mine, I'm sighing and sliding back down to the floor. "By the way, why are you all holding piping bags, exactly?"

"Well, I did come up with an idea," Owen says. "When Cam said you were baking."

I lift an eyebrow. "Oh, really?"

"I know baking is wrapped up with a lot of emotions for you," he says.

My heart melts. My guys pay attention to me. They listen, they observe. They care about what's important to me and what makes me tick.

"So it seemed appropriate that we use tonight's baking with all of tonight's emotions."

"I'm very interested in this," I tell him.

Owen takes me by the shoulders and turns to the guys. "Kiss your boys, sweetheart. They need some sugar for being so patient."

I happily let him push me into Alexsei's arms.

My hockey player's big arms wrap around me and he pulls me into his hot, bare chest. His mouth covers mine, devouring me, heating every inch of me. His tongue sweeps against mine and I taste the minty toothpaste he just used. I inhale the smell of his soap and the scent that's all Alexsei.

I truly believe I could be blindfolded and still know which of my men was kissing and touching me. They're all so hot and can make me lose my mind, but they're all different.

"Love you so much," he tells me huskily against my lips.

"I love you, too," I say, running my hands through his thick, damp hair.

Then he's pushing me into Cam's arms.

Cam catches me with a smirk. "You happy now, Pixie?" he asks, his hands on my ass. "You've got all three of us wrapped nice and tight around that pretty little finger."

I run my hand over his jaw. "Really happy," I agree. Then I have to add, "I think I mentioned how good Owen is at eating pussy."

Cam's eyes narrow, but his mouth still curls up. "You did. Because you're a naughty little brat." Then he swats my ass.

But he covers my mouth with his, catching my gasp in a deep, hot kiss. God, I'm so glad he enjoys kissing me. He holds me against his body and I can feel how hard he already is, and I know it's for all of us.

I've just wrapped my arms around his neck and arched into him when I feel him sweep me up into his arms. He lifts his head, staring down at me as he starts for the bedroom.

I glance over his shoulder to find Owen and Alexsei right on his heels. I shiver with desire and anticipation.

Cam tosses me onto the bed and tugs his shirt off. "Undress," he orders me.

No please, no endearments. But I would be concerned if he got too sweet.

I'm still wearing my apron, so I reach behind my neck to untie it.

"Oh, fuck, leave that on," Alexsei says, almost pleading.

The other guys have moved in next to Cam. They're all staring at me with heat in their eyes. And they all nod.

"Need to fuck our sexy little baker in that apron," Alexsei says.

"Yes," Owen agrees simply.

Oh, damn. I take a breath. "I'm never going to be able to bake without getting horny again, am I?" I ask.

"Nope." Cam isn't even a tiny bit apologetic.

"It's only fair," Owen says, pulling his T-shirt over his head and tossing it to the floor. "I get hard every time I see you in an apron."

I pause in wrestling my tank top off from underneath the apron. "You do?"

He grins down at me. "I get hard every time I *see* you."

I give a happy giggle and finish, somehow, tugging my tank off—honestly, I'm impressed I could do that. I'm not wearing a bra, so that leaves only my sweats and panties.

Owen kneels on the mattress and reaches under the apron. "Let me help." He sweeps them down my legs smoothly.

"Thanks," I say breathlessly.

"No problem." His eyes are fixed where the apron is bunched above my hips. "Sorry guys," he says to Cam and Alexsei without looking at them. "I know this is all about us being a team and sharing and stuff, but I've *really* missed my girl."

"Go for it," Alexsei says.

Owen doesn't wait for any word from Cam to run both big, rough hands up my inner thighs, spreading me wide and then leaning in to lick my pussy.

"Owen!" I gasp, my hand going to the back of his head.

"Just need a taste," he murmurs against my clit before he swirls his tongue around the bud, then sucks.

"Oh my God!"

Cam settles onto the mattress next to my hip, leaning onto an elbow, watching. He reaches out and pulls the apron up higher on my stomach. "That seems to be pretty much what I did," he muses, squeezing some of the blue icing from the bag he's holding onto his index finger and then sucking it off.

Having one of my men watch so closely as another one's tongue is buried between my thighs is something I will never get tired of. I curl my fingers into Owen's hair. He gives me a hard suck and I moan.

But because it's Cam, I have to say, "Then why does it feel different when he does it?"

Cam lifts his gaze to mine. He squeezes another blob of icing onto his finger, then lifts it to my mouth, and paints the frosting over my lower lip. "This mouth really needs to be kept busy with things other than sassing me."

He slides his finger into my mouth and I close my lips around it, licking along the length of the digit, then sucking. His eyes darken and I feel a surge of satisfaction.

Alexsei settles next to my other hip, also watching Owen eat me. "It really has to do with finding her clit," he says. Owen lifts his head and Alexsei points the icing bag tip at my clit. "It's right here."

"I see," Cam says. "I *think* I found it. She sure screamed out when my mouth was down there."

"I was grinding it against you," I tell him, squirming against the mattress. "So you couldn't miss it."

"Ah," he says with a nod. "Well, thank you." His tone is very dry.

I have to fight a smile.

"Here, see if this is what that felt like," Owen says, leaning back a bit to give Cam room.

My eyebrows arch. Owen is going to share pussy eating?

But he's smirking at me when I meet his eyes.

He *likes* this.

Well, holy shit.

Cam leans in, and Owen uses his fingers to spread my folds. My pussy clenches. God, this is making me hot.

"Right there, huh?" Cam asks.

Alexsei points, but his index finger brushes over my clit. "Right here." He swirls his finger over me and I gasp.

"Right here?" Cam runs his finger over my clit then.

I grit my teeth.

"Yep. That's it," Alexsei tells him.

"Of course, all of this is good," Owen says, running his finger down one of my outer lips and then circling my opening. "I mean, I've seen you find this spot." He slides a finger into me.

My hips lift instinctively, and I moan.

"But it's good with tongue, too." Owen leans in, slides his finger out, and replaces it with his tongue.

I whimper despite the fact I'm trying to hold it back.

"Yeah, I definitely did that," Cam says. "This doesn't really seem that difficult."

I realize my eyes have closed when I have to open them to glare at him.

He's watching my face with a mix of amusement and heat.

"Or is it just you, Pixie? You just have an especially greedy cunt that reacts to any mouth or tongue on it?"

Heat slams me at his dirty talk. I suck in a breath. "I think it's definitely about *you*. There's three of you down there and I'm just lying here orgasm-less," I say. But my voice is very breathless and they can *obviously* tell how wet and hot I am.

"Definitely need to keep that mouth busy," Cam says. "Alexsei, do something."

Alexsei immediately stands up and drops his towel and I'm momentarily distracted by the sight of my hot, ripped, fully aroused hockey player crawling up the bed toward my head.

But then Cam leans over and licks, then sucks on my clit. Hard. I cry out.

Cam looks up at me, giving me two more swipes of his tongue. "Yeah, that feels familiar. Love your pussy, goddess."

"Goddess?" Alexsei asks, pumping his cock with one hand and brushing my hair back from my face with the other. "I like that."

"Luna, the moon goddess," Cam says.

"Perfect," Alexsei murmurs, his thumb running over my lower lip.

Suddenly, Owen slaps my pussy. I cry out, more in surprise than pain. My eyes fly to his. "Tell Cam thank you for sucking on your clit."

I swallow. Oh, bossy Owen has shown up. *Yes.*

"Thank you," I tell Cam.

"Thank you for what?" he asks, brow up.

"For sucking on my clit."

"Now ask him, nicely, to suck on your pretty nipples," Owen says, as he eases two fingers into me. "While I make you come the first time."

My pussy clenches around his fingers. "Cam, will you suck on my nipples?"

Cam looks up at Alexsei. Then he nods. "If they're frosting flavored."

Alexsei reaches for the piping bag he tossed on the mattress. Cam tugs the top of the apron to one side and Alexsei swirls frosting over my nipple. Cam leans in and licks it clean, then sucks hard.

Alexsei replaces the frosting. Cam licks and sucks it up again.

I know Owen can feel the way my pussy is responding. I'm clenching around his fingers as he pumps them in and out slowly.

Then Cam grabs the blue piping bag and lifts it, but instead of adding icing to my skin, he paints a squiggly line down Alexsei's hard shaft.

Alexsei sucks in a breath but doesn't say anything.

And I know exactly what to do. I lift up, propping myself on my elbows, and then lean in to lick my tongue over the line of icing.

"Fuck," Alexsei swears under his breath. He grasps his cock at the base, holding it for me, watching my tongue.

Cam replaces the line of icing, adding a swirl to his head, and I follow along obediently.

I suck Alexsei into my mouth and he guides his cock deeper.

"That's right, keep her quiet," Cam says as he adds icing over my stomach, licking it clean.

Owen goes to work on my clit, his fingers thrusting deep and curling into my G-spot.

It only takes them about two minutes to send me spiraling into my first orgasm.

"Yes! Oh God! Yes!" It's hard to call out three men's names, but they're all a part of undoing me, so I just stick with a generic, "Fuck, yes!"

Before I've even floated down, Owen has moved from his spot between my legs. He's moving behind me on the bed, pulling me up to rest my back against his chest, his big hands opening my thighs. "Fuck them," he says.

I can't tell who he's looking at, but I can assume he's talking to Cam.

Cam looks at him with a questioning gaze.

I feel Owen nod. "Fuck them. I take her last."

Alexsei, our forever go-with-the-flow guy, has already dug out condoms and lube and tossed it all on the bed. He's studying me, the apron bunched at my waist, the top pulled to one side, exposing a breast. He's rolling the condom on, not asking any questions.

"We could all take...each other...at once," Cam says. His gaze goes from Owen's face, to mine, to Alexsei's.

"I...know," Owen says. "She needs prep for that."

Cam gives him a curious gaze. "You've been researching."

I look up at Owen. "You have?"

He shrugs. "Of course."

"I might need a diagram," Alexsei says. "Or some porn."

Owen gives a short, surprised laugh.

"We'll *coach* you through it," Cam tells him, giving Owen a wink.

Owen groans and I fight a smile realizing that it might take Owen a little time yet to get over the whole I'm-sort-of-in-a-sexual-relationship-kind-of-with-one-of-my-players thing.

"How about *me*?" I ask. "Somebody want to fill *me* in? Or am I just the fuck toy?"

At the term *fuck toy*, I feel Owen stiffen behind me. And not in a bad way. Oh, the *nice guy* likes that, huh? I look up at him. "I mean, just tell me my role here."

Cam crawls up the bed, bracing himself with hands on either side of my hips, his face only inches from mine. "Your *role here* is whatever we tell you it is," he says low and growly. "If we want you to be the fuck toy, then yes, that's exactly what you'll be." But I can tell from the look in his eyes, that *he* is playing a role.

Because he knows I love that dominating side of him.

I've never felt more powerful and in charge than I do with these three men. They're here because of me. *With* me. I'm the hub of this wheel. No... even better...I'm the center of this little universe. But they don't orbit a sun. They revolve around a moon.

And that makes me feel humble. And loved. And like I need to take care of *them*.

"What are you going to do with me, then?" I ask.

"We're going to take a few days to prep your pretty ass," he says, running a hand up and down my thigh. "Plugs, fingers, playing. And then when you're ready, Owen will take your ass, while Alexsei fucks your pussy, and I fuck his ass. We'll all be *together* in the most intimate way."

I'm breathing fast by the time he finishes.

Oh...

"I want that," I say softly, almost panting.

Cam looks immensely pleased. "I know, goddess. It will be so fucking good."

I seriously want that. Right now.

"We could–" I start.

But as always, Cam reads me. He shakes his head. "You're not ready for that."

"But–"

"Owen is huge," Cam says bluntly. "Even if he wasn't, taking a cock in your ass takes prep. But with him and you? We definitely need to work up to it."

All of that makes me hot but also makes me feel strangely a little sappy. Cam referring to all of this with "we" makes me so happy.

"Say you understand," he says.

"I understand," I reply. "But—" I add.

He sighs, as if he knew I wouldn't just leave it with a simple obedient answer.

"I *really* want to do that. So can we get plugs...tomorrow?"

He stares at me for a beat, then leans in and kisses me. When he pulls back, he says, "I'll order them tonight. *After* you come three times. Like a good fucking girl."

I shiver. And nod. "I'll be good."

Owen is hot and hard behind me, and I can feel how fast his heart is pounding.

Cam leans back. "Alexsei, get over here and make our girl come hard on your cock."

"Reporting for duty," Alexsei says, crawling across the mattress and taking Cam's place between my legs. He grasps my thighs and pulls me down so I'm more on my back, my head against Owen's stomach. Alexsei looks down at me with a smile. "You know I'm gonna want in that sweet ass, too."

My breath catches.

"*I* am not ready to switch places with *you* in that scenario," Owen interjects.

Alexsei looks up at him with a grin. "You can just watch, Coach."

"There are so many fun things we can do with our girl and

three cocks," Cam agrees. "But— He rolls on a condom. "You just let me know if you do ever want to try something new."

I bite my lip, waiting for Owen's response.

He finally just grunts.

He clearly doesn't know what to say, so I tell Alexsei, "You know, sometimes Cam needs something else to do with *his* mouth, too. Kiss him."

I love to see these two men together. They're so hot. They kiss and touch and fuck differently. That sounds stupid even in my own head, but they're different together than they are with me and I love watching.

Alexsei happily grabs Cam around the back of the neck and hauls him in for a kiss. Cam cups the back of Alexsei's head and deepens the kiss immediately.

I grip Alexsei's cock, stroking him firmly.

He growls in the back of his throat with us both touching him.

Cam reaches down and takes a hold of Alexsei's cock at the base. Then he lines him up with my pussy.

"Fuck her," he growls against Alexsei's mouth. "Hard. Make Owen feel how deep she takes you."

Alexsei thrusts into me and I gasp, gripping Owen's thighs.

"Yes!" I cry out as I'm filled so full I feel it to the soles of my feet.

"Fuck yes," Owen grits out.

He can see Alexsei stretching me perfectly. Can see him withdraw, wet from me, then thrust again. He can feel the force Alexsei is using.

"God, you're perfect," Owen tells me.

He lifts his hands, cupping my breasts, playing with the nipples. The way he tugs and pinches and rolls them makes me clench around Alexsei and he rips his mouth away from Cam to groan and look down at me.

"Fuck, Luna. Goddamn, your pussy is perfect."

I arch closer to him. "Harder. I need you deeper."

"I'm going to split you open, girl," he says tightly, clenching his jaw.

"Give me everything you've got," I plead. "I want you deep and hard."

"Jesus Christ," Alexsei swears. "I don't want to hurt you."

I'm shocked when Owen reaches down, grasps both of my thighs and lifts them, spreading me wider, bringing my knees toward my chest.

"She can take you," he says. "Give her what she needs."

My big protective teddy bear is telling Alexsei to go harder.

God, that's hot.

Cam's hand strokes down Alexsei's chest to his abs and back and forth. His gaze locks on mine over Alexsei's shoulder.

"Help him," I say without thinking. "Make him go deep."

The lust in Cam's eyes flares bright. "You're fucking perfect for us, aren't you, goddess? You're using *us* just right."

I catch my breath. Then nod. "Damn right."

"Fuck, I love you," he mutters. Then he moves into position behind Alexsei. "Bend over. Take me."

Alexsei groans and shudders. But he leans over me. My knees are up between us, but he still kisses me deeply, then lifts his head to say, "Hang on, Pixie. You're about to get your slap shot."

I almost laugh, but just then Cam thrusts, which causes Alexsei to thrust. With Owen holding me tight from behind, I feel every powerful inch.

"Oh my *God*," I moan.

And from there I kind of lose my mind.

I hear lots of, "good fucking girl", "take all of it", "you're perfect", and "goddamned goddess", but I'm not focused on who's saying what and what exactly I'm doing to deserve the praise.

Honestly, they're doing all the work. I'm just here. Their fuck toy.

And I love every second.

Cam comes first, and I fully intend to tease him about that

later. But then Owen's hand sneaks in between Alexsei and me and he starts talking right in my ear as he plays with my clit.

"Look at you stretched around him. You're taking him so well, gorgeous girl. This pussy was made for us. You're going to be so hot and wet and sensitive when I get in there. You're going to come for him and then I'm going to fill you up and make you come so fucking hard."

And I'm flying. Coming apart. Crying out. Filled with heat, lust, joy, and love all at once.

Alexsei roars my name and I feel him stiffen over me as he comes. He immediately shifts off of me and Owen pulls me up his body. He positions me to straddle his lap, facing Cam and Alexsei who have collapsed on the mattress on either side of us. Owen rolls on a condom and then moves me as if I weigh nothing. He positions me over his cock and I sink down, his girth filling me again even as my pussy is still rippling from my orgasm.

"*Fuck*. Luna. Baby," he groans.

"God, Owen," I breathe, bracing my hands on his thighs.

"Ride me," he commands.

My body feels boneless, but I can't *not* move. I lift and lower my hips, loving how my sensitive pussy drags over his cock.

"Faster," he tells me, gripping my hips.

"I can barely move," I tell him. "You all fucked me senseless."

"Not. Yet," he says. He squeezes again, then lifts and lowers me.

Hot tingles explode deep inside me.

A few months ago, I would have laughed at the idea of having a *third* orgasm tonight, but I know these men now. They *will* make sure that happens.

"You're so fucking gorgeous like that," Cam tells me.

My head comes up to find him and Alexsei watching me ride Owen.

Alexsei shifts and grasps the front of my apron. As if communicating telepathically, Owen reaches to untie it from behind my neck and at my waist. Alexsei pulls it off and I'm now naked, riding one of my men while the other two watch.

"Ride him faster," Alexsei tells me. "Want to see you get off like that."

"Love seeing your inner thighs wet and glistening," Cam says. "Your nipples red, whisker burn all over your pretty skin."

I moan and start moving faster.

Owen's fingers curl into my hips.

"Look at you taking another cock, like a good girl," Cam praises. "Never too much, is it, goddess? You're going to need filling up like this forever." He reaches up and runs a hand down my thigh.

"Good thing you've got us," Alexsei adds. "You need all three of us to give you everything you need." He cups my breast, tweaking a nipple.

The idea of all three of them, forever, doing everything they can to keep me happy, needing me to be happy, needing each other to feel complete is what makes my inner muscles clench hard and my orgasm start tightening low and deep.

"Yes, she loves the idea of having three men addicted to her," Cam says. He shifts, reaching to the bedside table. "Doing whatever she needs them to do to fully satisfy her."

I shudder, lifting and lowering myself faster.

"Fuck, Luna," Owen grits out. "Yes, baby. Like that. Grip me tighter."

"I've got you, Coach," Cam says. "Turn her around, Alexsei."

He doesn't ask questions. Alexsei just moves to kneel beside me, then takes my hips and lifts me off Owen's cock. He turns me to face Owen, then lowers me back over the huge cock.

As he slides inside me again, we both groan.

I lean in to kiss him. "I missed you so much," I tell him, kissing my way down his throat.

His big hands are splayed over my ass possessively.

"Me, too. Jesus, I've been so fucking miserable. Thinking about you every night."

"Have you jerked off thinking of me?" I murmur against his skin, kissing up to just below his ear.

"Of course I have," he says, squeezing my ass. "I've even imagined you with the guys."

I lift my head. "Yeah? And that turned you on?"

"Of course. And, strange as it sounds, it made me feel better thinking that at least you weren't alone and you were being taken care of."

That's...nice. It does sound strange, but I understand what he means. He really does love that Cam and Alexsei love me. They love that Owen loves me, too. This is all still taking some getting used to, but it feels so right.

"They were taking care of you, weren't they, baby?" he asks, kneading my ass.

I nod. "They were."

"They were fucking you so good? Filling you up? Making you come? Worshiping you?"

I suck in a little breath, but answer truthfully, "Yes."

Then I feel him spread my cheeks. "Good."

Then I feel thick fingers at my back entrance. My eyes go wide and I look over my shoulder.

Cam puts a hand on my upper back. "Take it."

It's Alexsei's finger massaging and probing that tight ring of muscles, though. I feel the cool slide of lube as Cam squeezes it from the bottle and I shiver. But I'm not cold.

I turn back to Owen. He's buried deep, but not moving.

"Oh, God," is all I can say.

"We will always take care of you, Luna," he says.

I nod. I know that.

Alexsei works one finger inside me and the feeling is incredible. Slowly, Owen starts moving again. Alexsei matches his rhythm and I just let myself get lost in the sensations.

So much so that minutes later, when Cam presses a slim vibrator into my ass, I simply moan and let the pleasure wash over me.

"Such a good girl," Cam croons. "You really will let us just fill you up. All the ways we know you need."

I rest my forehead on Owen's chest, not able to form words.

"Fuck her faster," I hear Alexsei say.

I don't know who he's talking to because both Owen and Cam pick up the pace of the thrusts they're giving me.

And seconds later, I break apart.

I cry out as a mind-blowing orgasm slams into me. I feel it everywhere and I think I black out for a second.

Owen roars my name a moment later, and I feel him shudder beneath me as he comes.

A few seconds later, I hear Cam groan and say, "Fuck, that was beautiful."

And Alexsei add, "You need to order those plugs *now*."

And Owen give a simple, "Yes."

I don't say yes, but I think it. Really hard.

But Cam can read me. I'm certain he knows how I feel about the subject.

Alexsei carries me to the shower ten minutes later. We don't do anything other than wash off. Well, and kiss some. But we have to get the frosting off. And the blue is going to stain my skin for a day or so.

When we get back to the bedroom, Cam's changed the sheets and both Owen and Cam have showered and are in T-shirts and sweatpants. Owen is in what I assume is Alexsei's clothes, and that makes me as happy as everything else tonight.

I climb up into the bed between Alexsei and Owen. Cam is on Alexsei's other side. And we all just...cuddle.

Suddenly I sit up. "Shit, the cupcakes." I start to climb over Owen, but Cam reaches out and grabs the back of Alexsei's T-shirt that I'm wearing.

He tugs me back. "Took care of it." He yawns.

"We threw the icing out, though," Owen says. "Figured you'd have to start over on that. Sorry."

I smile into the darkness. I should have known they'd take care of it. "You don't sound sorry."

He chuckles and pulls me into his chest. "I'm not. Not one bit."

"That's growth," I tell him. "I would expect you to be out there remaking it for me."

There's a beat of silence and then Cam and Owen both chuckle.

"What?" I ask.

"He was going to," Cam says. "But I stopped him from texting Dani or Elise for the recipe since it's almost two a.m."

"These guys don't have enough powdered sugar anyway," Owen grumbles.

I don't know what to say. Or think. Or feel.

I love them all so fucking much.

So I just say that. And add, "You're my favorite people in the whole world." I pause. "But if you tell Dani that, I'll deny it."

They all chuckle.

"We love you, too, Pixie," Cam says. Then he yawns.

"I like goddess, better," Alexsei says, squeezing my leg under the sheets.

"I like calling you baby," Owen says. "Which do you like best?"

I smile at the dark ceiling. "What do I like you guys calling me best?" I ask.

"Yeah," Alexsei says.

"Well, that's easy," I tell them. "I like you calling me *yours*."

Epilogue

OWEN

"OH, you've got to be fucking kidding me." I get out of my truck and stand in front of the cabin, hands on my hips, just staring.

Now I'm really glad Cam and I came up early.

We have groceries, sheets and towels, and some dishes because the last time I was here, the group used a lot of paper plates and plastic utensils. Of course, that group was six guys, and we were only here to fish and drink beer.

This trip is different. A romantic getaway for our girlfriend before the craziness of the hockey season starts. The least we could do was real plates. I also got wine, flowers, and candles.

I even picked up some of Luna's favorite bath essentials, and I'd made a stop to get some of our favorite massage oil and had swiped some cake frosting from her fridge when she hadn't been looking.

Cam had said that he would take care of packing for our girl.

Which even before I saw the tiny bag he'd brought for her, I knew means there will be at least two vibrators, her silky robe, and…not much else.

Though Luna does seem most comfortable around the house in one of our hoodies or T-shirts and not much underneath.

My cock twitches at the idea of having her all to ourselves, away from the bakery, away from our families—as much as we love them—and hopefully away from her phone for the next four days.

That includes being incommunicado with my son, too, who is in contact with Luna often, not just because she's his boss but also because she's his… pseudo-stepmom.

In fact, he calls her first for advice or to use her as a sounding board often before he talks to me or Chelsea.

Luna doesn't let him get away with things, exactly, but she is a little more chill about hearing problems and screw-ups. Which has made me a little more chill.

My heart squeezes as I think about Luna's relationship with Brady. She fits into the role of friend and advisor perfectly. Hell, she fits into everything perfectly. She and Chelsea have become friends. Amara thinks she's amazing—helped in part by the fact that Luna can turn a simple cake into almost *anything*, a challenge Amara has put to her half a dozen times and one that Luna has crushed every time. Dev thinks she's charming and delightful. My parents and sisters love her.

Chelsea, Dev, Amara, and everyone else in my life also love Alexsei and Cam.

The life that Luna, Alexsei, Cam, and I have figured out is damn near perfect. It's like four puzzle pieces have come together and locked into place as soon as we turned them the right way.

We all have a role, and we can all depend on the other three to fill in where we can't.

I have to admit that looking forward to this coming hockey season is easier knowing that when I'm on the road, I'll have one of my best friends there with me, and Cam will be at home with my girl and for my son if Brady needs anything.

"This isn't what I was expecting," Cam tells me, meeting me in front of the bumper.

A gust of wind blows past and a creaking sound pulls my attention to the roof of the cabin—where a large tree branch is resting on one corner.

Fuck. This plan is definitely going off track.

"It's been five years since I was here, and I was admittedly pretty drunk for a big portion of the last trip, but I do not recall the cabin looking like this," I admit.

Even drunk, I would have remembered a sagging front porch that I'm afraid to step on, a tree resting on the roof, and a boarded-up front window.

"Mark said he hadn't been up here in a couple years and the guy who takes care of it for him quit, though, right?" Cam reminds me.

My buddy Mark had no problem with us using the cabin for a few days, but he had warned me he hadn't seen it in a while.

"Yeah." I grimace. "But…fuck." I scrub a hand over my face. "I can fix a lot of shit, but this is a little beyond what I can do by tonight."

Mark had inherited this fishing cabin from his uncle years ago and we used to do guy trips annually with some other friends. They were always a ton of fun and exactly what I needed as a getaway before the hockey season started each year. But I hadn't been picky about the four walls and roof for those trips.

This one is different.

When Alexsei and I told Cam that the four of us should take a vacation before Alexsei and I were wrapped up in the chaos of another hockey season, getting away to a remote cabin all to ourselves had sounded great to all three of us. Making it a surprise trip for Luna had sounded even better.

My phone dings with a text. Cam's does at the same time.

We immediately know it's either Alexsei or Luna since we have a group chat.

Or it could be Brady, I suppose.

Or just Alexsei.

I'm actually in three group chats. One that includes the bigger family—i.e., Brady—one that's just the four of us, and one that's just us three guys. That one's for making plans like this weekend or for sending messages like, "she had a shitty day, someone needs to grab tacos. Who will be home first?"

We have to be careful when we're texting dirty stuff to get the right one, too. So far no one's screwed up and included Brady, but I've almost hit send a couple of times before realizing I'm in the wrong one.

I pull out my phone.

It's the group chat with just the three of us.

There's a text from Alexsei.

> I'm thinking I might keep this simple. AKA, blindfold and rope.

Alexsei is in charge of getting Luna to the cabin tonight. Without her knowing where they're going.

I chuckle as Cam shakes his head and responds.

> You can't just kidnap her. You have to come up with a believable excuse to go for a drive. We gave you three good stories last night. And you cannot cave when she gets suspicious. Not even for a blow job.

"He's our weakest link," I say.

Cam rolls his eyes. "For sure. Especially with Luna. Why did we think this was a good idea?"

"Because he was the one with time to help her with the event."

"Right." Cam and I both had morning meetings and Luna had a huge fiftieth anniversary party to set up.

Alexsei texts.

> A little kidnapping could be fun and sexy.
> <winking emoji>

Both Cam and I pause. He's not wrong.

"If he gags her and puts her in the backseat, she can't try to seduce the secret out of him," I tell Cam.

"Good point." Cam frowns, but he's also almost wearing a smile. I know he's thinking about how naughty Luna can be. And how much he likes that.

My phone dings again.

> Found one of her romance novels. I think she might be into a little captive role playing.

Well, now…that's interesting.
I respond.

> No rope burns.

Cam snorts and types.

> Take handcuffs in case she fights you.

Now I snort.

> No way is she gonna fight Alexsei coming at her with a blindfold.

Alexsei texts.

> <winking emoji> Exactly.

Cam is grinning widely now as he types.

> Unless you tell her to fight.

I feel my body respond to that. He's right. Luna is always up for role-playing and if Alexsei holds up a blindfold and says,

"Fight me, gorgeous," she absolutely will and they'll have a great time.

"But we won't be there to watch. That's not fair," I tell Cam.

"Damn. True." He pauses. "Guess we'll have to come up with a way for them to make it up to us when they get here."

I nod slowly, at least a dozen scenarios going through my mind. "Darn."

We're both quiet for a minute and I know he's envisioning the whole thing, too.

"She'd definitely fight it if *you* told her *not* to," I say.

Cam makes a satisfied sigh-growl sound.

Luna loves to disobey Cam because she knows what that means later.

Cam types something into his phone and my phone pings.

But when I look at the messages, it's not in the group text with Alexsei and me. It's in the group text that includes Luna.

> Luna, be a good girl and just get in the car when Alexsei tells you to. Don't argue and don't fight him on it.

My cock gets a little harder.

Luna's response comes a little slower than Alexsei's are, and I imagine she's been finishing something up at the party site and he is just waiting for her.

Luna responds finally.

> Obviously I'm going to get in the van. That's how we're getting back to the bakery. <eye roll emoji>

I know she includes the emoji because she knows it will annoy Cam. In a good way.

And it does. His text is clipped.

> That smart mouth is going to get you into trouble.

Luna's response is immediate.

> Promise?

Cam texts again but this time it's to our group chat with only Alexsei.

> I won't be surprised if her hair is messed up and her panties are missing when she gets to the cabin, but you will have to sit and watch Owen and I catch up.

Yeah, that makes my cock twitch, too.
Alexsei responds.

> Then I'll have to make the kidnapping worth it.

Yeah, this is going to be a very fun getaway. I add my own text.

> Do whatever you need to do with her.

And yes, Cam and I now fully expect Luna to show up here handcuffed and thrown over Alexsei's shoulder.

I feel the now-familiar surge of contentment and happiness that comes from being a part of this foursome. We have a hell of a good time. And I've got three amazing people that I know I can count on for fun as well as help.

The wind blows again and the cabin creaks and my grin dies.

Cam's attention goes to the cabin, too. "That seems...bad."

I sigh. Our vacation plans are going to have to change.

And yeah, I need help with that. I made all of these plans—from the location to the agenda to the menu. I'm good at this stuff, and I like it, and the other three depend on me to do it. I've been planning trips for me and Brady since he was five. But I've learned that I don't have to do everything myself and that my partners are there when I need anything.

I blow out a breath.

In the past five months, I've gotten used to sleeping in the bed with Cam and Alexsei there, too, but I haven't quite gotten used to the way they'll prioritize me even when what I need isn't about Luna. But I'm getting more used to it all the time. Because it happens over and over.

This time it is about her, though.

I clear my throat. "Let's check out the back, but I don't think this is going to work."

Cam lets me lead the way, but he accompanies me to the back of the cabin. I'm hoping that the back entrance is a little more welcoming.

It is, barely.

I open the back door and step inside. I'm immediately met with a musty smell and heavy humid air.

"Fuck." I run a hand through my hair. "There's no way we can stay here." I walk further in and see one area of the living room ceiling where water has clearly been leaking with every rain storm and as snow has melted.

"Okay, what do you need me to do?" Cam asks.

I turn to him. "I need you to take over," I say.

And it doesn't hurt at all.

It hasn't taken me long to let go of the need to fix everything. I'm the one who steps up most of the time. It's just what I'm good at. I almost always have the answer, no matter the issue, question, or problem. It's the way I like it, and they're all comfortable with it. But we've figured out where we all fit and how we work best together.

"What do you want me to do?" Cam asks. "I'm not great with power tools, as you know. My mom wasn't the fix-it type and I just hire people to do that kind of work."

I do know that. I don't think Luna is the only one in the family who gets a little turned-on when I put my tool-belt on.

"I would never make you do something like that," I tell him with a grin. "We just need a new vacation. And quickly. You've got contacts and big ideas. Can you come up with something? Maybe a swanky hotel up here somewhere? Or we could find another nice cabin to rent?"

It's really last minute though, so I'm not sure even my billionaire buddy can do this.

"How about Paris?"

I stop in the middle of the living room and stare at him. "You came up with that fast."

"Luna's mentioned how much she'd love to see Paris before."

I frown. "Why didn't you bring that up when we were discussing this trip?"

"You already had a plan in mind and this idea was yours and Alexsei's," Cam says with a shrug. "We can do Paris any time. But if that's a good backup now, I can make it happen."

I'm still getting a little used to the lack of competition between the three of us. The only time it really comes up is in a playful, sexy way in bed and it's always because it's extra good for Luna.

"Huh. Paris is pretty different from this." The rickety roof of the cabin creaks again.

"But can you imagine our sweet little baker in Paris, among all that amazing food and all those sweets? Macarons and eclairs everywhere?" Cam asks, grinning.

I can. Luna would love Paris. God, I'd love to see her face as she goes from fancy bakery to fancy bakery.

"Let's do it," I say.

"Great." He pulls out his phone.

It really is that easy with this guy. He's got the money, the connections, the private plane hookup. We really can take Luna to Paris today.

I look around and shove my hand through my hair. "Sorry this fell apart." Another gust of wind whips around the cabin, there's a loud creak, and then I hear something fall against the side of the cabin. Or *off* of the cabin? I grimace. "Literally."

"It's fine. We'll let you plan Christmas," he says, looking at his phone as he swipes over the screen.

I perk up. "Really? I can plan Christmas?" I know I sound more excited than I should, but I'm already thinking about how to get Christmas organized with all of the people that need to be included.

Cam looks up with a chuckle. "Yes, Dad, you can plan Christmas."

I grin. "Okay." I watch him trip plan. "I, uh...I'll let Alexsei know about the change in plans."

"Yeah, have him meet us at the airport in..." He pauses, looking at his phone, waiting. Then the message he needs comes in and he says, "Four hours."

Four hours. We can get back, repack—Paris is a much different trip than a cabin in the woods—and catch a private plane.

"Damn, vacationing with you might change my mind about travel," I tell him.

He grins. "Oh, it will."

I feel strangely satisfied. Despite this plan going totally to shit, things are still going to be great. Luna is going to fucking love this trip.

Four hours later, we're sitting on a private plane, sipping champagne and grinning at one another as Luna tries to guess where we're going.

She was blindfolded when she and Alexsei showed up, but not handcuffed. Her lipstick was completely gone from her mouth and there is a smudge of it on Alexsei's shirt. And I don't want to know where else her lipstick might be on the big happy hockey player.

But clearly he *did* cave in to at least some of her techniques.

Weakest link for sure.

"New York?" she asks.

"Nope," Alexsei says. He's sitting next to me across from her, while Cam's in the seat next to her.

"LA?" she asks.

"Nah," I tell her.

She looks at me. "A remote cabin somewhere in the woods where we can walk around naked all day and fuck outside on the deck and in the hot tub?"

I freeze with my champagne flute halfway to my mouth. I stare at her. "Why would you guess that?"

She grins. "You're so cute when you try to keep secrets from me, Coach."

I narrow my eyes and give a little growl. "Cam?"

"Yeah, Coach?" He's grinning.

"Luna's asking for a spanking."

"I've got you."

Yes, I've gotten used to sleeping in the bed. Cam's also gotten a lot more enthusiastic about pussy eating. But we still all have our specialties.

Luna's eyes widen and she tries to scoot away from Cam, but his hand comes down and grips her thigh. "Where do you think you're going? Besides, you know I love to chase you, Pixie."

She swallows hard and looks from Cam to me to Alexsei.

She focuses on the one who's the easiest for her. "Where are we going, Alexsei?" she asks, her voice getting sweeter.

He shakes his head. "You'll find out soon enough." Then he adds, "Well, not *that* soon."

"Alexsei," Cam growls in warning.

If anyone's going to spill the beans, it's definitely Alexsei.

"It's a long flight?" she asks, perking up, clearly taking that as a clue.

"Luna," I say.

Her gaze comes to mine. "Yes?"

"Do you trust us?"

She smiles. "I do."

For some reason, whether it's the loving smile, or just how fucking good this all feels with the four of us together, or just how damned much I love this woman, those two words from her hit me hot and hard all of a sudden.

I also note the way Alexsei shifts in his seat and the way Cam sits up straighter.

I'm not the only one that heard Luna say, "I do" and had a visceral reaction.

Her eyes widen. She looks from me to Alexsei to Cam. "*What* is all of *that*?" she asks, pointing a deep crimson-painted index finger at each of us.

I clear my throat. "What are you talking about?"

"You all got funny looks when I said I trust you." She frowns and looks at each of us again. "You know that, right? I don't actually need to know where we're going. I love that you're surprising me with a trip."

Alexsei sits forward, leaning his forearms on his thighs. "I think you noticed our reactions to you saying, "I do", sweetheart, and all of us thinking about how much we'd love to hear those words from you someday while you're wearing a white dress and standing up in front of a bunch of our family and friends."

Of course, Alexsei is just going to lay his heart out there.

But, it's not just *his* heart.

Her eyes widen. "What?"

Cam mutters, "Even though we are making a *white* dress very much a lie."

She elbows him, but then she studies him. Her lips slowly spread into a smile. She leans closer to him and says, "So, you want to *marry* me, Cameron?"

He rolls his eyes. "I'm just using you to get to Alexsei, Pixie. You know that."

Her grin is big and bright, and she laughs lightly. "You are such a bad liar. You want to marry *me*, too," she sing-songs. She leans in and nuzzles his neck. "You are so madly in love with me you can't imagine living without me."

She can't see it, but his lips curl up in a smile. His hand comes up to cup the back of her head. "You're very, very tolerable," he says.

She kisses the underside of his jaw. "I love you, too, Cam. And yes, I'll marry you someday."

He finally lets his smile loose. "I love you, too, Luna."

She turns to Alexsei. "And, of course, I'll marry you someday. You're my sunshine, Alexsei. I never want to be without you."

He reaches out and pulls her into his lap. "I love you, goddess. I can't wait to have my ring on your finger."

She's sitting sideways on his thighs and reaches out and takes my hand. "I love you so much, Owen."

"I love you, too." My heart feels so full in my chest. I lift her hand to my lips. "I definitely want you forever. I am *definitely* going to marry you. But—" Of course I'm the one with a 'but'. "I can't live anywhere else until Brady goes off to college. Will you wait for me?"

She smiles. "Forever."

"A year is nothing," Alexsei says. "No one's going anywhere. We can wait for Brady to leave."

Luna nods. "Exactly."

"And if we move Luna in with us before that and have her with *us* twenty-four-seven, then that's just how it goes," Cam says with a sly smile.

Asshole. I grin at him. "Good thing Brady stays with his mom a lot, I guess."

"I guess so," Cam agrees.

I really do love these people.

And I love that we're going to Paris.

And I love that we're in this for good, forever.

And I really love my son, but when he goes off to college, I think I'm going to be just fine.

Want a little more of Luna, Alexsei, Cam, and Owen? Read a bonus scene at subscribepage.io/TFqg3L!

And for more sexy why choose fun read how Luna's best friend Dani found her three guys in Puck One Night Stands on Kindle Unlimited!

Puck One Night Stands

I don't do casual hookups, so I have no idea what to expect when I meet not one, but *three* hot guys who are into me.

I'm an introverted, failing-book-shop-owning, romance-writer wanna be.

But after my dating disaster at a hockey game—all caught on the jumbotron—I somehow have the attention of three men.

Nathan Armstrong is the hot, older, sophisticated billionaire owner of the team.

Why does this man want a night with me? I'm baffled...but I'm not saying no.

I should also say no to the romantic, suave, brilliant team doctor, Michael Hughes.

And the team's new hot-shot all-star player Crew McNeill.

But I don't.

And I'm loving every minute. Especially the minutes they decide we should *all* spend together. Golden Retriever Crew is all in, bossy, broody Nathan is reluctant (to say the least), and sexy, confident Michael knows what we all need. They're all here, promising to make every one of my fantasies come true.

And they do. Night after headboard-banging night.

But it can't last.

Good thing I was okay with a short-term fling because as soon as the fans find out what we're doing, our lives–and my heart–are going to be all pucked up.

Read all the sexy why choose fun in Puck One Night Stands!

Also by Emma Foxx

Chicago Racketeers

Nathan

"I'm not doing this. It's ridiculous."

"You're doing it. You know it's a good idea."

"Someone else can do it. It doesn't have to be me."

"It doesn't *have to* be you. But it *should* be you. Quit whining."

I frown at the older woman next to me as the elevator from the top floor of our building hits the ground floor and the doors swish open. "You look like such a sweet woman," I tell her. "But I don't get an ounce of compassion or coddling."

She snorts as she steps off the elevator into the lobby that is now teeming with people. "I used up all of my compassion in nineteen eighty-eight. You're too late."

"No," I say, my hand on her back as I guide her through the crowd of people dressed in black and silver and hyped up for tonight's game. "I distinctly remember you being nice when I was a kid."

"I was faking it. You have to be a real asshole to be mean to a kid," she says, giving me a grin.

I chuckle. I've known Valerie for thirty-four years, ever since my grandfather hired her as his personal secretary. She's one of the few people who can make me chuckle. Or who can get away with telling me to quit whining.

We step out into the fading sunlight. The Racketeers play at seven tonight and the crowd is getting thick outside the arena. I guide her through the crowd and then hand her off to Bill, one of the security guards. "Take Val to her car, please." She doesn't typically stay this late on a game night and I don't like that she'll be out in all this traffic, but while they fans are all coming in, she'll be going out so it should be fine.

"Evenin' Val," Bill greets her.

"Hi, Bill," she says with a smile. But before she heads off in the direction of the employee lot, she turns back. "You," she says pointing at me. "Go do the promotion."

"I don't want to." It's not whining, it's just a fact. I'm not a people person. I might even go so far as to say I only truly like about three people on the planet and Val is one of them.

"I don't know why we have to go over this every time," she says with a sigh. "It's part of your job. You have twelve VIP tickets to hand out as a surprise to fans." She waves her hand around at the people milling about. "How hard can that be? You're going to make twelve peoples' nights. That's so nice."

I roll my eyes.

She shakes her head. "Go. Do it. And yes, you have to smile."

"Dammit, this just keeps getting worse and worse. I'm leaving before you tell me I have to actually *talk* to them too," I say.

"Nathan William Armstrong," Valerie says. "You find twelve people who love this team, you walk up to them, *smile*, say something *nice*, and give them those fucking VIP tickets, or I'm not bringing you any tortellini soup on Monday."

I groan. Valerie has a big family gathering this coming weekend and her family knows how to eat and, more importantly, cook. She always brings me leftovers the Monday after their get togethers.

I give her a long-suffering look. "Fine."

Then I notice someone standing a few feet behind Valerie and Bill.

Someone with long red hair, and a sweet ass that looks like it would fit perfectly in my two palms.

She seems to be alone. Or waiting for someone, I amend, as she looks at her phone.

"Fine," I repeat, this time with a much brighter tone. And a smile.

Valerie blinks at me. "Okay. Well, that's better."

Yes, this is definitely feeling better already.

I may not love people but I love attractive women in my bed.

Valerie and Bill move off and I approach the redhead. She turns slightly, giving me more of a side view.

Great breasts to go with her sweet ass...yep, this handing out surprise VIP tickets suddenly seems like one of the best ideas our PR department has come up with in a long time.

"Excuse me."

She turns to face me fully and I actually feel the entire universe pause for a moment of collective appreciation as her green eyes lock on mine.

Damn. She's... adorable. Round face with a sprinkle of freckles just across the bridge of her nose. Long lashes on those emerald eyes. Full pink lips.

She's looking at me inquisitively. "Hi," she says.

Her voice strokes over me and I feel my blood start pumping harder.

What the fuck is that? I've definitely felt immediate attraction before but this feels different. Do I know her? Have we met somewhere before? I doubt it. I don't think I could forget those eyes or that fiery red hair. But damn, there's something about looking at her that makes me think *I could do this, just this, for hours.*

Though my fingers are itching to do more than look. I want to touch. I want to run my hands through her hair. I want to see if her cheek is as soft as it looks. I want to glide my thumb across her lower lip and feel her warm breath as she breathes out...

"Can I help you?" she asks, clearly confused about why I'm just standing here like a dumbass staring at her and not speaking.

I've never *felt* the word flummoxed before but...this must be exactly what that word means.

I pull my shit together. "Yes. Actually, I'm going to help you."

"You are?" Her lips curl slightly as if she's amused.

"First row, a VIP ticket for tonight's game." I pull one of the tickets out of my inside suit jacket pocket and hold it up.

"Oh." She frowns and glances toward the cars pulling up at the curb, dropping people off for the game. Then she looks back up at me. "I, um, have tickets. I mean, my friend does. I'm waiting for her to go in. But we've already got tickets."

"Not tickets as good as these," I tell her. "It's a special promotion. We're upgrading twelve fans tonight. I'll upgrade your friend as well." I reach into my pocket.

"Well, we're… I mean, it's not… there are four of us, actually," she tells me.

Okay, even better. The faster I get rid of these damned things, the sooner I can go back upstairs. I pull four tickets out and hold them out. "Done."

She looks from me to the tickets and then back to me. "Really? Are you sure?"

"I am." I want to know exactly where she's sitting. That will make it easier to find her after the game. Why and for what I'm not exactly sure, but I've got three periods of hockey to figure that out.

She reaches out tentatively. "Well, okay then."

I make sure our fingers connect and I don't let go of the tickets immediately. "What's your name?"

She meets my gaze. "Danielle."

"Hi, Danielle. I'm Nathan."

"It's nice to meet you, Nathan."

Damn, I like the way she says my name. "My pleasure, Danielle."

Her smile grows and I let the tickets slide from my fingers. "I hope you enjoy the game."

"Thank you."

Just then a red Honda Civic pulls up at the curb and a guy in blue jeans, a plaid shirt, and wearing a blue baseball cap spills out of the backseat.

"Dani!" he exclaims, righting himself just before tripping on the curb.

He bounds over to her and wraps her in a huge hug.

I can smell the beer on him from three feet away.

She grimaces. "Hey, Ben."

"Sorry I'm a little late. I met some of the guys after work," he tells her as he lets her go.

Obviously to pound a six pack. He actually sways a little on his feet.

"That's okay. I'm still waiting for Luna and Kyle too."

"Yeah, Kyle texted. They're almost here."

"Great."

I know I'm scowling taking this all in. Maybe this guy is her brother. Her drunk brother who she doesn't like hugging. Because it was clear she did not enjoy that hug.

"I'm so glad you finally said yes to them setting us up," Ben says, looping an arm around her. He looks her up and down. "Damn, you look hot."

She tugs her black cardigan sweater back up onto her shoulder where Ben's arm pulled it down. But the move doesn't quite pull the V neck of her t-shirt up enough to cover the sweet swell of the tops of her breasts.

I really fucking hate Ben.

I also really fucking hate that I just gave Ben a VIP ticket to the game to sit next to Danielle.

I catch her eye. "Are you okay?" I demand, my voice sounding harsher than I intend. But fuck this guy who thinks he can show up loaded and ruin Danielle's night.

She nods but mouths, *thank you* in return.

I nod as she turns back to Ben, who belches loudly and doesn't say excuse me.

I'm definitely not letting her out of my sight tonight.

As if I was going to anyway.

I turn and make my way through the crowd. I shove two VIP tickets at the next set of two guys decked out in fan gear that I notice. I think they almost have heart attacks from excitement. I get rid of the other six by giving them to a family standing in line at the concession stand.

There. I did my duty. I even smiled. I think. Maybe. Kind of.

Everyone can get off my ass.

Now I can take care of Danielle.

I head up to talk to the media people. Then I track down Wade, the kid who works as the mascot, Sammy the Malamute.

After all of my plans are in place, I finally take a deep breath. There's only a few minutes until game time. I need to get up to my box and make sure Danielle got to her seats.

I round the corner and someone plows into me.

Beer soaks my dress shirt and pants, even splashing up into my face.

What the fuck!

I wipe the suds out of my eyes. And find myself staring at the shocked and appalled face of none other than Ben the Loser.

I look to his left.

Danielle is standing there, staring at me in horror.

But the front of her oatmeal colored t-shirt is soaked as well.

Ben, on the other hand, is completely dry.

Of course, he is.

"Oh, shit!" he finally exclaims. "Damn, man. Sorry!"

I wait for a beat. Is he going to apologize to Danielle? Is he even going to look in her direction?

I don't say a word to him, but I reach for her hand. I tug her toward me, then turn and start in the opposite direction. My chest is damp and my hatred of Ben has solidified, but I also think the idiot just did me a favor. Danielle's hand is small and warm in mine and has me envisioning taking both our palms and showing her how to rub my cock into a hard rod.

As I swallow, beating back my thoughts of doing dirty things to Danielle immediately if not sooner, I hear a confused Ben say, "Where are you going?"

Danielle trips along behind me for three steps before she catches up and says, "Yes, where are we going?"

"We need new shirts."

She clearly doesn't know what to say to that.

I continue striding down the hall until I get to the storage room. I shove my free hand into my pocket, pull out my keys, unlock the door and shove it open. The motion sensor light flickers on and I tug Danielle through the door, letting it bump shut behind us.

She's breathing fast, but I don't think it's from the walk.

"I'm really sorry," she says nervously, glancing around the room.

"Why?" I ask, crossing the room to the Racketeers hockey T-shirt shelves. I need to keep moving. And not look at her.

The T-shirt she's wearing is a beige color. It's not white. It didn't become see-through when it got wet, but it's plastered against her like a second skin. Because, of course, Ben got the large beers. Two of them. That or he was carrying one for her. But she has a bottle of water in her hand, so I'm guessing both of those were good ol' Benny's.

"For getting beer all over your clearly very expensive suit."

I grab a white T-shirt with our mascot emblazoned on it for her. It's an x-small because she's petite. And because I want to see it straining across her chest, I admit it. I also pull out one for myself, a solid black with a small logo on the upper right hand side of the shirt. With my suit jacket back on, it won't even be noticeable.

Am I the only guy walking around the level where the concessions are and where the fans are coming up the ramps and into the stands, in a suit? Maybe. But it's important for the administration to be out and about when the fans are in the arena, to see how our employees interact with them, to see how they react to various experiences like the mascot meet-and-greet, the Feeling Pucky? contest, and the Stick It to Cancer fundraiser.

Or so our PR department keeps telling me.

"*You* didn't get beer on my very expensive suit," I tell her as I cross back to stand in front of her. "Or on your shirt."

I hand her the T-shirt and let my gaze glance over her wet shirt.

I'd been right about the breasts. Very nice.

Her cheeks are pink and I want to touch them again. Hell, I

want to touch her breasts too. And everything in between. Instead I yank on my tie, unknotting it, then slide it from my collar. I toss it down on the clothing rack.

She watches the entire process raptly.

"So you and Ben…" I trail off, hoping she'll fill in the blank.

Her eyes are on my fingers as I start unbuttoning my shirt.

"Um, nothing," she says, absently. "He's roommates with my roommate's date for tonight."

Perfect.

"He's a dick," I point out.

She nods. But I don't think she's really hearing what I'm saying. I'm almost done with my buttons and her eyes are glued to my chest.

I shrug out of my dress shirt and I watch as her mouth drops open slightly.

Every single second I've spent in the gym is now one hundred percent worth it. She's staring at my bare chest with wide eyes, visibly swallowing. Her cheeks bloom with color and her arm holding the T-shirt goes slack.

I grin.

She doesn't see it. She hasn't looked up for nearly a full minute. I don't mind. I make a show of sliding my arms up into the Racketeers T-shirt and pull it over my head so my muscles flex.

Only when the black cotton covers my torso does she finally blink. But she doesn't say a word.

"You should change too," I tell her.

She looks up and meets my gaze in confusion. "What? Oh." She looks down at the shirt I gave her. "Right. Yeah." Then she glances around. "Here?"

I shrug. "No one will come in here."

She looks at me again. "Um."

Well, damn. I thought maybe she'd be distracted enough to just start stripping without thinking about it. "I'll turn around." But I'm not leaving.

She glances back at the door, clearly debating. Then she turns back to me. "Okay." Her voice is softer. And she's looking at me with wide eyes and pink cheeks.

I hope she never ever fucking looks at Ben like that.

If I have anything to say about it she won't.

She won't ever look at anyone like that.

I turn and I hear clothing rustling. I'm not even trying not to envision her peeling off the wet shirt, and then pulling the dry T-shirt on. It's all I can think about.

What kind of bra does she wear? How many hooks are there? What color is it? White or nude? She doesn't seem like the expensive lacy lingerie type but more practical.

But I want to buy her expensive lacy lingerie.

Jesus, what is happening to me?

This girl is not my type. I tend to hook up with busy, independent women my age who know the score. Women who aren't looking for soft things like cuddles, and hugs.

Danielle *exudes* cuddles and hugs.

I wouldn't even call what I do dating. But when I run through the list of women I have fucked in the last five years I doubt very much if any of them have a cardigan in their entire closet.

And none of them like hockey.

But Danielle is going to be sitting right behind the glass tonight at one of the Racketeers biggest games.

And my eyes will be on her all night.

"Okay, I'm done."

I turn back to find her in the Racketeers tee, her cardigan back in place, her wet shirt in hand.

"Do you need to have this replaced?" I ask, taking it from her.

She frowns. "What do you mean? I'll just wash it."

"I'll buy you a new one. Or ten new ones. You don't have to hold onto this one."

She shakes her head. "That's ridiculous. You don't need to replace my shirt. The beer was Ben's fault."

Yes it was. Dickhead Ben. She needed to remember that.

"You're not going to sit and hold a beer soaked shirt during the game," I tell her, tossing the T-shirt into the trashcan near the door of the room.

"Well, you're not replacing it. You've already gotten me this T-shirt," she says, plucking the Racketeers shirt away from her stomach. "Though, it's a little small."

I study her. The shirt is snug. Very snug. It makes her breasts look amazing. "It's perfect," I tell her.

She looks up quickly and catches me staring at her chest.

Her eyes widen, but her lips curl. "Yeah?"

"Definitely. That is exactly your size."

With both of us changed, she seems to have regained her equilibrium. She actually snorts. "Okay. Whatever you say."

"Let me walk you to your seat."

She starts for the door with a laugh. "No. I can find my way. God knows what might happen if you get too close to Ben again."

I have a list of about six things I'd *like* to have happen to Ben. "Fine. I'll see you around, Danielle."

She looks back quickly, her hand on the doorknob. "You think so?"

"I guarantee it."

Read the rest of Puck One Night Stands, available now!

Find Emma on Social

Emma Foxx is the super fun and sexy pen name for two long-time, bestselling romance authors who decided why have just one hero when you can have three at the same time? (they're not sure what took them so long to figure this out)! Emma writes contemporary romances that will make you laugh (yes, maybe out loud in public) and want more...books (sure, that's what we mean 😉). Find Emma on Instagram, Tik Tok, and Goodreads.